BLOOD OF THE PROPHET

Fourth Element Book #2

KAT ROSS

Blood of the Prophet

First Edition

Copyright © 2016 Kat Ross

Cover design by Damonza

Map design by Robert Altbauer at fantasy-map.net

ISBN: 978-0-9972362-2-4

For my son Nick, who inspires me every day

FOREWORD

If you're anything like me, you may have forgotten some of the places and terms from the last book, so just a quick shout-out that there's a glossary at the very end you can refer to if needed. Enjoy!

Cheers, Kat

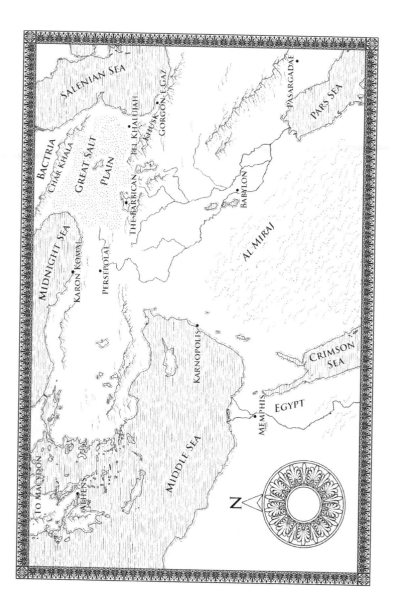

SALENIAN SEA

BACTRIA

CHAR KHALA

GREAT SALT PLAIN

BEL KHALULAH

KHUSK

GORGON-E-GAZ

PASARGADAE

PARS SEA

THE BARBICAN

BABYLON

MIDNIGHT SEA

AL MIRAJ

KARON KOMAL

PERSEPOLAI

KARNOPOLIS

CRIMSON SEA

MEMPHIS

EGYPT

MIDDLE SEA

TO MACEDON

ATHENS

N

❧ I ❧

ARAXA

"We are here."

Shuffling feet paused before an iron-bound door. A single torch cast a pool of wavering light on rough stone walls stained black with mildew. The torch had been soaked in an aromatic resin called galbanum which, when first lit, would give off a bitter and peculiar scent. After it burned for a few minutes, however, the resin mellowed to something reminiscent of green apples or evergreens. But even the sweet smoke failed to mask the air in the tunnel, which had a dank, unpleasant quality, as though it had absorbed the darkness pressing in from all sides.

The Numerator holding the torch raised it to examine the door more closely, then gave a satisfied nod. His face was all hard planes and angles, yet none of them seemed to fit quite right, like the walls of a shoddily built house. Thinning brown hair swept back from a high, pale forehead.

"Are you certain?" asked the second man. "This section has been bricked up for decades."

"I am certain." An elegant finger traced the hinges. "See?

There are no signs of rust. Check the map yourself, Hierarch. This is the place."

The honeycomb of tunnels beneath the temple district of Karnopolis had been used for many things over the last thousand years. When invaders came to loot and burn, as they often did in the city's early days, the magi would hide there until it was safe to come out. Later, the tunnels had served as wine cellars, smugglers' dens and, naturally, dungeons.

But peace had now reigned for more than two centuries. Most of the tunnels had fallen into disuse, and few remembered they even existed. Only one prisoner remained. He had been there a very long time. In fact, he should have died decades ago and no one knew for certain why he hadn't, although they had their suspicions. The prisoner was both feared and pitied, a relic from the war left to quietly gather dust in the darkness. When they thought of him at all, it was mainly to wonder when he would die and spare them the indignity of his upkeep.

The two Numerators who stood outside his cell were the first people other than his jailers to come see him in recent memory. Food and water arrived twice a day through a slot in the heavy oak door, and a bucket of waste was removed, but the prisoner had not spoken in a generation except to request certain harmless items, such as pens and vellum, which no one objected to. Until recently, only the King and a handful of magi knew he still lived. He had been one of them once, so they refrained from killing him outright. That might be considered a sin in the eyes of the Holy Father. The prisoner also had certain arcane knowledge he refused to share, so it was only prudent to keep him around in case they needed it someday.

That day had now arrived.

"Is this truly necessary?" the older Numerator demanded. He was the head of their order and a hard man, but the thought of seeing the prisoner made his voice quaver.

"If we are to take charge of him, it would be wise to assess his condition first," replied the much younger man, whose name was Araxa.

"I know that," snapped the Hierarch. "But do you not find it strange he still lives?" He made the sign of the flame, touching forehead, lips and heart. "There is some dark magic at work here."

"It must be related to the cuff he wears," Araxa said. "They have assured me it keeps him docile. If he could have broken free, he would have done it years ago. I do not deny he is dangerous. That is why we must take him from the magi before their incompetence causes yet another disaster."

The Hierarch nodded his grey head. "It is a blessing that the King has charged us with purging the magi of traitors. They've probably been infested for years."

The Numerators of Karnopolis despised the magi, and vice versa. As the Hierarch's spymaster, Araxa had been given the task of leading this purge. One of his first acts was to demand the transfer of the prisoner to the Numerators' custody. He had been shocked to discover the old man still lived, both because it shouldn't be possible and because Araxa traded in secrets. He had informants in the magi, but none had ever breathed a hint of this. It was only after two of their own Purified had brazenly stolen the holy fire that the King revealed the truth. The Prophet Zarathustra had been—quite literally—under their noses for the last two hundred years.

"By the time I am finished, the magi will be grateful if we allow them to crawl back to their flyspeck villages," Araxa said. "Their power will be broken, and the Numerators will be given full control over the daēvas as well. Then we can dispose of them as we see fit."

The Hierarch frowned a little at this. "But we need the daēvas to fight for us."

"Only to defeat the Druj once and for all. Let them serve their purpose and return to hell, where they belong." He gave a sly, reptilian smile. "They may heal quickly, but they are not immune to a knife in the heart. Or fire."

"Perhaps." The Hierarch waved a blue-veined hand. "Are there no guards?"

"Not in a hundred years. They say he has never attempted to escape. No one even remembers these tunnels exist, Your Excellency. And a man could stumble around in the dark for weeks without finding a way out."

"It is still a foolish risk."

"As you say. In any event, it will soon be a moot point. I agree he cannot be left down here. Not with devil-worshipping heretics running loose, and traitors amongst those who are supposed to be his keepers."

The Hierarch cleared his throat with a wet *harrumph*. "Let's get this over with. Open it."

Araxa produced a crude bronze key and turned it in the lock. He thrust his lantern through the door first, expecting darkness, but the chamber beyond was filled with candlelight. A straw mattress had been pushed against one stone wall. The Hierarch wrinkled his nose at the smell wafting through the doorway, stale and waxy and animal. He clutched his pristine white robes and peered over Araxa's shoulder with morbid curiosity. What state would the prisoner be in after two hundred years in a windowless cell? He had been offered chances to repent, to return to the fold. But Zarathustra was a stubborn man. And apparently a mad one.

Araxa drew in a sharp breath at the scene before him.

"It's a wonder he hasn't burned to death," he said. "The magi truly are fools to have indulged him so."

Stacks of vellum towered from floor to vaulted ceiling, many of them mere inches away from wavering candles. One wall appeared to be devoted to charts of the heavens, drawn from memory. Another was covered with incomprehensible diagrams, while the stretch nearest the door consisted of sketches of goats, some with disturbingly human eyes. There was no rhyme or reason to it that Araxa could discern. It was the cell of a lunatic.

He knew the old man had been considered a genius in his time, an inventor and alchemist. Ironically enough, he had even designed the gold cuff trapping him in this place.

"I've run out of ink," a tremulous voice said. "You promised me ink two months ago. Have you brought it?"

The Numerators exchanged a look. "I'll see that it's done," Araxa said soothingly, with no intention of doing so.

The Prophet Zarathustra, believed by all the world to be dead, sucked his rotten teeth and turned back to the vellum between his knees. One filthy, ragged fingernail scraped its surface as he traced intricate symbols on it, long grey hair hanging in cobwebs across his face. Within moments, he seemed to have forgotten anyone else was there.

"You see?" Araxa said. "He'll give us no trouble."

"Make the arrangements," the Hierarch said. "And burn these papers once he's gone. They're nonsense, but they could lead to questions we don't wish answered. How many know of his existence?"

"The High Magus of Karnopolis, of course. The King and his closest advisors. A handful of magi who see to his daily needs."

"Put the last ones on your list to be questioned," the Hierarch said. "I wouldn't be surprised if they had ties to the so-called Followers."

"They are already on it," Araxa said. "At the top."

"Good." The Hierarch took a last look at the prisoner, shook his head in disgust, and exited the cell, Araxa at his heels. The iron-bound door was once again locked. Araxa lifted the torch and they retraced their steps through the darkness. Altogether, the spymaster was pleased with the situation. He had worried the Hierarch was too old and weak-minded to do what needed to be done, but that no longer mattered, since he had ceded authority over the entire affair to Araxa.

"Would you join me for a cup of wine in my study?" the Hierarch asked as they reached the final passage leading out of the labyrinth. "It does ease my gout."

Araxa smiled. Thoughts of poison danced in his head, but the time was not yet right.

"I'd be delighted to, Your Excellency," he said.

❦ 2 ❦

NAZAFAREEN

I used to think the stars were angels. A great army waiting for the last battle against the Undead Druj. The light shone from their swords, which were made of silver and inlaid with precious stones. When the time came to return to Earth and pass judgment on the wicked, this celestial horde would be led by the Holy Father himself, riding a stallion that breathed cold blue fire.

Really, it made perfect sense.

Then my daēva, Darius, told me the stars were actually suns, only very far away. That they were, in fact, flaming orbs of vast magnitude. This flew in the face of all reason. Next he would claim the Earth was a sphere as well.

But as I lay on my back, listening to waves lap at the ship's hull and staring up at the dome of the night sky, I knew he was right. I could sense their ferocious energy myself now. It made me uneasy. I dreamt of fire often these days. The dreams always ended with my daēva dead, his blood boiled in his veins, and me untouched.

"What's wrong?" Darius asked. He sensed my discomfort thanks to the bond that joined us, although not what caused it.

He couldn't read my mind—a fact for which I was eternally grateful.

"Nothing. Tell me more about Karnopolis."

He sighed. "I've already told you everything I know, Nazafareen."

"Tell me again."

I glanced over at Darius's profile, the beaky nose and short-cropped hair. I had only kissed him once but I wanted to again. Desperately. Yet the walls between us had fallen back into place. It wasn't so long ago I was his mistress, and he little more than a slave. It didn't help matters that I was also bonded to his father, Victor, whom he hated, and that we were going back to his childhood home, a place with terrible memories for him. Either way, Darius was in a fragile state of mind. Outwardly he seemed calm. But I knew he felt afraid. I did too.

"It is the greatest city in the empire," Darius said. "Ten times older than Persepolae, at least. Its architects had a love of symmetry, so Karnopolis forms an enormous square, precisely fourteen leagues on each side and boasting two hundred and fifty watchtowers along the walls. I know the temple district best, where they keep the daēvas. It's usually full of pilgrims, so we should be able to blend in."

I snorted. "Yes, a girl with only one hand and a boy with a withered arm. No one will notice we happen to match the description of the most wanted pair in the empire, I'm sure."

"Such things can be disguised," Darius said. "Are you having second thoughts?"

"No," I said. "Those came days ago. More like eleventh or twelfth."

"You did volunteer for this."

"Oh, I'm not complaining. Just stating the obvious. If the Prophet even lives, they will have him in some hole so deep and dark he could not be found in two years, let alone two weeks." I propped myself up on one elbow. The sky in the east was beginning to lighten. I could see a series of rugged islands in the distance, their little white and blue houses clinging like barnacles to the cliffs. "But we have to try. And if I get to kill some Numerators, so much the better."

Darius smiled. "How bloodthirsty you are, Nazafareen."

"Only for the daēva-hunters. And the magi." I thought for a moment. "The King, of course. We may as well throw in all the satraps while we're at it."

"Yes, it's a short list you've got." He paused. "Speaking of killing, have you been practicing?"

I knew he meant with the power. I shouldn't even be able to touch it. Manipulating the three workable elements—water, air and earth—was a daēva talent and I was human.

"Yes," I grumbled. "It's like trying to bail out a boat with a leaky bucket. Plenty of frenzied activity, but you still end up at the bottom of the ocean."

"Give it time."

"That's what you always say. And it's the one thing we haven't got."

"We did fine before," Darius pointed out. "You can still fight with a sword. I'm strong enough in the power for both of us."

He could be tactful and even kind when he chose to, so Darius didn't even glance at my missing hand. Yes, I could still hold a blade with my left—which luckily was my strongest. But it was ridiculous to pretend my skill was the same.

"I can't shake the feeling we're skipping into a pit of quicksand," I said. "Let's just get that cursed old man as fast as we can and be on our way."

"Don't speak ill of the Prophet." Darius frowned. Unlike me, he was still devout. "He didn't mean for any of this to happen."

"How do you know? Because Victor says so?"

Darius's blue eyes glittered dangerously at the mention of his father. "Zarathustra was...*is* a good man. His intentions were distorted."

"That's one way of putting it. It's thanks to him the daēvas were enslaved." I blew out a long breath. "Let's not argue. What he is makes no difference to me. He just needs to live long enough to convince the Immortals in Persepolae to throw down their swords before Alexander burns the city to the ground. After that, I don't give a fig what happens to him."

We watched the sun rise in brittle silence. I didn't understand why Darius still clung to the Way of the Flame after all that had been done to him. His left arm was a withered husk because of the bonding process. The cuff had maimed him—another thing the magi had lied about. They claimed the daēvas' infirmities were their Druj curse. But they weren't Druj. Not even close. Frankly, I had no idea what they were, or where they came from. Darius didn't either, which was part of his problem. He couldn't face giving up all he believed when he had nothing to take its place.

"Quarreling again?" Tijah flopped down beside me, joined moments later by her own daēva, Myrri. They could have been sisters, both tall and slender, with tilted eyes and pretty skin the color of strong tea. Tijah wore her hair in dozens of small braids, while Myrri's hung in springy curls to her shoulders. The bond had taken Myrri's tongue, so they used a system of hand gestures to communicate. Myrri's fingers flashed and Tijah laughed.

"Not in the least," I said. "We were just admiring the view."

"Well, take a look on the port side," Tijah said with a grin. She was from the desert lands of Al Miraj and had never seen a pool of water much larger than she could hop across. She found the ocean fascinating, and had spent much of our journey from the Bosporus cajoling the crew into teaching her their seafaring lingo, which she liked to show off at any opportunity.

I raised my eyebrows at her pleased expression.

"Land ho," she said.

Darius and I jumped to our feet and ran to the opposite rail, where the ancient city of Karnopolis crouched in the morning sun.

"Holy Father," I breathed, forgetting for a moment I was supposed to be a heretic.

Until I was thirteen, I had never set foot inside a house. My people were nomads. We lived in goat-skin tents and drove our herds over the mountains twice a year. When I left my clan to join the King's Water Dogs, I had lived in Tel Khalujah, which seemed a bustling metropolis. And when I first saw the summer capital of Persepolae, I'd realized Tel Khalujah was just a backwater.

But Karnopolis…It was fifty times larger than Persepolae. As we sailed into the harbor, past fishing boats and cargo ships and the sleek triremes of the King's Navy, I gawked at the famous wall surrounding the city. It curved down to the Middle Sea like a sheer cliff, casting sharp-edged shadows on the white stone buildings within. Odd-looking trees with large fronds and no lower branches swayed in the breeze along the waterfront.

"My father—may the gods cause his manhood to wither and fall off—said they race chariots atop the wall," Tijah observed. "I'd like to see that sometime."

"Karnopolis has every amusement, despite the best efforts of the magi to suppress sinfulness," Darius said dryly. "Unless I'm mistaken, the address we're going to is deep in the belly of the pleasure district."

Tijah grinned. "Why does it not surprise me the smuggler has unsavory friends? Well, we are less likely to be scrutinized there, I suppose."

"Do they have special daēva gates, like in Persepolae?" I asked. It had only just occurred to me, but if they used the fire test for people entering the city, we had a problem.

"Not here," Darius replied. "There are not enough of us to make it worth the trouble, I think."

As the ship dropped anchor, we went below and collected our

belongings. In my case, that was a sword wrapped in a length of cloth and a small leather sack with a change of clothing and a few toiletries. It felt odd to wear a dress instead of trousers. I kept tripping over the skirts and hoped we didn't get in a fight before I had a chance to change.

"Here, give it to me," Tijah said as I fumbled one-handed with the hooks on my veil. She stepped back and studied me. "Stop scowling under there, Nazafareen. Try to look meek. Eyes downcast."

I made a rude noise and Tijah laughed. "Just pretend you're wearing a *qarha*. It feels more or less the same. Unless you'd prefer to be arrested at the gates?"

"No, I'm quite happy with the veil," I said, blowing out a hot breath through my mouth. The thin linen flapped up, then settled back down like an albatross coming in to roost.

"Good. You can thank me later." Feet pounded on the deck overhead, accompanied by thumps and shouts as the sails were lowered. "Ready?"

I looked at Myrri, also veiled, who raised an eyebrow. "Ready," I said.

Our ship had once been called the *Amestris*. Two weeks before, she had rescued us from a village on the Midnight Sea and brought us all the way to the Hellespont, where King Alexander's army was camped. As a result, the *Amestris* was a blacklisted ship, so her owner—the smuggler, Kayan Zaaykar—had changed her nameplate to the *Photina*. But her captain was the same man as before, and we bid him a warm farewell as the crew prepared a longboat to carry us to shore.

"Are you sure I shouldn't wait for you?" he asked, rubbing the dark stubble on his jaw.

"When we leave, it will be over land," I replied. "The sea route to Persepolae would take three times as long. And it's not safe. Someone could recognize the ship."

He nodded. It wasn't the first time we'd had this debate. "I'll tell Kayan Zaaykar you landed safely," he said. "Be well."

"And you."

The four of us got into the longboat and sailors lowered it to the water. In a few minutes, they had rowed us to a beach where fishing boats were pulled up. I had hoped never to set foot inside the borders of the empire again, and here I was, heading straight into the dragon's den. I glanced at Darius. His expression gave nothing away, but I knew he felt it too, even more than I did. Dread.

"Which way?" Tijah asked, as the sailors rowed back to the *Photina*.

The veil concealed everything but her brown eyes, which were cool and intelligent. Tijah didn't ruffle easily, nor did her daēva. Once she committed to something, she didn't look back. I wish I had her confidence.

Darius pointed to a fish market at the edge of the harbor.

"We can take a shortcut through there," he said.

The people of Karnopolis were mostly dark of hair and skin, although Darius said the city was a melting pot, drawing merchants and mercenaries and pilgrims from all corners of the empire. The babble of a dozen foreign tongues surrounded us as we pushed our way through the bustling marketplace. Persepolae, the summer capital, was quiet and stately, full of gleaming white marble and strict geometrical designs, but this city hummed with boisterous life. The people were louder, their hand gestures bigger and clothing gaudier. Sleek cats wove between the stalls, hunting for scraps of fish. The tables were shaded by awnings of brightly dyed cloth, forming a maze of light and shadow that echoed with the sounds of full-throated haggling. As we approached the nearest gate into the city, Myrri touched my arm. I felt Darius stiffen.

A body was nailed to the top of the wall with iron spikes, its arms and legs splayed wide. The face had been pecked at by birds and was barely recognizable as human, but the robes were unmistakable. A magus. I had no great love for the priesthood, but judging by the wisps of white hair clinging to his scalp, the poor man had been old enough to be my grandfather. The sight was made even more macabre by the beauty of the massive wooden gate, framed by blue-glazed brick with a mosaic of galloping horses and a border of blue and white flowers.

A few people stared, but most acted as if they didn't even see the corpse, dangling like a broken puppet. From the condition of the parts I could see, I guessed it had been there for at least a week.

"Is that how they punish law-breakers here?" Tijah asked in a low voice. "Gods, I only hope he was dead before they strung him up."

Darius shook his head, troubled. "The satrap of Karnopolis is not known to be lenient, but I've never seen such a thing before."

"It's a message," I said. "That's the only reason you'd do something like that. To scare people."

We moved away from the crowds to a relatively quiet patch of ground where we could observe the gate. Although the guards seemed mostly lazy and disinterested, I noticed with a sinking heart that not everyone was permitted to pass without question. Every ninth or tenth person was pulled aside as the guards inspected their palms.

"They're checking tattoos," Darius said. He clenched his right hand into a fist. "They must have been warned about us. If they see the triangle..."

He didn't have to finish the thought. The single triangle with a slash through it marked him as daēva. Tijah and I both had two triangles on our palms, one nested inside the other—proof we were human. The tattoos had been inked with the power. Nothing could alter or remove them.

"The magus at Tel Khalujah used to say a messenger could travel the Royal Road from Persepolae to Karnopolis in three days by relay," I said. Our quiet lessons in his study on history and geography seemed like another lifetime to me now, but perhaps they would prove useful after all.

"We have to assume one already has." Darius eyed the four guards, with their spears and wicker shields. "At least they aren't daēvas. Then they wouldn't even need to see my hand to know what I am."

"What next then?" Tijah asked.

"Let's try another gate," he suggested.

We followed the curve of the great wall along the waterfront, but it was the same at the next gate, and the one after that. The guards did not check everyone, but they did seem to be singling out dark-haired young men of a certain age. Young men who looked like Darius.

"This is bad," Tijah said, exchanging a look with Myrri. "Perhaps just the three of us should go through for now. Veiled women won't have a problem." She turned to Darius. "You stay here, and we'll find a way to sneak you in later."

"I don't like that so much," I said. "He's the only one who knows the city. And there's nowhere to hide out here. The *Photina* will be gone by now. Her captain is as wanted as we are, he wouldn't risk staying in port, not even to take on supplies."

"I suppose we could toss the dice," Tijah said dubiously. "We might manage to slip inside."

"I don't like that either," I said, blowing on my veil. I felt sweaty and frustrated. "Darius, what do you say?"

"I have an idea." He smiled, a devilish glint in his eye. "Just wait."

So we stood and watched people and animals and carts go in and out, raising clouds of fine, gritty sand. At least there was no faceless corpse nailed over this particular gate. In the heat, the other one had given off the faintly sweet rot I remembered from Gorgon-e Gaz, turning my stomach to a sour mess.

The sun sat at its peak in the sky when I sensed Darius grow more alert, like a hunting hound scenting a boar.

"Are you going to use the power?" I asked warily. "I hope you remember what happened in Karon Komai. It was as good as lighting a signal fire for the Immortals."

"I remember. And I won't use much. Just a trickle."

I almost objected. If they were close enough, other daēvas could sense the power being used. But I couldn't see any choice. And if we were going to gamble, I'd put my wager on Darius.

A moment later, a cart loaded with huge cedar timbers rolled up the gate. Darius's mind stilled. I knew he had gone to the nexus, the place where he became one with the elements. The cuff warmed against my skin. One of the guards was just raising his hand to wave the cart through when there was a snapping sound and the ropes holding the timbers broke. Yells erupted as ten-foot logs rolled in every direction, smashing into the wheels of other carts and sending the lines of people running for cover. The guards cursed at the driver, who was tearing at his hair and in turn cursing the evil spirits that had brought bad luck and ruin down upon an honest laborer. Two of the guards rushed to the side of a wealthy merchant who was gesticulating in fury at his own ruined cart. The last two looked at each other and shrugged, then began to help the driver retrieve his runaway wares.

"Now," Darius hissed.

Moving fast (but not *too* fast), we joined the handful of people who had been about to pass through the gate before the "accident" occurred. Most had stopped to gawk at the mayhem, and paid us no attention as we slipped into the shadow of the massive wall. Up close, the pitted and weathered mortar looked a thousand years old. Like it had broken the teeth of invaders no one even remembered anymore. Like it had stood there forever and would still be standing when the rest of the world was swallowed up by the desert sands.

As I stepped through the rectangular cut of the gate, I had the sensation of entering the jaws of some great beast and couldn't help but wonder if we would all come out again.

"Let's split up," Darius said the moment we were through. "Follow, but don't let it appear we're all together."

Tijah nodded, and she and Myrri slowed their steps until I could no longer see them. I drew a deep breath, my nose filling with strange perfumes and spices and the dry, dusty odor of sun-baked mud. Mules and oxcarts filled the narrow streets with no regard whatsoever for anyone on foot, or anything coming from the opposite direction. Within a few blocks, I had witnessed two violent arguments over right-of-way, although no one but the combatants paid them any mind. To my relief, the city was crowded enough that four more souls were just a drop in the ocean of humanity. Of course, it also meant finding the Prophet would be like identifying a single grain of sand in the Sayhad desert.

The address we wanted wasn't far from the docks in a seedy area of wine sinks, gambling dens and brothels popular with sailors. I kept my head down and my stump tucked inside my sleeve as we passed a pair of uniformed men with swords and cudgels, City Watch by the looks of them. I no longer wore the scarlet tunic of the Water Dogs, but only two weeks ago I had been a resident of the King's dungeons in Persepolae. And I still wore the pair of gold cuffs marking me as bonded—one linking me to Victor, the other to Darius. Tijah and Myrri wore them too, concealed under long sleeves. A single glimpse of the cuffs by someone who knew what they were and we'd all be in cells.

I held my breath, but the guards strolled by without showing any special interest in us. We could kill them if we had to, but more would come. Too many to fight. For now, we just had to stay out of trouble long enough to find Kayan Zaaykar's contact and pray he didn't turn us in.

The dirty, narrow streets twisted and tangled together like the branches of a thorn bush, and even Darius, who was the best tracker I had ever met, had to stop and ask for directions. Finally, we came to a four-story building that was larger and somewhat grander than its neighbors. A teenaged boy with painted eyes lounged against the wall outside, just under a sign depicting a large—and frankly phallic—shaft piercing a wine cup. His gaze lingered on Darius, then turned to Tijah, Myrri and myself with open curiosity. I guessed not many women turned up on the doorstep of Marduk's Spear, not unless they were hunting wayward husbands.

"We're looking for the owner of this fine establishment," Darius said with a friendly smile.

"Who's asking?" the kid demanded.

"Friends of Kayan Zaaykar," Darius said, dropping his voice.

The boy gave us an unreadable look. He couldn't have been more than fourteen, but his dark, knowing eyes looked closer to forty. "Come inside," he said at last, stepping through the doorway into the cool, dim interior.

Marduk's Spear was nominally a tavern, with tables and couches occupying the ground floor, although the boys serving wine to the sparse morning clientele were all exceptionally pretty. A pear-shaped tanbur sat propped in the corner, its strings silent at this early hour. Arched doors on the far side of the room opened onto a courtyard filled with flowerbeds and more of those strange limbless trees I had seen at the harbor. The boy indicated we should follow and led us into the garden to the shade of a date tree.

It was still early in the day, but the temperature had already grown too warm for my taste. Karnopolis was sticky, damp and vaguely smelly, like the fists of an infant, and I felt a fleeting but sharp longing for the mountains of my childhood. Karnopolis's temperate climate had earned the city its status as the winter capital. The King and his entire court would be here now if not for the barbarian army at his western border—an army I had sworn allegiance to, for whatever that was worth. I somehow doubted I would live long enough for Alexander to collect his due.

"Wait here," the kid said. He darted off, past a few chickens pecking half-heartedly in the dirt and up a flight of stairs, bare feet slapping on the tiles.

"Are you sure this man is a Follower of the Prophet?" Tijah whispered. "He doesn't seem exactly...devout."

"Unless there's another Marduk's Spear, we've come to the right place," Darius said. "Let's just be careful how much we say until we're sure of him." He glanced at me. "I'll take the lead, if you don't mind."

I knew he thought I was a hothead who couldn't hold her tongue, which was true, but I didn't appreciate being reminded of that fact.

"Fine." I wiped a sheen of sweat from my forehead with the sleeve of my turquoise gown. "You do the talking."

A moment later, an enormous man in a leather vest descended the stairs. His arms looked like they were stuffed with rocks, and he wore a scowl on his scarred face.

"Who's asking for Arshad Nabu-zar-adan?" he growled.

"Kayan Zaaykar sent us," I blurted.

Darius sighed.

"Sorry," I mouthed, clamping my lips shut.

It would have been so much easier if Kayan had just come along, but the smuggler had stayed behind at Alexander's camp. He claimed to be too well known in Karnopolis to risk coming here. But he had insisted the owner of Marduk's Spear was a man we could trust.

"And who's *us*?" the giant demanded.

"Friends," Darius said shortly. "And our message is for your boss, not you."

I wondered how Darius knew the giant was not, in fact, Arshad Nabu-zar-adan, but he was obviously correct in this assumption, because the man crossed his arms—the better to

KAT ROSS

display his bulging biceps—and lowered an impressively ridged brow. It was the sort of head that cracked other heads like eggs. I knew the type.

"Then you're shit out of—"

"It's alright. Bring them to my chambers."

We all looked up at the balcony above. The person attached to the cultured voice had already withdrawn, but it was as if the Holy Father himself had appeared in the clouds, for the giant's demeanor immediately changed to that of a palace courtier.

"Right this way then," he said, baring a handful of teeth in a sweet smile.

❦ 3 ❦

BALTHAZAR

Four leagues due north of the ninety-sixth gate of Karnopolis was a small pond surrounded by trees. No bullfrogs croaked at its reedy edges. No insects skated across its glassy surface. The level of its dark waters never changed, not in the hottest, driest months of summer, nor after the heavy spring rains. It was a lifeless place, because it was not really a pond but a gate, similar to the one leading into the city, except that this gate connected two worlds.

The glen lay deep in the woods, and only a passing fox saw the necromancer named Balthazar ride his horse out of the pond. He emerged perfectly dry and stopped for a moment at the edge, dark hair lifting in the wind. The fox did not like the smell of either the man or his beast. They reeked of unpleasant magic. *Heart thieves*, the fox thought to herself, as she hurried silently back to her pups.

Balthazar took a deep breath, tasting the forest air. Leaving the Dominion always left him with a profound feeling of relief. The shadowlands stole a piece from him, an intangible but important piece, and he was grateful to have it back. It had thudded into him as he crossed the shivery border at the surface of the pond—his magic, what there was of it.

This was the first reason Balthazar was glad to be back in the mundane world. The second was that things moved in the Dominion between the gates, things that hunted his kind, and although Balthazar trafficked in death, he did not relish the thought of his own. He had been lucky this time. None had caught his scent, partly thanks to the talisman of Traveling he carried in his pocket. The journey from Bactria was the longest he had ever spent in the shadowlands, nearly a full day. But it had saved him two weeks of hard riding, and his instincts told him time was running short.

The horse was glad to be out too. It whickered softly, nosing the grass at the edge of the pond. The day was a pleasant one, and the necromancer was in high spirits as he rode out of the woods and found the road to the city. The closer he came to the wall, the thicker the traffic on the road became, but no one gave him a second glance, except to ask for a quick blessing. Balthazar complied with a fatherly smile. He wore the white robes of a magus and knew their nonsense by heart.

Karnopolis had changed little since he was last there, although a full two centuries had passed. It was one of the oldest cities in the known world and exuded the lazy arrogance of a sun-warmed cat. The only major new additions Balthazar could detect were the austere Hall of the Numerators and the much smaller Tomb of the Prophet. Both were near the Temple of the Magi, which was his destination.

Balthazar paused when he reached the enormous marble building and spent a moment looking up at the broad steps and the feckless priests who hurried to and fro. He had decided to come alone for a number of reasons, chiefly because the more of his brethren were in the city, the greater the chance of discovery. They called his kind necromancers because they commanded the

Undead, but he disliked the term. Antimagi was a far more accurate title. The powers he served were the exact opposite of the elemental magic of the daēvas and their masters. They took living matter and drained it dry of whatever life force it possessed, swelling the Antimagus with stolen vitality. When Balthazar was chained to his slaves, his strength equaled four men. It was a heady sensation. He could hardly drag his human chattel through the streets of Karnopolis, but he did have the chains and collars in his saddlebag. As he watched the magi scurrying about, Balthazar thought he would not have a great deal of trouble finding new ones, should the need arise.

Queen Neblis had been reluctant to see him go alone, but she had faith in Balthazar's abilities. He had failed her only once, when the daēva called Victor had escaped on the plain, and he felt he had more than made up for it by bringing her the holy fire. Now they needed the Prophet to teach them how to use it.

Balthazar dismounted and led his horse to the stables behind the temple, where he gave a coin to the boy there, tousled his hair, and asked him to take good care of his mount, which was a beautiful black Ferghana. The other horses whinnied uneasily at its presence, but the boy hushed them, grateful for the copper. Balthazar entered the temple through a rear door and went straight to the fire altar. They would give him shelter if he asked for it, and he planned to. It was the ideal place from which to conduct the search. He would be just another magus from the provinces, come to make his annual pilgrimage to the Prophet's Tomb.

It had been a very long time indeed since he had knelt before the brazier. It sat in the center of an otherwise empty room, and the fire within burned eternally, a symbol of the Holy Father and the purification of sin. As Balthazar stared into the flames, listening to the droning prayers of the other magi, he had a sudden, vivid memory of himself as a much younger man. He had worn a short beard then, and the cuff of the warrior magi encircled his left wrist. They had stripped him of it just days before the Druj hordes surrounded the city. He remembered looking out the narrow window of his cell and seeing the endless lines of revenants beyond the wall, their iron swords and fearsome mounts. He remembered the black shadows of the liches, weaving back and forth like snakes, the sound they made. Balthazar had nearly soiled himself watching them.

Now, they obeyed his command.

The magi had called him a heretic and worse for his dabblings. Cast him out. But Neblis had picked him up. And now those magi were all dead, and he was still here.

Balthazar no longer prayed to the Holy Father, but he knew the sign of the flame. Forehead, lips, heart. *Good thoughts, good words, good deeds.* It came as easily to his fingers as if he had just performed it yesterday. He scanned the faces of the other magi at the altar, but recognized none. Back in his day, many of them—all those with the gift, at least—had worn the cuffs. They were at war, and the magi, along with the Immortals, were the first and last lines of defense. But that seemed to have gone out of fashion, or perhaps fewer had the gift. He was glad to see it, because it meant all the magi here would be too young to remember him. The infamous Balthazar. He lowered his head to cover a smile. If anyone knew where the Prophet was, it would be one of these fools.

Balthazar rose and made his way to the guest quarters. The elderly magus there was happy to accommodate a pilgrim from Qaddah. He asked a number of questions, but Balthazar was a fluent liar, and he knew the correct responses. Once he had shaken the man off, he prowled the corridors until he found one of the hidden doors leading down to the tunnels. He could search them himself, but that would take weeks. A better course would be to at least confirm the Prophet was down there first. In the meantime, he could put the labyrinth to other purposes.

Balthazar looked both ways to ensure he was not observed, then slid the knife hidden in his robes into the crack and worked it open. Dust rained down, a good sign. This part of the tunnels had not been used in a long while. His darkly handsome face cracked into a grin.

That was about to change.

⚜ 4 ⚜

NAZAFAREEN

We followed the giant up two flights of stairs and down a series of low, arched hallways. The building extended far back from the street, enclosing the square courtyard, and turned out to be much larger than it seemed from the outside. Finally, he threw open a door and stood aside. The room beyond was decorated in shades of purple and gold, and smelled strongly of Lily of the Valley. I knew right away that Arshad Nabu-zar-adan was an educated man, because he had a pile of scrolls on a cedar pedestal. Seeing them reminded me that I couldn't read myself, and I took an instant, irrational disliking to him.

A couch had been placed near the window to catch the humid breeze. The man who reclined on it was middle-aged but still slender, with neatly combed silver hair kept at shoulder length. He wore rings on his fingers and a fancy embroidered tunic. I guessed business was good at Marduk's Spear.

"Please sit," he said, signaling the boy at his feet to pour cups of wine. We waited in silence until the boy had departed, discreetly shutting the door behind him. Tijah and I unhooked our veils and took two finely carved chairs. Myrri ignored the wine, hands tucked into the folds of her gown. I wondered how many knives she had hidden away under there.

"To your health," Arshad Nabu-zar-adan said, lifting his cup.

"And yours," Darius murmured.

We raised our cups and sipped. I was used to the dicey vintage they served watered down in the barracks of Tel Khalujah, but this wine was smooth and mellow. Expensive, like everything else in the room. Warmth bloomed in my belly as I studied Arshad Nabu-zar-adan over the rim of my cup. He had a prominent nose and small, almost prim mouth that was just beginning to sag at the corners. The eyes squinting at us with open suspicion were framed by dark brows that came to little peaks, as though he were continuously surprised at the dregs of humanity that washed up on the shore of Marduk's Spear.

"How is Kayan Zaaykar?" our host asked. "I haven't seen him in years."

I exchanged a glance with Darius. Kayan claimed he'd received a message from the brothel owner no more than a month ago, saying he wholly supported the barbarian invasion.

"He is in Sestos," Darius said carefully. "With the Macydonian King."

"A traitor then? That is unfortunate news indeed." Arshad Nabu-zar-adan's black eyes grew even colder. "I think it best you leave. I am an honest businessman and loyal subject of King Artaxeros the Second, the Father bless his name."

"He told us to say he still owes you fifty siglos for that bet last year." Darius held out a purse. "Here it is, with interest."

The brothel owner didn't even glance at the money. "I'm sorry you've wasted your time, but I have no information about this man or his acquaintances. As I said, I haven't seen him in a long time."

"We're not asking for information—" Tijah began.

"Now, please." He tapped a walking stick twice on the floor and the door flew open. The giant stood there, looking at us with the bored expression of someone who ejected people from Marduk's Spear on a regular basis. "Escort our visitors to the street."

"Listen," Darius began, a bit desperately.

"No, you listen." His gaze bored into us, one by one, starting with Tijah. "A girl with the cadence of Al Miraj on her tongue. Another who speaks not at all. A young man with blue eyes and a grey hand. A young woman with the look of the northern clans. I know exactly who you are, and where you come from. It is my business to know such things. Do you think to entrap me simply by repeating a name? I have no interest in aiding fugitives and traitors. If you will not leave, I will summon the City Watch and let them deal with you."

My temper, stoked by the wine and heat, grew darker with every word he spoke. Darius shot me a warning look but it was too late.

"If you know who we are, you should know enough not to threaten," I snapped. "Unless you want this *fine establishment* to be pulled down around your ears!"

Darius started to rise, and the giant took a step into the room. He had knives in his boots, I noticed, and a nasty-looking cudgel at his waist, which one meaty hand was already groping for. Myrri moved in front of Tijah, her own knives materializing out of thin air. From the look of intense concentration on her face, Myrri was gathering the power. When it came to Tijah, she was pitiless as a mother bear protecting her cub.

I threw myself across the carpet, lunging for Arshad Nabu-zaradan's throat. As I reached him, my sleeve fell back, revealing the stump and the two gold cuffs worked with snarling lions that encircled my forearm.

"Wait!" he choked out, eyes fixed on the cuffs. "Stop!"

This last was directed at the giant, whose cudgel was poised to brain anyone foolish enough to come within reach. Darius had stepped back to give himself room to draw his sword. He looked aggravated.

"Don't," he growled at Myrri. "You'll bring them down on us."

I grabbed a fistful of Arshad's fancy tunic. My skirts had gotten hopelessly twisted around my legs, leaving no option but to tumble with all the grace of a hamstrung ox onto the couch next to him.

"Are you a daēva?" Arshad managed.

I shook my head and jerked my chin toward Darius. "He is."

Arshad Nabu-zar-adan stared at Darius, then at me. Confusion and fear flickered across his face. The giant frowned, waiting for his master's instructions.

"The proclamation said nothing of daēvas," Arshad muttered. "Only that murderers had escaped the dungeons at Persepolae. They say you killed two Purified."

"Lies," Tijah growled.

Myrri made the knives disappear and laid a pacifying hand on Tijah's arm. As fierce as she could be, Myrri was actually the more level-headed of the two of them.

"We *were* Water Dogs," I said. "From the satrapy of Tel Khalujah. Now we are traitors who seek the Prophet. Are you still going to turn us in?" I smiled, although my heart was thumping hard. The prospect of violence was not unappealing. "If you say yes, you'll be dead in less time than it takes to speak the word."

Arshad Nabu-zar-adan didn't answer for an excruciating moment. Then he signaled the giant to leave the room.

"What happened to your hand?" he asked.

"My own captain cut it off in the dungeons," I said. "To break the bond with my daēva." I glanced at Darius. "One of the Purified you speak of was murdered in those cells, but not by us. It was the King's own men. Kayan Zaaykar let us hide at his manor house after we escaped. The Immortals found us, but we made it to the *Amestris*, and then to Alexander's camp. Kayan is there now. It was too dangerous for him to come with us."

Arshad Nabu-zar-adan let out a breath from his thin nose. "I'm sorry for doubting you, but I had to be sure. The King issued a proclamation a fortnight ago. There's a reward on your heads, a large one. The King also said he had discovered the existence of a heretical sect seeking the overthrow of the empire and the enslavement of its people. He vowed to root them out by any means necessary."

"The Followers of the Prophet," Darius said quietly.

"Yes. There have already been six public executions of magi." He lowered his voice to a near whisper. "Five were perfectly innocent, but one knew of our cause and sympathized with it. Holy Father bless him, he must have kept my name to himself, or soldiers would have been at my door days ago. But I fear it's only a matter of time." He toyed with his rings, spinning them with stubby fingers that looked like they belonged on another body entirely. "The proclamation has unleashed a reign of terror. Anyone with a grudge against his neighbors can accuse them of being Followers and they will be subject to the question. These are dark times indeed, and growing darker each day."

"We saw a corpse on the wall," Tijah said. "A magus."

"Yes. The bodies of the so-called traitors are being displayed. Karnopolis has ninety-nine gates, and I fear each will have its own corpse by the time this inquisition is done." He sighed. "But first I would hear your tale in full. It seems you know more than I about what has transpired in Persepolae. Rumors have reached us, but each is more far-fetched than the last."

Arshad Nabu-zar-adan called for food and we told him in turns all that had happened since the day our company of Water Dogs was sent from Tel Khalujah to bring back six daēvas who had escaped from the prison at Gorgon-e Gaz. How we met necromancers on the Great Salt Plain who were chasing the same daēvas. How one of them turned out to be Darius's own father. How after many further misadventures, Kayan Zaaykar's ship had brought us to the tent of the young Macydonian King with mismatched eyes and boundless ambitions.

"So he plans to burn Persepolae?" Arshad Nabu-zar-adan asked in disbelief.

"Unless we can find a way to turn the Immortals, yes," Darius said. "Alexander knows he cannot beat them in battle. He has free daēvas, but not nearly enough, and the Immortals number five thousand daēvas alone. If we can find the Prophet and take him to Persepolae, his words might convince them to surrender. If not, he might be able to break the cuffs himself."

"And what would happen then?"

Darius shrugged. Unfortunately, he explained, no one knew what would happen then. But at least King Artaxeros couldn't force the daēva Immortals to fight for him.

"When does Alexander intend to march on the city?"

"In less than three weeks' time," Darius replied.

"Holy Father." Arshad made the sign of the flame, touching his fingers to forehead, lips and heart. "We must move quickly. Now I will tell you the news I had for Kayan. It is both good and bad." He poured another cup of wine and downed half of it in one go, which seemed to steady his nerves. "The Nabu-zar-adan family has kept the faith for generations, waiting for the return of the Prophet. There are few Followers left anymore, but one of our members is a magus in the Temple. For years, Saman has been our eyes and ears there, although he never managed to discover any new information. I myself believe only the High Magus and perhaps one or two others know the truth. It is the only way they could have kept such a secret for so long." He laced his fingers around the cup. Arshad's hands were steady, but the nails had been chewed to the quick. He glanced at the open doorway and seemed reassured by the giant's looming shadow against the wall outside.

"Two weeks ago, an emissary arrived from Persepolae, the same one bearing the King's proclamation," Arshad continued.

"Hoping to learn what had happened at the Barbican, Saman concealed himself and eavesdropped on the man's audience with the High Magus of Karnopolis."

I shared a look with Darius. We both leaned forward a little in our chairs.

"The message from the King was brief. In a way, it was everything we had hoped for. It was also our worst nightmare."

"Well, what did he say?" I demanded.

"The Prophet lives. He is somewhere within the city walls."

Darius sagged with relief. Until that moment, none of us were sure the Followers' claims were anything more than wishful thinking.

"And the bad news?" Tijah asked.

"He is to be handed over to the Numerators."

"Oh gods," she whispered. Myrri made a soft noise in her throat, like a wounded animal. We all feared the Numerators, but as a daēva, she had more reason than most.

"When?" Darius asked.

"I'm not sure, but I would guess any day now."

"Could it have been done already?" I asked, feeling the cold hand of dread grip my stomach. If we were too late...

"No," Arshad said firmly. "Saman would have told me."

"We can't let it happen," Darius said. "We must stop them."

"Yes, but how? I can't tell you where the Prophet is being held. Saman said it was never mentioned." Our host stood and walked to the window. "As you know, the Numerators are fanatics. They hate the daēvas and think the magi coddle them. The Numerators are not subtle men. They extract what they want by fire and iron. The Holy Father only knows what they will do to the Prophet. I think the magi have kept him alive because he was one of their own, but the Numerators do not share that sentiment."

"Can you contact this magus?" I asked. "We need to speak to him right away."

"We do have a prearranged spot," Arshad said. "Although we

must be careful. If Saman is found out..." He didn't have to finish the thought. I imagine all of us were picturing the mutilated body over the gate.

"We'll leave a message in the morning," Darius said. "We need to find out when this transfer is happening and anything else he might have discovered. Where do you usually meet him?"

Arshad smiled. "The one place where both a magus and a pious businessman like myself might have reason to go."

We looked at each other blankly.

"The Tomb of the Prophet," Arshad Nabu-zar-adan said with satisfaction. "It attracts pilgrims, magi, even the occasional Numerator. They go to pay their respects, leave offerings. There is a loose stone in the fourteenth step of the eastern stairs, with a space beneath large enough to accommodate a folded square of vellum. It is our habit to place a fresh lotus blossom there when a message has been left."

"Fine," I said. "But I want to watch the tomb. See who picks up the message. We can't be too careful."

"Don't you trust Magus Saman?" Arshad asked. "I can vouch for his loyalty."

"I don't trust anyone except the people in this room," I smiled. "Some more than others."

"She's right," Darius cut in hastily. "It makes sense to wait for the answer so we can arrange a meeting a soon as possible."

"As you say." Arshad ostentatiously made the sign of the flame again and I tried not to roll my eyes. "I believe there is a reason the Holy Father has sent you to me at this very moment. The truth is our numbers are few. Saman is the only magus the Followers have at the Temple. Even if we knew where Zarathustra was, I don't know how we would manage to help him. But you four..." He looked us over. "I've heard how deadly bonded pairs can be. I imagine you could tear the walls of his prison down with a thought."

"If you can tell us where he is, we'll get him out," Darius agreed. His tone wasn't boastful, just calmly certain.

Arshad Nabu-zar-adan nodded. "First things first. We must disguise who you are. Frankly, it's pure luck you weren't picked up by the City Watch on the way here." He tapped a fingernail against pearly teeth. "I know an excellent Egyptian wig maker. He's only a few streets away."

"Wigs?" I frowned. The veil was hot and itchy enough.

Arshad laughed. "Not for you, my dear. For him." He pointed at Darius. "He shall be a girl, and you shall be a boy. The same for the others."

Tijah clutched her braids in dismay. "Cut them off?"

"Hair grows back," Arshad pointed out. "Heads don't."

"Why can't I just wear a veil?" she demanded. She tried to hide it, but Tijah had a vain streak a mile wide.

"Do you see any women in this establishment?" he asked. "Tongues will wag if *four* suddenly appear at Marduk's Spear."

"Can't we pretend to be prostitutes?" I whined.

Arshad Nabu-zar-adan looked truly shocked at this suggestion. "Only women of breeding are permitted the veil," he muttered. "Such a thing is simply...*not done*."

"But—"

Arshad flapped his hands. "I cannot take the risk, not with the Followers being openly persecuted. Anything out of the ordinary would bring them down on us within hours."

"Fine," I said. "If we can't wear veils, we'll cut our hair off and pass as boys. It's simple enough." Tijah shot me a dark look but didn't object further. Myrri seemed amused. She flashed a sign at Tijah that made her scowl even more deeply.

"We'll need a story to explain your presence here. Something romantic, but not actually criminal." Arshad pursed his lips, then grinned. "Star-crossed lovers, I think. The boys will like that. You"—he looked at Darius—"are my favorite nephew. And Naza-fareen is your betrothed. But your families hate each other and forbade the marriage, so you've run away. These two...what are your names again?"

Tijah repeated them, one hand clutching her braids as though she already mourned them.

"These two are your loyal servants. You are stopping here for a week or two while you wait to catch a ship across the Middle Sea. But Nazafareen's brothers are vengeful brutes, so you're all in disguise." He clapped his hands. "It's like a play."

Darius shrugged. I was still trying to untangle it all. "So the boys who work here will know he's really a man and we're women?" I said. "But they'll think we're just hiding from our families?"

"Yes. Trust me, you wouldn't fool them for an instant. Half of them saw you come in anyway. But people on the street? You should manage to pass without too much trouble." Arshad glanced out the window. "I'll give you rooms on the top floor. The pleasure district has been crawling with guardsmen since the proclamation, so I'd suggest you get straight to it."

The giant, whose name was Bobak, showed us upstairs. Now that he knew we weren't there to arrest his master, his attitude changed. Like some of the other large men I'd known in the Water Dogs, Bobak seemed naturally easygoing, perhaps because he had nothing to prove.

"The top floor's a bit stuffy, but we have to keep the lower rooms for the paying clients," he said apologetically, throwing open the shutters of a small room with a bed and wash basin painted a vibrant blue. "Not a bad view though."

I looked out over the city. From up here, I could see far beyond the pleasure district, to the hilltop mansions of the wealthy and the gleaming white marble of the temple district and the King's winter palace. It squatted like a massive anthill in the center of the city, with fortress-like walls spiraling upwards toward the clouds. Even from this distance, I could see the famous gardens surrounding it, a dark green oasis in the sand-colored metropolis.

Bobak winked at me. "I'd better get back downstairs. Have to keep an eye on the boys, make sure none of the clients get rough." He grinned. "Most of them know better, but the boys feel safer when I'm close by."

I smiled and thanked him, thinking I felt safer with Bobak around too. If they came for us, we'd have another head-thumper —assuming Arshad paid him well enough to ensure that kind of loyalty. After he left, I splashed some water on my face. It was tepid, but still felt wonderful. A moment later, a knock came on the door.

I knew it was Darius. I could sense where he was at all times, just as I could still sense Victor. He was very far away, but he lived and was well. I wondered if he had reached Bactria, the strong-hold of Queen Neblis. Victor claimed he had escaped from her once before, although he hadn't shared any details. From the hints he kept dropping, I got the impression Neblis had loved him once. But that was a long time ago. Now she just seemed to want him dead.

"Come in," I said, turning from the window as Darius entered the room. His tunic clung to him damply, and the hair at his neck curled in the humidity. In short, he looked annoyingly adorable.

"What do you think of Arshad?" he asked.

I raised an eyebrow. "A man who sells the flesh of young boys while praising the Holy Father? Not much. But it does seem things may be breaking loose, Darius. If not for this purge set off by the theft of the fire, we'd be chasing our own tails."

"Secrets are like bugs living under a rock," he agreed. "You never know they're there until someone kicks it over."

I fanned myself with my sleeve. No wonder clients preferred the downstairs rooms. This one was an oven. "That sounds like something my mother would say."

"We'll go to the tomb and leave that message first thing

tomorrow. But Arshad is right in one thing. We can't go anywhere without altering our appearances." He took his knife out and patted the edge of the bed. "Ready?"

"I hope it's sharp," I said, holding up a nearly waist-long chunk of hair with my left hand. His left was useless, as was my right. Between us, we just might manage to give me a haircut.

"Very," he said, and then his hand brushed mine and the sensation sent a shockwave down to my toes. I gritted my teeth and tried counting to twenty, but all I could think about was the feel of his fingers in my hair and the echo of his own desire through the bond. Because every time he touched me, I felt not only my reaction to it, but his as well. It was the strangest, most erotic thing.

We both avoided it and sought it out at any excuse. That was the twisted nature of our relationship. I wished it were otherwise, wished it with all my heart and soul, but whatever the magi had done to him, it left him with an unshakeable belief that the bond equaled pain. That closeness equaled pain. And I didn't want to cause Darius any more. He'd had enough.

Then there was the awkward fact of my bond with his father. I couldn't take off the cuff because I was afraid doing so would block Victor's power when he most needed it. A daēva stayed trapped in the bond whether the cuff was worn or not. Unless I kept the channel open, he would be unable to touch elemental magic.

But it also meant we shared an emotional and physical connection no matter how far away he was. Part of Victor lived in my head, and there was nothing I could do about it. So I put my walls up against Darius, and he did the same, while strands of light brown hair gathered in a pile on the floor.

When he got to the nape of my neck, that sensitive juncture of jaw and throat, I reached back and cupped his hand in mine. He froze.

"Nazafareen..." Darius's voice was a rough, broken thing.

The blade scraped through the last of my hair. He stood and stepped away.

I half turned on the bed, running a hand across the top of my head. It felt so soft. Light. Like kitten fur.

"How do I look?"

He smiled. "Like one of the pretty boys downstairs," he said.

We looked at each for a long moment. I could still feel the spot where his fingers brushed my throat.

"I may have missed a spot or two," he said.

"It's fine." I suddenly couldn't stand to be in that room another moment. Heat flushed my skin. I felt almost ill. I wanted only to break something, or better yet, burn something to ashes. The power flickered at the edges of my vision. "I'll see how Tijah and Myrri are doing," I muttered.

Before he could answer, I jumped to my feet and went next door. Tijah was slumped on the bed. Half her braids were gone. Myrri sat beside her, arms crossed and a stony expression on her face. A knife was stuck into the far wall, as though it had been thrown there.

"You have to finish it," I said.

"I don't want to!" Tijah howled.

"Well, you can't go around like that."

"Do her first," Tijah growled, glaring daggers at Myrri.

I pointed to the stool. Myrri slunk over.

"Give me the knife," I said.

She handed it over, and Tijah and I made short work of her hair. But the problem with using a knife was that it still stuck up in tufts everywhere.

"Holy Father, do I look like that?" I asked, surveying our handiwork. Myrri's hands crept across her head. She gave me a resigned look that seemed to say, *I've been butchered, but it's no less than I expected.*

"Worse," Tijah said.

"We need scissors," I said decisively. "I'll be right back."

I ran downstairs and found the kid who had been lounging outside. He was in the lap of a fat man who looked annoyed when I walked over.

"Sorry to interrupt, but is there is a pair of scissors in this place?"

The boy burst out laughing. "You look like the mangy cat Bobak gives scraps to."

I shot him a dark look. "Scissors?"

"Try the third door, second floor. Ester has some." He went back to his canoodling without another glance.

I ran back upstairs and knocked on the third door, ignoring the moans coming from the other rooms.

"Come in."

A young woman sat at a table covered with cosmetics. She had a long braid and wore a modest, high-necked gown. Her own face was clean of paint, despite the array of pots and brushes before her.

"We're, uh...friends of the owner, staying for a little while," I said. "I need a pair of scissors."

She looked me over. "Yes, you do. Sit down, I'll fix it. Is this a new thing Arshad is trying out? Girls as boys? A niche market, but nothing surprises me anymore."

I flushed. "No, it's for other reasons. A family matter."

"All right." She seemed trained to stay out of other people's business. "I'm Ester. What's your name?"

I sat down in front of the table. "Nazafareen."

She started snipping with a practiced hand. "I take care of the boys. Keep them looking their best. Not all the houses have someone to do that, but Arshad treats his boys well. Much better than other places."

I shuddered inside to think of what those *other places* were like. Growing up in the clan, I'd never seen a brothel until Tel Khalujah. The city was much smaller than Karnopolis, but like most places, it had a booming flesh trade. Once we'd arrested a man who'd beaten one of his girls nearly to death. He'd paid a fine to the satrap and been released within hours. We couldn't do anything about that, but afterwards, Darius had quietly taken the man aside and explained to him in detail what sort of terrible accidents might befall him if it ever happened again. He was white-faced and trembling when we left him on the doorstep of the brothel.

"Do you think you could help my friends...uh, handmaidens too?" I asked. "They're upstairs."

If Ester noticed the slip, she didn't comment on it. "Of course."

I made sure the sleeve covered my cuffs as she circled me, running her hands over my head and evening out the rough patches. After a few minutes, Ester stood back. "Much better. Here, have a look."

She opened a drawer and took out a small copper mirror in a gilt frame. I held it up and my eyes widened. I did look like one of Arshad's boys—one who was nearing the end of his prime. It had been years since I'd seen my reflection so clearly. I looked older, wearier. My nose was still too big, but my cheeks were thinner, the bones sharp as spearheads. Darius had told me I was beautiful once, but I think that's just because he liked me.

I tilted my face, examining it from different angles. I was almost twenty years old, and as long as I was bonded to Darius, I wasn't supposed to age anymore. In theory, I could live as long as the daēvas did, which was a very long time indeed. In theory. But a dagger in the heart would kill me just like anyone else.

"Thanks," I said, handing her the mirror. "I'll bring them down now, if you have time."

"Sure. I get busiest in the evening. You wouldn't believe how fussy some of these kids are about their makeup, and it's always getting smeared." She smiled. "It's nice to have another woman to talk to."

I smiled back. "From what Arshad told us, I thought there weren't any."

"Well, I don't stay here. And he only took me on a few months ago. He dreams of making Marduk's Spear the most famous brothel in Karnopolis. There's only a few that have boys, and they're bitter rivals. When the Silver Hawk hired a hairdresser, he had to have one too."

"He doesn't keep children, does he?" I asked uneasily. The thought made my stomach turn. I didn't think I could stay here a minute longer if Arshad had little kids stashed somewhere. In fact, I might just see how he liked hanging from the roof by his bony old ankles.

"None under the age of thirteen," Ester said. "Although there's a market for them."

"That's still young," I said, thinking of my little sister, who would be nearly that age now if she hadn't been killed by a wight.

Ester shrugged. "None of them have anywhere else to go. It's much worse on the streets."

I shook my head. It never ceased to amaze me how men who claimed to be devout, like Arshad, could blithely pretend the rules didn't apply to them whenever it was convenient. But the magi and the King were the same, preaching good thoughts and good deeds while they exploited the daēvas as slaves. It's why I was in Karnopolis, risking my life to find a man I didn't even like. To try to right the terrible wrong I'd been a part of for so long.

"I'll be back in a minute," I said. "And please don't tell anyone we're here. Arshad will explain later."

She went back to fussing with her bottles and brushes. "Don't worry, I can keep a secret. He guarantees privacy to all who come to Marduk's Spear. Anyone who betrays that might as well throw themselves in the nearest canal. Save Bobak the trouble."

I smiled at this. Ester didn't.

Two minutes later, I had located my quarry and hauled them both down one flight to Ester's room. Tijah sulked through the entire ordeal, but she brightened when Ester offered her some candied dates. Myrri endured her own haircut in dreamy solitude. She never seemed to be paying much attention to anything, but I knew appearances were deceiving. In a fight, Myrri was focused and deadly. She worked best with water, as Darius did with earth. The only person besides Tijah she had ever been close to was a daēva named Tommas, and he was dead.

I caught her eye now, pointed to her hair, and made the sign for good, thumb and pinky touching. She gave me a shy smile and returned the gesture.

I tried to include her when we were all talking, and Darius did too, but we only knew a few of the signs they used, so when Myrri communicated, it was always through Tijah. They had been bonded since they were children and seemed nearly able to read each other's minds. I had come to think of them as two halves of the same person. Tijah was Myrri's voice. And Myrri...she was Tijah's anchor. The one who could endure anything, who did what had to be done.

I watched Tijah chat with Ester, her face animated as she sniffed the various pots and talked Myrri into letting her face get painted. When she was in the right mood, Tijah could have charmed a priggish old Numerator into singing her bawdy drinking songs.

I'd expected her and Myrri to leave us after Alexander's camp. To put the empire and Tijah's father behind them and start fresh someplace far away. No one would have stopped them. But they hadn't. They'd chosen to stick with me and Darius, and I'd never forget that.

"Your turn," Tijah said.

Myrri batted eyes heavily shadowed with green sparkles at me.

"No," I replied flatly.

"Oh, yes..."

Arguing with Tijah when she was like this would be futile, so I gave in, although with as little grace as possible. When they were done, I examined the results in the mirror. I looked even more like a washed-up boy whore than I had before, which was saying something.

Of course, Darius chose exactly that moment to come looking for us. He doubled over with laughter when he saw me.

"How much for this nubile youth?" he asked, barely managing to get the words out as he pretended to rummage through his pockets for coins. "I want the full treatment, mind you. Spare no expense."

"Oh, you'll get the full treatment," I growled. "I just hope you like it rough."

"Not too rough," he said, and our eyes met and suddenly we weren't laughing anymore.

Ester broke the awkward silence. "Candied date?" she asked Darius.

He reached for it but I snatched it out of his hand.

"He's on a diet," I said, sharing a grin with Tijah. "Now, do you think you could rummage up a dress? Blue would suit his eyes best, I think."

5

BALTHAZAR

Balthazar cut a morsel of lamb and listened to the magi whispering to each other. They reminded him of a herd of frightened sheep, huddling together as the wolves circled ever closer—the wolves in this case being the Numerators. Dinner in the vast torch-lit dining hall was a subdued affair, and the few hushed conversations at his table all revolved around a single topic.

"I hear they are fanning out across the empire," a magus with a wispy white beard said in a tremulous voice. "Every one of us, from the Khusk Range to the southern desert, will be subject to the question."

"It's an outrage," muttered another magus, who was somewhat younger but already looked stooped and bent, as though he rarely bothered to look up at the world around him. "It is likely some plot of the Numerators to discredit us. I would put nothing past them."

"Yes, it's terribly convenient both Purified died before they could be examined by the King," added a third magus at Balthazar's elbow. "Now we must take the Numerators' word that our brothers had any connection to the theft of the fire."

Balthazar glanced at the man nearest him. He couldn't have been more than thirty years, but he spoke with the sort of high-handed pomposity Balthazar had always detested about the magi.

"What is your name, brother?" he asked, composing his features into a friendly smile.

"Why do you ask?" The dough-faced magus eyed Balthazar with thinly veiled suspicion. His cheeks were flushed, and although his girth implied a healthy appetite, he had hardly touched his meal of curried lamb and bread.

"I am new to the city, just arrived this very day from Qaddah. It seems I have missed the latest news. Can you tell me what has transpired?"

The magus relaxed and took a gulp of wine. "There are as many rumors as whores on Saffron Street. Some claim Alexander is behind it all, and that he has taken the Bactrian witch as his consort. Others swear an army of Druj attacked the palace in Persepolae." He waved a chubby hand. "The second is certainly false. As to the first, who knows? Only two things appear certain. The holy fire has been taken from the Barbican, and a group of dangerous daēvas escaped from Gorgon-e Gaz. Thank the Holy Father, they are all dead. But the magi are being blamed for both disasters." He leaned in, and Balthazar got a whiff of the man's sour breath. "Some actually claim there were necromancers involved. Said they flew down on wings black as night and carried the daēvas off to Bactria, and the holy fire with them." He laughed uneasily. "Can you imagine?"

Balthazar primly made the sign of the flame. "Holy Father keep us," he said, feigning horror. "It cannot be true. They wouldn't dare cross the mountains, would they?"

"Only a rumor," the magus said, with the overly careful diction of a habitual drinker. "But the King is convinced we harbor traitors, some ridiculous sect called the Followers of the Prophet that believes all daēvas should be freed. Now he has thrown us to the tender mercy of the Numerators." He stared glassily into the dregs of his cup. "I myself have been summoned for questioning tomorrow. Of course, I have nothing to hide."

"Of course." Balthazar wondered what these sheep would do if they knew that just four days prior, he had personally placed the urn containing their holy fire in Queen Neblis's hands. It was all too amusing. "You never did tell me your name, brother."

"It's Shahrooz," the magus said, pushing his untouched plate away with a heavy sigh and glancing at the empty decanter between them.

"And I am Balthus." He looked around. The other magi had gone back to their whispered laments. No one was paying them the least bit of attention. "Would you care to join me in my rooms for another cup of wine? I have a fine Attican red I brought from the temple in Qaddah."

Shahrooz perked up at this. "Attican? I haven't tasted that in years." He lowered his voice conspiratorially. "The vintage they serve here is worse than the swill in the lowest wine sinks. At least, that's what I hear," he amended quickly. "The brothers in Qaddah must be treated well."

"Yes, I was rather surprised at the low quality of the food and drink here," Balthazar said, warming to his role. "Considering Karnopolis is the seat of our faith."

Shahrooz scowled. "The Numerators again. They collect the taxes, so they ensure their own order gets the lion's share, while we are left with scraps."

Balthazar shook his head in mock disbelief. "The Holy Father will no doubt see the scales are balanced in the next life. Greed is a mortal sin."

"I wouldn't mind if He did it in this one," Shahrooz mumbled, seemingly oblivious to the fact that he was skating near the precipice of out-and-out heresy. Lucky for him, the only one to hear it had renounced his own faith two centuries ago.

Balthazar gave a razor-edged smile. "Nor would I. Times are changing, brother. And once all this nonsense blows over, these lands will be swept clean. I have visions sometimes. They tell me it will be so."

"I have visions too," Shahrooz said with a laugh. "Of a fine northern vintage. Come, let us celebrate while we still can. We shall toast the Prophet, and you can tell me of Qaddah. I've always wanted to see the famous oasis there."

"Yes, we must toast the Prophet," Balthazar agreed as they left the cavernous dining hall and made their way into the winding corridors of the temple complex. "Tell me, have you served here long?"

"Twenty-two years. Since I was a boy of seven."

"And what are your duties?"

"The same as yours, I suppose. Daily consecration of the fire altar. Preparing the dead. We have a large number of students and initiates here. Daēvas too, of course. I teach classes in the mornings..."

The man droned on, but Balthazar was no longer listening. His thoughts turned to the Prophet. Zarathustra, once the High Magus of Karnopolis. A proud, hawk-nosed man, who had tended to inspire either blind loyalty or abject scorn. The near godlike figure they had turned him into bore little resemblance to the man Balthazar remembered. Zarathustra had been devout, of course, but he also had a keen, questioning mind. Not all the magi who served under him had approved of his alchemical experiments, and they especially hadn't liked his friendship with the daēva named Victor.

Unlike all but a handful of people, Balthazar remembered the time before the daēvas were leashed. They were standoffish, fey creatures who shunned humans, preferring to live in the wilderness. Except for Victor. He would visit Zarathustra at the temple in Karnopolis from time to time. The two would shut themselves away in Zarathustra's study for days at a time. No one knew what they talked about, but when the cities began to fall to the Druj, to the wights and revenants and liches, Zarathustra had summoned him, and Victor came.

Shortly after that, Zarathustra vanished, a new High Magus was declared and Xeros announced the discovery of a weapon against the Druj. Cuffs forged from holy fire that compelled the wicked daēvas to fight on the humans' behalf. By then, distrust of any creature that wasn't human had grown widespread among the magi. Half of them already suspected the daēvas were witches, and it had taken no great leap of imagination to convince them the daēvas were also Druj.

Testing of the magi to see who had the ability to wear the cuffs and link with the daēvas had commenced immediately. Balthazar was one of those with the gift.

The chains he wore as an Antimagus were based on the design of the daēva cuffs, but far cruder. For one thing, they required Balthazar to be physically connected to his slaves, while the daēva cuffs worked at any distance. There was also a limit to how many he could hold. Not so with the daēva cuffs. Worst of all, his chains didn't work on daēvas, only humans.

Like Brother Shahrooz.

"Here we are," Balthazar said, opening the door to his small chamber.

The magus entered, steadying himself against the doorway. "Do you have cups? We should have brought some from the dining hall."

"Right here," Balthazar said, reaching into his saddlebags. Shahrooz bobbed his head happily and shuffled into the room. "Please, sit." Balthazar smiled. "We have much to discuss, and the night grows short."

Perhaps Brother Shahrooz heard something in his tone, some primal sense of danger that pierced the fog of drunkenness, for his eyes widened and he took a step for the door, but it came too late. A moment later, the iron collar was snapping shut around his neck. Balthazar slid the other end around his own wrist and breathed deeply as he felt the magus's mind shiver in terror.

"Holy Father," the magus gibbered, his eyes glazing over as all but the automatic functions of his body—breath, heartbeat—surrendered to the will of the Antimagus. "Holy Father..."

Balthazar studied him for a moment. It would be so much easier if he could just read the man's mind. Unfortunately, the chains didn't work that way. Balthazar could share his own strongest, clearest memories with a slave, but not the other way around. He would have to use more traditional, if messier, methods to find what he was looking for.

"Hold still," the necromancer whispered, drawing a knife from his belt. "Now. Tell me all you know about the Prophet."

🌿 6 🌿

NAZAFAREEN

I took my revenge by dragging Darius to the Egyptian wig maker later that same afternoon. His name was Hammu, and once we said we were friends of Arshad Nabu-zar-adan, he clapped his hands and vowed to give us the "cousin's discount," which I took to mean he would rob us only half-blind.

Over cups of wine, I told him I had suffered an unfortunate accident while cooking pastries and set my hair on fire. It was such a charred ruin that my brother and I had decided to just hack it all off and start fresh, but I couldn't tolerate the thought of walking around like this until it did. Hammu understood perfectly and assured us his merchandise was the finest in Karnopolis, taken from the heads of noble ladies who subsisted only on milk and honey.

Darius watched with an amused expression while I tried on various hairpieces, finally settling on one with dark ringlets that I thought would complement his pale complexion. After a nice energetic bit of haggling, during which Hammu produced actual tears, we settled on a price and were back at Marduk's Spear by suppertime.

Tijah, Myrri and Arshad Nabu-zar-adan waited in a private sitting room that opened onto the courtyard to allow cooling breezes to pass through. The setting sun cast long shadows across the gardens. I could hear muted laughter from the main room, where the evening clientele had begun to gather, but Bobak lounged just outside the door to ensure no one eavesdropped on our conversation.

Arshad seemed to have a soft spot for cats, for the creatures roamed everywhere. One of them, a slim black thing with white paws, dozed in Myrri's lap as Darius and I joined the others on embroidered silk cushions arranged in a semicircle around a low rectangular table. A pitcher of water sat next to a stone vase carved on opposite sides with the stern face of a woman—perhaps some goddess whose name was long forgotten. Beads of water had condensed on the pitcher. I poured a cup and drank deeply. It must have just been drawn from the well for it was deliciously cold.

"How did you find Hammu?" Arshad asked, selecting a pistachio from a silver bowl and cracking it with his teeth.

"Most helpful," Darius said, at the exact same moment that I said, "He'd rob his own grandmother if she gave him the chance."

Arshad laughed. His own silver hair was immaculate, as always, and the purple thread of his tunic practically screamed *obscenely wealthy brothel owner*. "Well, I know you went to the right place. He is Egyptian, so thieving is in his blood. But Egyptians also make the best wigs. No one knows why, but it is true. Now, then." He rose and went to a lacquered cabinet, from which he took a sheet of vellum and a stylus. "Let us compose our note." Arshad dipped the stylus in black ink and held it poised over the parchment. He thought for a moment, nibbling his bottom lip. The stylus scratched out a message.

"What did you say?" I craned my neck to look at the parchment, as if I could read what it said anyway.

"Friends are here to help," Arshad read. "Come at once."

"Myrri and I will leave it," Tijah said, taking a delicate bite of bread. She had the manners of a rich girl, and I could tell Arshad noticed. "Darius and Nazafareen can wait for the answer. I want to get a look at the temple district. That seems the likeliest place for his prison."

Arshad folded the message into a square and placed it on the table. "The fourteenth step of the eastern side," he reminded her.

Tijah, who remembered everything she had ever heard, gave him a patronizing smile. "I know," she said.

"Where can we sit without being too obvious?" I asked. "It could be hours before Saman responds."

"I have thought on this," Arshad said. "The temple district is full of trinket sellers who cater to the pilgrims. Carved wooden faravahars, things of that nature. Bobak has a nephew in the business and we can easily obtain a supply for you. Set up a blanket at the foot of the steps and no one will look at you twice."

Darius smiled. "I should have thought of that myself," he said. "The peddlers are part of the scenery. Even in these harsh times, they wouldn't draw undue attention. But there's another problem." He looked tired, with dark shadows under his eyes that somehow made him even more handsome. "If Zarathustra has lived so long, it must be because he is bonded. That means he has a daēva somewhere."

"So we should be prepared to rescue two," Tijah said, sharing a look with Myrri. "But if he does have a daēva, he or she can help us."

"It depends on the daēva," I said. "They might be loyal to the empire. We have no idea."

I wished Victor had come. He was old enough to remember it all firsthand. He had fought in the war two centuries before and was incredibly strong in the power, especially earth. He was also a bit of an arrogant prick, but you couldn't have everything.

"How will you get him to Persepolae?" Arshad asked. "Assuming he can be found and freed."

"We'll ride," I said. "It's the fastest way. We have gold to buy horses."

"I know a dealer who's slightly less dishonest than the others. I'll send you to him whenever you like."

I shifted on the couch. There was a question I needed to ask, although I feared the answer. "Have you heard any news from Tel Khalujah? Rumors of trouble involving the mountain clans?"

Arshad shook his head. "Nothing. Why?"

"They're my people. If the King can't punish me, I assume he'll go after them." I didn't feel like telling Arshad what had happened in the dungeons when the Numerators paid me a visit. They had wanted me to torture Darius into confessing his treason. When I refused, they threatened to wipe out my family. I'd asked Darius's mother Delilah to send a warning, but I had no idea if she'd managed to do it. If she hadn't, their deaths would be on my head.

"Well, I don't know about the clans, but things in Persepolae are as bad as they are here, if not worse," Arshad said. "They say there are traitors in the Immortals as well as the magi, and many have been given to the fire. The King's daēva was publicly flogged, although my informers say she still lives."

Darius's face could have been set in stone. Only I knew his pain. If we had not come to Persepolae, if Ilyas had not denounced Darius before the King, none of it would have happened. If Tel Khalujah had not been the closest satrapy to Gorgon-e Gaz, if the Water Dogs chosen to bring back the escaped daēvas had not included Victor's own son...So many ifs, setting in motion a chain of events that still rippled outward like a stone dropped in a pond.

"In his eagerness for retribution, King Artaxeros is making a tactical error," Darius said. "He risks the Immortals' loyalty by abusing them so."

"It does play to our cause," Arshad agreed. "I have just heard from one of the Followers in Persepolae that at least a third of the daēva Immortals would be willing to follow Alexander of Macydon if they can be freed from the cuffs."

"And the others?" Tijah asked.

Arshad shrugged. "I do not know what they will do. But if the King loses at Persepolae, I doubt very much that the other satrapies will persist in a rebellion. They know Alexander is merciful to those who welcome him, but he won't blink at razing their cities to dust if they bar their gates. The empire will fall. And the slavery of the daēvas will finally come to an end."

"*If* the King loses," Darius said. "That is hardly a foregone conclusion."

"No." Arshad seemed troubled. "Their forces are well matched in sheer numbers, and there's no question that Alexander is a superior general. But the Immortals...No one has ever defeated them."

"No one used fire on a massive scale," Darius pointed out.

"What he's trying to say is if we don't do something to stop this battle, no matter which side wins, the daēvas will lose," I cut in. "They will either be dead, or still under the thumb of the empire."

"And you believe the Prophet can stop it?"

"He is the *only* one who can."

Arshad nodded. "I'll let you know if I hear anything about the mountain clans. All gossip reaches Marduk's Spear eventually. And now I'd best make an appearance with the customers. Make sure the boys are behaving themselves." He made the sign of the flame and I wanted badly to punch him in the face. "The Followers have waited for this day for many long years. To think our saintly Prophet could soon walk among us again..." His voice trailed off and he pressed a sleeve to his eyes.

I shared a look with Tijah. Well, I supposed I was a hypocrite too, but Arshad took it to a whole other level. "Yes, a miracle," I said tartly. "No doubt he's been lonely in his prison. When he gets out, you can offer him a free—"

I cut off, wincing in pain, as Darius casually leaned forward, placing his large sandal over mine and stepping down with all his weight. I thought I heard something crunch.

"We should be thanking *you*," he said to Arshad with a pleasant smile, as I tried vainly to retrieve my foot. "And your trust is not misplaced. If he lives, we will find him."

Arshad looked between us, vaguely bewildered. I pressed my lips together in a pained grin even as I vowed to make Darius pay dearly when we were alone. Tijah, who sat on our side of the table, had a full view of the proceedings. She took a large, loud bite of a carrot as Myrri made a sort of wheezing sound that passed for her rare laughter.

"Well then, may the Holy Father watch over you all tomorrow," Arshad said, rising. "I'll see the trinkets are left by the front door."

As soon as he was gone, I gave Darius a hard shove and examined my foot, gingerly wiggling the toes and perversely hoping some of them were broken so I could make him feel bad.

"That old goat," I muttered. "*Your trust is not misplaced.*" I pointed an accusing finger at his chest. "Has it occurred to you that your loyalties *are*?"

"Getting us thrown out isn't going to accomplish anything," Darius countered calmly. "Has no one ever told you that one catches more flies with honey than vinegar?"

"I'd drink a bottle of the stuff if it meant I didn't have to listen to his pious horseshit," I said, enveloped in the warm glow of self-righteousness.

Tijah yawned. "I'm done for. You two can stay and argue, we're going up to bed."

Something occurred to me. "Hey...Bobak?" I called.

My heart sank as a hulking shadow shifted outside the door.

"Yep?"

"You're still here."

He stuck his grizzled head inside. "Yep."

"Guess you heard all that?"

"Yep."

I stared at him. It was hard to tell what he was thinking. So far, I'd only seen mean Bobak and nice Bobak, and they looked pretty similar. "Sorry. No offense."

Bobak shrugged. "Don't care. Long as you don't harm him, or the boys." He smiled gently. "Then I'd have to kill you."

⚜

I LAY IN MY NARROW BED LISTENING TO THE SHOUTS AND giggles coming from downstairs. There were few choices in this world if you weren't lucky enough to be born rich. Life with the Four-Legs Clan had its own hardships, but we took care of each other. Everyone had a place and no one went hungry, not unless we all did. I thought of my mother and father, my brother Kian, and wondered if I would ever see any of them again. If they would even recognize me if I did. I wasn't the naïve, trusting girl I used to be. I had fought and killed Druj. I had been betrayed, and betrayed my own loyalties in turn. The only people I truly cared about other than my family were all in this brothel. Darius most of all, although I was still unsure what we were to each other.

I could sense him on the other side of the wall. He only slept two or three hours a night, if he bothered to at all. Tomorrow we would go to the temple district, where he had spent the first sixteen years of his life. A miserable stretch of time, although he never spoke of it. If my sister Ashraf still haunted my dreams, this city haunted Darius. He would have to face it eventually and I feared what would happen when he did. Most of the time, Darius had an almost preternatural calm, but it masked a temper even worse than my own. I'd only seen him erupt twice—once, when he learned Victor was his father, and the second time after I'd severed him from the power, in an incident also involving Victor. Both times had been bad, and I had a feeling it was only the tail of the elephant.

The tallow candle on my bedside table wavered as a faint breeze swept the room. I'd lied when I told him on the ship that I couldn't sense the power, couldn't sense the everything-nothing place daēvas called the nexus. I sensed it all the time now. It was the source elemental power flowed from, the underlying fabric of all things. I think I could have touched it if I wished to, but I didn't. Partly because that was how the Immortals tracked us down at the manor house. They had felt it when Darius wielded air.

But mainly because I felt a strong attraction to fire. The forbidden element. The only one daēvas couldn't work. If they did, it would kill them. I didn't know why this was so. But it's how the Numerators enforced a sort of population control. Under the laws of the empire, daēvas could only be used for the King's Immortals and the Water Dogs. As the latter, we had protected the northern border from Queen Neblis and her Undead Druj. But daēvas were strictly forbidden in private households, except for a handful of the wealthiest merchants. The reason was simple. Daēvas equaled power. No human could stand against them in a fight. They were faster and stronger, they lived for hundreds of years (maybe longer), and they knew magic. If the satraps, the regional governors of this sprawling empire, started breeding them, rebellion would not be far behind.

So the Numerators roamed the empire, testing everyone at the fire temples. If you passed—meaning you were human—you were given a tattoo on your palm. But if an unmarked daēva got close to the flames, within a foot or two, they would be unable to resist the attraction. They would reach for it and they would burn. It was a ruthless system, but effective. The empire had been stable for two hundred years, since the chained daēvas helped drive the Druj back to Bactria.

As Darius's human bonded, I controlled the flow of his power through the cuff. That was supposed to be *all* I could do. He was the river, and I was the floodgate. I could open or close it as I pleased, but I shouldn't be able to dive into those waters myself.

And yet I could. During the fight with Immortals of Kayan's manor house, I had killed a man with the power. I had reached straight through the cuffs and manipulated the element of water to reverse the flow of blood through his veins. It had stopped his heart in an instant. At the same moment, both Darius and Victor had experienced a sudden burst of power, enough to flatten the rest of the soldiers, without being harmed themselves. For the daēva magic had a price. If you used air, it quickened the breath in your own lungs. Water exerted a tidal pull on blood, and working with earth could shatter flesh and bone.

We all should have been dead. And now I dreamed of fire almost every night. Just looking at the candle, I felt its seductive pull. A fierce energy so unlike the other three elements. It called to me through the cuffs. Just one taste...

And I knew Darius would die. Probably me and Victor too.

I took a breath and blew. The flame guttered for a moment, then died.

۞

After a quick breakfast of bread and yoghurt, we paid a visit to Ester. She sat at her table, long braid coiled over one shoulder, grinding up various items with a mortar and pestle. A spark of interest lit in Darius's eyes as he surveyed the pots and jars of fragrant oil. He liked to know what things were made of, how they worked. His greatest talent was with working with earth. Darius could often tell what metals were in something just from looking at it. Now he made a show of sniffing each small mound of powder and studying them in the bright morning sun pouring through the window, although I knew he didn't need to.

"Let me see...Antimony, burnt almonds, lead, copper, ochre, ash...malachite?"

"Yes." Ester looked at him in astonishment. "Have you made cosmetics before?"

"My mother did," Darius lied with a cocky grin. "Now that last one...I'm not sure. Some type of insect?"

"Ant eggs!" Ester said, clapping her hands. "It gives the eye shadow a frosty effect."

I stepped in before Darius's showing off got us in even deeper trouble. "My *betrothed* and I would like to go for a walk around the city. Can you help me with his disguise? Uncle Arshad says we must be very careful about showing our faces anywhere but Marduk's Spear."

"Of course." Ester gave Darius a critical once-over and went to work. Half an hour later, my daēva was transformed into a proper lady. He wore a short face veil that let only his blue eyes show, which were now rimmed heavily with kohl.

"It itches," he complained when Ester set the wig atop his head and set about adjusting the fit.

"You only have to wear it outside," I said placatingly. I could feel the itchiness too, an irritating tickle at the back of my mind.

"At least it's not summer," Ester said. She smoothed the ringlets over his shoulders. "You don't look half bad."

Darius picked up the mirror and examined himself from several different angles.

"You'll have to protect my honor, Nazafareen," he said. "My alluring beauty might incite the men in the street to untoward behavior."

"No one touches my virgin mistress," I growled in a husky voice.

Ester moved to tint Darius's lips with a pearly goo she said was made from fish scales, but he slapped her hand away.

"I'm not a harlot," Darius said. He grinned and amended it to, "Well, not a cheap one."

"Now for the gown," Ester said. "I brought a few that used to belong to my older sister. Let's try the blue first." She winked. "It ought to fit. She's a large-boned lass."

"Are you saying I look fat in this dress?" Darius demanded.

Ester made soothing sounds. "Don't be silly. But you're broader in the shoulders than most women. Taller too. Alright, get the tunic off."

I was surprised she was so immodest, but then I remembered we were in a brothel. She probably saw naked boys all day long. And Darius did have pants on.

He pulled off the wig and veil first. Holy Father, he looked good, even with the eye makeup. It actually made him seem more exotic. Darius used his right arm to lift the tunic above his hand and drop it on the floor. His left arm hung dead and twisted at his side. Ester glanced at it, but didn't react in a way that might embarrass him.

Aside from that arm, the rest of his skin was...perfect. All the wounds he'd taken—fighting Druj and necromancers, getting beaten by the guards at the palace in Persepolae and tortured by our captain, Ilyas—had already healed. Another of his daēva gifts. Darius slouched there, waiting for Ester to dress him and looking like one of those statues of chiseled youths the Greeks adored so. I realized I was staring like a beggar at a feast and turned my eyes to the ceiling.

"Need some help?" I asked Ester hopefully.

"It's all right, I've got it," she said, dropping the gown over his head and guiding his arms through the holes. I gritted my teeth, ignoring a stab of jealousy. Did her hands linger on his chest for a heartbeat too long? And what was that look passing between them?

Darius caught my eye at just that moment and grinned evilly. I was an open book to him, and not a very complicated one.

"Would you help me with my hair, rose petal?" he asked sweetly.

"My pleasure," I grumbled, yanking the wig on his head with more force than was strictly necessary.

"And my veil?"

I had to lean into him to hook it around the back, close enough that I felt his breath on my cheek.

"There. You look lovely."

"All right, time to shoo," Ester said. "Both of you. The afternoon clientele will be arriving soon, and I have to get the boys ready."

We gave her our thanks and found Tijah and Myrri waiting outside.

"Do you have the note?" I whispered to Tijah.

She patted her pants pocket. "We'll follow you."

I nodded. Tijah was taking the biggest risk. If Saman had been found out and anyone was watching the tomb, she'd be the one they grabbed. According to Darius, neither the Numerators nor the magi had fully-trained adult daēvas. Once they came of age, they were shipped off to become Immortals or Water Dogs. There was a garrison of daēvas at the palace, but the main force of the King was back in Persepolae.

Darius was one of the strongest in generations. I'd seen him throw a stone wall twenty yards and tear the roof off a building, although it had hurt him to do it. I told myself we'd still have a chance to escape if it turned out to be a trap, but I'm not sure I believed it.

"I don't like the feel of this city," I said. "It's poisonous. If anything happens..."

Tijah slapped a hand over my mouth and muttered something in her native tongue. "Bad luck! Don't even say it. Foolish words tempt the gods, and everyone knows they have a warped sense of humor."

Tijah worshipped her own set of deities, and they were a

capricious and vengeful bunch. The Holy Father didn't strike me as much better. If He did exist, which I had come to doubt, He seemed about as reliable as the cats lurking around Marduk's Spear.

I held my hand up. "Fine. Just be quick about it. And subtle."

Tijah sniffed. "I'm not entirely stupid. Have a little faith."

"I'm trying to."

Tijah turned to Darius and gave him a leer. "How much for your...trinkets?"

Myrri shook her head, but she was grinning. When she smiled, her whole face changed, giving her a kind of luminous beauty that rivalled even Tijah's.

"More than *you* can afford," he shot back breathily.

I hefted the bag Arshad had left for us over one shoulder and prodded him forward. "Enough, children. So where is this tomb?"

"About twenty minutes' walk," Darius said.

"Lead on, then. And no flirting with strange men. It's far too hot to get in a fight, and this is my best tunic."

Darius snorted behind the veil, but he started off down the street, Tijah and Myrri following. With my hair chopped off and in the guise of a boy, I felt relaxed enough to enjoy the languid pace of the city. Once we left the pleasure district, whose denizens were still mostly sleeping at this early hour, we passed through a busier area devoted to different trades: silks and spices, housewares and jewelers, woodworkers and weavers. Some sold their wares in shops, others beneath shaded awnings on the streets. No one paid me any mind, but Darius got several admiring glances and I could see he was pleased with himself.

After a while, the shops and bazaars thinned out and the buildings grew larger and more extravagant. Mudbrick turned to stone, and then to marble. The people on foot were mostly servants, rushing about on different errands. I started seeing magi, and a few Numerators too. Their white robes looked similar, but the Numerators' had blood red hems. We rounded a corner and came to a wide boulevard flanked by large marble buildings on each side. Darius pointed to the one on the left.

"That's the Temple of the Magi," he said. "Next to it is the Imperial Archives and the Hall of the Numerators."

"And that one?" I pointed to the building on the right. It was dingier than the others, with small barred windows.

"The daēva quarters," Darius said. His even tone betrayed no emotion, but I could sense turmoil in him as he glanced away. "And this is the Tomb of the Prophet."

It was a rectangular mausoleum squeezed between the daēva quarters and the archives, reached by wide stairs rising up on all four sides. A flame burned at the entrance, and bouquets of flowers, scraps of food and cups of water had been left haphazardly on the steps by visiting pilgrims. The main entrance had lifelike carvings of horses, of course, because Persians put horses on *everything*, as well as a procession of magi bearing myrtle wands and what looked to me like lion cubs swaddled in blankets, whatever that was about.

I took a quick look around. A few magi moved in and out of the temple across the street, but I didn't see any soldiers or Numerators or anyone who seemed to have a particular interest in the tomb. Of course, that didn't mean it wasn't being watched. There were any number of vantage points in the surrounding buildings.

"What does that say?" I pointed to the flowing script carved into the lintel. I knew the magi had taught Darius to read.

"One good deed is worth a thousand prayers," he replied.

I'd been preparing a sarcastic comment in anticipation of some empty platitude. That's the way it is when you lose your faith. I was not simply a non-believer. I actively hated them for duping me. But even for a heretic, that sentiment was hard to argue with.

I shook the cloth out on a patch of ground a stone's throw from the tomb's main entrance and began arranging the trinkets

Arshad had given us, feeling irritated the Prophet had said something I could even remotely agree with. They included little wooden figurines of the man himself, woven leather bracelets painted with the faravahar, and assorted other cheap goods identical to the wares on display in other parts of the plaza.

And then Tijah was ascending the steps. With her braids shorn to the scalp, wearing pants and a plain brown tunic, she looked like a delicate youth of twenty or so. She moved confidently as always, and kept her eyes on the brazier. I held my breath as she knelt as though in prayer and felt around for the loose stone Arshad had spoken of on the eastern side, just beneath a slightly wilted lotus blossom. It was a clever spot, I realized, shielded from both the Temple of the Magi and the Hall of the Numerators by the tomb itself. Still, my skin crawled as her fingers slid the note inside and placed a lotus on top.

If anyone was watching, Tijah had just damned herself as a Follower of the Prophet. This was the moment soldiers would come pouring out of the Hall of the Numerators to arrest her. But all remained quiet as she skipped back down the steps and disappeared into the thickening crowds without a backward glance. From the corner of my eye, I saw Myrri slide like a shadow from behind the daēva quarters and stroll after her.

"Did anyone follow them?" I asked Darius. He had a sixth sense for such things.

"I don't think so." He closed his eyes and reached for the nexus, that place of quiet where he could focus his mind without distractions. "No."

I felt a surge of hope I hadn't dared indulge before. Our mission here had seemed hopeless. Worse than hopeless, actually, since I had fully believed it would not only end in failure, but back in the King's dungeons. If we truly had an ally in the magi...

Well, even if we discovered where Zarathustra was, we still had to rescue him, I reminded myself. One step at a time.

"Five siglos," Darius entreated an old woman passing by. "A

memento of the Prophet to treasure and leave to your grandchildren." He batted his eyelashes, but she was unmoved.

"Five siglos? More like one. If *you* paid *me*."

I had never heard Darius actually *harrumph* before, but he did it now.

"Three siglos then. But my children will go hungry tonight. All nine of them."

She eyed him disdainfully. "If you have nine children, I'm the King's daēva." And with that, she spun on her heel and marched away, wide hips swaying like the *Photina* in a swelling sea.

I couldn't see his face beneath the veil, but I could feel the sudden sharp ache in his heart.

"We'll get her back," I said in a low voice. "I swear to you, Darius. Your mother will be freed."

He nodded, but he barely spoke for the rest of that day. I knew how guilty he felt. Delilah had sacrificed her freedom to smuggle him out of the dungeons. The King seemed to care for her in a twisted way, for he didn't execute her. But he had locked her up, and I knew there were other ways to make a daēva suffer. She was the real reason Victor had gone to Bactria to steal the fire back. It was the only thing short of death that could release the piece of Delilah trapped inside the cuff.

So Darius brooded while I took over the haggling duties—and discovered I had quite a knack for it, especially since I didn't care how many trinkets we sold. Pilgrims and magi and Numerators came and went, and the shadows lengthened across the plaza. But no one paused on the fourteenth step of the eastern side of the tomb.

As the day wore on, I noticed the magi studiously avoided looking at the Numerators, while the latter had a certain smug air about them. They were an arrogant bunch normally, but this was different. More pronounced. I saw several magi cross the street to avoid groups of Numerators moving between their own headquarters and the Imperial Archives, where they kept the taxation records. Their shoulders were hunched and they practically ran up the steps to the temple, glancing back anxiously like rabbits that sensed the shadow of the hawk passing overhead.

And I remembered one of the last things Ilyas had told me before Tijah killed him. We were at Kayan Zaaykar's manor house on the Midnight Sea. Ilyas had arrived with two dozen Immortals. He was hunting Victor, the only one of us who had managed to escape.

I asked Ilyas what had happened to Delilah after she helped us flee the palace. He said the Numerators wanted to burn her in Darius's stead.

The King trusts them above the magi, and even the Immortals, because they haven't harbored traitors, Ilyas had said. *There's a purge coming, Nazafareen.*

Of course. The Numerators weren't only taking custody of Zarathustra. They were in charge of the whole witch hunt. They were the ones who had nailed six magi to the city walls. I felt a chill in my bones. I knew little about the Numerators, and had only ever spoken to one in my life. He'd threatened to wipe out my clan if I didn't torture Darius into confessing his supposed crimes. If the magi were the King's lapdogs, the Numerators were his wolves. And it seemed they'd been given free run of the henhouse.

The sun was setting as we packed up our wares. I wanted to stay longer, but the foot traffic had thinned to a trickle and none of the other peddlers remained. As Darius placed the last of the trinkets in our sack, a group of a dozen children emerged from the Temple of the Magi. They trudged down the wide marble steps, but even their downcast manner couldn't hide the way they moved—with a grace that was more than human, despite the physical infirmities marring their bodies. Twisted backs and blind eyes. Missing fingers or toes, and those were the lucky ones. The children were escorted by women in flowing red robes, each with a gleaming golden cuff at her wrist.

Darius looked at them for a long moment. I thought he might say something, but his walls slammed up with bruising force. He had been one of those children once, not so long ago.

"Let's go," he said roughly, and I was glad no one was close enough to hear how masculine his voice sounded.

We passed the daēva quarters just as one of the children paused to study a flock of starlings making a tremendous racket in the trees. She had wild black hair that looked like it hadn't seen a comb in days, but her eyes were bright as she watched the birds. She seemed to enjoy their rowdy twittering.

I caught the child's eye and gave her a smile. She looked down at her feet, then peeked back at me through the curtain of hair. She wore a faded blue dress. The cuff bonding her to her human keeper was too large, and she kept pushing it up her skinny fore-arm. A dog barked, and the flock exploded from the branches, a hundred wings beating the air as they rose into the sky. The child lifted her head to watch, and stumbled forward as her bonded, a heavyset woman with a petulant mouth, seized her arm and dragged her toward the door of the daēva quarters.

"Keep moving, Druj," the woman hissed.

I glanced at Darius. He stared straight ahead, his eyes like ice above the veil. The child and her keeper disappeared inside. The door closed with a heavy thud. I thought of all those daēva chil-dren, generations of them, being told day in and day out they were Druj, evil. The truth was that their ancestors had *saved* us from the Druj. And we had thanked those daēvas by locking them up in Gorgon-e Gaz for the next two centuries—like Victor.

Darius's walls were up, but I could still feel his anger leaking through. He had endured all this and worse growing up in Karnopolis. He hated them for what they'd done to him, and yet he still half-believed it. The seeds of self-loathing had been planted when he was very young. It is not easy to change, even when our adult minds know better.

I could think of absolutely nothing to say as we walked back to Marduk's Spear. But I knew I would do whatever I could to help those children and all the others like them. The only question was how.

Zarathustra had much to answer for, and I would see he did, no matter what Darius said.

✣ 7 ✣

ARAXA

In an octagonal stone chamber on the highest level of the Hall of the Numerators, the Hierarch's spymaster sat lost in thought. His deep-set eyes stared unseeing at the long list of names on his desk. Some had already been crossed out, having been questioned and found innocent, or, in a few cases, guilty of treason. Others bore scribbled notations in Araxa's spidery hand, most of it the gossip he had gleaned from the first set of names.

He had known about the Followers for some time, but never thought they posed any real threat. After all, they had existed since the war two hundred years before and never done anything but whisper and fret. His assessment had changed with the theft of the holy fire, and the revelation that the magi had been lying to everyone but the royal line about Zarathustra's fate. The Followers of the Prophet had managed to corrupt six guards at Gorgon-e Gaz, at least two Purified at the Barbican, and even to infiltrate the Water Dogs and Immortals. It was now Araxa's task to determine how far this corruption went, and to carve it out by the roots—a task he had taken on with relish.

The last rays of the sun crept across the marble floor as he idly tapped his fingers on the parchment. The study was as stark as its occupant. Bare stone walls, a battered writing desk and a single hard wooden chair, which Araxa sat in himself. Anyone who entered would be forced to stand while they addressed him, a small reminder of his authority. The only personal item in the room was an enameled box on the desk. Araxa enjoyed the rumors regarding its contents. Some claimed it held the heart of a daēva that had tried to kill him when he was a young Numerator. Others said he kept a poison inside so potent and sly a single grain could cause a man's sudden, inexplicable death a week or more after ingestion. Araxa did nothing to lay them to rest. They all added to his reputation.

The truth was more mundane. The box held a lock of his mother's hair. It soothed him to touch it, to inhale the bittersweet scent of almond oil. He opened the box now and wound the soft black coil through his fingers. He did not miss her, but she reminded him of where he came from, and how far he had come.

Araxa moved to the window and watched the square slowly empty. Half a league to the right, the towers of the King's palace loomed against the darkening sky. To the left, the pleasure district shook itself awake beneath an orange moon. He heard the strains of distant music, raucous laughter, the excited barking of a dog.

His hand stole to his neck, nails lightly brushing his skin as he reflected on his next course of action. Since he was a boy, Araxa had suffered periodic outbreaks of a painful condition that left his chest and torso covered in angry red boils. It had made him an outcast among the other children. They said he was cursed, that he was part Druj. The girls were the harshest. Laughing at him behind their hands, or simply looking at him with open disdain. He'd taken his revenge by spying on them in their baths, although his own arousal disgusted him.

Araxa had chosen to join the Numerators both because of the complete absence of women and the power their order wielded in the administration of the empire. Now, at the age of thirty-four, he was the youngest aide to the Hierarch in the Numerators' history. The path to this summit was littered with the bodies—literal and figurative—of men who had stood in Araxa's way. Only one remained: the Hierarch himself. He was old and gout-ridden but not particularly frail, and might live a good many years. Still, no one would be shocked if he died in his sleep.

There were several different ways such a thing could be accomplished. Araxa had fantasized about all of them. He was torn between poison and a pillow on the face. The second had a brutish appeal. He would press down, the silk cool against his palms, until the old man's feeble struggles finally stopped. Not a single mark would be left on the body. The only drawback to this method was not being able to witness the light dying in the Hierarch's watery grey eyes, but Araxa had a vivid imagination. He had already pictured it hundreds of times, in great detail.

Before he could take such a bold step, however, he had two other tasks to complete first. The destruction of the magi, and the question of the *other* old man.

The Prophet Zarathustra.

Scratching made his condition worse, but Araxa couldn't help himself. He raked his nails across the tender flesh beneath his robes. It gave him a moment's respite, but then the burning returned, fiery in its intensity. Tiny blisters broke open, and he withdrew his hand, wiping it on a cloth he kept for that purpose.

Visiting the cell had only hardened his resolve to see the Prophet disposed of. Like the other Numerators, Araxa had never trusted the daēvas, leashed though they might be. Their power was simply too dangerous. Araxa was no fool. He understood the daēvas were the only thing keeping Neblis and her Druj hordes from their throats. But the breeding program was madness. They already had more than enough daēvas to keep the empire safe. Of course, the magi vehemently disagreed, and thus far the Numerators' arguments had fallen on deaf ears in Persepolae. But without the holy fire to make new cuffs, the point would become moot—as long as no one could ask the Prophet how he'd done it in the first place.

Night fell on the city. Torches flickered in the windows of the magi's temple, although the Imperial Archives grew dark, its scribes having departed for home. Araxa tucked his hands into his sleeves and made his way down three circular flights to the level of the street. Most of the Numerators he passed in the corridors avoided his gaze. They were the record-keepers, the bureaucrats who made up the bulk of his order. But two or three gave him a deferential nod. Like Araxa, their robes bore the sigil of an eye with a flame where the pupil should be. The Hands of the Father. The daēva-hunters. They strode down the middle of the torch-lit passages, knowing they would be given a wide berth by the others. No one, not even their own brother Numerators, wished to catch the attention of a Hand. Especially not now, with their new powers of arrest and dispensation of justice.

Araxa's octagonal study was in the main building for practical reasons, but he conducted much of his business in another part of the Numerators' sprawling warren. Three wings of the Hall were devoted to administration of the empire and its vast resources, but the fourth belonged exclusively to the Hands. It had no windows, and the walls were particularly thick, muffling any sounds that might arise within. To the people of Karnopolis, it was known in hushed tones as the *Grestako*, which meant cave of the demons. Few who went inside were ever seen again.

Araxa barely noticed the smell, although it had made him lose his breakfast the first time he'd encountered it more than a decade before. Old blood, sweat, despair. It had sunk into the very stones of the place. At least it wasn't summer. The smell became much worse then.

Two Hands of the Father awaited him outside one of the cells. Unlike the stoop-shouldered clerks, both had muscular builds and the stolid faces of soldiers, which was more or less what they were. By tradition, the head of their order held no formal title, but most of the Hands respectfully called him Patar, an affectionate term meaning father.

"Magi from the Barbican, Patar Araxa," the first said with a scowl. "One's already soiled himself." He gave a coarse laugh. "So much for the *Purified*."

"Keep them waiting," Araxa said. His voice was high and soft and oddly affectless. It was a voice made for whispers in the dark. Those who survived his attentions tended to remember that voice more than anything else. "Let them stew. Separately, of course. By the time I question them, they'll be eager to please. Now, what of Magus Roham? Is he here?"

"Since this morning. He's been demanding to see the Hierarch. Says he's nothing to hide, but knows of a few others who might be involved."

Araxa gave a thin smile. "I'll start with him. Bring him to the Chamber of Truth."

The Hands nodded and strode off down the corridor, scarlet-hemmed robes billowing behind them. Araxa followed at a slower pace. He could hear faint moans drifting through the fist-sized iron screens set into the doors on either side. The cells were small and dark. A prisoner had once told him an hour inside felt like a week. Zarathustra had no idea how lucky he was to have been given over to the magi instead of the Numerators. Well, that reprieve was about to end.

Once in the Chamber of Truth, Araxa composed himself and waited for Magus Roham. The floor of the circular room sloped ever so gently toward a drain in the middle. The Hands employed varying degrees of intensity in their questioning, depending on the evidence of guilt. The last magus to be brought there had turned out to be very guilty indeed. The stone was brown with dried blood. It had pooled around the manacles fixed to the far wall and ran in a viscous river to the drain. Araxa had ordered the

Hands not to rinse the room with a bucket just yet. It was amazing what an incentive such a sight could be to the next magus.

Ringing boot heels in the corridor announced the arrival of the two Hands and their charge, whose eyes widened as they dragged him into the chamber. His gaze flicked over the table and its various implements, then flinched away. Magus Roham had watery blue eyes that turned down at the corners, giving him a slightly melancholy appearance. A small, red mouth peeked through a black beard peppered with grey. Not a young man, but with many years left still. Years he clearly saw slipping away like blood down the drain.

"This is not necessary," he said in a voice made high and cracked by fear. "I—"

"Do you know why I asked for you to be brought here today?" Araxa asked gently.

"I don't know, Minister," Roham babbled. "I haven't—"

"Your name came up in an interesting discussion I had with Magus Vahdat."

Already pale, Roham turned the sickly shade of a deathscap mushroom. "Vahdat? I barely knew—"

"Before he was executed as a traitor and displayed over the sixteenth gate, Magus Vahdat gave me an extensive list of names," Araxa went on relentlessly. "Brothers who appear sympathetic to the daēvas. Yours was on it."

"Mine? But...It's impossible!" Roham licked his red lips. "I despise the daēvas as much as you do, Minister. I would never... Vahdat was a traitor and a liar. Surely, you do not believe him?"

Araxa didn't respond. The two Hands of the Father flanked the doorway. One motion of Araxa's finger and Roham would be wearing those manacles. The magus knew it, for his back stiffened, as if he could feel their cold gazes.

"I swear on the Holy Father, I am not a Follower of the Prophet," Roham said, falling to his knees and clasping his hands.

"Mercy, Minister. When I heard your order had been appointed to hunt down the heretics that defiled the Barbican, I said a prayer of thanks!"

Araxa shared a wry look with the Hands. "Indeed. Be that as it may, it is my duty to find the truth." He sighed regretfully. "I am a reasonable man. But I cannot simply release you on your word. The influence of the Followers is insidious. They are a blight, one that we must cut out before it devours us all. And the only way to do that is to discover its source. We must get every last bit of pestilence, lest it grow again in secret."

The magus nodded fervently. "Yes, yes. That is what I was telling your esteemed brothers. I have thought hard on this, so very hard. There are several magi who have acted suspiciously in the last few weeks."

"In what way?" Araxa demanded.

"Nervous, frightened, as if they have guilty—"

"That describes half the magi," Araxa interrupted. His voice grew even softer and more nasal when angry. Roham was forced to lean forward to hear him. "You must give me something specific."

"Well, there's Nikan. I heard him say he thought the Numerators themselves were behind the whole thing. Another wondered aloud why the Followers believe the Prophet lives, in a way that implied he might believe it too. It is all heresy, of course, and I told him so!" Roham snatched at the hem of Araxa's robes. "Please, there is more, much more. I have names!"

Araxa gestured at one of the Hands. "Fetch some parchment. Magus Roham will be writing all this down."

Within minutes, the magus was scribbling away, filling page after page of vellum. It all came back to the Prophet, Araxa reflected. If the secret of his existence was revealed...

The Hierarch had wanted to move the Prophet immediately, but Araxa had counseled patience. Certainly, he could be placed in one of the Grestako's cells, but word would no doubt spread of a mysterious prisoner. And Araxa sensed an opportunity. One he could exploit to his advantage when the time was right.

As his mind turned the problem over and over, studying every angle, Araxa's nails methodically carved furrows across his chest. And when spots of red began to bloom through his snowy white robes, he was too lost in thought to notice.

8

NAZAFAREEN

I woke at dawn bathed in sweat. I'd had the dream again, of molten fire running through my veins as the sea boiled and Darius screamed in agony somewhere behind me. It was accompanied by mindless fury and the urge to do violence I had felt with disturbing frequency—ever since I'd wielded the power in the village of Karon Komai. The aftertaste of it lingered as I washed up in lukewarm water and put on a fresh tunic. I didn't know what was wrong with me. True, I had never been especially gentle or meek, but this was extreme. It was like the year I first had my blood, when my moods would change with the wind and I nearly broke the door to the barracks from slamming it so many times.

Was I angry at Darius? The Prophet? Our sleazy host? Or was it something else entirely? I didn't know. Only that if nothing else presented itself, I might be forced to find Bobak and insult his mother.

We'd all agreed Tijah and Myrri would be the ones to watch the tomb today. But the thought of sitting in my room with nothing to do made me want to smash something.

I eyed the sword leaning in the corner, still in its wrappings. I used to be competent with a blade in my hands, back when I still had both of them. As a Water Dog, I'd trained with Darius and the others every day in the barracks yard at Tel Khalujah. I'd learned most of what I knew from Ilyas. The man who had maimed me, who'd tried to force Darius and Victor to fight each other to the death at the manor house. Tijah had killed him and I was in her debt for it, although I still wished it had been me.

I decided right then I would never try to touch the power again. I couldn't be trusted with it. Something was broken in me. I'd become too reckless, too self-destructive. Now I knew how Darius felt when he'd begged me to hold him in check. When he still believed he was Druj. Evil. A lie, but I wondered if part of him believed it still. Either way, his own demons gnawed at him. He pretended they didn't, but he was a master at pretending. It's how he had survived so long.

I reached back to finger-comb my hair, as I always did in the mornings, and found only air. Right. One less grooming problem to deal with! I had gotten better at coping with just one hand. It was certainly possible—Darius had done it all his life. I had little trouble dressing anymore, and if food required cutting, I just speared it with my knife and ate it in bites the way the clan used to do. I no longer stupidly reached for things with a right hand that didn't exist. And my stump could be used for all sorts of tasks that didn't require fingers, like smoothing the blankets on my bed or closing a door.

But there was one skill I hadn't yet tested: fighting.

Only a few weeks had passed since our battle with the necromancers on the plain, but it felt much longer. My body had grown soft, not to mention covered in scars. I felt a wave of self-pity coming on and wallowed in it for a while, but then the girl who had grown up in the tents of the Four-Legs Clan reminded me that rabbits get eaten while wolves get fat.

So I got off my arse and found Darius. He was eating an orange in the courtyard, his short, dark hair damp from performing the water blessing. I thought of the first day after we were bonded, when I'd marched down to the river, furious at being awoken by the sensation of freezing liquid trickling down my spine. The way he stood by the bank, stripped to the waist, and how I'd pitied him for his withered arm. Or told myself I did. Even then, he'd stirred something in me. Despite his infirmity, he looked like a young wolf. Cold and dangerous and unpredictable.

"Tijah and Myrri just left," he said, offering me a piece of orange. "You look tired."

"I'm fine." I popped the wedge in my mouth. It was perfectly ripe, tart and juicy. "Just a little restless."

His feral daēva eyes studied me. "You're not telling me something."

"I'm not telling you lots of things," I said lightly. "Hundreds, at least. Just because we're bonded, doesn't mean you get to know every thought that passes through my head."

Darius rubbed the back of his neck. He wore the same sleeveless tunic he'd slept in, and I tried not to stare like a lech at the smooth, corded muscles of his right arm. "Nice try. But this is a very particular thing, and it's been eating at you for days. Out with it."

I shrugged. "Just nightmares. I can't remember them. Isn't that what you told me once?"

"That was before we knew each other."

He was right, but I still didn't feel like recounting my dreams. They were too horrible.

"Do you ever feel angry about your infirmity?" I asked instead.

He seemed surprised by the question. "Angry?"

"If not for this, you'd be whole," I said, glancing at the cuff hidden beneath my sleeve.

"Well, it's been that way since I was an infant." His expression softened. "I know it's different for you."

"What's done is done," I said quickly, not wanting his sympathy. "But I want to start training again. With a sword. We can't make a plan until we know where the old man's being held, but it's hard to imagine a rescue that doesn't involve using the power. And once you use it, they'll know what you are and we'll have to fight our way out. I need to know I can still protect you."

He nodded. "Stealth would be my preference, but I can't deny our luck hasn't been the best lately. We should be prepared for anything, I suppose. The question is where. We can't go at each other in the courtyard." Darius grinned. "We're supposed to be madly in love, remember?"

"Let's ask Bobak," I said, forcing myself to smile back, but still a little hurt at the joking way he said it.

We found Arshad's hired muscle in the main room, drinking tea and playing dice with the boy who'd directed me to Ester. It was far too early for customers, and they seemed to be the only ones awake in the brothel besides us. Scrubbed clean of makeup, and without the simpering persona he assumed during working hours, the kid looked painfully young. His jug ears reminded me of my brother Kian.

"Hmmm," Bobak said, when we told him what we wanted. "You can try the roof. It'll be too hot in a few hours, but mornings and evenings can be quite pleasant up there. Just don't fall off."

"Thanks," I said. "Hey, kid, what's your name?"

He cast me the bored, slightly scornful glance universal to teenagers everywhere. "Dav."

"I'm Nazafareen, and this is Darius."

"I know."

"Dav, I'll give you ten siglos if you make sure no one else goes up there until lunchtime."

The kid laughed. "Sure, but they're all sleeping anyway. I'm the only one who gets up early around here."

"Just do it."

He shrugged and tossed the dice. "Your money."

We took the stairs back to the top floor, retrieved our swords, and found the ladder leading to the roof. It formed a hollow square, with the courtyard in the middle. Now that I knew what to look for, I recognized the reddish brown tiles of the Hall of the Numerators in the hazy distance beyond the lush grounds of the winter palace. Tijah and Myrri would be there by now, selling trinkets and keeping an eye on the tomb. I hated to let them go alone, but Tijah had insisted four people would stand out too much and she and Myrri could take care of themselves, thank you very much. She could be prickly sometimes, and pig-headed too. Just like some others I could name.

Darius braced a foot on the low edge and buckled on his sword, trapping one end against his hips with his dead arm and securing it with the other. I tried to mimic him, determined not to ask him to do it for me. As I fumbled with the belt, I noticed the wall was covered with graffiti. We obviously weren't the first people to come up here.

Darius read the roughly carved inscription next to his sandal and laughed.

"What does it say?" I asked, cursing under my breath as the end of the belt slithered through my grasp yet again.

He made a sad face. "Weep girls! For my penis has given you up."

I snorted.

"It's actually pretty mild," he added, pointing at another scrawled comment. "Now *that* one—"

"Yes, yes. I can imagine." I unhooked the sword and laid it flat on the ground. The blade itself was made of bronze, about eighteen inches long and double-edged. It had a dog's head pommel, and a supple leather scabbard I kept well-oiled. With the weight of the sword gone, it was a much simpler matter to catch the end of the belt, pin it with my stump, and use my left hand to fasten the single button. I suppressed a grin of triumph as I reattached the scabbard and drew the blade. The hilt was warm from the sun. It felt good in my hand, and my feet moved without conscious thought into dueling stance.

Darius gave me a little salute and we slipped into the familiar dance, circling each other slowly at first, then matching blades with more attention to form than actual force. I knew he was barely trying. If this were a real fight, I would be dead a hundred times over. There was no matching a daēva's strength and speed. When I was Darius's bonded in the Water Dogs, my main purpose was to protect him from attacks by other humans. I had fought revenants and wights, but not daēvas. Just the thought of it was chilling.

So we parried and stabbed and blocked at what Darius likely considered a leisurely pace, until the sun was high in the sky and sweat stung my eyes. When I tried to deflect an overhead attack and my knees buckled for the third time in as many minutes, Darius called an end to it.

"That was fun," he said cheerfully. "How do you feel?"

"I assume you're only asking to be polite," I muttered.

"All right, yes. Your arm is sore, and it will be worse tomorrow, but that's only to be expected. We've always used one-handed swords because they're better for close quarter combat, so little has changed in your fighting style. Overall, you're quite pleased with yourself, although you're trying not to show it."

I stared at him. Then I burst out laughing. "That's a fair enough assessment. Thank you, Darius. It was kind of you to indulge me."

He gave an offhand shrug. "I needed the practice myself."

"And now you're lying. But we'll both pretend you aren't. See you at supper." I smiled and left him on the roof, using a whetstone on the edge of his sword. After stowing my own in my room, I bribed Dav again to guard the door of the bathhouse in the rear of the courtyard while I gave myself a thorough wash. Marduk's Spear didn't have a separate one for women since there usually weren't any, and I didn't feel like flashing the teenaged boys who worked there. Some of them couldn't care less, but I got the impression others wouldn't mind an eyeful. Just because they serviced men for a living didn't mean it was their preference.

My arms and legs wobbled a bit, but my body felt more alive than it had in a long time. When I finished bathing, I went back upstairs and rested on my bed as the sun sank lower and the sounds of business at Marduk's Spear came filtering up from the lower floors.

I'm not sure what got me thinking of Tommas. Maybe it was practicing with Darius. The two of us used to spar with Tommas and Ilyas every day back in Tel Khalujah. Tommas had the kind of beauty that instantly overshadowed everyone else in the room, male or female, but he never cared much about it. He was one of the most cheerful people I had ever known, which is something of a miracle considering he was bonded to Ilyas.

Ilyas had loved him and punished them both for it. He simply couldn't reconcile his faith with his own feelings for a so-called demon. I'd never realized the truth until Tommas died and it was too late.

Like my sister Ashraf, Tommas had been killed by a wight. A wight in the body of a child. I could still see its face. The black almond eyes, shining with a kind of dead light.

Lying here in this walled city, a thousand leagues from the Char Khala range marking the empire's northern border with Bactria, it was easy to forget who our true enemy was. But as much as I hated the King and the Numerators, their crimes paled beside Neblis. She was a daēva too, but Victor said she dabbled in dark forces beyond his understanding. That she had become something more.

Whatever she was, all the people I'd loved who were now gone had died at the hands of her Druj. And whether or not we found the Prophet, whether we saved Persepolae from destruction or the city burned...Either way, she would be waiting.

This train of thought left me in a black mood. Everything

seemed so futile. As soon as we overcame one hurdle, another rose in our path.

Tommas had been sold to the Water Dogs because he was good at killing the Undead. They'd brought him to Tel Khalujah from the islands of the Middle Sea when he was just a boy. To ease his homesickness, he used to carve pretty things from pieces of wood—fish, shells, boats. He'd given me one years ago that I carried in my pocket, but I'd lost it somewhere. The dungeons, most likely. My stay there had taken on the quality of a nightmare only half remembered, but filled with terror and dread.

When I'd mentioned it to Myrri, she gave me one of his carvings from her own collection, a little ship whose wood was as smooth and glossy as a river stone. I cradled it in my palm and hoped that wherever Tommas was now, he was having himself a good laugh. There were worse things than being dead. And listening to the grunts coming through the floor from the room below, I decided being stuck at Marduk's Spear came pretty close.

I must have drifted off because when a rap came on the door, it was full dark out.

"They're back," Darius called softly. "Meet us downstairs."

I jumped up and found Tijah and Myrri in the private room, along with the white-pawed cat. Dav was there too, passing out bowls of lamb stew.

"Well?" I demanded.

"The *flower* was gone when we got there," Tijah said, glancing at Dav. "But nothing was left in its place."

"More waiting, you mean," I said glumly.

The thing I hated most in the world. Especially when time was the one thing we had so little of.

"Where's Arshad?" Darius asked.

"Oh, he always gets into a tizzy this time of year," Dav replied, pouring cups of wine with a practiced hand.

"This time of year?" I tried to calculate what day it was and came up blank. Since the dungeons, I hadn't given a moment's thought to the calendar. Only that it was late winter, and every day we did not find the Prophet was a day closer to the bloody sacking of Persepolae.

"The festival of Nowruz. It's in a week." He looked at us in astonishment, thick black eyebrows climbing to his hairline. "Where are you from, anyway?"

"No place you've heard of," Tijah cut in. "A real backwater."

"Well, it's the biggest holiday in Karnopolis after the King's birthday," Dav said. "There's feasting and drinking for days. We get really busy." He lowered his voice. "But that's not what everyone's talking about. They say a magus was found on the steps of the Archives at dawn this morning. Cut to pieces. Everyone thinks the Numerators did it."

Darius and I shared a look. "Cut to pieces?" he repeated.

"Oh, yes. Both eyes were gone, and his manhood too. A warning to the Followers, people are saying."

"Holy Father," Darius muttered.

"Do you know the name of the magus who was killed?" I asked, my stomach knotting at the greasy aroma of the stew.

Dav shook his head. From his smooth cheeks, I guessed he was about fifteen. I wondered how much longer the brothel owner would have a use for him, and what would happen to him after that.

"Has Arshad heard?" Darius asked.

Dav shrugged. "Don't know. Haven't seen him since this morning."

"Let us know if you do. We need to speak with him right away."

"Sure. And if you need anything else, ask the cook," Dav said, and then he was gone, stork-like legs pumping as he dashed back to the common room.

"Do you think it could be Saman?" I asked in a low voice.

"Who knows?" Tijah put in. "Either way, I don't like relying on someone we haven't met. Time's running out. What if this magus has cold feet? I could hardly blame him considering the Numerators are butchering the magi with the King's blessing. But we've been here two days already with nothing to show for it."

"You said the message was gone," Darius pointed out.

"Yes, but we don't know who took it." She picked up a spoon and began stirring her bowl of stew, but didn't eat any. "What if he's been arrested?"

"This is all speculation," I said. "We can't just walk into the Temple of the Magi to look around. I don't see any other choice than waiting, at least for a little while longer."

"There's something else to consider," Darius added. "I've seen mercenaries from Al Miraj on the streets."

Tijah buried her face in the winecup. Myrri stopped petting the cat.

"Do you think your father is still hunting you?" I asked Tijah.

"Of course," she said. "He will never forgive me for running away from my wedding. No matter how monstrous the groom happened to be!"

"Your family is rich, aren't they?" Darius asked. Tijah had told him some of the truth about her past on the *Amestris*.

"Filthy," she replied.

"Then there's going to be a bounty. We need to keep you both hidden," Darius said. "Those mercenaries would be on you like a pack of jackals if they knew—"

Both his and Myrri's heads swung toward the doorway. Myrri's face darkened as she strode to the archway and whipped her hand around the corner. I heard a yelp, and a moment later Dav was squirming in her grasp. Myrri hauled him by the neck of his tunic back into the room.

"How much did you hear?" Darius asked quietly.

"Nothing!"

Tijah advanced on him, oozing menace. "Don't lie, kid."

"I'm *not*." Myrri gave him a shake. "Ow! All right, hardly anything. Just the bit about mercenaries and a bounty..."

Myrri's fingers flashed a complex series of signs. Tijah nodded grimly. "I say we gut him right now, the little skulker," she said, pulling a knife from her boot.

I hoped she was just trying to scare him, but you never knew with Tijah. She had her own moral code, and the prospect of being dragged home was—quite understandably—the worst thing she could imagine. The men of Al Miraj were notoriously brutal toward their women, especially on questions of honor. I exchanged a worried look with Darius. Myrri's eyes had gone flat, and although she could usually be counted on to make Tijah see reason, I didn't think she'd be of much help in this case. Before they ran away, Tijah's father had ordered Myrri whipped as a punishment, knowing Tijah would feel her pain.

Dav had no idea of the hornet's nest he'd just kicked.

"Wait!" His eyes were huge. "I swear I'll never tell a soul. On my life!"

"Leave him be," Darius said wearily, stepping between them. "He won't tell."

Tijah's eyes narrowed. "How do you know that?"

"Look at him."

Dav was white with terror. A boy like him must have seen and heard some bad things in his short life. He obviously had no illusions that Tijah was bluffing.

"Fine." She sheathed her knife and Dav sagged with relief. "But *I* swear on Kavi, the nine-headed goddess of vengeance, if I find out he's betrayed us..."

"Point taken," Darius said.

Dav nodded fervently, looking at Darius like he was the Holy Father come down to earth and made flesh. Myrri released him and he darted off without another word.

"Just two more weeks," I said. "That's the longest we can stay here if we hope to reach Persepolae before Alexander does. With any luck, it will be much sooner." I looked at Tijah. "And if anyone shows up looking for you, I promise, they will disappear without a trace. We can handle mercenaries."

She stared at the untouched food. "I still don't trust that kid. He's a sneak."

"I'll keep an eye on him," Darius said. "But from now on, you and Myrri stay here. Nazafareen and I will watch the tomb." Tijah opened her mouth to protest and Darius held up his hand. "I know you hate sitting around. You're going to say that it's been five years since you left home. You look different, especially with your hair chopped off. No one would recognize you." He glanced at Myrri. "But both of you together? And one with a daēva tattoo on the palm? You tell me. Is it worth taking the chance?"

Tijah raked a hand through her inch-long hair. Her delicate bones gave her the look of a long-necked bird. Her jaw was set hard. I could see she was afraid and trying not to show it. She flashed a sign at Myrri, who gave the barest nod.

"Fine. We're in the hands of the gods now," Tijah said with resignation. "Let's try not to piss them off."

We picked at our food in silence for a few minutes, each lost in his or her own dark thoughts. When Darius turned toward the door, ears cocked at some sound too low for me to hear, I briefly wondered if it was Dav again. It seemed unlikely. I had a feeling the kid would keep as far as from Tijah as he could get for the rest of our stay. About ten seconds later, Arshad appeared in the doorway. A man in a deep cowl stood behind him. They came into the room and I heard Bobak's distinctive sigh as he took up a position just outside the archway.

"I'm glad to find you all here," Arshad said, wringing his hands. He turned to the hooded figure beside him. "This is Magus Saman. He has risked much to come tonight."

The cowl fell back and I blinked in surprise. I'd been expecting someone close to Arshad's age, but Saman was barely older than we were. His hair had been shorn nearly to the scalp, leaving only dark stubble. I knew this meant he had been raised to the robes in the last five years. But despite the magus's youth, his brown eyes were lit with a fierce intelligence. He had a full, well-formed mouth and dimpled chin. As Arshad made the introductions and Saman's gaze settled on each of us in turn, Tijah shifted in her seat, leaning forward slightly, and I suppressed a smile. Something about Saman reminded me a little of Tommas. Very male, very attractive...and very unattainable.

"I saw you at the square today," he said to Tijah. "You were near the tomb."

"Oh?" She smiled. "As it happens, we were looking for *you*."

He smiled back, dropping easily to the empty couch across from her. "I thought you were a boy."

Tijah's smile widened and Myrri smirked. "Not a boy," she said in a throaty voice I'd never heard before.

Holy Father, was she flirting with a magus? I thought Saman might blush or stammer, but he seemed unruffled by Tijah's frank stare. "I only have a short time before they will miss me at the temple," he said. "But I do bring news important enough to risk coming to you. There are hidden tunnels beneath the temple district, and someone is using them."

"Tunnels?" I asked.

"Yes. I discovered one of the entrances by accident. Since the emissary came from the King, I've been on the lookout for anything out of the ordinary. Yesterday, as I walked back to my room after evening prayers, I noticed a wooden panel with faint scratches at the edge, as though someone had recently pried it open. It was in one of the main residential hallways, so it could have been anyone. But the gouges looked fresh." He scrubbed a hand across the short hair at the back of his head. "I waited until it was late and the halls were deserted. I used a bread knife I'd taken from the kitchens. It took some wiggling, but the panel popped open. Behind was a ladder leading into darkness. I fetched a torch and climbed down. There was a tunnel below, but it soon led to another that crossed the first, and then another. I feared I would get lost if I wandered too long. I have no idea how far they go, but it seems safe to assume they run beneath the temple, and possibly the entire district."

I felt a surge of excitement. As much as I disliked close places, the tunnels sounded like a promising place to hide someone. They were also a way for us to sneak into the temple without being seen.

"When I was a child, my grandmother used to tell stories about the caves beneath Karnopolis," Arshad said thoughtfully. "She claimed they were full of smugglers' treasure. Heaps of jewels and gold. But she said there was a great flood many years ago and the caves were sealed up. I always thought it a legend. But what if there is a grain of truth?"

"Do you think they could be holding the Prophet down there?" Tijah asked.

"It's certainly possible," Saman replied. "I will try to explore further when I get back tonight. But there is more. The High Magus is meeting with the Numerators tomorrow."

"At the temple?" Darius asked.

Saman nodded. "The High Magus of Persepolae holds a higher rank than any Numerator, even the Hierarch. He carries out the will of the Holy Father on earth, and even the King would think twice about openly insulting him. Of course, it is in name only, as he is powerless to stop the Numerators in their quest to purge the magi of traitors. But they will still come to him as a gesture of courtesy, however empty it may be." Saman rose and began to pace up and down. "The meeting is ostensibly about this latest killing. The Numerators deny it was their handiwork. But I think they might also discuss the arrangements to transfer the Prophet."

"We need to find out exactly when and how it will be carried out," Darius said.

"Yes," Saman agreed. "I will conceal myself in the same place as last time, when the emissary came from the King. With the Holy Father's blessing, I will get away with it a second time."

"We'll be ready the moment you find out where the Prophet is," Darius said.

Saman nodded. "Arshad told me who you are. I am grateful we have both humans and daēvas working together in this. It is what the Prophet always wanted."

"This magus who was murdered so horribly," Tijah said. "Do you think the Numerators did it?"

Saman hesitated. "They are certainly capable. The High Magus believes so, as do most of my brothers. But something is off. It doesn't strike me as their style. Every other magus was executed publicly, after being branded a traitor. The Numerators wanted people to *see*, and be fearful. Why leave the last one on the steps?"

"Perhaps they didn't mean to kill him," Darius said. "Perhaps it was an accident during questioning."

Saman sighed. "Perhaps. But the condition of the body...Such things do not happen by accident. The purge is being carried out by the Hands of the Father, a powerful order within the Numerators. They are assassins, torturers. Pain is their business. If they wish to keep you alive, they know how to do it."

No one spoke for a moment.

"Aren't you afraid?" Tijah asked softly.

"Of course. I'd be a fool if I wasn't. But I joined the priesthood to help others. To do good in the world." Saman spoke in a calm way that made him seem older than his years. I disliked the magi for their treatment of the daēvas, but I thought he would make a good one someday. "I had the calling at a young age," he continued. "My family was taken by plague when I was a child. Both my parents, and all six of my brothers and sisters. Only I survived. I thought there had to be a reason for it. When I first came to Karnopolis, I had never seen a daēva. I knew nothing about them. Part of my duties included teaching religious studies. When I saw how the daēva children were abused ..."

Darius's jaw tightened but he said nothing.

"I was shaken by what I witnessed. Another magus saw my distress and took me aside. I confessed that it seemed a sin to treat other living creatures so cruelly, whether or not they were supposedly Druj. I expected a reprimand, but he was sympathetic. He also warned me not to share my doubts with the others. That magus was Brother Jal. We became very close. Over time, he recruited me to the Followers." Saman's dark eyes held no fear. "They have not called me for questioning yet. With luck, I have a little more time before that happens."

He seemed to accept the inevitability of his own death. It made me angry.

"Why don't you just run?" I said. "Leave the city and get as far away as you can before it's *your* body dumped on the steps, or adorning one of the city gates."

He studied me. "The Hands took Brother Jal four days ago. His spirit rests with the Holy Father now. I am the last one. There is no one else." Saman stood abruptly. "I must go before they miss me. Do not expect a message until tomorrow night at the earliest. Then, Holy Father willing, I will have solid information on which you can act." He drew the cowl up again to conceal his face and Arshad escorted him out to the street.

After Saman left, we went over all he had told us. Despite her earlier promise to stay hidden, Tijah was itching to get into the tunnels herself and have a look around. Darius seemed preoccupied with the fresh scratches on the panel. His logical mind had correctly understood that the whole thing was a bit strange. If the Prophet was down there somewhere, they had been safeguarding him for two hundred years. Why would a new door be opened now? And by someone who had to force it, leaving scratches in the wood? It made us both uneasy.

I listened to them talk with half an ear. I kept thinking of

Saman, and what I would do if I were him. I wasn't sure I would have his courage. Not for some abstract principle. I knew why I was here. Not for Delilah, and certainly not for the Prophet Zarathustra. I was here for Darius. He hadn't asked me to come, but I would do anything for him.

My left hand strayed to the stump of my right as I thought of Saman carrying a torch through the darkness of those tunnels. It was easier to be brave when you'd never experienced torture first-hand. When you'd never felt a knife sever skin and tendons and bone. He might change his mind when they caught him. But of course by then it would be too late.

I couldn't sleep that night, so I went back up to the roof. It was much cooler there than in my stuffy little room. The streets four stories below were thick with revelers starting early on the celebrations. The festival of Nowruz marked the start of the New Year. We had always observed it at Tel Khalujah with a feast in the satrap's palace. The daēvas never came, of course. They weren't invited.

Although I had been bonded to Darius for two years before our ill-fated mission to catch the escaped daēvas from Gorgon-e Gaz, I had barely known him. Strange to think someone whose emotions you shared could be such a cipher in every other respect. Part of the reason was my own single-mindedness. I'd wanted only to kill as many Druj as I could. To avenge my younger sister, Ashraf, who had been possessed by a wight as the clan crossed the mountains. My uncle had stabbed her. He'd had no choice. If he hadn't, the wight would have taken him, and the rest of us in turn.

But her death had left me with a blind hatred for the Undead. I'd cared for nothing else. Not even Darius. He had been a means to an end. Not a person, just another weapon. Until the rainy night he fell off the roof of the daēva barracks, and I held his hand as we waited for the magus to come. A spark had come to life in me then, although I'd tried hard to stamp it out. My feelings weren't just improper, they were heretical to our entire faith. The daēvas were demons and must always be kept at arm's length.

Of course, it didn't work. I'd cared very much for him, even if I'd still believed he was Druj.

As I looked up at the stars, I felt his presence behind me. "They're bright tonight," I said without turning around. We were in the habit of greeting each other in this way.

"I used to study the heavens," Darius said, joining me at the edge of the roof. "The last magus I was bonded to before I came to the Water Dogs had an interest in astronomy. He made charts and tracked their movements." He pointed. "Do you see that one? Very bright, near the cluster of four?"

"I think so, yes."

"It's not a sun like the others, but made of rock and much closer."

I squinted at the twinkling pinpoint of light. It looked like all the others to me. "You mean like the moon?"

"Yes, but twice as big."

"Do you think people live there?"

Darius shook his head. "It's a barren place."

"And you can tell all that just from looking at it?" I asked.

"Not from looking, but from feeling it, yes."

We were quiet for a moment. "What would you do if things were different?" I asked. "If you had all the time in the world and no one was trying to burn you on a pyre or cut your head off?"

He smiled. "I'd like to learn how to use the power for healing, like Victor can. And to make things. Not weapons. Useful things. What about you?"

"I would have a little house somewhere in the mountains." I closed my eyes and pictured the view from the high cols of the Khusk Range, the air so clear it magnified everything until the horizon felt close enough to kiss. I remembered the sweet smell of balsam and spruce. The hardy little wildflowers that grew from cracks in the rock. The rush of the snowmelt in spring, and the blue of the sky, bigger and deeper than it was anywhere else. "I'd have a few goats too. I never liked the smell of them much, but they're friskier than dogs. I would get fat on yoghurt and cheese, and I might learn how to read." When I opened my eyes with a sigh, Darius was staring at me.

"I'll teach you, if you wish," he said.

Someone laughed in the night, a drunken cackle. "Really?"

"Of course. I haven't offered before because I didn't want to offend you."

I frowned. "Oh. Am I so easily offended?"

His tone was amused. "Sometimes."

"Hmmm. Thanks, but it looks hard." I hadn't expected to be taken up on my idle fancy, and was already having second thoughts.

"We've nothing else to do," Darius pointed out. "At least not until Saman contacts us again."

"I suppose."

"I'll ask Arshad if we can borrow his scrolls tomorrow." He paused. "Do you sense anything from Victor? Is he in Bactria?"

"I don't know. He's faint to me now, like a star seen from the corner of the eye. At least Lysandros is with him."

Darius snorted. "Let's just hope they don't kill each other before they get there."

"I'm still surprised he offered to go along. He obviously hates your father, and the feeling seemed mutual." I drew my knees up to my chest. "It's still hard for me to imagine the Prophet and Victor being friends."

"Victor told you that?"

"Yes. They were close enough that when Zarathustra asked for his help, Victor agreed. He was the first to be cuffed. Then they used him to catch the others."

"Xeros the First, you mean?"

I nodded. "When I asked Victor where the daēvas came from, he said he couldn't remember. Don't you think that's strange? He said it was the same for all the daēvas, the old ones, and I believe he was telling the truth."

"Maybe he's so old, he's forgotten."

"Maybe. But Victor's mind is sharp. He certainly hasn't forgotten his hatred for the empire. It's something more, Darius. And Neblis...if she really is a daēva, how did she learn to create the Undead? Ilyas spoke of the veil, that last night. He was talking about why daēvas can't sense Druj, and he said it was because they are *behind the veil*. But what is the veil anyway? Is it a place?"

"I don't know, Nazafareen." Darius seemed troubled. "But I believe there are other powers in the world besides the elemental magic the daēvas use. They are part of the nexus, but a different part."

We were quiet for a while. "I'm afraid," I admitted.

"Of what?"

"The Numerators. The Hands of the Father. That they will use the cuffs against us again. Or take you away from me." I sighed. "I'm afraid for my clan. And I'm afraid for Victor. I try to have faith, but I think he's done a foolish thing in going to Bactria."

We gazed up at the stars. For a moment, I had the dizzying sensation of looking into a great abyss, an ocean of light full of strange currents and tidal surges that lasted a million years. Then Darius's hand found mine, warm and calloused from his sword, and the world righted itself again.

"I'm afraid too, Nazafareen. But the Prophet taught that heaven and hell are both here on earth." He tilted his head back, drinking in the night. I knew he felt the nexus most strongly in the quiet of darkness. "We decide our own fates. Not the Holy Father. You and me. And there is only one road forward. Shall we take it together?"

I gave his hand a small squeeze. "Always," I said.

❊ 9 ❊

ARAXA

raxa and the High Magus of Karnopolis stared at each other in stony silence. Their relationship had never been especially warm, but in the last two weeks, any pretense of civility had given way to open loathing. Araxa felt not an ounce of sympathy for the man. If his priests were corrupted by the daēvas, they had only themselves to blame. They had grown too close to the demons in their charge and the taint of the Druj had infected their souls. It had been inevitable. Now the Numerators would clean up the mess, and when the dust settled, the power of the magi would be forever weakened, if not broken outright.

All Araxa wanted was to make the final arrangements for the transfer of Zarathustra to his own custody. What he would do with the prisoner after that...well, Araxa had not yet decided. But instead of discussing those details, he found himself on the defensive over the magus who had been found in a broken heap outside the temple the day before.

From where he sat, in an airy chamber looking out over the square, he could see the exact spot of the grisly discovery. Araxa shifted impatiently in his cushioned chair. Thick rugs covered the stone floor and the walls bore tapestries depicting scenes from the Prophet's life. In one, he knelt as the Holy Father placed the fire in his outstretched hands. Another depicted him in meditation upon a mountaintop, and a third had him restoring sight to a blind man as seven archangels looked on from above.

They should show him drawing pictures of goats, Araxa thought sourly. That seemed to be what he did best these days. Why the magi had kept him around was a mystery. As a symbol of their faith, the Prophet remained potent and inspiring. But if anyone ever discovered the reality of what the man had devolved into...Araxa could not think of a greater disaster.

The High Magus noticed him studying the tapestries and scowled even more deeply. His name was Jahandar, and he wore a tall pointed hat with droopy earflaps that hugged the sides of his long face. Jahandar's wiry grey eyebrows were drawn into a frown, and two spots of color marked his ancient, wrinkled cheeks. He was very angry, but attempting to restrain his temper. Anyone with half a brain feared the Hierarch's second-in-command.

"As I've told you repeatedly, the Numerators had nothing to do with the murder," Araxa said, shattering the brittle silence. "It's outrageous to even suggest such a thing. We carry out our work with the full authority of the King. Even if I were disposed to ordering an assassination, as you call it, I have no need to."

"Then who did?" the High Magus demanded plaintively.

"Have you considered the possibility this man was a traitor, done in by his fellow conspirators within the magi? Perhaps he knew too much and had to be silenced before he was summoned for questioning." Privately, Araxa thought this the likeliest scenario. That, or a lunatic was on the loose.

Jahandar made a noise of dissent. "I've known Magus Shahrooz for twenty years. He was a pious man! It's unthinkable that—"

"Yes, yes. Just as it was unthinkable the holy fire could be stolen from the Barbican," Araxa interrupted, lacing his hands together and leaning forward the slightest bit. "I'm sure the City

Watch will get to the bottom of it. My only concern now is the Prophet. He wears a cuff. That is obviously what has kept him alive all these years. But what is its purpose? How does it prevent him from escaping? Who wears its match?"

The High Magus seemed to shrink in on himself, a whipped dog cornered by its master. Araxa had conducted hundreds of interrogations, and he recognized the instant when the questioning began to near the heart of the matter.

"No one," Jahandar replied, staring at the floor and refusing to meet Araxa's eye.

"What do you mean, no one? Why does he wear it then?"

The High Magus opened his mouth but no sound came out.

"Do not consider lying to me," Araxa said, his reedy voice even softer and more menacing than a moment before. "What will happen if I remove it?"

Jahandar turned a waxy color. "I would not do that."

"Why not?"

The High Magus of Karnopolis darted his eyes to the window, then to a tall cedar cabinet in the corner, as though seeking an escape route. His shoulders sagged and he finally met Araxa's deep-set gaze.

"It dampens his power, but he is not bonded to another," Jahandar said.

"His power?" Araxa struggled to maintain his composure. Losing his temper now would accomplish nothing. "Explain, please."

The magus rubbed his enormous nose. "The daēva cuffs we use today were not the first Zarathustra made. He attempted several different designs. Each had a different effect. The initial pair did nothing. The second linked the wearers' minds, but blocked the power completely. The third...well, that set allowed power to flow through the daēva. When Zarathustra defied King Xeros, it was one of the second set that was locked on his wrist."

"I still don't understand," Araxa said slowly. "Why would he require such a thing?"

Jahandar stared at him, not replying, and Araxa felt a bolt of astonishment. "*Are you saying he is daēva himself?*"

The High Magus of Karnopolis licked his lips. "Partly, yes. That is what we have always suspected, at least. There is no other explanation. How could he have forged the cuffs in the first place, unless he could touch the power?"

"I thought they were given to him by the Holy Father," Araxa said with a thin smile.

"Yes, well...In any event, no one was sure until he started hurling things about the room with air. Xeros, in his infinite wisdom, seized one of the cuffs lying nearby and placed it upon the Prophet's wrist. It prevented Zarathustra from doing further damage." The High Magus trailed off. He was well aware that the words spoken in this room were beyond heresy.

Araxa sat in stunned silence for a moment, gathering his thoughts. He knew that before they were leashed, the demons had occasionally seduced and bedded humans. Such unholy unions were severely punished, their offspring smothered at birth or left to die of exposure. But the empire was a big place, and a law did not exist that had never been broken. Perhaps it was hardly surprising—inevitable, even—that a few had managed to elude the Numerators.

Araxa shook his head in disgust. He had always privately wondered at the claim that the cuffs were a gift from God. And if Zarathustra made them himself, it was only logical he had used the power in some way *before* he had a device to channel the daēvas' power. But the idea that the magi's most venerated saint was part Druj....

It did not matter, he told himself firmly. He would cleanse their faith, make it pure again. That was his purpose. What he had been born for.

"Holy Father," Araxa muttered. "I suppose that is why he does not age?"

Jahandar nodded. "What will you do with him?"

"That is for the Hierarch to decide," Araxa replied. *What indeed?*

"Please...He has been quiet these many years. A model prisoner. Promise you won't harm him. Despite his weaknesses, Zarathustra saved the empire from certain destruction. We owe him our gratitude."

"I have no intention of harming him," Araxa said primly. "We shall plan the transfer for the evening of Nowruz. A fitting start to the New Year."

The High Magus of Karnopolis bowed his head. "As you say."

"He will be brought through the tunnels to the wing of the Hands of the Father. We will hold him there until a more appropriate place is selected. But with the Followers running rampant, I cannot take the chance one of them might attempt to free him."

"We have guarded the secret of his existence for two centuries," the High Magus said stiffly. "The only ones who know are myself, the King, and the two brothers who care for him." He drew a wheezing breath. "And now you and the Hierarch."

Araxa longed for a dampened cloth to press to his chest. The itch was maddening today. He knew the condition worsened when he felt agitated and tried to calm down.

"It's a miracle he hasn't escaped considering your extreme lenience," he told the High Magus sternly. "Now leave me. I must think." Araxa did not care that he was in the High Magus's own chambers, and the man didn't dare to refuse him. A moment later, he was scuttling out the door, looking frankly relieved he wasn't under arrest himself.

So Zarathustra was part daēva. Araxa found this fact extremely disturbing. It meant the Numerators' ultimate test—exposure to fire—was flawed. It only weeded out full-blooded demons.

How many more walk among us? He wondered.

The Hands of the Father had been created shortly after the war, when it became clear that an objective order was needed, one with no ties to the daēvas. As a Hand, Araxa had spent the first decade of his service traveling from town to town with the tax collectors. While they counted livestock and bushels of grain, he and two Water Dogs would gather the villagers together while soldiers searched their homes to be sure no one was hiding. The palms of the adults would be checked for tattoos marking them as human, and those children who had been born since the last census would be taken to the fire temple. All those who passed the test would receive their own tattoo.

Illegally bred daēvas were rare, so it was usually a routine procedure. Only once had Araxa seen the effects of fire on a daēva. The creature was young, nine or ten years old. It had belonged to a rich landowner who confessed that he had purchased it from the corrupt provincial satrap. He had wished to use the power to divert a nearby river to irrigate his fields. The man had hidden the cuffs away when the Numerators appeared, but the daēva had panicked and tried to run. The Water Dogs captured it easily because one of its legs was much shorter than the other.

The owner was a sentimental man, and he had begged Araxa to spare the demon. To send it off to serve in the Immortals. But Araxa knew examples had to be made, if one wished to leave a lasting impression. He was also curious about what exactly would happen. So they had taken the daēva to the village temple and dragged it to the brazier. Araxa now knew the precise distance at which the demons died: arm's length. The flames had suddenly leapt, as if doused with oil. And the daēva... The smell is what Araxa remembered. Like roast pig, but with the dry, acrid aroma of burnt hair. If there had been any doubt in his mind the daēvas were Druj, seeing the creature ignite without even being touched by the fire laid them to rest. The holy flames had rejected its presence in the strongest terms possible.

It was at this point Araxa began to privately question keeping them as guard dogs. They were feral and vicious no matter how tame they seemed, and he felt certain that one day they would bite the hand that held their leashes.

The following year, he had returned to Karnopolis and quickly risen to a position of prominence in the order. He discovered that besides hunting daēvas, the Hands of the Father carried out other delicate tasks for the King. A knife in the dark. A drop of poison in the cup. This suited him perfectly. He had a sixth sense for uncovering secrets and charting the hidden currents at court.

Which is how he knew someone was hiding in the cedar cabinet. They kept themselves perfectly still, but he had heard a soft indrawn breath when Jahandar admitted the Prophet was part demon.

Araxa wondered if it was an assassin. Perhaps that was why the High Magus had looked in that direction. He'd never been a subtle man. Perhaps they thought if they got rid of Araxa, the purge would die with him, although he doubted even the magi could be that foolish. And killing him in Jahandar's own chambers...too clumsy and obvious.

So if not an assassin, then whom?

Araxa strode to the door, where four of his brothers waited in the corridor. With a wordless gesture, he bade them to come inside. Assassin or no, one did not survive as long as Araxa had by taking needless risks. A moment later, they had silently surrounded the cabinet. Araxa nodded and one of the Hands, a short, squat man with a terrible burn scar on his neck, stepped forward and yanked the doors wide.

"Who have we here?" Araxa murmured. "A magus?" He sighed regretfully. "A Follower, perhaps?"

The young man inside began to shake his head, eyes wide, but Araxa had already spun on his heel and started for the door.

"Bring him to the cells," he instructed the Hands, who had thrown the magus to the floor and were all four kicking him senseless. "Search his rooms here first. Bring anything of interest back to the Hall." As he stepped out the door to the ringing screams of the spy, two magi came around the corner. Their steps quickened as they passed him, and they did not dare raise their heads, not even to see who was the latest to be taken.

It pleased Araxa very much. He wanted only what was best for the empire, although if that meant the magi had to bend their stiff necks to him, he did not mind. Perhaps it was sinful of him to take pleasure in their humiliation, but all things considered, Araxa thought the Holy Father would understand.

❧ 10 ❧

NAZAFAREEN

The next four days passed with no message from Saman. Every morning, Darius and I went to the tomb, hoping for a sign. We sat cross-legged on the ground and watched pilgrims trudge by from every far-flung corner of the empire. I caught snatches of different languages as they passed, from the almost guttural tongue of Al Miraj and Qaddah to the lilting speech of the far east. Rich and poor, young and old, healthy and dying, they came in droves, with prayers on their lips and religious fervor in their eyes.

Many brought offerings for the Prophet, but none paused on the fourteenth step of the eastern side of the tomb.

Tijah and Myrri didn't relish sitting around at Marduk's Spear, but they had agreed to keep a low profile and Darius held them to it. With nothing else to do, they became Ester's unofficial helpers, painting faces and gossiping with the boys like they'd been there for years. I think Ester liked the company, and Tijah seemed to enjoy flaunting her feminine side. In all the years we had known each other, I had rarely seen her out of uniform. She enjoyed the heat of battle as much as I did and was utterly terrifying with a scimitar in her hand. But for the first time, I was seeing the woman she might have been in Al Miraj. Even with her hair chopped off, Tijah was cultured and elegant in a way I knew I would never be. It made me slightly jealous, but I loved her and forgave her for it.

In the evenings, Dav followed Darius around like a puppy. He seemed pathetically eager for the attention of a man who wasn't interested in him physically. At first, Darius was embarrassed by the attention, but I could tell he was warming to the kid. He let Dav hold his sword, and even taught him a few sparring tricks up on the roof while Tijah and I played at dice or reminisced about Tel Khalujah. Dav remained leery of her, which was wise, but Tijah ignored him and he did nothing to earn further retribution.

Meanwhile, two more magi turned up dead, both butchered like the first. Any lingering idea we might somehow get inside the temple to look around for ourselves was now laughable. Soldiers had been sent to guard every entrance, and the magi rarely ventured outside anymore. If they did, it was in groups of three or more. Most people seemed to blame the Numerators for these crimes, but anyone who came too close to the temple was scrutinized as a potential threat. Even the pilgrims stayed away, and we sold only a handful of trinkets each day. Every time I checked the loose stone to see if a message waited, I expected the worst. That we had been betrayed and soldiers would rush out of the tomb to seize both me and Darius. That it didn't happen just put me more on edge.

ॐ

"IF WE DON'T FIND HIM IN THE NEXT WEEK, IT WILL BE TOO late," Darius said.

We were in our usual spot on the roof. It was where we practiced our sword fighting, and now, deciphering the tedious writings of the Prophet. Arshad owned his collected works and it was dry going, especially since I'd renounced my faith and couldn't care less about the endless rituals required to avoid damnation.

I was already regretting my burning desire to learn how to read, but didn't have the heart to tell Darius. He was patient and encouraging, glossing over my mistakes and heaping praise on every minor victory. I almost missed the old caustic Darius. This one seemed like a weird facsimile.

"Maybe Victor will have better luck," I said glumly. We sat against the low wall enclosing the edge of the roof. It was early morning, and the air was thick with the smell of the sea. "If he gets the fire, we won't need the Prophet to free the daēva Immortals."

A muscle feathered in Darius's jaw. "Victor's still alive?"

"Still alive," I agreed. "At this distance, it's hard to say much else. But he's not in pain. I'm sure I would feel that. And don't forget, he has Lysandros with him. I wouldn't take on the pair of them for all the gold in the King's treasury." I picked up a scroll Darius had identified as *Meditations on the Thirty-Nine Virtues* and tossed it down again. "Is there nothing more interesting? For a pimp, Arshad has incredibly boring taste in literature."

Darius sorted through the pile. I envied the ease with which he scanned each scroll. I had learned most of the alphabet, but trying to string it all together into words still took me forever.

"You might like this one better," he said, unfurling one end from its wooden roller to expose the first two pages. The writing was tiny and cramped and made my head hurt just looking at it. "It's a treatise on alchemy." Darius frowned. "Must be quite rare. I don't remember ever seeing anything like this at the temple in all the years I lived there. Maybe it's not surprising. Most of his contributions to science have been swept under the rug. The magi wanted him to be remembered as a holy man, not a thaumaturge."

"A what?"

"Something like a sorcerer."

I looked up. "Is that what Zarathustra was?"

"So the Greeks claim." He grinned. "But they're barbarians, of course. In any event, the High Magus who took over after Zarathustra was deposed burned many of his scrolls. For all we know, this one could be the last of its kind."

"Victor said he could touch the power, like me. I wish I knew why. And if there are others. There must be, it can't only be the two of us. I wonder if I could still work it if I weren't wearing the cuffs?" I shook my head, confused. "But that seems all wrong. Only daēvas have the ability..."

I babbled on for a bit, but Darius didn't respond. He was reading the scroll with an intent expression on his face.

"He talks about the elements," Darius said. "Their various properties...This is interesting."

"What?" I leaned over his shoulder.

"Well, he says fire, the fourth element, is different from the others."

"We already know that. It's unworkable."

Darius looked at me. "Zarathustra doesn't seem to think so. And he says it's both an element and a force, whatever that means. That it can alter the other three elements."

"But I thought fire can't be used at all."

"Not by a daēva," Darius agreed.

"Alter in what way?"

"I'm not sure. He's rather vague." Darius glanced at the angle of the sun. It was just peeking over the sandy hills to the east. "We'll have to finish this later. It's time we get to the tomb." He returned the scrolls to their bag. "Are you ready?"

"For another wasted day? Sure, why not."

Darius sighed. "If there's no answer today, we need to think of something else."

"I could try to sneak into the magi's temple," I offered. "Find those tunnels and have a look around."

"If they caught you, it wouldn't take long to connect you to the Water Dog with a missing hand who escaped the dungeons."

"I know, but it's all I can think of."

"One more day," Darius said firmly, raking his fingers through his hair. "And then we go into the tunnels together."

I went downstairs and gathered our supply of trinkets from Bobak while Darius turned himself into a lady. He wasn't bad, if you didn't mind your women on the burly side. I'm not sure he would have passed without the veil, but with only his blue eyes showing and a bit of makeup, he just pulled it off.

There were more people than usual in the streets because of Nowruz, which was only three days away. The festivities attracted visitors from near and far. Most of the men wore a simple tunic, but here and there in the crowds I spied the short kilts favored by Egyptians and the long cotton cloth Far Easterners wore wound around the body, with the end draped over the shoulder.

Farm wagons rumbled along piled high with vegetables, but we also saw hard-faced riders, alone and in groups, who had to be the mercenaries Darius had warned Tijah about.

"They gather like vultures to a dying animal," Darius muttered under his breath. "Dav says the King has summoned swords for hire to guard the city so he can mobilize most of the troops to Persepolae. He sent messengers the length and breadth of the empire, turning over every rock they could find. Now they've come here, hoping for gold and glory."

"How can you tell the ones from Al Miraj?" I asked as we wound our way along a street of gambling dens, the rattle of dice and curses of the losers audible even at this early hour.

"See the loose black scarves around their necks?" Darius nodded towards a trio of men lounging outside a tavern up ahead. "When the desert winds blow, they wrap the cloth over their faces to keep the sand away. And they wear curved blades, like Tijah and Myrri."

I looked at the men out of the corner of my eye as we approached. Two were tall and thin, the last short and stocky. They all had long black moustaches and nasty-looking scars.

Besides the scimitars, the men wore vicious hook-shaped daggers strapped to their boots. They were arguing about something, and I stepped aside to give them a wide berth when the tallest one, a gaunt man with a lazy eye, gave the short one a hard shove. He stumbled directly into my path, bumping my shoulder and knocking the bag of trinkets from my hand.

"Watch where you're going, boy," the man grumbled, breath reeking of wine. I muttered an apology, but before I could move on, he snatched up the bag and began pawing through it. "What's this here?" he said, pulling out a figurine of a man wearing a long beard and square hat, standing against the outstretched eagle wings of the faravahar.

My heart raced, but I kept my head and put on a polite smile. "Only seven siglos for a keepsake of the Prophet, carved by the famous blind craftsmen of Samashna," I said. "For you, sir, I will lower the price to five, which barely covers the cost of the wood. Anything less and my sisters would starve—"

"And who's that?" Lazy Eye demanded, pointing at Darius. "You don't look like siblings."

"My betrothed, sir," I replied quickly.

"She looks like she could break you in half," the short one smirked.

"Zorah is a healthy lass," I agreed, giving him a knowing wink. "I'm saving to buy a farm after we're married. As much as I admire a delicate lady, I've no wish to be stuck doing all the work. Give me a strong back over a small waist and I'm content."

The mercenaries laughed. "Then your wish has come true," said the third, whose cheeks were pitted with deep pockmarks, perhaps from a childhood illness. He raised his cup. "To sturdy oxen and sturdy wives. I hope you have an extra-long goad!" The others roared with laughter.

I forced a smile. Darius tried to look modest, casting his eyes toward the ground, but they had a dangerous glint I knew all too well. We needed to get out of there before he lost his temper.

"A kiss!" Lazy Eye shouted, waving his own cup in the air. "Or does she have the face of an ox too? Is that why she hides behind the veil?"

A few passersby had paused to watch the spectacle, but most kept their eyes straight ahead and hurried on. The short mercenary still clutched our wares in one meaty fist. I was tempted to kick him in the balls and run, but we were too close to the temple district. I couldn't risk giving up our spot by the tomb for these louts.

"Kiss! Kiss!" The other two took up the chant, red-faced and leering.

I sighed and turned to Darius.

"Would you favor me, dewdrop?" I asked.

He gave the barest nod. I lifted the veil just above his mouth. The mercenaries quieted. I felt the warmth of his breath and then I pressed my lips against his. My knees loosened a bit at the contact, chaste as it was. When I opened my eyes, his were staring straight at me through the gauzy veil. I suppose I'd expected Darius to close them like a proper lady, but the look he gave me was decidedly *improper*, if not outright brazen. Heat crept up my neck.

"Look at the boy blush," Lazy Eye exclaimed. He sighed almost mournfully. "Ah, true love is a rare and wondrous thing."

I dropped the veil and stepped back, feeling a little light-headed.

"We should find ourselves some women," the short one mumbled.

I held my hand out for the bag. He just stared at me, a mean twist to his mouth.

"City Watch," the pock-marked one hissed. "Give him his wares, Aji."

I looked down the street, where four soldiers were making their way through the crowd, each with a tall spear braced on his shoulder. The mercenary threw the bag to the ground, spilling figurines across the packed dirt. The three of them downed the dregs of their wine and slunk off into the nearest alley.

Darius and I knelt down and silently gathered the figurines. I tried to forget the taste of his lips on mine, the hard blue of his eyes just inches away. Tried to forget the power, pulsing at the edge of my awareness. The approaching soldiers raked us with cool gazes. I tucked the stump of my right hand behind my back and cinched the bag closed just as they came abreast of us. Unlike the mercenaries, these men looked sober and disciplined.

"Is there a problem?" one of them asked, glancing at the alley with distaste. I got the impression the City Watch was less than thrilled about the influx of heavily armed foreigners to Karnopolis.

"No, I just dropped my sack," I said.

They gave us a skeptical look and moved on.

"Ready to go, *Zorah?*" I asked, giving Darius a cheeky grin.

"Quite," he said, and I turned away before he could see the flush in my cheeks again.

We hurried to the tomb in silence. As we rounded the last corner, I missed a step and almost dropped the bag again. Resting on the fourteenth stair of the eastern side, its spiky white petals bleeding to a delicate pink at the tips, was a fresh lotus blossom.

It was just one of a dozen flowers strewn across the steps, but to me it shone like a signal beacon. I shared an excited look with Darius. Saman must have found something out. Something important. So it had taken him longer than he'd expected to contact us. Maybe they were watching him. Or maybe he'd only just discovered where the Prophet was being held.

Darius shook out our cloth across the street from the tomb and arranged the trinkets as he would on any other day, even as his sharp eyes swept the square. It looked perfectly ordinary to me. The soldiers guarding the Temple of the Magi greeted a departing magus, but it wasn't Saman. Otherwise the place was quiet, as usual for the mornings.

"We should wait," Darius said in a low voice.

"For what?" I felt a surge of impatience. I was tired of waiting. Tired of Marduk's Spear, and this hot, crowded city. I wanted to be on a horse racing for Persepolae, with the Prophet in a sack tied behind my saddle. "If it's a trap, sitting around won't make any difference. Do you feel any danger? Are we being watched?"

He gave me a level look. "The buildings around us are full of magi and Numerators, hundreds of them. There could be more soldiers waiting inside. I have no way of telling if they pose a threat."

"Well, either we have a plan or we don't. I'm going to find out which it is."

I looked around the square one last time. The magus I'd seen emerge from the temple was out of sight now. I leapt to my feet and ran across the street, ignoring Darius's clipped "*Nazafareen!*"

Heart thudding in my chest, mouth dry as dust, I scampered up the stairs and dropped to one knee on the fourteenth step.

BALTHAZAR

The soldiers glanced at Balthazar as he emerged from the temple and started down the stairs. A magus traveling alone in the city had become an unusual sight, but since he was going out rather than in, they saw no need to question him. There was nothing sinister about the man. He had an attractive, boyish face, with olive skin and regular features made more interesting by a slightly crooked nose. He nodded respectfully as he passed, and the soldiers nodded back.

With the soldiers behind him, Balthazar's mouth tightened in frustration. Besides Shahrooz, he had dragged two magi into the tunnels to question them. Vigorously. He knew their deepest secrets and darkest desires. And yet he was no closer to discovering the location of the Prophet. He was starting to wonder if the Purified who claimed Zarathustra was alive had been delusional. The man had seemed certain, but his mind had not been fully intact at the time. It was possible this was all a wild goose chase.

Balthazar took no special pleasure in the murders. They were simply a means to an end. He had selected the magi carefully, based on the length of their service at the temple in Karnopolis and the likelihood they would be privy to the closest-kept secrets. In retrospect, perhaps he should have started with the High Magus himself. But the man was not easy to get to, and it would be even harder now. They were pissing themselves at every shadow.

It was past time he searched the tunnels themselves, no matter how long that took. He would need a lantern and paint to mark his trail. A man could wander for days, weeks even, and still only traverse a small part of the labyrinth. Balthazar had already done some exploring and found the tunnels to be in a poor state of repair, the ceiling and walls crumbling. Some passages had been bricked up entirely. Others bore black water marks from occasions when the river had flooded them.

Balthazar reached the bottom of the steps and paused. The square was deserted, save for two trinket sellers near the tomb. He had no destination in mind. He only wished to get away from the magi for a time. From their incessant chanting and praying. The place brought back memories better left buried. Of the first time he had made a gate, for example.

He had learned of the shadowlands from a forbidden text on the occult Balthazar had acquired in the second year he took the robes, when he was fourteen. The scroll referred to it as *the gloaming*. The land of the dead. It claimed there was dark magic there, magic anyone could take if he managed to pierce the veil between worlds. So he had filled a bowl of water and followed the instructions, slashing his palm and letting the blood drip into the bowl until the water darkened to a deep red hue. He'd let the liquid settle until it became flat as glass, watching his own reflection in the surface. Then he had spoken certain words in an ancient tongue that tasted strange in his mouth. And after many long minutes, he began to have the sensation that the mirror image was not himself anymore, but separate. Alive. He had felt the pull of the gate. Felt it *welcome* him. It wanted to let him through. It was greedy for him. And he was greedy for its magic.

So he had dipped his fingertips into the water, slowly submerging his hand, and then his arm, and it had passed straight through the bottom of the bowl into a cold place.

Balthazar had immediately yanked his arm out, skin tingling with apprehension. He had hoped it would work, and yet part of him was not ready. He was still a callow youth dabbling in things he had no real understanding of. A long time passed before he gathered the courage to try again, to pay the blood price in full, and the next time had been his undoing.

Balthazar was about to cross the square when he saw one of the trinket sellers, a young man of slight build, stroll towards the tomb. Something in the way the boy's eyes darted about drew Balthazar's interest. Being a liar and a sneak himself, he instantly recognized those qualities in others. Balthazar moved behind a tree and watched the boy climb the steps. Halfway up, he paused and knelt, as though in prayer. Balthazar thought he saw the boy's hand do something to the stone at his feet, but his vantage point was not clear enough to say what it was exactly. Several moments later, the boy rose abruptly and started back down the steps.

But that was not what made the necromancer's hackles rise.

As the boy returned to his wares, Balthazar heard the rattle of wheels on stone. A brick-laden cart came careening around the corner, drawn by four enormous draft horses. The boy froze, and Balthazar was certain he would be run down. But the stocky, veiled woman who had been sitting with him leapt forward and dragged him out of the way, in a blur so fast Balthazar could barely track the movement. The driver cursed loudly, but by the time the cart had moved past, the pair was gone, their trinkets abandoned.

Balthazar's mind raced. There was only one creature that moved like that. A *daēva*.

The necromancer began to run.

❦ 12 ❧

NAZAFAREEN

"We have to get out of here," Darius growled in my ear. "Right now."

I nodded, still shaky from my close call with the cart. We dove into the nearest alley as the driver muttered something about *careless fools* and shook the reins, urging the horses forward.

"What about the—" I began, glancing back at the trinkets on the ground.

"Leave them. If anyone saw what I did back there...."

"You didn't use the power, did you?"

"No, but almost as bad. I moved as no human can move. Do you have it?"

I gripped the note in my fist. "I have it."

"We'll read it when we get back. This way." He led me at a fast jog through the maze of narrow streets. A short time later, we were back at Marduk's Spear. The streets of the pleasure district had been too crowded for Darius to be positive we weren't followed, but neither of us had seen anyone. We entered through the stables, just in case, and wasted a few minutes searching for Arshad, but he wasn't in his study or anywhere else.

"Wait in the private dining room," Darius said to me. "I'll find Tijah and Myrri. The cook says he saw them playing dice in the common room."

It seemed to take forever for Darius to return. I sat on one of the couches, then stood up again and paced from the door to the courtyard until I heard voices and the three of them came hustling in. Myrri gave me a tight smile. Tijah sprawled in a chair.

"Thank the gods," she muttered. "What does he say?"

The air in the room suddenly seemed thick enough to cut as Darius scanned the parchment. I leaned forward a little, praying we weren't too late.

"The Prophet will be transferred tomorrow night," he said finally. "On the first day of Nowruz. We're to meet Saman at sunset."

"That's cutting it damn close," Tijah muttered. "Why not sooner?"

"I don't know, but I'm sure there's a reason."

"Do we know what kind of escort the Prophet will have?" I asked. "Is he bonded?"

"As to the second, Saman doesn't say. But six Hands of the Father will be guarding him. The plan is for us to sneak in and spirit him away before they realize he's gone."

"Sneak in *where*?" I said in exasperation.

"The tunnels. He included a map." Darius unrolled the second piece of parchment on the table and weighed down the corners with apples from a clay bowl. The map was hand-drawn and not easy to read. Saman had printed an X in the center of a tangle of lines that must be the Prophet's cell.

"Can you make sense of it?" I asked Darius.

"Just get me down there," he replied.

"Right. And how do we get down there?"

"Let me see." Tijah leaned over the map, tracing a finger along the lines. "Maybe the triangles are exits. Let me borrow this for a few hours. Myrri and I will check out the streets." Darius opened his mouth to remind her that she was supposed to keep hidden, but the scowl on her face made him shut it again. "We'll be careful. But I need to do something or I'll go crazy." Myrri absently patted her hand. She flashed some signs and Tijah gave a rueful smile. "Myrri says you have to let me out for a while or we'll *both* lose our minds."

I understood how they felt. The walls of the brothel felt like they were closing in on me a little bit more every hour I sat there. "Do you think that's what Saman's been doing for the last three days?" I asked. "Mapping out the tunnels?"

Tijah shrugged. "Probably."

"Because he would have known about all this right after the meeting between the High Magus and the Numerators. Why didn't he tell us then?"

"Maybe he didn't have enough information. Or the meeting was postponed for some reason."

"Maybe."

"You think it's a fake?"

"I think we should show it to Arshad," I said.

"Show him what?" The brothel owner stepped through the door, looking dapper as ever in an embroidered silk tunic and flashy gold faravahar brooch pinned over his heart. "Bobak says you were looking for me."

"We think we know where Zarathustra is," Darius said, handing him the parchment.

Arshad sucked a breath between his teeth as he read the message. "Well, that's Saman's writing if you're wondering. We've exchanged messages for two years now and I can vouch for it without a shred of doubt." His hand shook slightly as he gave the parchment back to Darius. "After all this time...two long centuries. That he truly lives...Holy Father, when people find out, this will change everything." The joy in his eyes dimmed. "Though with the news I just received, it may not have come a moment too soon."

"What?" Darius leaned forward, his brow creased with worry.

"Alexander has begun marching on Persepolae."

"*What?*"

"Yes. He is already across the Hellespont. He will reach the city in no more than four days."

"But...how? Why? He promised us more time!"

"I think the young king had no choice," Arshad said uneasily. "It seems Artaxeros is not sitting idly by, waiting for his empire to be invaded. He sent most of the Persian fleet into the Propontis. If Alexander had not moved, he would have been trapped on the wrong side of the strait."

Darius crumpled the parchment and flung it to the ground. "Curse him!"

"All is not lost yet," Arshad said soothingly. "You still have time to reach the summer capital."

I patted Darius on the shoulder. "More than enough," I said. "We can be there in three days, if we push hard."

"And if nothing goes wrong," Darius replied.

"It won't." I gave him a reassuring smile as Tijah shook her head and made the sign against bad luck.

"Well, now you've done it," she said.

❧ 13 ❧

BALTHAZAR

Balthazar followed the pair to a brothel called Marduk's Spear. He knew enough about daēvas to stay well back as he trailed them through the streets of the pleasure district. Most likely, it was a waste of time. Just as certain men had a taste for children, others would pay a great deal to bed a daēva. No doubt he had stumbled on some tawdry affair. But he couldn't afford to ignore anything out of the ordinary—especially when it transpired next to the Tomb of the Prophet.

Balthazar entered and took a seat in the farthest corner. The two he had followed must have gone straight to a back room, or perhaps through the stables. It was late morning, so the common room was only a quarter full. At a nearby table, two dark-skinned young men who looked too old to be whores and too young to be patrons were dicing and drinking tea. They had an easy closeness that reminded him of brothers, although their features were different. The owner's sons or nephews, maybe, there to keep an eye on things.

Balthazar ordered wine but did not touch it. He sat for a while, watching customers come and go from the upstairs rooms, and was just about to forget the whole thing when the taller boy rattled the dice cup and said something in the harshly musical tongue of Al Miraj. The other opened his mouth in a laugh but no sound came out. His fingers flashed and the other *did* laugh, loud and hard.

Balthazar froze. A brief memory, so vivid he could smell the burned flesh. Two Water Dogs on the Great Salt Plain, both women. One held up the head of a Revenant as her free hand spoke in signs he could not understand.

They weren't wearing the blue and red uniforms and their hair had been chopped off, but he recognized them now. Not boys at all. The Water Dogs sensed him staring and glanced over. Balthazar tried not to shrink under the inspection, but after a moment they returned to their game without comment.

The last time Balthazar had met these Dogs, he'd worn chains linking him to his captives. He had been covered in sand and blood, and anything that came near him died in flames, screaming. Now he kept his eyes downcast. His thick brown hair was neatly combed. He wore the clean white robes of a magus, which was apparently a common enough sight in the pleasure district in general, and Marduk's Spear in particular, that no one raised an eyebrow at his presence.

Balthazar watched as the veiled daēva who had been selling trinkets at the tomb came rushing in and dragged the Water Dogs off to a back room. If he'd still believed in the Holy Father, Balthazar would have thought divine providence had led him to this place. He sipped his wine, mind churning. Why were they not wearing the Water Dog colors? The only explanation was that they were hiding from something. He thought the heavy-shouldered one in the veil was the daēva whose power the necromancers had all sensed on the plain.

Balthazar didn't believe in coincidences. What were they doing at the Tomb of the Prophet? And what had caused them to flee and leave their wares behind, as if they had no intention of ever returning? If there was some connection to his own goal, he would ferret it out. It would not be difficult to take one of the Dogs in the night, but his chains didn't work on bonded, not humans nor daēvas. Antimagus Alloch had discovered that in the battle, when he tried to collar the girl with long hair and died for it. He supposed he could torture them, but Water Dogs weren't easy to break and their bonded always found them quickly. There was no place one could be hidden from the other.

"More wine?"

It was one of the boy whores. His eyes were painted with kohl, his hair curled into ringlets that brushed his slim shoulders. The boy gave the necromancer a tired smile. Balthazar had seen that smile a thousand times before when he lived in Karnopolis.

Balthazar smiled back. "What is your name?"

"Dav."

"How much is a room here, Dav?"

The boy quoted a ridiculously inflated number, but Balthazar didn't object. "Might you be available to entertain me? I prefer a secluded room. Do you have something like that? I can pay extra."

The boy's smile brightened into something nearly genuine. "Of course. Just this way."

Balthazar followed him through a doorway in the rear of the common room. As they walked down the hall, the daēva's companion emerged from a small dining room. Balthazar had taken her for a boy at the tomb, but as they suddenly came face to face, he realized she was a young woman with her hair cropped nearly to the skull. Her features were fine-boned and fragile, although her amber eyes were hard as granite.

Balthazar remembered her from that first brief encounter on the plain, how her hand had strayed to the hilt of her sword as if she wanted nothing more than to charge at him and his brethren. He vaguely remembered her later, amid the chaos and death of the dome. She was a killer, the girl was. Violent and merciless. He'd kept out of her way until he'd found the fire, and then he had ridden hard for Bactria and his queen. As he left the dome, he had seen her kill Alloch, the last of the Antimagi.

The Water Dog looked straight into Balthazar's eyes, but he detected not even the tiniest spark of recognition. All she saw was a magus in his early thirties, with broad shoulders and dark hair. A moment later she was brushing past him in the narrow hallway and the boy led him up a flight of stairs to the second floor. The room he entered was tiny, with only a lumpy bed and a small, plain wooden chest. The boy—Dav—immediately pulled his tunic over his head. His skin was pale and luminous as the moon.

"Sit down," Balthazar ordered, leaning against the wall. He did not undress or make any attempt to touch the boy, which made the child frown in confusion. This wasn't how it usually went. Still, the boy was trained to comply with what the clients wanted as long as it was within reason, so he sat on the bed, naked and unembarrassed, and waited.

Balthazar felt strange. The unaccustomed heat must be getting to him. That, and being back in the pleasure quarter. He had grown up not far from here, in the maze of filthy alleyways at the heart of the quarter. Balthazar's parents had both died of plague when he was very young. His older sister, Artunis, had sold her body to keep them both fed. He had been a pretty child, and by the age of eleven, some of her customers had started to notice him. She'd kept him hidden away after that, but then she too fell sick.

How hungry they had been. They'd eaten insects and snakes and even a pair of leather sandals Balthazar had stolen from a drunk who passed out on the street. After his sister died, he sat with her body for two days. He almost certainly would have ended up in a place like Marduk's Spear himself if a magus, one of his sister's regular customers, hadn't found him and taken him to the temple to become a novice.

Balthazar studied the boy. He looked to be fifteen. By that age, Balthazar had already been living a double life, observing the rituals of the magi by day and pursuing forbidden knowledge by night. The boy wore garish green eye makeup but he did not simper, and he looked like he might be intelligent. Not just cunning and cynical, although he was those things too, but genuinely clever. Balthazar thought this boy lived his own sort of double life.

"You must hear things, working here," he said. "Wine loosens tongues, among other things."

The boy shrugged.

"What gossip can you tell me?"

The boy scratched his head. "Well, someone's been cutting up the magi, but you already know about that, don't you?"

A muscle in Balthazar's jaw twitched, but then he saw the boy eyeing his robes and realized he didn't mean Balthazar personally, but rather the priests as a whole. "Yes," he agreed. "I've heard. It must be a madman."

"Not the Numerators? That's what everyone says."

"Or the Numerators. What else?"

"I heard some mercenaries talking. They said refugees from the eastern satrapies are starting to flood across the plain. That they are running ahead of Druj. The King is holding the Immortals in Persepolae to deal with the barbarian king, Alexander, and the east is undefended." The boy chewed his full bottom lip. "Do you think it could be true? Druj? I've never seen one. One of the boys says they are just stories to scare little children."

"They are real enough, but the city wall of Karnopolis is one of the oldest and highest in the world. It kept them out before," Balthazar replied, and the boy nodded thoughtfully, not realizing this was no answer. *Neblis has moved quickly since I left.* "What else? Who are the people staying here? The girl I passed in the hall?"

Dav's eyes grew large for a moment, but he shrugged and feigned ignorance. "I'm not sure who you mean."

"I know it's a girl," Balthazar said evenly. "How many are there? Six, or only four? Why are they here?"

"I...I don't know," the boy stammered. Balthazar pushed off the wall and sat down on the bed next to him. It creaked heavily with his weight.

"You wish to please me, don't you?" he asked softly.

The boy tried on a strained smile. "Magus, they are no one. Guests of the owner, that's all I know." He laid a hand on Balthazar's thigh. "Let me help you relax. You seem—"

Balthazar only glanced down, but Dav pulled his hand away as if he'd been burned. His gaze flickered to the closed door. Balthazar knew there was a giant of a man out there who worked for the brothel. He had seen him sitting on a stool in the corner of the common room, his air of boredom and half-closed eyes belying his watchfulness. The necromancer had no fear of the giant, but he needed to learn what Dav knew. So he smiled, and saw the boy's relief. Balthazar had a wide, sunny smile, a handsome smile, with small, pointy eyeteeth that made him look even younger. In reality, he was old enough to be the boy's great-great-grandfather, but who would ever believe the truth?

"You're right. I think we should have some fun," he said, gently pushing the boy back on the bed. "Close your eyes."

Dav let his painted eyelids flutter closed. How thin he was, and how terribly young. "Are you shy? It's all right if you are."

"A little." Balthazar took care to muffle the sound of the chains as he withdrew them from the sack. "I have scars. I was a warrior magus once."

"Really?" The boy seemed intrigued. "Have you killed anyone?"

"Yes." Balthazar laid the chains at the bottom of the bed. They were just inches from Dav's left foot. He would have felt them if he'd moved at all, but he didn't.

"I didn't think there were any of those left," the boy said.

"What about you?" Balthazar ran a hand up the back of his own neck. It came away slick with sweat. The air in the room was very close. "Do you have dreams?"

Dav cracked an eyelid. "Are you coming to bed?"

"No peeking," Balthazar said.

The boy shut his eyes again and took a deep breath that swelled his bony chest. "Dreams? Do you mean at night?"

"No. I mean what you would do if you could be anyone, go anywhere."

"Oh. I don't know."

"I'm certain you do. You can tell me." Balthazar didn't know why he was wasting time talking. He should be wringing the boy out like a wet rag, bleeding him for every drop of information he had. His instincts told him Dav knew why the Water Dogs had come here. And yet Balthazar found himself in no hurry to return to the temple. He hated the magi now even more than when he was one of them. And the boy was the first person Balthazar had spoken to since he'd arrived who wasn't a hypocrite.

"Well...the most sought-after courtiers are very rich and elegant. They choose who their patrons are and have their own servants, and go to all the parties. Some of the boys here are eunuchs, but I'm not. Arshad doesn't do that. They were cut before they came to him. I would like to meet a rich man, one who is kind, and live in my own house." He laughed, still without opening his eyes. "All the boys want that, of course. And most of them will die in places much worse than this one."

"A worthy dream," Balthazar said. "May the Holy Father watch over you." He had intended it as a joke, but as he spoke the words, Balthazar found he actually meant them. He scrubbed a hand across his eyes. Too many ghosts in this city. Two centuries wasn't nearly long enough to dispel them. It had been a mistake to come here alone. He should have brought his brothers.

Balthazar cupped Dav's chin with one hand. "I'm sorry," he said.

"For what?"

"For this." The boy's eyes flew open as the collar touched his flesh. No matter how warm the air was, the metal was always cold. It seared Balthazar's hand as he snapped it shut.

The things I do for her. Balthazar had stained his soul for Neblis a thousand times, and he would do it a thousand more. Even now, as he looked into the boy's frightened eyes, Balthazar ached for her touch. He was bonded to her as tightly as his slaves, and by his own free will.

"The Water Dogs," he whispered.

And at last, the boy began to talk.

14

While Tijah and Myrri tried to figure out how the map of the tunnels related to the streets aboveground, Darius and I went out to buy horses. We settled on four because I had a feeling that the Prophet would not be in any shape to ride alone after two hundred years of captivity, and Darius agreed.

Arshad had sent us to another of his cronies, whose stables lay across one of the city's murky, impenetrable canals. Maluduk-bal-idinna had the oily look of someone who prayed at the fire temple five times a day, but whose scruples vanished in a puff of incense the moment he sensed a sucker. His horses were good quality, at least. They had glossy coats and bright eyes, and none of them tried to bite me. I'd honed my haggling skills on the pilgrims, so we ended up with a better price than expected.

"What if he's mad?" I said to Darius as we led our new mounts —two chestnut stallions and a pair of creamy Ferghana mares— back to Marduk's Spear. The late afternoon sun was blistering. Anyone stupid enough to be outside moved slowly. Even the cats napped in the shade. As we passed the Egyptian wig-maker's shop, he caught a glimpse of Darius through the front door and startled. I smiled and waved. Next came the gambling den where two men who looked like Bobak's uglier brothers nodded at us in a friendly greeting. I was starting to feel like I'd lived on Saffron Street all my life.

"Just think about it," I said. "Zarathustra has been locked up all this time. I can tell you what I'd be like. Out of my mind, that's what."

"Victor was imprisoned since the war," Darius pointed out.

"That's different. I'm not saying Gorgon-e Gaz wasn't bad. It was probably horrible." I thought of the prison fortress on the shore of the Salenian Sea, where the old daēvas were kept. "It was *definitely* horrible. But at least he had other daēvas with him. What if they've kept the Prophet in the dark? Alone? I'm just saying, we have no idea what he's like now. He might hate the magi as much as Victor does. And he might not do what we want him to do."

"I know. But there's nothing we can do about that. One thing at a time, Nazafareen. Let's just focus on getting him out of the city."

"I wish we could meet with Saman one last time. I'd feel better if we could plan this face to face. We know almost nothing about what we're walking into. What if there are more guards than we expect? What if they have daēvas?"

"They don't know we're coming," Darius said. "There's a lot to be said for surprise. Look, at least he found out where Zarathustra is. Two more days and the Numerators would have had him. But Saman insisted we not try to contact him. It's too dangerous now."

"What if we get lost? Or separated?"

"You know I can always find you, Nazafareen," Darius said quietly. "Always."

His eyes held me and my heart gave a little lurch. For a moment, he let his guard down. Warm feelings of protectiveness washed over me, like the sun coming out on a winter's day, and I smiled. "I know," I said.

We stabled the horses in a small barn behind the central courtyard and went looking for Tijah and Myrri. They weren't in their shared room on the top floor, or the private dining room where we met when we needed to talk. It was the eve of Nowruz, and raucous crowds filled the brothel to bursting. I pushed my way upstairs and knocked on Ester's door.

"Have you seen Tijah?" I asked, sticking my head inside.

Damp curls stuck from out Ester's braid as she painted the mouth of a gangly, heavy-lidded boy named Paria. Four more sat cross-legged on the floor, waiting their turns. "Nope. Have you seen Dav? He's usually the first one here. He's so fussy and vain, he always wants extra time."

"I didn't see him at supper," one of the boys ventured.

"He's probably mooning over that client of his," another laughed. "Tall, dark and holy."

"Why do I never get the good-looking ones?" the first complained, pushing wavy brown hair from his eyes.

"Because most of them don't have to pay for it," said the second, who was old enough that his voice was just starting to deepen.

Paria turned to look at them and Ester jerked his chin back.

"We just got in," I said. "But no, I haven't seen Dav either."

"Well, if you do, tell him he'd better hurry up. I'm running out of kohl and..." She surveyed the scattering of open pots and jars in exasperation. "Everything."

"Yeah, I'll tell him. Where's Arshad?"

"Serving wine in the main room, I think." She finished Paria's lips and began braiding his hair. He made a face as she briskly divided it into three and jerked the strands tight. Ester wasn't normally so brusque. But the extra customers at the brothel had everyone on edge, including Bobak, who stood near the stairs cracking his knuckles and looking even more psychopathic than usual.

Our private room was taken by a party of merchants eating supper, so Darius and I went up to the roof to wait for Tijah and Myrri. On the way, he ducked into his room to pick up the scroll we'd been studying that morning.

"You might need to use the power tomorrow," Darius said, as we sat down against the wall. "Maybe we can find out something useful."

Here it comes. "About that...It may not be such a great idea. I'm not sure I can be trusted with it."

"You may have to anyway," he replied. "I know you're afraid of fire." My head jerked up. He looked at me calmly. "I am too. We'd be fools not to be. But you can learn to control yourself. And I'm interested in what the Prophet has to say on the subject."

Darius unrolled the scroll to the point where he had been reading that morning. It was too dark for me to see much anymore, but his eyes gathered the moonlight like a cat's.

"Here we are...*Let us discuss the subtle aspects of Fire, which lies at the very essence of the Art. Fire is the heart of all things, it is the blood of creation. Water, air and earth, those material elements, require energy to shape their substance, and to transform it. Fire is capricious. It may appear to smolder and then surge to life. Fire alone will sear the bones of the alchemist, but wielded in conjunction with one or more of the terrestrial elements, it can break all doors of this world and those beyond...."*

"Wait," I said. "What does that mean? Wielded in conjunction?"

Darius shrugged. "At the same time, I suppose."

"Have you ever done that? Used two elements simultaneously? Not fire, obviously. But others."

"Yes, of course. When I throw something, I use both earth and air. It's a little tricky at first, but it comes naturally once you've done it a few times."

"Interesting. Go on."

"All right, let's see...*There is only one power, and that is the glue binding everything together. It is the sea all life and matter swims in. But if one thinks of the power as a tree, with the nexus being the trunk and roots, the branches represent the different manifestations of that power, of which three are known to me. These are elemental magic; talismanic magic; and negatory magic.*"

"What's negatory magic?" I asked.

Darius shook his head. "I don't know. I've never heard of it." A finger traced the cramped writing on the scroll. "All he says is that it's extremely rare, and usually accompanied by an inborn but modest ability to wield elemental magic. *Fire begets fire, in mind and deed. The Alchemist must be wary of the price, lest it lead him to evil.*"

"Is he talking about humans? What does that even mean?"

"Again, he doesn't say. And part of the scroll seems to be missing." Darius showed me the torn, slightly charred edge, as though it had been snatched away from flames at the last moment. "But he might mean negatory magic is related to one's temperament in some way." He avoided looking at me. "Perhaps he wielded it himself. That's how he knows about it."

"I won't work fire, Darius."

"Holy Father, I'm not telling you to! But listen to the final line...*Of the three, negatory magic is both the weakest and the strongest. It stands apart, as the dark horse in the herd. All shall yield to the Breaker, for*—" He sighed. "And that is the end. Intriguing, I must say. Are you sure you have nothing to tell me, Nazafareen?"

I felt a burst of temper, made worse by the fact that it simply proved him right. "Not a thing!" I exclaimed. "And I'm tired of talking about me. What about you? We've been in this city a week now and you've said barely a word about it."

"What is it you wish me to say?"

"Oh, I don't know. But you never tell me anything! What was your life like before you came to Tel Khalujah? Who taught you to read? I've told you all kinds of things about myself, and you refuse to return the favor." I glared miserably at the scrolls. If I did have negatory magic within me, I didn't want it. *The Alchemist must be wary of the price, lest it lead him to evil.*

That struck me as distinctly ominous.

"You really wish to know?" Darius asked.

"Yes, I do."

"All right." He leaned back, not looking at me. "I don't remember my parents, either of them. I was only an infant when they took me from Gorgon-e Gaz to Karnopolis. All daēvas are bonded to an amah until they are of an age to be placed. Some go to the Immortals, others to Water Dogs, a few to the richest and most powerful merchants."

"What's an amah?" He had mentioned the word before, but I never really understood it.

"A foster mother. Each cares for several daēvas at a time. My first was a brisk, efficient type. She was not a warm person, but she wasn't a monster. She allowed us to play and only punished when she thought it was necessary for discipline. When I turned seven, she left. I'm not sure why." He paused. His voice was cold and emotionless when he spoke again. "She was replaced by a woman named Taravat. Taravat was young, with long black hair. She liked to paint her nails with henna. She was kind at first. She gave us sweets and hugs, and told us funny stories. She said she could not have children of her own, but the Holy Father had seen fit to give her daēvas, Druj though we might be. She would raise us in the light. It was her calling, she said."

Despite the warmth of the night, I felt a chill creep over me.

"But soon enough, the mask began to slip. The smallest infraction would merit a beating. And when the bruises became too visible, she started using the cuff."

"Was there no one to stop her?" I asked, quietly horrified.

"I tried to tell a magus once. He said he would look into it and never did. Finally, one of the boys in her care took his own life. My friend, Mani. She'd been at him for weeks, relentlessly. I'd tried to provoke her, to draw her anger away, but she had enough for both of us. And Mani was a gentle soul. He didn't know how to lock himself away." He paused. "Taravat relished using your emotions against you. Crawling inside your skull. It was worse than the physical torture." Darius tipped his head back, resting it against the wall. "Mani's death was viewed as a waste of a daēva, so the magi finally intervened."

"How long were you bonded to her?"

"Five years."

"Holy Father."

"After that, there were no more amahs. I was old enough to be bonded to a magus. His religious lessons focused on the wicked nature of the Druj, and more on the need to constantly guard against the temptations of evil." Darius barked a laugh. "I was used to that. But he also taught me to read and write, and permitted me to study books on science and geography. Eventually, they sent me to the winter palace to train with the Immortals, and then the Water Dogs."

We were silent for a while. "I hate them all," I said finally. "Do you think this woman is still given children to torment?"

"I don't know. Probably. I used to see her after they took my cuff from her. She would stare at me like a hungry jackal, but she didn't dare defy the magi."

"Someday, I will hunt this Taravat down and kill her. Slowly."

Darius gave me a crooked grin. "I almost pity her."

"Why did you not hate me?" I asked him. "When we met?"

"Oh, but I did." His smile this time was strained.

"You offered me your hand at the bonding ceremony."

He shrugged. "I could see you were as broken as I was by it. And then, the next day..."

"By the river. What an ass I was."

His smile faded. "Would you give me the blessing, Nazafareen?"

I sighed. "Why do you want to be blessed by a heretic?"

"I want to be blessed by *you*. Like we used to." He gave me a level look. "It may be the last time."

He meant we might not live through tomorrow. "All right," I said. I hadn't spoken the words in weeks, although I would never forget them. I used to pray with Ilyas every morning. Now I knew why he was so fanatically devout. He had hoped the Holy Father would cleanse him of his lust for Tommas. But the Holy Father either didn't exist or he was a sadist. Either way, I was done with Him.

Still, I couldn't refuse my daēva this. Not after what he'd just told me. So I waited while Darius fetched a waterskin and bowl. He filled the bowl and set it down on the wall. Then he dropped to his knees in front of me. I laid a hand on his bowed head. How silky his hair was.

"Good thoughts, good words, good deeds. May the Holy Father guide and keep you," I said, taking the bowl and letting the water trickle out in a stream over his head. It was tepid, but I still shuddered a little at the sensation. He stayed like that for a moment, and then his face was pressed against my tunic, his right hand clutching my waist. I slid my hand to the back of his neck and pulled him tighter. I loved him so much at that moment it felt like one of those hooked blades had caught in my chest. I was afraid to move or speak for fear of driving him away. Above all, I did not want to cause him any more pain. But the feel of his skin under my fingertips ignited a desire in me that I couldn't conceal.

When he looked up at me, his eyes were the color of the eastern sky, a fathomless blue with darkness pressing in at the edges.

"Take off the cuffs," he said hoarsely.

My breath caught as I understood what he wanted. Simply removing the cuff was not enough to break our bond. Only two things could do that. If one of us died, or if another person assumed the bond. But if Darius accidentally touched the gold alloy of my own cuff, the dominant cuff...it was agony for him.

I slid both of them off and let them drop to the tiles. Two circular gouges puckered my forearm just below the elbow where I'd pushed the cuffs up tight to keep them on my stump. Then I sank to my knees before him. Darius still had a fistful of my tunic and he used it to drag me toward him. Our mouths met, and we were pulling clothing off in a frenzy until it lay in a heap. At that moment, I didn't care who might come along. Darius was the most beautiful thing I had ever seen.

"I will always be yours, cuffs or no," he told me as the warmth of his body enveloped me. "In this life and every one after."

✤ 15 ✤

ARAXA

Araxa studied the magus who lay shackled to the stone floor of the Chamber of Truth. He hardly looked human anymore, just a lump of bruised flesh and shattered bone. The Hands of the Father had worked on him for four days and nights. He had been extremely resistant to confessing his sins, but he'd done it in the end. Araxa had known he would. They all broke in the end, as long as the questioners remained patient and didn't rush things.

The confession had come early that morning, just before dawn. Luckily, the only others present to witness it were the two Hands Araxa trusted implicitly. Hurdad and Kalbod had risen through the ranks alongside him since they were all beardless youths. They agreed with Araxa wholeheartedly about the daēvas and the need to be rid of them. The King was a blind fool who only seemed to recognize the external threats to his empire, namely the barbarians and the demon queen of Bactria. Araxa knew better. Like most southerners, he had never seen an Undead Druj, but every day, he saw the demons walking among them. What tenuous leashes they wore! One circlet of gold away from chaos and destruction.

Look what had happened in Persepolae. Two of the Immortals helped a Water Dog and her daēva escape, aided by the *King's own daēva*. It was madness. They needed to be put down like the rabid dogs they were. And keeping the Prophet alive was equally insane. He had no conceivable use, and many liabilities, not least that the filthy blood of the daēvas ran in his own veins.

The magus twitched and mumbled something incoherent. Araxa brought a cup of water to his lips and helped him drink. He was a Follower of the Prophet, Araxa had learned. Somehow he'd discovered Zarathustra still lived, and he had fellow conspirators in the city who planned to aid him in freeing the prisoner.

Araxa never did anything without considering every angle. Knowledge was power, especially when you were the only living soul who had it. He could simply order the conspirators to be hunted down and arrested, but another thought had occurred to him. Without the fire to make new cuffs, and with the Prophet dead, it would be the end of an era. Araxa hesitated to kill Zarathustra himself. For all the ruthless acts the spymaster had committed, he still felt a kind of superstitious dread when he contemplated murdering the Prophet with his own hands. But if he died during an escape attempt...

Araxa knew the Hierarch would never approve of his plans. Not because he was averse to harsh measures, but because he was afraid. Of the King. Of the Druj. Of what would happen to his wrinkly hide if word got out that the Numerators had killed the Prophet. Which was why Araxa had decided to have the prisoner's Followers do it for him.

The Hands had spared Magus Saman's fingers so he would still be able to write. That had been one of Araxa's innovations, when he took over as head of their order. Confessions were best made in the miscreant's own hand. But instead of the usual litany of foul deeds and pleas for forgiveness, Saman had written a note. The one he would have written three days earlier had he not been caught hiding in the wardrobe of the High Magus's audience chamber. It had taken some time, and several tries, but the three Hands were finally satisfied the handwriting appeared neat and there were no stray drops of blood marring the parchment.

Araxa had always maneuvered from the shadows, pulling the strings of his puppets so gently that most were unaware of his influence. But in this, he had felt a strong desire to handle the matter personally. He didn't fully understand why, but it had been close to a compulsion.

So he had hurried up the steps of the tomb in the final hour of the night, the hour of suicides and treachery. The dampness on his palms, the sudden quickness of breath were sensations he had not felt in a long time. As he crouched by the step and thrust his hand into the shallow niche beneath the loose stone, he had experienced a rush of lightheadedness. It was not unlike the feeling he had as a boy peeping through the windows of strangers. Present and apart at the same time, as though there were two of him, one who watched and one who acted. Even then he had loved rooting out secrets. The key difference was that when he was caught as a boy—and he had been caught, before he honed his instincts—the worst he could expect was a beating.

But if he was caught now...

Araxa had no doubt whatsoever that the Hierarch would give him to the flames before the King even had a chance to pass judgment.

But no one had seen him leave the note, and only a few hours later, the conspirators had retrieved it. He'd seen no need to follow them. He knew where they were going. A cesspool of sin called Marduk's Spear. They would come for the Prophet tomorrow, and the Numerators would be waiting for them.

❧ 16 ❧

BALTHAZAR

The magi were gathered for afternoon prayers when Balthazar returned to the temple. There were six inner sanctums where the eternal fire burned, and he chose the smallest. Some two dozen magi stood in a circle muttering their incantations, each clutching a bundle of slender myrtle wands. Balthazar's lips moved, but he could not bring himself to speak the words. The way of the flame held there was no light without darkness, no truth without lies. That the world was locked in an eternal struggle between good and evil. The Holy Father stood on the side of righteousness, the Druj on the other. And every sentient being freely chose which path they followed.

Balthazar had long ago rejected such moral judgments. There was only knowledge and ignorance. Power and weakness. And yet for the first time in two hundred years, he wondered what would happen to him when he died. When his soul was weighed and measured on Chinvat Bridge.

"Father bless you, my brother," the Keeper of the Flame said, touching Balthazar lightly on his forehead, lips and heart. Balthazar grasped his sleeve and the Keeper's white brows drew together in a frown. "Magus Saman," he whispered. "Where can I find him?"

The Keeper stared at him, and Balthazar had the uncomfortable feeling he saw too much. He was very old, but hardly old enough to remember.

"Magus Saman is gone," the Keeper said softly.

"What do you mean, *gone?*"

"They've taken him. He would not have run away from his duties here. Not Saman."

"You mean the Numerators?"

"Who else?" The Keeper glanced at Balthazar's hand, and he released the magus and let it fall by his side.

"When?"

"Several days ago. The Holy Father will watch over him."

"Like He's watched over those decorating the city wall?" Balthazar snarled.

The Keeper flinched. "It is when the hour is darkest that our faith must burn most brightly."

"Of course you are right," he replied, forcing his voice to calmness. "Good thoughts, good words, good deeds."

The Keeper nodded and moved on to the next magus. They all looked at him strangely when he strode off before the blessings were finished, but Balthazar no longer cared. He wanted to be quit of this city and the corrupt liars who ran things. Balthazar peeled his robes off the instant he got back to his room. He couldn't stand the touch of the cloth against his skin. He felt almost feverish. It was going back to the pleasure district. Old memories were resurfacing that had been better left buried. He splashed water on his face, dampened his hands and ran them through his hair. His heart thudded in his chest. *I'm still alive. Still living.*

The boy had told him things, but not enough. Not the meat of it.

The chains coiled in the corner where he'd tossed them, like a gleaming viper. Balthazar lay back on his narrow bed, nude and trembling. Ashamed of himself and his weakness, but unable to stop. There had been times when he talked to the boy that he almost believed he was talking to himself. The fate he had come within a hair's breadth of meeting had the magus not come looking for his dead sister.

No! Balthazar clenched his fists. As far as he was concerned, he was barely human anymore, and had not been for a long time. Whatever he was now—necromancer, Antimagus, killer, traveler of the shadowlands—the boy from Cuttlefish Alley was long dead. Balthazar's breath gradually grew more even as he folded his arms behind his head and watched the shadows lengthen across the room. He had not expected it to affect him so, coming back here. He had underestimated the pull of his memories, like an undertow threatening to drag him down into the quiet, infinite darkness. But his work here was almost finished, if he could only puzzle out the final pieces.

Thought came sluggishly, and soon Balthazar's eyes slid shut. His fingers relaxed, unfurling like the scarlet blossoms his mistress was so fond of. A shell lay cradled in the center of his palm. It spiraled inwards but not in a way that was easy for the eye to trace. The curves seemed symmetrical, and yet if you looked at them too closely, they twisted in impossible, dizzying directions. The outside was rough and striated, but the inside was a delicate shiny pink that he had always found powerfully erotic.

Balthazar's chest rose and fell steadily, and an almost peaceful expression stole across his face. The warmth of the afternoon had raised a sheen of sweat on his bare skin. He slept as the magi tended their braziers and the moon rose in the sky.

She found him in the gloaming.

He had been dreaming about his sister, and how Artunis would let him comb her hair in the evenings while they made a supper of whatever scraps of food he had managed to find that day. Sometimes it was nothing at all, and on those days, Artunis would sing or tell him stories to keep his mind off the terrible hunger scouring his belly. In the dream, they had been sitting in their little mudbrick hovel, just the two of them. None of the smelly, hairy men were there, and Balthazar was glad. He understood why she had to do what she did, but the men repulsed him and he did not like how some of them looked at him in a considering way.

In the dream, it must have been a good day, because they were shelling a mound of peas together. His sister looked radiant in the glow from their small fire, her slightly tilted eyes gazing at him with warmth, but also a little sadness, as always. Artunis had kissed him and then she'd given him a little push. *Go, sweet*, she had said. *Go, beautiful boy. She calls you.*

As he walked out the door and down the street, his surroundings slowly changed. The light source became indeterminate and the ground grew uneven beneath his bare feet. Tall, colorless grasses appeared, swaying in an invisible breeze. The sensation of being watched made his shoulder blades itch. Each step raised a puff of fine white sand. He could see what looked like shells drifting and rolling in the shadows, although they were oddly shaped and it made his head hurt to look at them for more than a few seconds.

He knew this place, knew its dangers, yet they seemed distant. For he also knew he had not wandered here by accident. He had been summoned, just as he hoped when he went to sleep with the talisman in his hand.

"Balthazar."

He turned and saw her, long hair fanning out in the fey current. She wore a clinging gown that shimmered like scales. It looked like it would tear at the slightest touch, and his breath caught in his throat.

"My Queen," he said, falling to one knee and bowing his dark head.

Neblis let him stay like that for what seemed an eternity. He wondered if she was angry at him over the boy. The child would remember nothing. Balthazar had seen no need to harm him as he had the others. In fact, it would have needlessly aroused suspicion. That was the only reason he had let him live. Not because he pitied the boy.

A whore, just like you...

He silenced the voice with an effort of will, and then her cool fingers tangled in his hair, turning his face up to meet hers. He drank in her loveliness like a man dying of thirst. She could alter her features at will, but each incarnation had its own charms. This one had eyes like quicksilver, with jagged streaks of emerald in the iris.

"Walk with me, Balthazar," she said.

He rose and fell into step beside her. They crossed a great abyssal plane whose horizon stretched into dimness in all directions. The Dominion had many parts, Balthazar knew, some more treacherous than others. He remembered this one well because it was where he had laid eyes on Neblis for the first time.

"Tell me what you have learned in Karnopolis," she said, cocking her head in that birdlike way. She barely reached his shoulder and he felt a surge of protectiveness, although there was nothing fragile about Neblis. She could tear him to pieces with a thought if she so desired.

"I am close to discovering where the Prophet is," Balthazar said. "But I believe others seek him too. Four of the Water Dogs we met on the plain."

"You *believe?*" Her rosebud lips tightened.

"I do not yet know their plans," he admitted.

"Why not?"

"They are in league with a magus, but the Numerators have him. The daēva hunters are on a crusade to find Zarathustra's followers. The same who stole the holy fire from the Barbican."

"One of them is Victor's son," Neblis said. "I would have you bring him to me as well."

Balthazar looked at her sharply. "A Water Dog? How do you know this?"

Neblis laughed, a throaty chuckle. "Do you think you are my only source of information, Balthazar? Well, it is no secret. The daēva's name is Darius, and he almost burned for it in Persepolae."

"I know the one you refer to. I saw him today. It will be as you wish, my lady."

Neblis gave him a shrewd look. "What do you know of his bonded?"

"The fair-haired woman? Not much. She has skill with a sword, but she lost her right hand since last we met."

"There are rumors she used the power in Karon Komai."

"Where?"

"It is the fishing village where the King's soldiers caught up with her. A full company of Immortals, and more than half of them ended up reaping their eternal reward. Granted, the Water Dogs had Victor on their side." She sniffed. "He's worth ten of those unshaven boys."

"And this Water Dog used the power *herself*?" Balthazar was taken aback.

"So they say."

"But she is human," he said, feeling stupid.

Neblis smiled and patted his arm. "Is she? You have much to learn. I presume you understand the principles of elemental magic, even though you cannot work it yourself. The four domains—earth, air, fire, water?"

Balthazar frowned. "Yes, of course."

"And talismanic magic?"

"Devices or words designed for a single purpose," Balthazar replied. "My chains. The daēva cuffs. The words of opening for a gate."

"Very good." She beamed at him like he was a particularly bright pupil and despite himself, Balthazar felt a rush of pleasure.

"Now I will share a secret with you. There is a *third* type of magic, one that is very, very rare. I wonder..."

Balthazar waited patiently while his queen considered the problem from various angles. Finally, she shook her head. "No, it is too unlikely. And I see no point in having both Water Dogs. The bond is a crude thing, but I hear it can carry a strong emotional attachment. Kill her, Balthazar. Kill her, and her daēva will be easier to manage." Her voice took on a singsong lilt. "Darius is the one I want, and Darius I shall have."

"But what is this other type of magic?" Balthazar asked, unwilling to let the knowledge pass him by. He had never heard of such a thing before. "This magic that is neither elemental nor talismanic?"

"Its nature is destructive. Your chains draw upon it, but none can wield it save a very few. This holy fire you brought me, Balthazar, it reeks of the void." Neblis tilted her head, sharp cheekbones jutting like ridges from the hollows of her face. "You must go to the Numerators, take the magus from them. He will lead you to the Prophet. Do whatever is necessary. Concealing your presence in the city is less important now than finding Zarathustra. I need him."

Balthazar knew little about the Numerators, but he had seen them strolling through the temple district. They acted as if they were untouchable. A law unto themselves. The magi scattered like chickens before a hungry fox whenever one appeared. He would enjoy teaching them a lesson. "With pleasure," he said.

Neblis laid a hand on his arm, drawing him to a stop. Thick beds of grey moss undulated on either side. He had the strong sensation of watching eyes in the murk. Cold, hungry eyes. If Balthazar had been alone and mounted, he would have kicked his horse into a gallop and run for his life. But his mistress had no fear of most things that dwelt in the Dominion, quite the opposite. She seemed to look on them as pets.

"I have not been idle in your absence," Neblis said. "Five

hundred revenants have crossed the mountains to sow chaos. Tel Khalujah will burn, and so will the other satrapies."

Balthazar had only seen so many at once during the siege of Karnopolis. Eight feet tall, with grotesque, rotting wounds from ancient battles past. Eyes like silver mirrors and each possessing the strength of four men. When they spoke, the words tumbled out dry as dust. And when they sensed anything living, they would hack with their iron swords until it stopped moving. The perfect soldiers, revenants did not need sleep or food. They cared only for killing.

Although Balthazar knew they were compelled to do the bidding of the necromancers who had raised them, a small part of him—the part that had watched through the cell bars so long ago —could not help but shudder at what Neblis had unleashed.

"The King cannot send his daēvas to defend them until he has Alexander in hand," Neblis continued. Her pupils dilated until the green iris disappeared, like the moon passing in front of the sun. "I'll flog this land within an inch of its life. Strip the skin from its back and splinter its bones. Oh, they will *beg* to call me mistress." She stared into the gloom. "But we shall discuss all that when you return."

Balthazar looked down at her and felt a knife twist in his heart. Neblis inspired a curious mixture of fear and desire and pathetic eagerness to please that would undo him completely if he wasn't careful. He knew she favored him because unlike the other Antimagi, he was strong enough to at least pretend he still had some dignity. So he gathered himself together and met her gaze. "As you command, my Queen. I shall count the hours."

She smiled. "Is it your new habit to come to me clad only in your skin?"

Heat suffused his face. He hadn't even noticed that he wore not a stitch of clothing. Neblis surveyed him with amusement. Then she gave him a little push, just as Artunis had, and a moment later he was on his back in the mossy beds with his mistress standing over him. It was as though his substance had no objective weight or density in this place. The veil often reminded him of water, with its invisible currents and eddies. It was not water, but it was not precisely air either. More like the stuff of dreams, which could be thick and heavy as his chains—or so light, you could spread your arms and fly.

Neblis knelt beside him and stroked his hair, making his heart beat faster. "I am in contact with my brother," she said. "He leads an army of the Avas Valkirin, if we can only find a way to bring them past the wards."

"How can it be? I thought the barrier was impassable."

"Farrumohr managed to get a message through," Neblis said.

Balthazar kept his face still. He knew better than to betray his dislike for the thing that lurked in the well of the House-Behind-The-Veil. Farrumohr was a native of the Dominion, a creature of flame and shadow. For centuries, he had provided the Undead souls Neblis used to create her Druj, her wights and revenants and liches. They were the restless dead that lingered near the gates, reluctant to go on, and thus easy prey for opportunists like Farrumohr. In exchange, Neblis gave him the human slaves of her Antimagi after they had outlived their usefulness. All in all, it was a harmonious relationship.

But Balthazar had always suspected the demon of harboring secret designs. Now he was carrying messages for Neblis to her brother in the Moon Lands. His aid might be indispensable, but Balthazar did not like consorting with entities whose minds and desires were too alien to comprehend.

"It has been long since last we spoke, but he is well." Neblis's fingers tightened painfully in Balthazar's hair, making him wince. She noticed and began smoothing it again as though nothing had happened. She often hurt or killed accidentally, simply because she forgot her own strength. Neblis behaved like a child that way, fond of her pets but careless of them also.

"Your brother?" Balthazar half lifted his head to look at her.

"Yes, Prince Culach."

He was her twin, Balthazar knew, trapped on the other side of the wards the Avas Danai had put in place after Victor had led his hundred daēvas through the Dominion and into what they called the Sun Lands—Balthazar's own world.

"And your people are willing to face the Immortals?" he asked.

"Whatever is left of the King's army after it defeats Alexander, yes." She smiled. "You look unconvinced. Are you still stinging from a defeat two centuries old?"

"The Immortals are formidable," Balthazar said evenly. "You cannot deny that."

"Which is why we need our own daēvas to fight them. The Avas Valkirin. *My clan*."

Nebis hated the Avas Danai—Victor's clan. She rarely spoke of them, and when she did it was in bitter terms. They had shut the doors between the worlds and locked them tight, trapping her on the wrong side.

"We are an ancient race, Balthazar. The Immortals seem impressive to you because you don't know any better, but they are raw, untrained brats. Culach's army will grind them to dust. And then this land will be ours, and the lands beyond it, all the way to the edges of the world." She tweaked his chin. "I think you will make a fine consort to the empress."

"Have the wards been shattered then?"

Her face darkened. "Not yet. Farrumohr used the gate of the dead to pass messages, but it is heavily guarded. We must find another way for Culach to come through from the Moon Lands."

"How? The barrier has been in place for centuries."

"I don't know yet. That is why we need Zarathustra. At the least, he can show us how to forge new cuffs."

"For the Avas Danai?"

Her fingers tightened in his hair again. "Every single one of them."

"And then will you take me to see your home in the Moon Lands?"

"Of course," Neblis replied silkily. "Once we have brought the empire into the fold, and our enemies grovel at our feet." She cupped his cheek. "So curious you are. Always seeking new things, new knowledge. You are a pilgrim at heart, Balthazar." Her smile faded. "But I must have Zarathustra. He is not only indispensable, but I fear what could happen if he fell into the wrong hands. The old seer could be used as a weapon against us if we're not careful. I have entrusted this task to you because I hold you in great esteem. We belong to each other, do we not, Balthazar?"

Her thumb brushed his lower lip. Balthazar bit the inside of his cheek to keep from reaching for her. He could never be certain what she wanted and found it was safer to just follow her lead. "Yes, my Queen," he said.

"Heart and soul?"

"Heart and soul."

"I hope you haven't been walking around the temple in this condition," she murmured. "You'll give those filthy old men the wrong idea."

Balthazar was still trying to think of a reply when her soft mouth met his, and thought ceased entirely.

ꙮ 17 ꙮ

ARAXA

Araxa ran one spidery finger along the map, tracing the warren of tunnels beneath the temple district for the hundredth time, searching for anything he might have missed. Hidden doors or crawlspaces. Secret exits. He had ordered Hurdad and Kalbod to search the archives for all records mentioning the ancient labyrinth carved into the rock beneath the city. Not a single one had been found. He suspected the magi had destroyed any document that referenced the existence of the tunnels. They had been diligent about keeping their secret from the Numerators and it had worked, until now.

The map he consulted was the one belonging to the High Magus of Karnopolis himself. The old priest had handed it over without argument, although his mouth was set in a grim line. The magi did not relish giving the Numerators one of their own, even if he was a dangerous heretic.

Araxa decided he would allow the Followers to remove Zarathustra from his cell. There were only two ways they could go after that, and the Hands would be waiting for them in the dark. When the King asked afterwards, he could honestly say the Prophet had died during an escape attempt. The additional implication—that the magi themselves were behind it somehow —fit perfectly with Araxa's aim of discrediting them beyond repair. It could never be proven, of course, but the King would always wonder. Who else would have known Zarathustra's location and the fact that he was about to be handed over to the Numerators?

The timing of it all could not be better. Araxa had just received word the Macydonians were marching on Persepolae and would be there in a matter of days. The King would be too preoccupied with defending the summer capital to care what happened to one old magus who was supposed to be dead anyway.

He shifted uncomfortably at his desk. The rash had begun to scab over, but Araxa had to practically sit on his hands to keep from scratching. The final stage of the outbreak was the most maddening. When he returned to his rooms, he would submerge himself in a cool lavender bath, which was the only thing that doused the fire.

Araxa had gone over his plans for hours and felt satisfied the Hands would have no trouble herding the Followers through the tunnels like sheep the next day. Two were daēvas, but Numerators knew how to handle the demons. Knew their single fatal weakness. And so Nowruz would begin with a most auspicious start, the dawn of a new era in which the Numerators held sway and the empire was made pure again.

He looked up as Kalbod entered the room. The Hand was a few years younger than Araxa, with hard, chiseled features and a bullish neck. His loyalty to Araxa was absolute. In theory, the Hierarch was the ultimate authority of all the Numerators, but the Hands of the Father kept their own code, and had Araxa ordered Kalbod to dispose of the head of their order, he would have done it without a moment's hesitation.

"There is a magus asking to see you, Minister," Kalbod said.

Araxa frowned. That was a first. The magi generally avoided him like the plague. A summons to his study was cause for anxiety, if not outright terror. Not once had a magus sought him out, not since the purge had begun.

"What does he want?" Araxa asked. "The hour is late. Better he returns tomorrow."

Kalbod's bulk shifted. "I already told him that, Minister. He says he has urgent information about the Followers. Information that cannot wait until morning."

"Indeed." Araxa leaned forward. "What is this magus's name?"

"Balthus, Minister. He is visiting from Qaddah. He claims to have stumbled across some sort of plot. He heard you were the one in charge of rooting out the traitors."

"Bring him in," Araxa said, rolling up the map and laying it to one side. "I will hear what he has to say." He hoped the "plot" this magus claimed to have knowledge of was not the very same he himself had discovered and was now using to his own advantage. It would not be a complete disaster—he could find other ways to quietly get rid of the Prophet after the transfer was made—but it *would* be a disappointment.

Araxa kept his palms flat on the desk as Kalbod's footsteps receded down the hallway. The urge to scratch was almost overwhelming, but if he succumbed to it, the scaly, lizard-like rash would only spread. For the moment, it was confined to his chest and torso, but more than once Araxa had been covered from head to toe, and he had no desire to experience *that* again.

He used to wonder if his affliction was a curse from the Holy Father, as the other children had claimed. None of the physicians he consulted had ever seen such a thing before. They prescribed various remedies, each more unpleasant than the last. They had given him powders and salves and pastes and potions. They had drained his blood and ordered him to ingest large doses of mercury, which caused endless pain and vomiting but did nothing to cure him.

He had concluded it was simply his burden to bear, a sort of martyrdom that made him all the more zealous in his faith. There was no requirement of celibacy in his order, but Araxa had not even thought of the pleasures of the flesh in years. His mother had warned him about girls at a young age, and the message had stuck. It had been twenty years since his father—a cheating pig who beat his children and servants and anyone else he could lay hands on—had died of some pox acquired from the whores he frequented in the pleasure district. Araxa had grown up in a respectable family, and the shame to his mother had been profound. She had showed Araxa, seventeen at the time, his father's nude corpse and coldly pointed out the ravages lust had taken on his flesh. From then on, Araxa had been terrified of suffering a similar fate. His mother said demons had infested his father, and the only way to keep them out was diligent prayer and avoidance of temptation.

Araxa did not especially miss his mother, who was dead now too. She had not been a warm woman. He thought that was one of the reasons his father had spent so much time away, leaving Araxa's mother in charge of the household. She was strict and fanatically religious, and it had been a relief when Araxa left to join the Numerators. But with the passage of time, his memories of her had softened. He still did not like her much, but he understood her. He, too, had been forced to make difficult choices, to withhold mercy for the greater good. He felt she had instilled in him bedrock morals that would have been lacking had his father done the job. This was why Araxa kept a lock of her hair on his desk. To remind him that *right* was not always easy.

The reason he reached for it now, though, had less to do with sentiment than the desperate need to do something other than claw his own skin to shreds. Araxa was fingering the strands of hair when Kalbod returned with the magus called Balthus.

Araxa disliked him immediately. He was tall and young and glowing with good health, and his straight-backed posture and direct gaze were far too confident for Araxa's taste. He had olive skin that made a striking contrast to the snowy white robes, and a slightly crooked nose, as though it had been broken at some point and healed awkwardly. The magus glanced around and noted there was no other chair in the room. Araxa thought his lips quirked in amusement, but it came and went too fast to be sure. Kalbod had paused just behind him. He would wait for Araxa's command and he would carry it out, whether it was to bring the man a chair or choke the life out of him on the spot, and his expression would not change either way.

"Minister," Balthus said in a deferential tone that did little to mollify Araxa. "I must thank you for agreeing to see me at this hour. If it were not such a pressing matter, I would have waited, but I think you will be glad to hear what I have to say right away."

"Your devotion is admirable," Araxa replied. "I wish more of your brethren understood their duty so well. Unfortunately, most of them have to be dragged here kicking and screaming." He looked at Kalbod. "You may leave us."

Kalbod nodded and backed out of the room, closing the door behind him. Araxa leaned back in his chair, idly twisting the lock of raven hair around his thumb, and waited for Balthus to spill his guts. At first he thought it likely the magus had been summoned for questioning and hoped to preempt it by coming himself with some far-fetched tale that would prove to be another wild goose chase. But the name *Balthus* was not on any of his lists, Araxa was certain.

The magus just stood there for a moment, his face half-cloaked in shadow, and Araxa felt a twinge of unease. Something was *off* about the man. Araxa was skilled at reading people. He had broken enough of them in his life to recognize the subtle signs of the body. The things a man did with his hands and eyes when he was lying or hiding something or fearful and trying not to show it. Balthus should have been afraid of him, but Araxa could see no indication of it. He was about to call Kalbod back into the room when the magus began to speak.

"I wish to make a confession," he said.

"Go ahead," Araxa replied evenly.

Balthus looked heavenward and spread his hands in a gesture of sad resignation. "I seem to have lost my faith."

"Do you jest?" Araxa snapped. "If you have wasted my time, I will have you flogged."

"I've done bad things," Balthus said, giving him a crocodilian smile. "Very bad."

"Unless this pertains to the heretics, I've no—"

"I find it ironic that when you use extreme measures on a man, it is considered justice, but when I do it, people think me a monster."

"What in the name of the Father are you talking about?" Araxa demanded. He was already regretting having let this man into his study. The priest was clearly not right in the head.

"Magus Shahrooz tried quoting scripture at first. He misunderstood when I asked him to tell me about the Prophet."

"Magus Shahrooz?" Araxa frowned. Now there was a name he *did* recognize...But from where?

"When I took his ears, he began to listen more closely." Balthus grimaced. "I'm sorry. That was a poor attempt at humor, was it not?"

Shahrooz...Shahrooz...An image sprung into Araxa's mind, fully formed, of a vaguely man-shaped lump of flesh. It lay sprawled on the steps of the Imperial Archives, bathed in the rosy glow of dawn, arms spread wide as if in supplication. The sight of it had been less disturbing to Araxa than the fact that it was not his own handiwork and he had no idea whose it was. His first thought had been an overzealous Hand, but none had come forward to claim responsibility.

That was four days ago. Since then, two more mutilated bodies had been discovered.

"Magus Efrim seemed a good bet," Balthus continued. "Considered one of the High Magus's closest confidantes. A schemer and busybody, by all accounts."

Efrim, Araxa recalled with a sinking heart, was one of the two.

"He told me who was fucking who, and who was thieving from the treasury, and a host of other useless things, but not the thing I wanted to know." Balthus made a *tsking* sound. "It was disappointing."

Araxa opened his mouth to yell for Kalbod, but the magus took two fast strides towards him and instead of help bursting through the door, fingers closed around his throat. Araxa's eyes bulged. The strength in that hand was terrifying.

"Don't," Balthus said gently. "Don't do that. Not until we're finished." The fingers relaxed slightly. "This thing I want to know. Shall I ask *you*?"

Araxa considered trying to fight, but the magus was obviously stronger and faster. He was also insane. So Araxa nodded his head as best he could.

"Where is Saman? Do anything but answer and I'll snap your neck. You'll be a corpse before your man outside takes a single step for the door."

Araxa pretended to consider the question for a moment. He cleared his throat, trying to ignore the intense heat of the fingertips brushing his jugular vein. What did this lunatic want with Saman? He must be a Follower too. The den of vipers was even larger than he had imagined...

"Saman is dead," Araxa whispered. "Now release me before you share his fate. He did not die well or prettily, but it could still have been worse. Do you wish to discover how?"

A harsh, grating sound erupted that Araxa thought was laughter. "You would threaten me? How amusing. But I suppose that is my fault. You still don't know what you're dealing with, do you? You are used to the magi, the bleating sheep. The fire worshippers. I worship something else. *Someone* else."

Araxa stared at the doorway, willing Kalbod to interrupt even though he knew the Hand was too well-trained to do so unless it was some sort of emergency. He could not see Balthus because the man stood directly behind his chair. But he could smell him, a hint of smoke from the temple mixed with a scent that was heavy and cloying and reminded him of a red blossom called heartsbane that grew only in the far eastern mountains and was very, very poisonous.

"How nice for you," Araxa said. "Well, I told you what you wanted to know. Saman is dead. He took his secrets to the grave. There is nothing else I can tell you."

"A pity, but I thank you for your honesty." The sudden offhand tone made Araxa blink in surprise. "What is that you hold in your hand?"

He glanced down. The lock of hair was wrapped tightly around his thumb, and he was unconsciously stroking it. Araxa felt a stab of embarrassment. He did not want this madman to know anything personal about him.

"Nothing."

"It must be something." And then, to Araxa's horror, the magus crouched down and examined his mother's hair. "Who did this belong to? A lover?"

"No!" That would be an abomination, even worse than the things his father had done. A hazy memory drifted up from the depths like a bubble of air from a waterlogged corpse and Araxa shoved it back down. An abomination.

"No? Are you sure?" Balthus twirled the hair around his own finger, his grinning face inches from Araxa's. "Or maybe it isn't from a *she* at all?"

In the highest tower of the temple, the bells began to chime midnight, deep and sonorous. The candle on Araxa's desk guttered. He felt old and alone.

"My mother," he muttered.

"Ah! A sentimental man. I am too. For example, it has been a long time since I have visited the city of my birth, and yet I am relieved to find it still the same. The people come and go, but the feel of the place is unchanged." He leaned even closer, so Araxa felt the whisper of breath on his cheek. "My last sight of it was through prison bars. The revenants were hacking at the gates, so many that I thought the sheer weight of them might topple the wall itself. Zarathustra was already gone. They said he'd died and no one questioned it."

Araxa kept still at the mention of Zarathustra, giving no sign the name meant anything unusual to him. In a way, it was fortunate that this lunatic had come directly to him instead of rambling to anyone who would listen in the temple. If he knew of Saman's plans, he needed to be silenced. Either way, Magus Balthus would never leave the Hall of the Numerators. Not after touching his mother's hair. Araxa would simply wait for him to wind down, and then summon Kalbod.

"I had a daēva once," Balthus said. "Did you know that? I'm sorry, of course you didn't. But yes, they gave me one. They said I had the gift. The daēva did not like what had been done to him, not at all. I can't say I blamed him. But he learned who was master soon enough. It wasn't like it is today, with your tame creatures on a leash bowing and scraping to their bonded. The daēvas back then had to be *broken*."

Araxa felt his unease creeping back. The magus was speaking as if...well, as if he had been there during the war. Which simply wasn't possible. None of the original warrior-magi had survived, except Zarathustra.

"You don't believe me. I suppose I wouldn't either, if I were in your position. But I am no longer a magus, you see."

Araxa heard a faint metallic *clinking* sound that raised the hair on his neck without knowing precisely why. Only that his every instinct recoiled from the noise and shrieked *danger*. Was it already too late? Yes, it was. Something was closing around his neck, something cold and unyielding that made Balthus's throttling hands seem like the caress of a lover.

"I think it is easier to just show you what I am."

The words came to Araxa as though from a great distance.

Goosebumps rose on his skin and images slid into his mind like oil slowly sinking into sand.

An abandoned cistern in an overgrown corner of the temple grounds. Dead leaves float on the surface of the dark water. Standing in front of you is a man with long brown hair. It is wild and unkempt, although his narrow face has a pale, otherworldly beauty. There is a golden cuff around his wrist. He is wearing a tunic of sky blue and his eyes are wary.

"Open the gate," you say. "Use your magic."

"I don't understand," he says. "I don't see any gate."

The murmur of voices drifts through the trees, but you are shielded by a dense thicket of thorny bushes and a few moments later, the voices recede again. It is a scorching day and there is not even a hint of a breeze in the clearing. Sweat rolls down your spine, although the daēva seems untouched by the heat. You have only been bonded for a week, but that is long enough to know this creature can work magic you never dreamt of.

The cistern is about ten paces across. You have been looking for the perfect place, and this is it. Running water won't do for a gate. It must be still. Stagnant. The texts you have read specify ponds, lakes, vernal pools and even wine or blood spilled on stone or poured into a bowl. So, no rivers or seas. You don't know why this is, but accept it for truth.

You have only made one other gate, the one you reached your arm through, but now you have worked up your courage enough to try it again. This time, you want to make a gate big enough to walk into. You want to see what is on the other side. Find out if there is truly power for the taking there.

"You have to make the gate, Davod," you say. "Come, you are a demon. You must know how. Do not think to conceal this ability from me."

The daēva stares at the water, then back at you. You can feel his desperation. In the last week, he has learned to fear you. You know this not only because he no longer disobeys you, but because you seem to share some direct emotional connection. He is in your mind, and you are in his. That had been unexpected, and you are still not sure how you feel about it. You are not a sadist, but your morality is not like other people's. This you have known since you were a child. You know what it is to be afraid, to be weak and helpless, and you never want to feel that way again. You don't relish inflicting pain on others, but you will do whatever you must to protect yourself.

You are now eighteen years old and a full magus in the great temple of Karnopolis.

All this Araxa absorbed in a heartbeat. He sat in his study with Balthus, something foul and cold and made of iron around his neck, but he also stood at the edge of the cistern untold years ago. And because it was a memory, he knew something significant was about to happen.

The daēva named Davod crouches down and trails a hand in the water. Dark ripples spread across the surface, causing his reflection to waver. You release the power, ready to clamp down again at the first sign he intends to use it against you. Davod has not tried to do that in three days now, not since you left him writhing on the ground in agony for over an hour. You feel him reach for it, take it, hold it.

"There are two ways to make a gate," you say. "The power and blood price. If I were you, I would choose the first."

"You must tell me how," Davod says. "Do I use earth? Air? Water? Tell me!"

"The text does not say. You must tell me."

You didn't know then that a talisman was needed. So it was not actually the daēva's fault that he could not open it. You watch him blindly try different things with the power until it becomes clear this whole outing will be a failure unless you do something. So you unsheathe your belt knife and pay the blood price instead. The full price, just to be sure.

Blood spills from Davod's veins into the cistern and his body follows. It sinks slowly into the water, facedown, arms and legs spread. You wait until the surface is smooth as a coin again, and you step in after him, murmuring the ancient words. The water is chillier than it should be and lighter, more like mist than liquid. You walk into it, counting your steps. By the tenth step, you should be on the other side, facing a slimy stone wall. But you are not. You are in a twilight world where dim shapes flit at the edges of your vision. You realize you have been holding your breath and let it go. No bubbles emerge and when you convulsively suck air into your lungs, they are filled and not with water. You are not in water anymore.

You see Davod's body drifting along the bottom, his hair fanned out like seaweed, and then a fast-moving shadow darts out and takes it and you want to scream but somehow keep it inside.

The price has been paid.

You are not sure how long you walk in this place. The gloaming between worlds. You pass through shaded canyons and forests of freakish coral, endless prairies of grey weeds that frighten you because they are taller than your head and conceal anything more than a few paces away. And you are certain this place is not barren. Not untenanted. You are being watched.

Just when you think you are doomed to wander lost forever, you see her. Her laughter is the tinkle of a marble fountain and she is wearing a crimson gown, which she shucks over her head without saying a word. She is pale all over, even to the points of her breasts, which are as white as the stones you played games with as a child. She takes you by the hand—

"That's enough." Balthus laughed. "I have no doubt you would like to see how I lost my innocence to a demon queen, but we haven't the time. See? The dawn is not far off."

Araxa twisted his aching neck toward the window, surprised to see a faint glow in the sky. His mouth felt dry as a month-old crust of bread and every muscle burned, as though he had not moved in hours. Where was Kalbod? Why had he not come?

"Now that we have cleared up what I am, it is your turn. Where is the Prophet Zarathustra and what do you mean to do with him? Speak clearly and tell me every detail."

Araxa felt the necromancer—his mind skittered away from that word, although he could no longer deny it—crawl across his brain like a beetle, brushing him with questing antennae and chitinous legs. His will was no longer his own. It belonged utterly to Balthus. Never had he been so helpless, so degraded. In all his machinations and scheming, he had not once thought of the Druj as anything other than an abstract threat. They were the problem of the border satrapies, not the mighty walled city of Karnopolis.

He was so appalled at his current predicament he hardly even wondered why the minions of Queen Neblis would be interested in the Prophet. At that moment, all Araxa could think of is that he did not want to die. So he began to talk, and he told the magus —*necromancer*—of the plot he had uncovered, and exactly how he planned to use the Followers to carry out the murder of the Prophet. He told him what he had done to Saman to loosen his tongue, and how the magus had forgiven him at the end, just before Araxa cut his throat.

There was a long silence when Araxa finished speaking. Eventually it became nearly unbearable. To break it, he asked, "Is Kalbod dead?"

"What? The one outside, you mean? Oh, no. Not dead," Balthus replied distractedly. "You sent him away yourself hours ago. I suppose you don't remember."

No, Araxa did not remember. The scene at the cistern could not have lasted more than ten or fifteen minutes, with another hour or so wandering in the...the *gloaming*. He had no idea what had happened in the intervening time, and found he didn't want to. Then the necromancer stood in a way that signaled to Araxa he had made a decision. The spymaster's bowels tightened. *The end the end the end...*

"You will carry out your plan to the letter," Balthus said. "To the letter!"

And he leaned down and whispered something into Araxa's ear and Araxa nodded dutifully and there was a click and the metal thing was gone from his neck. He swallowed hard, once, twice. He yawned and his ears popped.

"There's no time to sleep," Balthus said, dragging him to stand. Araxa stumbled on leaden feet, gripping the edge of the desk so he would not fall. He felt a painful tingling as blood rushed back into frozen limbs. "You have but a few hours to make ready. No one must know save for Kalbod and the other. What is his name? Hurdad. Fulfill your task and I will not return. If I do, my face will be the last thing on this earth you see." The necromancer studied him for a moment. "I find you loathsome, and coming from a creature such as myself, that is something." He tossed an object on the table and strode to the door.

Araxa stood there, blinking in the thin light of dawn. He did not understand what had just happened to him, nor why the necromancer had commanded him to stick with his plans for the Prophet, but he would do as ordered. Disobedience was not a viable option, in Araxa's opinion. He most emphatically did not want to see Balthus again, and he believed everything he had said. A man who lies with demons...Well, such a man was not to be crossed.

Itchy rash forgotten among all his other, more pressing woes, Araxa started for the door when his eye fell on the object Balthus had left on the table. It was his mother's hair. Defiled now. With a calm that Araxa suspected masked profound shock, he picked up a stub of candle. The droning chants of the magi drifted through the open window as Araxa's study filled with the acrid smell of burning hair.

❧ 18 ❧

BALTHAZAR

Balthazar's mood was much improved as he left the Hall of the Numerators. It seemed fate had taken pity on him at last. Days of grim work with nothing to show for it, and now a chance encounter had revealed the path to his goal. Not only that, but a way to take revenge on the very same Water Dogs who had fouled things up on the plain. Best of all, he wouldn't have to spend one more night in this cursed city.

Balthazar had not slept, but he didn't feel tired in the least. Unlike the torture of the three magi, which had been simply a task to execute in a brisk, workmanlike fashion, he had enjoyed collaring the Numerator. They both did things most others would not, but Balthazar felt he had little else in common with the man. Araxa struck him as cold and reptilian, a creature of deep insecurities who filled the void in himself by manipulating others. He cared only for power. The necromancer understood that, but found it shallow. Power for power's sake bored him. He sought knowledge above all things, for it could not be lost or taken away.

You are a pilgrim at heart, Balthazar.

He smiled. Yes, he was that. And other things besides. He was even capable of love, if an obsessive, all-consuming sort.

As he passed the daēva barracks, a group of solemn children emerged, accompanied by their amahs. Most kept their gazes pinned to the ground, but several glanced over at him. Their eyes were deep and knowing and for a terrible instant he thought they would stop in their tracks and point at him accusingly. Daēvas sensed the true nature of things, Balthazar knew. They saw behind the mask. With the power of those children at their disposal, he hadn't the least doubt the amahs could take him without a fight.

Necromancer.

They had been waiting for him when he emerged from the Dominion that day so long ago. He still wasn't sure how they had known, but they had. He'd walked out of the cistern straight into the arms of a dozen warrior magi and their daēvas. They had charged him with witchcraft, and the murder of Davod. A tribunal took less than an hour to find him guilty, which surprised no one since a search of Balthazar's room had uncovered a trove of banned books on subjects the High Magus termed "diabolical and indicative of a depravity never before seen within these hallowed walls."

And so they had locked him up the day before the Druj encircled the city. He had watched through the bars as his then-brothers formed up before the gates alongside King Xeros's army, griffin banners roaring defiance in the hot wind. How few they had seemed! Outnumbered twenty to one by the Undead hordes that awaited them. Victor had led the vanguard, galloping through the thirty-third gate before it was fully winched open. He wore no armor or helmet, only a blue tunic, and the ranks of revenants had swallowed him up in a heartbeat. Standing in his cell, Balthazar had written them all off for dead. Brave fools whose sacrifice wouldn't even be remembered in songs because there would be no one left to sing them.

And then he had sensed turmoil on the beach. Heard the awful, voiceless screams of the liches as they were torn apart by air. Watched in awe as great, jagged rents had opened in the sand, swallowing the revenants whole. Inch by bloody inch, the Druj were pushed back to their black-sailed ships. A storm blew in as they tried to flee, dashing the entire fleet against the rocks that lurked at the mouth of the harbor.

Balthazar had glimpsed Victor as they carried him back inside, bloody and broken. He'd nearly killed himself in the battle. All Balthazar could think is that he had never seen such a display of power. It humbled him, made him sick with longing and despair. They would burn him now that the battle was won. He was a proven witch, unfit to live.

Later that night, Neblis came to him in a dream and showed him how to make a gate with the cup of water they'd permitted him. He had poured it on the ground, snapped the neck of the magus who brought him breakfast, and stepped through. That was the last he had seen of Karnopolis.

Balthazar blinked as the daēva child smiled at him. It knew he was different, just not *how* he was different. Balthazar smiled back. He would not be visiting his old cell today, although walls could not hold him the way they used to. Better he didn't test his Queen's patience any further.

The streets began to fill with people as he made his way to the pleasure district. The first day of Nowruz had dawned bright and clear, with a cool sea breeze that carried away the usual stench of refuse and human waste. Many of the shops were shuttered tight for the holiday, but others had opened early to take advantage of the crowds. Those women who were not veiled wore fresh flowers in their hair, and the men had donned their finest tunics, with colorful embroidery at the sleeves and hem.

Balthazar considered what the boy at Marduk's Spear had told him—that two of the Water Dogs were runaways from Al Miraj. One was a daēva, and the other was important enough that her father had put up a substantial reward for her return. It had to be the two he had seen dicing in the common room of the brothel.

Again, chance had offered him a perfect solution. Balthazar did not wish to face four Water Dogs alone, but if two could be gotten rid of...

He found what he was looking for in the fifth tavern. Three men with curved swords and loose black scarves wound around their necks. They sat at a table near the back drinking the watery swill the barkeep called wine.

"Do you mind if I join you?" Balthazar asked, laying his hand on the back of the fourth, empty chair. Three faces turned, giving him equally hostile stares as they took in his robes, although one had a lazy eye so it appeared he was looking in two directions at once. Their smell reminded him of the men who used to call on his sister and Balthazar felt his gorge rise.

"We have no use for your Holy Father," said a tall one with scarred pits in his cheeks. His words were heavily accented, thick with the harsh inflection of the southern satrapies. "Sit somewhere else, magus. You'll find no converts here."

Balthazar raised his palms. "No offense meant. Perhaps you misunderstand. I'm looking for gentlemen of fortune to assist me in a small matter." He dropped a fat purse on the table. Greedy eyes lit with interest at the chink of coins inside. "There's gold up front, and more from the man who set the bounty if you bring him his prize. Will you hear my proposition?"

The mercenaries exchanged a quick look with each other. The one with the pocks, who Balthazar presumed was their nominal leader, said, "Buy us a round and we'll give you as long as it takes to drink it."

Balthazar gestured to one of the serving girls and sank into the chair. "I suppose you're here in answer to the King's call for fighting men," he said.

The one with the lazy eye scowled. "The pay's not what we hoped for. Scarcely enough to scrape by. And the City Watch treats us like filth unfit to lick their boots. If you have a job that pays real gold, I'd like to hear about it." The others nodded agreement.

"I chose you because you are from Al Miraj," Balthazar said, as a girl of seven or eight refilled their cups and danced away before one of them could grab her. "Two of your women are here, in this district." He did not tell them that one was daēva, not yet. "I have reason to believe they are fugitives. They are about twenty years old now, pretty, with the look of sisters."

The mercenaries watched him with hooded eyes, saying nothing. Their pockmarked leader took a gulp of wine and smoothed his black moustache.

"One does not speak," Balthazar said. "She is mute."

The smallest of them perked up at this. "The daughter of Rayyaan Bashara," he said. "It could be her servant." He looked at the leader. "Remember? She dishonored him on her wedding day. She was betrothed to the son of the satrap."

"Bashara put six of his household guards to death over it," the leader said, his expression darkening. "One of them was my cousin Hashim."

"When was this?" Balthazar asked. He had ordered wine for himself to be polite, but it sat untouched at his elbow. He would have to make certain these men didn't drink themselves senseless before he had need of them.

"Five years ago. Bashara sent his men after the girl, but they never found a trace of her. The bounty stands, however. Five hundred Darics, as I recall. For each."

The third mercenary, who had been quiet up to this point, gave a low whistle. "Enough to let a man live in comfort until the end of his days, even he live to be a hundred."

"Enough for three men," Balthazar corrected. "And then some." He pushed the purse to the center of the table. "Consider this an advance payment. But if you spend it all on wine, I will tell Rayyaan Bashara that you let his daughter slip through your fingers. Do we understand each other?"

The pockmarked mercenary spit on the floor. "You don't need to threaten," he said. "We're not amateurs. But why does a magus of Karnopolis care about the affairs of Al Miraj?"

"I don't," Balthazar responded. "But it never hurts to do a favor for a powerful man. You shall have the gold, and I shall have a share of the satrap's gratitude. There is plenty to go around."

"Where do we find them?"

"They are staying at a place called Marduk's Spear. Do you know it?"

"We know it." The man reached for the gold purse, and Balthazar laid his hand on top of it.

"Heed my next words well. You will follow them and watch until I give the signal. Only then can you take Bashara's daughter. I will deliver her servant to you myself."

The mercenary opened his mouth to question Balthazar further, but seemed to see something in his eyes that gave him pause. He swallowed. "It will be as you say."

Balthazar nodded. "She is not soft. Be prepared for a struggle."

Lazy Eye puffed out his chest. "Women do not frighten us, priest."

"Well, this one should," Balthazar said brusquely, scraping the chair back and rising to his feet. "Finish your wine and go watch the brothel, and don't be obvious about it. In fact, stay as far back as possible."

"And where will you be?" the leader demanded.

Balthazar smiled. "Exactly where I am needed," he said.

NAZAFAREEN

We spent the day locked in Darius's room. I suppose we could have practiced our swordplay, or gone over the plan yet again, or one of a hundred more sensible things. But we loved each other and that's not how either of us intended to spend what might be our last day on Earth.

I wanted to engrave every detail of him on my memory. To kiss the hollow where his pulse beat in his throat, to weave my fingers through his hair and feel his stubbled cheek against mine. He needed a shave so I started to give him one, although we only got halfway through before he pulled me into his lap. He felt everything I did, and the other way around, the lines between us blurring and finally, dissolving completely. If the cuffs were good for nothing else, I thought, they were good for this.

Tijah and Myrri were dicing in the front room as usual when I came downstairs with a stupid grin I seemed unable to wipe off my face. I expected Tijah to tease me mercilessly, but she just gave me a happy smile in return. Mouth-watering aromas drifted from the kitchen of Marduk's Spear, and the sight of two empty bowls on the table made my stomach rumble.

A simmering stew of fish and fresh herbs was the traditional dish for the first day of Nowruz here, Tijah informed me, signaling to one of the serving boys to bring another. Karnopolis was the farthest south I had ever been, and they had strange fruit here, like the muskmelon, which was sweet and orange-colored on the inside.

"Where's Darius?" she asked.

"Upstairs," I said. "He'll be down soon. It's almost time to leave."

He was in his room, probably looking out the window. I could sense him three flights up and near the street side. There was a quiet contentment in the bond. A sense of peace I had rarely felt from him. Always, there had been a struggle between us. He didn't believe himself worthy of love. But I made no effort to hide what I felt for him anymore, and he didn't either. His walls had come down—perhaps not forever, but it was a start.

The boy returned with a bowl of stew and placed it before me. A spoonful was halfway to my mouth when I froze. Last night, I had pushed Victor into the smallest, heaviest box in my mind that I could make and slammed the lid shut. I'd hoped it would keep him out of my business. Anything else was too creepy. And it had worked. He hadn't even crossed my mind until now, when I'd reached out for Darius through our bond. He had been there, of course, but I was only now realizing that Victor wasn't. He'd winked out like a snuffed candle.

"Oh no," I whispered.

"What is it?" Tijah asked.

Myrri's right hand slid inside her tunic, no doubt to the hilt of one of her knives.

"He's gone. Victor...I can't feel him anymore. I think the bond is broken." I hadn't sensed pain or fear from him, hadn't felt anything really. Not in what seemed like a long time. Would I have known if he died? I felt sure I would, we were *bonded*, and yet doubts spun through my mind like snowflakes, slowly accumulating in icy little drifts that chilled my soul. I had been selfish, oblivious. How long ago had this even happened? How could I not have noticed?

"Upstairs," Tijah said in a low voice, glancing around. "It's too crowded here."

I pushed the stew away uneaten and we hurried to our rooms on the top floor. Darius was just emerging from his as we came pounding up the stairwell. He knew something was wrong. That's why he was on his way down. He took my hand without a word and we settled ourselves in the room Tijah and Myrri shared. It was identical to my own, but with two beds instead of one. Myrri's side was neat as a pin, her blankets stripped and folded, and a saddlebag already packed for the journey to Persepolae we hoped to begin later that night. By contrast, Tijah's side had clothes strewn about, a half-eaten bowl of candied figs on the windowsill, and drips of candle wax and feathers in the corner where it looked like she'd performed some kind of ritual to her pagan gods.

Myrri and I sat on her bed, as Tijah packed up the remaining things and Darius stood guard by the door.

"Something's happened to Victor," I said to him. "I can't sense the bond at all."

Darius's expression didn't alter, but I knew the news came as a blow. He might have had mixed feelings about Victor, but they were still father and son. Victor had saved his life more than once, and mine too.

Myrri made a rapid series of hand signs.

"She says perhaps Neblis has done something to cloak him from you," Tijah translated, as she stuffed a tunic into her bulging saddlebag. "It could be possible."

"Or she's used the fire to break the bond," Darius said.

I nodded, not wanting to consider the remaining possibility—that he was dead and I had failed to even mark his passing.

I took a deep breath, touching the cuff with my left hand as though I could draw some clue from it. Then I closed my eyes and reached for the nexus. It came quickly now, almost as swift as thought. One by one, the sounds in the room drifted away until all I heard was the oceanic rushing of my own breath. The world contracted until my awareness was consumed by the small sensations in my body. An itch between my toes. A fleeting ache in my stump.

But after a while, I sensed a great expanse cradling me, as though I was just a kernel of light in the infinite beyond. This was the true nexus, the place where all things resided.

I waited for it to settle, and I sought Victor again. It wasn't easy. Try too hard, I knew, and it would burst like a bubble. The nexus was not a thing you bullied into submission. So I took care to stay calm as I searched for the unique consciousness I had come to know so well in the last weeks. I had some vague idea that if he was out there, I could find a sign of him.

Well, it was like swimming in the sea and hoping to come across one particular fish. When the futility of this effort became clear, I dragged myself up from the depths. Darius leaned against the door, one boot propped behind him.

"I can't find him," I said.

"He is dead or in Neblis's lair," Darius said. "It must be one or the other."

"What do you know of Bactria?" Tijah asked.

"Nothing," I said. "Victor is the only one who's ever been there. I should have asked him more questions about it, but there was so little time before he left."

Myrri signed something to Tijah. "She says he managed to escape from Gorgon-e Gaz, maybe he will escape from Neblis too." I looked at Myrri, saw a flash of anger in her tilted eyes. "Her mother died at Gorgon," Tijah added quietly. "It's a hellhole. We are both just sorry we didn't finish what Victor and the others started. The place should be torn down, stone by stone."

"It will be," I said, remembering my first sight of the prison fortress, how it looked like a vast grey sarcophagus half-buried on the shore of the Salenian Sea. Like some ancient tomb the waves had carved out of the sand. "Once this is over, we will go back and free the rest. I swear it."

Tijah just looked at me. I think we both knew that if the tide turned against the King, he would simply order the daēvas to be burned. They were too dangerous to leave alive. It could have happened already, for all I knew. But there was nothing we could do about it now.

"We must go," Darius said. "The sun sets in less than an hour."

Tijah made a signal and Myrri rose smoothly from the bed beside me.

"She'll find Arshad," Tijah said. "It's time we said our good-byes. Come, help me get these to the stables."

Darius grabbed Tijah's bags as though they weighed nothing and jogged down the stairs while I stopped in my room for my own things. I was glad to be leaving, even if I was also anxious about going down into those tunnels. I didn't like lightless places, and from Tijah's description, they seemed all too easy to get turned around in. I trusted Saman though I'd only met him the one time, but there were many ways I could imagine his plans going wrong, and still other ways I had doubtless overlooked. It may have been too late for second thoughts, but they crowded my brain nonetheless.

Arshad waited just inside the stables, silver hair brushed and gleaming in the lamplight. I was glad to see Dav was with him, although the boy looked pale and drawn. I had not seen him since his disappearance the day before and the difference was shocking. He had the wasted look of a person recovering from a long illness. Dav was deep in conversation with Darius as I crossed the court-yard, dodging the ever-present chickens who had discovered a colony of ants and were busily wiping them out.

"I'm happy for you," I heard Darius say to him. "We will visit if we ever return to Karnopolis."

"Please do," Dav said.

"And Arshad?"

"He knows. He says he won't try to stop me."

They broke off as I approached and I was just about to ask *Stop you from what?* when the brothel owner lunged forward and swept me into a crushing hug. Before I could kick him in the shin, he had moved on to Tijah and Myrri, and then Darius. Tears streamed down his cheeks and I hurriedly found my mare before he tried to kiss me as well.

"The Holy Father will watch over all of you tonight, I am certain of it," Arshad said. "If I were a decade younger, I would ride with you myself. But I fear I would only be a burden." He bowed his head. "Tell the Prophet that Arshad Nabu-zar-adan has always kept the faith."

"We will tell him," Darius said. "Thank you."

"You must try to make Saman go with you," Arshad said. "When this is over...The Numerators will not rest until they discover who betrayed them. It would only be a matter of time before he was exposed."

And you in turn, I thought.

"I will do all I can," Darius said soothingly. "He is welcome to ride with us to Persepolae. Frankly, I cannot imagine why he would want to stay once his goal has been accomplished. There would be no point, and there is still a battle to be fought against the King. We need every ally we can get."

"Good." Arshad hesitated as though he thought he should do something more, like offer us a blessing. But I'd made no secret of my heresy, Tijah and Myrri were unrepentant pagans, and Darius.... My cheeks heated as I recalled giving him the water blessing the night before.

In the end, Arshad settled for making the sign of the flame. Dav waved, his thin face breaking into a smile, as we led our horses out of the courtyard to the bustle of Saffron Street.

"What was that about?" I asked Darius as we made our way out of the pleasure quarter toward the river. "With Dav?"

"He found a patron," Darius replied. "His last client left him a purse full of gold. He and Ester plan to start their own cosmetics shop."

I thought back to the day before, when I'd seen him in the hallway with a tall magus. How odd. Not the type you'd expect to have much gold, let alone to give it away to a boy prostitute.

"That's great," I said, trying hard to put some enthusiasm into my voice. I'd felt guilty about leaving the kid to his harsh life, so why didn't I feel happier? "Where was he anyway?"

"What?" Darius's attention was focused on the street ahead, and what dangers it might hold for us. The crowds eddied around snake charmers, jugglers, dancers and fire-eaters. I knew the celebrations in others parts of the city would be more sedate, with cleansing rituals to usher in the New Year, but in the pleasure district, Nowruz was an excuse to cut loose and spend—or earn—a fortune.

"Dav. Remember when Ester was looking for him?"

"Oh, he'd fallen asleep in his room," Darius replied absently. "Slept right through the night. He thought he was coming down with a sickness, but he's feeling better now."

Now that I thought on it, the man he'd been with did seem a little familiar, but it was probably from all the hours we had spent watching the tomb. I'd seen hundreds of magi go in and out of the temple. It would have been strange if I *hadn't* seen him before at least once.

Once out of the pleasure district, we mounted and rode through quieter side streets toward the royal palace. The magus at Tel Khalujah said that it was very old, hundreds of years older than the empire itself. The outside had bas-reliefs of men with the curving beaks of eagles and bulls with the heads of men. Infernal goddesses stalked the walls, dating back to the time when the people of Karnopolis worshipped many deities, not just the Holy Father. There were ostriches and griffins and winged scorpions. The people all had square beards and wide, staring eyes. We saw a few soldiers, but the garrison was lightly manned because of the King's absence.

The entrance Tijah had found was in a corner of the famed gardens, which were open to the public. On any other day, I would have been captivated by the beauty of the place in early spring. Forsythia bushes bloomed bright yellow amid orderly rows of tulips and hyacinth. Roses rioted everywhere—pink and red and orange and creamy as a saucer of fresh milk. Bees hummed in the grass, and the air was heavy with the smell of nectar, laced with the sharp tang of pine needles.

I wished I had come here every day, even if it was just for a few minutes. My childhood had been spent almost entirely out of doors. We lived in goatskin tents, and I'd never slept with a roof over my head until I went to Tel Khalujah to become a Water Dog. I still preferred the wild places to the cities. The King's gardens were hardly a wild place, but they were closer to it than I'd been in a long time. I could tell Darius felt the same. Victor had told me once that before the daēvas were enslaved, they had been solitary creatures, living far from human civilization. Perhaps some part of Darius remembered, even though he had been born to the cuff.

Yes, on any other day, I would have been in heaven here. But nervous tension quickened my step as we walked our horses along a gravel path to a rectangular clearing bordered by dark cypress trees. Tijah stopped before the stone lip of an old well. Vines had found a toehold in the weathered rock, and their snaky tendrils erupted in a profusion of tiny blue flowers shaped like bells. Compared to the murky interior, they looked downright festive.

"This is it," she said, glancing at Myrri. "The first two entrances we found were bricked up, but someone must have overlooked this one."

I peered into the pitch-black of the well's throat and my guts tightened another notch.

"Don't worry, it's dry," Tijah said. "We already checked."

"That barely scratches the surface of what worries me," I muttered, but Tijah was moving away and paid me no attention. Darius dismounted with catlike grace and strode to the well. I sensed only curiosity as he peered into its depths.

"We let a rope down last night," Tijah said. "Tied it off to that tree." She pointed at the spearlike bole of a nearby cypress. "I don't know if the well was intended as a secret way in and out, or if the workers just hit the tunnels by accident while they were digging. Myrri thinks it's the second, because there's no ladder or other way to climb out once you're down there."

"Wouldn't it be dangerous to leave it open?" I said.

"It was boarded over. We ripped them off."

I noticed a splintered heap of wood off to one side, hidden in a meadow of tall feathergrass.

"We'll go down the way you did," Darius said, taking a coil of rope from his bag. He tossed one end to Tijah and secured the other around the tree. I watched her lower it down into the well. Myrri had crept off to watch the path and make sure we weren't interrupted. She wasn't at all happy about leaving Tijah behind, but there was no way around it. Someone had to wait with the horses. We couldn't leave them at the brothel's stable because it would be crazy to go back there. Once we had Zarathustra, we had to get outside the walls as fast as possible, hopefully before the Numerators even knew he was gone. I didn't want to contemplate what would happen if we had to fight our way through the gates.

So we'd decided Tijah would wait by the river, under the Bridge of a Thousand Sighs. If all went as planned, we would be back within an hour. If it didn't, she would still be able to sense Myrri, just as I could sense Darius, and she would find us wherever we came out.

"Do you have the map?" I asked Darius, buckling on my sword. At least that came more easily now.

"I don't need it," he said with a cocky grin. "But yes, I do."

The sun sank behind the walls of the ancient palace, once considered the most luxurious building in the civilized world until Artaxeros built Persepolae. It was past time for us to get moving. Darius tested the rope, then dropped into the mouth of the well and slid down with one hand like it was something he did every day.

Tijah embraced Myrri while the horses grazed happily on tender new shoots of clover. There had been times when I wondered if the two of them weren't more than friends, but I didn't think so. They loved each other deeply, but it wasn't a romantic love. Just two women whose loyalty to each other was absolute.

I took a last look around, telling myself I would be chatting with the most famous dead man on earth before full night had fallen, and doing my best to believe it. I looked into the well but could no longer see Darius.

Pure darkness. And it smelled bad too.

A sudden cold certainty gripped me that if we went down there, we would never come out again. And yet I knew I would follow him. He wouldn't turn back now. And I wouldn't let him face whatever waited in the tunnels alone.

"What's it like?" I called softly.

A long moment passed. The rope gave two shakes. That meant he'd made it to the bottom. I tugged it once to let him know I was on my way.

The edge of the well was quite low, and it was easy enough to climb over so that I perched on the lip with my feet dangling over blackness. "I'll need you to lower me down," I said to Tijah. "I don't think I can do it one-handed like monkey boy."

She grinned and tied the rope under my arms in a hoist.

"Be safe, sister," Tijah said. I wished she was coming with us. Arshad or Dav could have watched the horses, Nowruz be damned. This was the first time in my life I'd headed into danger without her and it felt horribly wrong. I could see from her eyes she felt the same way, and also that we both knew it was way too late to do anything about it.

"See you soon," I said, smiling. I tipped my face toward the sun, filling my lungs with fresh air. Tijah and Myrri braced their legs against the well and began to lower me down. The first thing I felt was the chill. Damp and earthy, like the abandoned burrow of an animal. Darius must have broken a million spider webs ahead of me, but gossamer wisps still tickled my cheeks as I descended into the netherworld beneath Karnopolis. The circle of sky above me shrank in on itself until I couldn't stand to look at it anymore. So I stared down into the gloom instead, but that was worse. Finally, I settled for watching the stone wall slide by. At some point, it switched to a red claylike earth, and then stone again, but a rougher sort streaked with veins of white quartz.

It seemed to take forever to reach the bottom. I nearly screamed when hands grabbed my legs, even though I knew it was Darius. He set me on my feet, untied the rope and gave it a yank to signal that Tijah could haul it up again. Then he slid his arms around me and gave me a proper kiss.

"Before Myrri catches us," he said softly into my ear.

I could hardly see his face in the twilight, just the gleam of his teeth, but I could feel him just fine under my hands, warm and solid.

"Like she doesn't know," I said, pressing my cheek to his chest. Darius had slowed his heart down to cope with the cold and it thundered in my ear like a cataract plunging from a distant cliff. I wished I could do the same. Be a hibernating bear instead of a shivering human. "Can you really see down here?"

We stood in a low tunnel that branched off in two directions. One led towards the river, the other back to the temple district. Both ways were as dark as the bottom of the sea. We couldn't carry torches because Darius and Myrri couldn't be that close to fire (and I much preferred not to be, either) and because anyone within a mile would spot the light. Instead, we had decided to rely on Darius's superb night vision.

"I can see well enough," he replied. "And I have the tunnels committed to memory. We'll be fine."

"You have Saman's *map* committed to memory," I corrected gently. "There's a big difference. Now if you had made that map, I'd trust it with my life. But you didn't. And it looked a scrawled mess to me. He didn't even tell us how to get into these tunnels, which doesn't inspire a great deal of confidence."

"I will kill anyone or anything that gets near you, Nazafareen," Darius said, stroking my fuzzy hair the way I'd seen him pet the cats at Marduk's Spear. "I won't use the power unless I have to, only because I don't want to alert any daēvas, but you know I can lay waste to this place." It was a simple and undeniable fact, so I didn't say anything. "I am not afraid of the Numerators, nor the magi. They should be afraid of me."

Well, I supposed he was right on that too. Now that we were doing something, I felt better. It's the waiting around I hated the most. "How far is the cell from here?"

"I'd say about twenty minutes' walk. If Saman keeps his word, he'll be waiting for us there."

Faint sounds above signaled the arrival of Myrri. I hugged Darius fiercely and stepped back. A moment later, her feet appeared, encased in soft boots that barely made a whisper as they touched the smooth stone floor. Myrri gave the rope a sharp yank and our tether to the outside world was reeled upward until it vanished altogether and we were left with only one way out— the exit by the river, where Tijah would be waiting.

"Right," Darius said. "Follow me."

We set out down the tunnel at a brisk walk. Within twenty paces, I could no longer see a thing, so I took hold of the back of Darius's tunic. Myrri came behind, silent as a wraith. For the first few minutes, the tunnel ran as straight as the flight of an arrow. The blackness heightened my other senses, but both Darius and

Myrri could hear things well beyond the range of human ears. If anyone else was near, they would know.

The floor had been worn smooth, from the passage of feet or water or both, so it was easy walking. The worst part was the dankness of the air. I felt it keenly after the tropical climate of Karnopolis, and while cold did not normally trouble me—I was a child of the mountains, after all—the tunnels had a staleness, a hint of mold and decay, that I found deeply unpleasant.

All the more reason to find the Prophet quickly, dispose of his guards, and find the exit to the river as fast as possible.

After a bit, we must have reached a junction, because Darius slowed and guided me sharply to the left. I had the sense from the echo of our footsteps that the walls had narrowed considerably. Several more times, we reached branches, and always Darius chose the left-hand turning without hesitation. I thought we must be going in some kind of huge circle, but I didn't doubt his abilities so I said nothing. Water dripped in the distance. Sometimes it seemed we passed through wider spaces and I would feel the stir of cold air on my cheeks. Then we reached a tunnel with no more turnings, which seemed to go straight for an interminable length of time.

"We're getting close," Darius whispered. "We should be just beneath the Hall of the Numerators now. I've seen a few old doorways, but they were all bricked up. I think this section must have been closed a long time ago."

"Do you hear anything?" I asked.

"Nothing at all."

I groped behind me until I found Myrri's hand. "Doing okay?" I whispered.

She squeezed my fingers.

We crept forward, more slowly now. My breath sounded terribly loud in my ears, and the gentle scrape of my boots seemed like it would carry for miles. What a place to be held prisoner. If they had kept him in the dark, he would have to be barking mad by now, in which case rescuing him would probably be useless. I hated to think like that, but I preferred to expect the worst than to be disappointed when we liberated a gibbering lunatic.

Darius stopped so abruptly I bumped into his back. A faint gleam of light appeared up ahead. I thought it must either be Saman or someone we would have to kill, but then I realized it was not a torch. The light spilled from underneath a door set in the wall of the tunnel.

"I'll go first," Darius whispered, so softly I had to strain to hear him even though his breath tickled my ear.

A dark shadow moved toward the glow. I sensed Myrri stepping up to stand next to me. My heart hammered wildly. Was the man we sought behind that door? And why were there no guards? Were the Numerators so confident no one knew of his existence?

A moment later, Darius pressed his hand against the wood. From my position in the darkness about ten paces away, I could see him better now. His eyes were closed as though he were focusing on something and I knew he had gone to the nexus.

Then his eyes opened and he beckoned us both forward.

"There's only one person inside," he said. "I can't tell if it's human or daēva."

Something was wrong. I just knew it. Where was Saman?

"Nazafareen..." Darius felt my doubt and fear. I touched the hilt of my sword and murmured a prayer. Not to the Holy Father. To Kavi, the nine-headed goddess of vengeance.

If Saman betrayed us, please see to it that he spends all eternity screaming for mercy in the Pit...

"Break through," I said.

Darius reached through the cuff for the power, a churning, shining pool of lightning, and seized threads of earth and air. His breath sped up a bit, but he was not using much and it didn't injure him the way it did in battle. Darius wove the two elements together into something too complicated for me to grasp (although I thought I could have, given time to study what he had done). The lock clicked open.

My own breath caught as he pushed the door wide.

A grotesque face stared at me, human eyes over a hairy snout with grinning teeth and a long beard. I nearly jumped out of my skin before realizing it was just a painting. The wall seemed to be covered with them.

Goats.

"I've run out of ink," a tremulous voice said. "You promised me ink two months ago. Have you brought it?"

❧ 20 ❧

ARAXA

He sat patiently in the dark, knees drawn up to his chest, fingernails idly scratching the rash that had now spread to his inner thighs and up the back of his neck. Balthus had commanded him not to go near the cell. The demons would sense his presence if he did. Araxa did not mind. He was just happy he was being permitted to carry out his original plan. Hurdad and Kalbod would aid him. No others knew of it because no others could be trusted.

At his side were a dozen large clay jars sealed with wax. Hurdad had stolen them from one of the magi's storerooms. The liquid inside the jars was similar to the substance in the lake surrounding the Barbican, except even more potent. Some of the magi called it Greek Fire. In truth, it was a unique recipe devised by the Prophet Zarathustra himself two centuries before to use against the Druj.

Araxa smiled in the darkness. Things had a way of coming full circle in the end. By dawn tomorrow, it would be clear the Followers had tried to cover their tracks by setting the tunnels on fire, but had miscalculated and burned themselves—and the Prophet—to ash in the process. Araxa doubted the Hierarch would scrutinize the tragedy closely, especially once he learned that a magus named Saman had confessed to the plot (although it came too late for Araxa to intervene, of course). His smile widened. The Hierarch *had* directed him to burn the contents of the cell. So in a way, Araxa was only carrying out his orders.

But as he imagined these future events, turning them over and over in search of flaws or discrepancies, a strange feeling crept over the spymaster of the Numerators. A worm of doubt, burrowing into his brain.

What had Balthus whispered to him as the sun rose? Why could he not recall the words? He vaguely thought it had been a command of some sort. Something his mind had recoiled from. But that feeling had passed an instant later, and now Araxa could no longer remember. He felt it there, inside him, but every time he tried to get the shape of it, his fingers slid off as from an icy ledge.

"The heretics have come. They are at the cell now."

Hurdad loomed out of the black, his deep voice betraying no sign of unease at what they were about to do. He held a flickering torch, which he kept well away from the jars.

"Right on time," Araxa replied. "The magus spoke truly. Is Hand Kalbod in place?"

"He is, Patar. We have them cornered. There will be no way out."

Araxa stood. "What we do, we do for the good of the empire. You do understand that, Hurdad?"

"They are vermin that must be eradicated. I will shed no tears."

Araxa wondered if Hurdad had ever shed a tear for anyone in his life. *Will he weep for me when...?* But the thought slid away and Hurdad was lumbering off down the tunnel, having been dismissed by a wave of Araxa's hand.

Time. It is time now.

The thought came as though it had been spoken directly into Araxa's ear, and in the pleasant voice of Magus Balthus no less.

Holy Father, I will sleep for a week after this. I am not going mad, but I am very tired and yes, something has been done to me. I...

Araxa crouched down and opened the jars, one by one. The smell made his eyes water. Eleven of them he poured out on the ground, watching as the puddles of viscous liquid spread outward, following the natural declivities of the tunnel. He had a lantern, whose shutters he had lifted enough to see by. An exit lay just behind him, leading to a ladder that emerged in one of the unused storerooms of the Hall. In just a few moments, he would be ascending it, as the inferno raged beneath him.

And yet Araxa did not move.

He watched, mesmerized, as the pool crept toward the red hem of his robes.

And then Balthus's final command rang out clear and true in his head. Sweat broke out on Araxa's brow as he bent down and, in one swift motion, tipped the last jar over his own head.

I find you loathsome, and coming from a creature such as myself, that is something.

It stung his eyes, numbed his lips. And the effect on his rash... Araxa felt as though he were on fire already. *Let it be over.*

He thought he heard the necromancer's laughter as he kicked over the lantern and all the world turned to white.

❧ 21 ❧

NAZAFAREEN

I scanned the room for the person who had just spoken but saw no one. A dozen candles wavered fitfully in the breeze through the open door, illuminating not a bare cell as I had expected, but a crazed jumble of stacked bits of parchment that resembled the nest of some strange bird. Drawings covered the walls, stars and moons and long arching lines that might have described the movements of those heavenly bodies at certain times of year, or might have been anything at all.

Then there were the goats.

Large and small, fierce and drowsy and beseeching. No two were exactly the same, but all had the same disturbing eyes. Not like proper goat eyes at all, which ought to have over-large horizontal pupils. These looked the eyes of pretty women, or boys, if they had very long eyelashes.

Something moved, and I took an involuntary step backward. A man crouched not six paces away. My eyes had passed right over him because he was the same color and general shape as the stack of vellum at his elbow. Yellowing and ragged, with pointy angles and a healthy layer of dust.

"Holy Father," Darius breathed. He too had stopped in the doorway, reluctant to go any further. The smell that greeted us was certainly one reason. Like a subterranean barnyard, or perhaps an abandoned bat cave. Potent and organic. I tried breathing through my mouth but found I could actually taste it that way, so I reverted back to shallow nose inhalations. Myrri made a coughing noise behind me, and the man's attention shifted to her. The only bright things about him were his eyes, which gleamed with some emotion I couldn't identify. Curiosity? Cunning? Profound madness?

"I guess we found him," I said. "Good thing we didn't buy five horses."

Darius entered the cell, keeping one wary eye on the candles. Their flames were small and not much of a threat, as long as he didn't get too close.

"We've come to take you away from this place," Darius said. "But we must leave immediately. Do you understand?"

The Prophet said nothing. His body crouched motionless as a toad, but his eyes darted between us in growing alarm.

"We won't harm you," Darius said in his most reasonable tone, as though he were speaking to a child who refused to eat their peas. "But there are other men who are coming for you as well, and their intentions are not...honorable."

"I only want my ink." His voice made me think of an old crow, harsh and rusty.

"And you shall have it," I said firmly, stepping forward to squat down before him. He shied back a little, but didn't skitter away. "My name is Nazafareen. This is Darius and Myrri. You must let us help you. I know you have been in this place for a long time and it seems strange to leave it, but leave it you will—either with us, or with the others. And they will not give you ink, that I can promise."

We looked at each other for a long moment, and then the Prophet gave me the barest nod. I thought I saw that gleam in his eye again, sharp and knowing, but a moment later it was gone and he seemed like a tired old man.

"Help me pack my things," he said.

"What things?"

He made a sweeping gesture that encompassed the entire contents of the cell. As he did so, the sleeve of his ragged robe fell back, revealing a gold cuff. While mine was worked in the image of a snarling lion, this one had two horned goat-head terminals. The source of his obsession became a little clearer.

"Are you bonded?" Darius asked him gently, pointing to the cuff. "Who wears its match?"

"I am alone," Zarathustra replied, and the way he said those three words made me feel truly sorry for him. They carried the weight of long years spent in silence. Of thousands of solitary meals, of creeping madness kept at bay with the light of a candle and the company of pen and parchment.

"Do you know a magus named Saman? Has he been here?"

The Prophet stared at him uncomprehendingly.

Then Darius stiffened and Myrri made an awful moaning noise deep in her throat. I felt it a second later. Fire. Not the weak, flickering wicks of tallow in the cell, but something much fiercer.

"Run!" Darius hissed, scooping the Prophet up like a bundle of twigs and darting out the doorway. The tunnel beyond was still clear, but I could smell a faint whiff of smoke. It nearly paralyzed me. Of all the bad possibilities I had imagined, and there were many, that the Numerators would set the tunnels on fire had not occurred to me. I had stupidly assumed they wanted to keep Zarathustra alive—at least until they could kill him themselves.

So Saman had betrayed us, or been betrayed. It made no difference now. The lightless maze we had ventured into was burning, and they'd used some kind of accelerant. No normal fire would be that hot, or move that fast. I couldn't see it, not yet, but I could sense it. Racing towards us as swiftly as the sandstorm on the Great Salt Plain.

"Which way?" I asked Darius, amazed at how calm my own voice sounded.

We all stood bunched up in front of the Prophet's cell. Darius's head swung left, then right. I felt his fear, felt him crush it down. He didn't need to explain that the fire was all around us. That there was nowhere to run. I knew it myself. The old man squawked and wriggled in Darius's arms. He kept reaching toward his nest of parchment.

"My life's work!" he cried. "Let me go! You mustn't—"

Without a word, Darius took off into the darkness. He chose the left-hand turning. The air in the tunnels thickened with each passing second. Damp and cold gave way to dry and warm, then hot. I tried to seek the nexus, to find a place of nothingness where I could shed my fear and focus only on finding a way through the flames, but kept getting distracted by the Prophet's howls of outrage as we left his scribblings behind. He veered between imperious demands—*who are you and where are you taking me?*—and disjointed rambling—*my ink, my ink, they promised me ink...*

Sweat soaked my tunic. We lurched around a corner and caught our first glimpse of the inferno, a reddish glow painting the walls of the tunnel ahead. Darius spun on his heel and we all tangled up for a second, until Myrri grabbed my hand and we ran back the way we had come.

Now Myrri was in the lead, and she chose branchings seemingly at random, although I knew she could sense even more acutely than I which ways were blocked and which remained open. The fire must have started a fair distance away or we would already have been fried to a crisp. But it was closing fast, and often as not, we found ourselves being forced to backtrack as flames roared into the tunnels ahead.

It began to feel like a game of cat and mouse—a game we would lose.

"There's got to be an exit nearby," Darius snarled. "Even if we find one that's sealed, I'll break it open."

"Just keep moving." I took a deep breath. I'd lost all sense of direction and hadn't a clue where we were in relation to the streets above. "If need be, we'll all work together to smash a way out of here." Darius nodded once in the dim light. He'd been waiting for me to say it. All this time, I'd avoided thinking about the dreams I had been having. The ones that started with me working fire and ended with Darius dead. Now I wondered if it had been an omen.

Without warning, the Prophet reached for me, clawlike fingers tangling in the neck of my tunic.

"Listen, boy," he hissed, but he didn't get any further because I stumbled backwards into Myrri, half turning as a shape loomed out of the tunnel behind her. It was tall and faceless, and it held a knife that it buried in her back before I could even open my mouth to scream.

Myrri staggered, brown eyes round with astonishment. I saw the embroidery on her assailant's chest, an eye with a flame for a pupil, and understood it was not just a Numerator, but a Hand of the Father. Rage filled me as I yanked my sword from its scabbard. The Hand calmly withdrew his blade from between Myrri's shoulders and shoved her out of the way. He had a thick, squashed nose that looked like it had been broken a time or two, most likely on someone else's head, and a neck wider than his skull.

"You killed the Patar," he said in an emotionless voice that raised the hair on my arms. "Vice Minister Kalbod. I wish you to know that name, because it is the name of the man who is about to kill you." He held the knife low and pointed down—a bad sign. This was not a man who cared for flash or flourish. No, this was a man who knew how to gut from navel to sternum in a single slash.

"You will be judged by the Holy Father for this," Zarathustra said. Somehow his voice had lost its tremulous edge. It rang strong and true. "Murder is a sin beyond redemption."

"Then my soul is doomed already," the Hand replied. There was the sound of flint striking pyrite and a torch bloomed to life. Darius staggered back, throwing a hand across his eyes. The light was blinding after so long in the dark tunnels.

"Do you know who I am?" the Prophet said. He seemed to grow taller as he stood there, back straight and unafraid of the hulking lunatic before him.

"I know, but it matters not as you shall soon be dead as well."

"The evil and hatred in your heart will only harm yourself, friend," Zarathustra said. "Let us pass."

Vice Minister Kalbod looked at the bloodstained blade in his hand. Then he reached out and wiped it clean on the Prophet's robes, leaving two crimson streaks on the ragged cloth. "I am not your friend," he said, raising the knife again.

I was afraid to use the power directly with the flames so close, but perhaps it could still help me. The Prophet stood between us. He would die in the next instant unless I did something. And this Hand terrified me. He was a veteran of killing and maiming, and even with my years in the Water Dogs, even with my sword, I didn't think I stood a chance.

So I pushed the Prophet aside and let a trickle of power through the cuff. Just enough to give me an advantage, the way I used to do in sparring practice. The Numerator's face snapped into sharp focus. I noticed the cluster of premature grey hairs above his ears, the flatness of his muddy green eyes. He took a breath and it seemed to last a thousand years.

My sword was buried in his chest before he'd exhaled.

Vice Minister Kalbod gurgled a bit, but I'd already shoved him away and kicked the fallen torch down the tunnel where it lay smoldering. Myrri was still on her feet, leaning against Darius, and I heaved a sigh of relief when I saw her eyes were clear and aware.

"How bad is it?" I whispered, running my left hand over her as gently as I could. She took it in her own and signed *okay* on my palm until I understood. I knew Myrri was not okay, but the knife had missed her heart or she would be gone already. With luck, her own strength and healing abilities just might save her. Myrri made another sign, thumb and ring finger touching and the others curled into a fist. I only knew a few of the hundreds she used to communicate, but that was one of them.

"Tijah?" I asked.

Myrri nodded emphatically. She made the sign again and pointed at the ceiling. I frowned in confusion.

Darius glanced down the tunnel, where the red glow of the advancing fire had grown brighter. "That was nicely done, Nazafareen, but we need to move. Now."

"She says Tijah is up there," I explained. Then it hit me. "Wait, she can sense Tijah, right?" I turned to Myrri. "So you mean we're near the river!"

Myrri grinned and nodded.

"The exit should be close," Darius said.

"Can you tell where it is?" I asked Myrri.

She rocked her palm from side to side, which meant *maybe*.

"Are you able to walk?" Another nod. "Lead on," I said.

The Prophet took a few steps and stumbled, his strength waning again. Darius swept him back into his arms. And then we were running again. Running and running. I could hear the roar of the flames now, and felt them pull at me, a lover's fingertips brushing mine. With that raw, untamed power flowing through me, I thought I could do anything. Toss away the earth and rock over our heads like a wolf shaking snow from its fur. The craving was almost unbearable but I blocked it out and kept my eyes fixed on the ground ahead. It seemed to slope ever so slightly upward. I imagined the air smelled a touch cleaner, although my eyes still stung and my lungs ached.

"There!" Darius pointed. We had hit yet another junction, but this one divided at an archway that had been bricked up sometime in the distant past. The bricks were the same dusty color as the tunnel walls and I wouldn't have noticed it if Darius's sharp eyes hadn't picked out their rounded edges. Thick smoke crept along the ceiling of the intersecting tunnel from both directions, and I felt flames surging forward from behind us as well. This was the end.

"We'll break through," Darius said. He gently set the Prophet on his feet. Zarathustra sagged against the wall, but his expression was serene. This was a man truly unafraid of death. I wondered if he might even welcome it.

Then Darius raised a hand and Myrri did the same, not because they needed to, but I think the action helped them focus. They were about to work with earth, the most violent of the elements. Bones would shatter along with bricks, but it was a small price to pay for freedom.

Darius gathered the power and a distant memory tickled my mind. A time when there was a fire in the satrap's granary at Tel Khalujah. It had simmered quietly until someone opened one of the doors, and then the whole building had exploded.

"Wait!" I cried, clamping down on Darius's power through the cuff. His head snapped around in fury at being severed. I grabbed his arm and yanked him backwards as jagged cracks raced down the brick wall. "Myrri, stop!" I screamed.

She turned and looked at me over her shoulder. At the last instant, understanding seemed to dawn, but it was too late. The brick wall erupted in a shower of dust as she broke through it with the power. Warm air rushed into the tunnel.

And the fire leapt like a beast on a hunk of raw meat. Flames surged forward from the adjoining corridors. They didn't touch Myrri, but they came within inches of her and that was enough. Her whole body jerked. Flames shot out of her eyes and mouth. Her hair became a torch. At first, the fire centered on her head, but then her tunic caught. At the very end, as the bond broke, her voice returned and I heard a single, piercing scream that would haunt me to the end of my days.

I stumbled backwards, covering my face against the terrible heat. But I never let go of Darius. I instinctively kept his power tight in my fist, although I could feel him straining for it, like a man struggling to leap off a cliff. In truth, I wanted to seize it too, badly, and I might have if I hadn't just seen Myrri get immolated. But I knew if I let go for the briefest instant, we were both dead, and so I hung on, gripping the bond with white knuckles as the flames swept closer. They blocked the path to the archway and I knew we'd burn before we got to the other side, but there seemed no other choice.

I was just getting ready to run into the fire when hands reached down from above and grabbed Zarathustra. The Prophet made a noise of surprise as he was hauled up through a small circular hole in the ceiling. An instant later, that white, muscular arm came down again, fingers spread wide.

"Take it!" A voice growled.

So I did.

❦ 22 ❦

NAZAFAREEN

The man set me on my feet. A moment later, Darius came through as well. He immediately knelt down to make sure Zarathustra was unhurt. The old man was perfectly quiet now. He seemed to have finally succumbed to shock, unable to cope with all that was happening. I knew how he felt. I couldn't believe Myrri was dead. If Tijah had been with us, she could have stopped Myrri from reaching for the fire, just as I had done with Darius. But we had left her behind.

"It happened in an instant," Darius said, his voice cracked. "You tried to warn us."

"Too late," I said wearily. "Holy Father, we've been stupid. We walked straight into their trap."

I tried to get my bearings, to figure out if we had just put the noose around our necks a second time. "Saman?" I asked, although I did not think it was him. The tunnel was too dark to make out the man's features, but his voice was different. Deeper, and with an accent I did not recognize.

"Saman is waiting for you above," the man said. "I am Balthus."

"You're a magus," Darius said warily. I supposed he could see the robes.

"Yes. He recruited me to the Followers."

"He never mentioned that."

"I asked him not to. If you had been captured...Well, he told me everything. He was going to come himself but he suspected they were watching him. It was too dangerous, so he sent me instead. That was a smugglers' hole I pulled you through. You must be blessed by the Holy Father to have stopped beneath one."

"Our companion was not so blessed," Darius replied harshly.

"I am sorry about your friend. But I can show you another way out."

"We need to get to the river," I said. All the fear and excitement was gone, leaving raw, jagged-edged grief in its place. Grief and anger. If not for the Prophet, Myrri would be alive. I groped around until I felt his filthy robes and gave him a shake. "Wake up!" I snarled. "Get on your feet!"

"Nazafareen—"

"Get. Up." I punctuated each word with a shake. I thought I heard the old man's teeth rattle in his head, the few that were left at any rate. Did I say anger? Blind rage was more like it. I hated him in that moment, hated everything he stood for. Hated that Myrri had traded her life for his, and how easily it might have been Darius, blackened and smoking in those dank tunnels. "Get up, you cursed old bag of bones—"

And then Darius's hands were pulling me back.

"I'll carry him," Balthus said. "You deal with your bonded. She is clearly distraught. But we cannot stay here any longer."

I heard him move off into the darkness. Darius leaned forward and gently kissed my mouth. He said nothing more, but it had the effect of calming me down enough to take his hand and follow Balthus's receding footsteps. The tunnels went on and on, but the air seemed clearer on this level. True to his word, the magus seemed to know them well, striding along without hesitation. My feet moved of their own accord through that oppressive darkness, as my thoughts drifted away. To Tijah, and what she must be going through right now, having the bond snapped without warning. Knowing Myrri was dead, but not how or why. They had been together since they were children. I didn't even have a body to bring her. We'd left Myrri in the tunnels to burn.

I could read Darius's grief as clearly as my own. Myrri alone had broken through the bricks and triggered the backdraft, but he had failed to foresee it. Darius already had a tendency to blame himself. I knew he would take her death almost as hard as Tijah.

Finally, I caught a glimpse of daylight ahead. It had been growing steadily brighter for a while, so slowly my eyes had adjusted without even realizing it. I could see well enough to walk on my own now, but I kept Darius's hand anyway. Balthus went ahead of us, the Prophet cradled in his arms like a child. All I could see of him was white robes and dark hair. From his straight back, he seemed young. I still held Darius's power, terrified we would turn a corner and encounter more fire. I could all too easily imagine him sharing Myrri's fate.

And then we emerged from the tunnels near the edge of the river, as Balthus had promised. Just ahead, the Bridge of a Thousand Sighs soared gracefully over the water, its white stone luminous in the moonlight. I didn't see Tijah or the horses, but who knows what she had done when she felt Myrri's death? I suspected her first impulse would be to avenge her daēva. I would feel the same way. Had she tried to enter the tunnels? To follow after us?

The place we had come out was a dark arch cut into the bank, its mouth hidden by brambles. I heard the cries of gulls and caught a faint but unmistakable whiff of sewage. There was an undertone of smoke as well, and a reddish glow in the sky. The sight threw me into confusion. Had we been in the tunnels all night? It didn't seem possible. And the glow came from the west, not the east.

If I hadn't been trying so hard to suffocate the power, I would have known the truth immediately.

"The temple district is in flames," Balthus said, and there seemed to me a note of grim satisfaction in his voice. "The fools thought the fire would burn itself out but it's spread out of control. It's aboveground now, with plenty of air and fuel."

He turned back and I got my first real look at his face, silhouetted against the bridge. He *was* young, although perhaps a decade older than Saman. Middle thirties, I guessed. He gave a half smile, revealing pointy canine teeth quite a bit longer than his front teeth, and I knew where I recognized him from.

"You were at Marduk's Spear!" I exclaimed. "Yesterday, with Dav. I saw you."

Darius had stopped walking. He was looking at Balthus strangely.

"I don't deny it," the magus said. "I confess, I wanted to see you for myself. I considered speaking to you, but I was afraid."

"Afraid of what?" I asked.

"That you were not who Saman believed you to be. Is it true you were once Water Dogs?"

"And what if we were?" Darius said warily.

Balthus shrugged. "It is no business of mine. I do not wish to pry into your affairs, only to help the Prophet, as you do."

"Where is Saman?" Darius demanded. "You said he would meet us."

"Well, he must be around here somewhere. Are those your horses?"

He pointed to the shadows under the bridge. His eyes must have been nearly as sharp as Darius's, because all I could see were vague shapes in the darkness. But then I heard a soft whicker as they caught our scent, and one of the horses raised its head. It had been cropping the grass along the riverbank.

"All four are there," Darius said. "But I don't see Tijah." He looked at the swirling waters of the river. "You don't think she...?"

"No," I said firmly. "Not Tijah. Not until she knew what happened to Myrri."

We entered the shadow of the bridge. I could hear distant shouts now as news spread that the temple district was burning. I didn't care a fig for the Numerators, nor the magi either, but I hoped the daēva barracks had been cleared. All those children...

"There were men here," Darius said, scanning the ground. "Signs of a struggle." His eyes met mine. "I think Tijah's been taken."

My heart sank. "Alive?"

Darius nodded. "No blood."

"And Saman? Was he here too?"

"I don't know."

I swore under my breath. "Was it soldiers? Numerators? Never mind, it doesn't matter. We go after them," I said, seizing the bridle of one of the Ferghana mares. "All of us. And when we find them, they will pay dearly."

"At least you fight with your left," Balthus observed, dark eyes glittering.

I turned to him. "How do you know that?"

The magus only smiled, but I had the distinct feeling he was laughing at me. "From the side your sword is buckled on, of course."

My hand fell to the hilt. "Of course."

"And because I've seen you wield that blade." The false diffidence left his voice like a snake shedding its scales. From one instant to the next, it was deeper, harsher. "Did you lose your right hand in the battle, Water Dog? Or was it later? Unless I misremember, you had both when we last saw each other."

I heard the whisper of Darius's sword being drawn, felt him fill with the power.

"Do not think to use elemental magic against me, daēva,"

Balthus said. "I will drain him in a heartbeat." He turned and I saw one of the loathsome iron collars circling the Prophet's neck. I don't know when Balthus had slipped it on, but he'd managed to conceal it in Zarathustra's robes. The old man lay limp in Balthus's arms, one of which held the other end of the chain. My hackles rose.

"Who are you?"

"My name is Balthazar. Do you remember now?"

I stared at him, eyes narrowed. Saw five enormous black horses arrayed before me on the Great Salt Plain, each carrying four riders. Only the leader had spoken. He had tried to make a bargain with us. The others had been too far back to make out their faces, although I had the impression they looked like normal men. There was nothing remarkable about them. Nothing to mark them as evil. And that in itself had chilled me more than anything.

I had killed the leader myself, so this must be one of the others.

"You took the holy fire," Darius said, leveling his blade at Balthazar's throat.

The necromancer inclined his head in agreement. "You are Victor's son, are you not?"

Darius didn't respond, although I felt a flicker of rage at the mention of his father's name. Balthazar seemed to take his silence for assent. He nodded once, to himself. "I knew him, a long time ago. He was either very brave or very stupid. Perhaps both. They are not mutually exclusive qualities."

"Why are you here?" Darius demanded coldly.

"Come with me to Bactria. My queen would like to make your acquaintance. She does not wish to harm you. In fact, I believe she wishes to make you an offer. Power such as you have never dreamt of."

"Neblis has nothing I want."

"What about the fire you spoke of? She has *that*. She could rid you of the shackles you wear."

Darius laughed. "You know nothing about me, necromancer. Do not presume to know what I want."

"Oh, I wouldn't dare," Balthazar said mildly. "But you must choose sides at some point. Better sooner than later."

"I've already chosen. We stand with Alexander."

Now it was Balthazar's turn to laugh, in genuine amusement. "The boy king? Once he's sacked Persepolae, Queen Neblis will destroy him. There will be no one left to stand with. *Or* behind. Her armies will cover the empire from mountains to sea in numbers you cannot even imagine. Think on it. Your kind has been enslaved for two hundred years. Neblis is one of you. She will see justice done."

"You speak of justice...You! A thief and murderer. Give me back the Prophet and I will consider it an act of good faith. He is of no use to you anyway."

"Lower your sword," Balthazar ordered. Darius reluctantly complied. He was quick, but perhaps not quick enough to skewer the antimagus before he snapped Zarathustra's neck. "I went to a great deal of trouble to rescue the three of you from the tunnels. Why should I just hand him over?"

"We must go to Persepolae." Darius's jaw clenched. "You cannot have him."

"And I'm afraid you cannot take him from me."

"Where is Saman? What have you done to him?" I demanded.

"That was not my doing," the necromancer said quickly. "The Numerators found him out days ago. He told them everything under torture. It was their plan to let you rescue Zarathustra and then to kill you all. The Hands of the Father set the fires, not I. Saman is gone, but I avenged his death for you." He smiled. "Consider it a small favor. The Numerator behind it all did not have a pleasant end."

"And nor will you," I snarled. *Poor Saman.* I had only met him the one time, but he seemed like a good man. Why was it always the good ones who got themselves killed?

We looked at each other for a moment, the necromancer and I. Bells tolled in the distance, a frantic warning sound.

"Remove the cuffs," Balthazar said to me. "Both of them."

"No," I said.

"Watch, then." The necromancer's eyes never left mine, but his cheeks flushed pink with blood even as Zarathustra's sank into his skull like pieces of fruit left too long in the sun. The old man's skin, already sallow from two centuries without daylight, turned the grey of a week-old corpse. A rattling sound escaped his lips.

"Stop," Darius cried. "You're killing him."

"The cuffs," Balthazar repeated. It was mesmerizing, watching the Prophet's own life flow into the necromancer's body. With each passing second, Balthazar seemed to grow more vibrant, more *real*, as the Prophet faded to an empty husk.

I pretended to reach for the cuffs at the same moment I made a desperate bid to seize the power. It slid through my fingers, but the necromancer staggered a bit as Darius lashed out with air. I whipped my sword free of the scabbard and took a step forward. Two more and my blade would be through Balthazar's throat. I wanted to spill his blood so badly I could almost taste it. First Tommas, then Myrri and Saman. Now Tijah had been stolen from me too. All because of this creature, this minion of Neblis.

I knew he couldn't collar me because I was already bonded to Darius. One of the other Antimagi had tried it on the plain and died for his mistake. I took a breath, and saw the power pulsing at the edge of my vision. I no longer cared how much damage I did to my own body. I wanted only to destroy him utterly. To batter his body against the stone of the bridge and hurl him into the water, down deep into the silty rushes at the bottom, filling his lungs until he drowned.

Balthazar stood before me, grinning, as if he could read my thoughts. I drew on the power again and this time, it did not slide away. Sheltered in the sudden calm of the nexus, I could sense the necromancer's unnatural magic, like a hole in the fabric of things. It flowed through the chains, which served as a channel in much the same way my own cuffs did. Was that what the Prophet had meant when he wrote of *talismanic magic*? Power invested in an object? Or an object designed to do a particular thing?

These thoughts passed through my mind even as the urge to obliterate the antimagus threatened to pop the nexus like a soap bubble. Dimly, I saw the Prophet 's hair turn from grey to white. His skin grew thin and translucent as an onion. It was past time to end this. I gathered the power. Or not gathered, precisely. Let it flood into me, from everywhere and nowhere. A humming, buzzing, crackling thing, like slow lightning. I knew that if I did not use it quickly, it might kill me. There were four possible paths to direct it outward: earth, air, water...and fire, of course. How the flames racing through the temple district called to me! *Too dangerous*. I shoved that thought aside, and focused on the other three elements. Earth was the strongest. It would be earth, then.

But before I could shape the power into a weapon, I heard Darius scream. Pain lanced through the bond. Terrible pain. Balthazar's smile widened, and it crashed over me in a wave. As though a sharp-toothed giant was sucking the marrow from my bones. My sword fell to the ground. The world tilted and my mouth filled with the brackish mud of the riverbank.

He didn't need to collar either of us, apparently. With the life and vitality he had stolen from the Prophet, Balthazar could strike at whim. My fingernails raked the dirt as a deep agony sank its teeth into muscle and tissue. I had not thought anything could be worse than what Ilyas did to me in the dungeons, but this was worse. This was dying.

Darius's breath rasped harshly beside me. The power had been ripped from my grasp like a toy from a small child. What a fool I had been. I knew nothing about the dark powers of the Antimagi, what they were capable of. Balthazar had defeated the oldest, most powerful daēvas at Gorgon-e Gaz. He and the other necro-mancers had killed them all, except for Victor. I'd seen firsthand what the chains could do to captives, I'd seen the Druj that were created when one of those captives died, but I'd never had the life-draining magic turned on me. It was like being flayed by a thousand invisible knives. I didn't even have the strength to cry out.

A shadow fell across my face as Balthazar crouched down. His face swam into the narrowing tunnel of my vision. A pale hand stretched toward me, iron chains glinting in the moonlight. I sensed Darius trying to crawl closer. I didn't know how he managed it. I could feel his pain through the bond, loud and bright, and it wove together with mine until I could hardly tell us apart. I couldn't move at all, but Darius was stubborn. If we would die, we would die together.

Why didn't Balthazar let us burn in the tunnels? Why save us at all, once he'd taken the Prophet?

Because he needed Darius, of course. Whatever had happened to Victor in Bactria, whether he was dead too or something else, Neblis wanted his son and Balthazar was her faithful servant.

The necromancer's fingers brushed Darius's cuff and there was nothing I could do to stop him. The skin on my arm pebbled as a bone-deep chill rolled over me. The power coursing through Balthazar might have derived from the nexus, but it was all ice and shadow. If his chains were truly a talisman, their purpose was to take the essence of life and transform it to its opposite.

A lock of brown hair fell across the necromancer's eyes as he looked down at me. I saw no hatred there, just curiosity and possibly even a hint of regret.

"Tell me your name," he commanded.

The word spilled unbidden through dry lips. "Nazafareen."

"You have spirit. I admire that. I want you to know I did not misuse the boy, Dav. I do not inflict unnecessary pain." His fingers closed around my stump. "Unfortunately, in *your* case, it's necessary."

I bit down on my own tongue as he did something that made the previous agony pale in comparison. At least I knew it wouldn't last long, because human bodies were not made to withstand what was happening to me, not for any length of time. The cuff began to slide from my wrist. In the instant before our bond transferred to the necromancer, Darius's right hand seized my left, our fingers lacing tight.

It seemed I lay like that for an eternity, with Balthazar on one side and Darius on the other. Caught between the dark talismanic magic of the chains, and the pulsing power of the elements. Just as the pain reached an unbearable pitch, something stirred in my chest. It was the color of fresh blood and unspent rage and it was *hungry*.

I recognized it right away. After all, I had been living with it for weeks now. I think Balthazar sensed it too, for he fell back just as I released my grip on its hackles. The monster roared forth and met his magic, quenching it like a barrel of saltwater thrown on a hot forge. There was a flash of light that turned the sky white. I rolled to my side, sobbing uncontrollably. When my vision cleared, the necromancer was gone. So was the Prophet and one of the horses.

"Nazafareen!" Darius knelt beside me. I still shook, but with fury now as much as pain. "Are you injured? Speak to me!"

I gingerly tested my limbs, expecting terrible fractures, joints torn from the sockets. Everything moved the way it was supposed to, although I ached all over. Darius guided me to my feet and I bit back a whimper.

"It hurts so much," I said, embarrassed at the tears leaking from my eyes.

Without speaking, Darius put his arms around me and I felt the warmth of our bond envelop us. Just as he had when the necromancers entombed me beneath the snow, Darius poured his life and strength through the cuff. The pain receded and I drew a shuddering breath.

"Thank you. You see? You are a healer already." I pressed my cheek against his tunic so I could hear the steady thud of his heart. "Do you think it was real or only in my mind?"

When Ilyas had tortured Darius in the dungeons, not a mark was left on his body. The necromancer's power seemed to work in the same way, although I had no doubt we would both be dead if I had not broken it somehow.

"Pain is pain," he said flatly, and I knew he was thinking of the dungeons too, and his own amah. "What happened?" He gently lifted my chin. "What drove him off?"

"I'm not sure." The thing in me had grown quiet again, but a residue of its wrath remained. Its primal need to destroy terrified me. If it had broken loose in the tunnels, seized the fire....

Darius had to know I was lying, but he let it pass. "The contingent of Immortals at the palace couldn't possibly have missed the show of power here," he said. "But we can still catch the necromancer. He'll be heading for the nearest gate."

He started for the horses. "Wait." I grabbed his sleeve. "You said Tijah lived."

"She did when she left," he agreed, pointing out several sets of boot prints in the soft earth of the embankment. "Those belong to mercenaries from Al Miraj. Do you see the pointy toe? It is the style there. The necromancer must have led them to her before he descended into the tunnels."

"Can you follow their trail?"

He nodded. The look on his face was clearly distressed. "But Nazafareen...I cannot track both quarries. They have fled in opposite directions. If we do not go after Balthazar now, we will likely lose him again. Neblis will have the Prophet."

I thought of the men who sought Tijah. Of the day she told me how her father had tried to wed her to the satrap's son, a young, handsome man with the soul of a butcher. This man had already married Tijah's sister, Saalima, so Tijah knew him for what he was. When she refused to comply, her father had Myrri whipped. The pair of them had run away the night before the wedding.

I'd promised Tijah she would not fight them alone if they came for her. And she didn't have Myrri to protect her anymore. She was utterly at their mercy. The thought made me sick with fear.

Darius and I would both be dead if she hadn't killed Ilyas. I owed her everything.

"Then let Neblis have him," I said. "I won't leave Tijah behind. Not to the fate that awaits her. Will you come with me? For Myrri?"

I knew what I was asking him. With Victor dead and the Prophet gone, his mother would surely burn. If he said no, I would go after her myself, although I did not see how I could follow the mercenaries once their tracks reached the tangle of streets.

Darius's eyes glowed in that catlike way as he sheathed his sword and leapt into the saddle. "Of course I will. But not only for Myrri. For Tommas and Tijah and all of us. We are no longer Water Dogs, but we are still comrades." He sighed and shame leaked through the bond. "I should not have made you ask."

I closed my eyes. The red beast inside me nodded its approval. It was not done yet.

I found I was looking forward to finding these men.

❧ 23 ❧

NAZAFAREEN

The trail led away from the river and into an area of warehouses serving the harbor. It was largely deserted, although every so often we saw people fleeing the fire, their belongings piled haphazardly into oxcarts or simply bundled on their backs. The red glow in the sky had spread outward from the temple district to engulf some of the crowded residential and commercial areas of the city. Karnopolis was a tinderbox, with thatched roofs and wooden supports girding its mudbrick structures. Even the stone mansions of the wealthy were filled with rugs, tapestries, clothing and other combustibles. A steady sea breeze fanned the flames, but they had not yet reached the district we rode through.

"Up ahead," Darius called softly. He was in the lead, with the reins of the third horse tied to his saddle. In contrast to the paved brick of the temple district, these streets were bare dirt, muffling the rhythm of our hooves.

"They've stopped?" I asked in surprise. I had expected the mercenaries to run back to Al Miraj with their prize as fast as possible.

"One is badly injured. Tijah must have put up a fight."

"Well, there's no question of that. Can you tell how she is?"

Darius shook his head. "Only that there are four humans in a building on the next street, and the trail ends there."

"We'd best go the rest of the way on foot."

We concealed the horses in a stand of trees and crept up to a large, windowless structure that occupied the entire block. With the full moon high overhead, even I could clearly see four sets of footprints leading to a door at the rear. One set was smaller than the others and seemed to be staggering.

Rage churned in my stomach. At the necromancer, the Numerators, these swine who had laid hands on Tijah. They had no clue what was coming for them.

"Ready?" Darius asked.

"Very."

He eased the door open with the toe of his boot. Darkness greeted us, but I could see the glow of a lamp at the far end of what seemed to be a cavernous space. Casks of oranges and sacks of barley and bunches of garlic were piled high against the walls to either side. A jumble of spices perfumed the air. I caught whiffs of coriander, fennel, juniper and cumin. Darius moved toward the light in perfect silence. I followed a short distance behind, my ears straining for any sound. And then I heard harsh laughter. The sour stink of unwashed bodies and cheap wine.

From the shadows, we were invisible. But I could see every detail of the scene before me.

Tijah lay on the floor, one eye swollen shut. I thought she was unconscious until the other eye opened a crack. She blinked hard a few times, trying to focus. Her hands and feet had been bound with rope. I recognized the three men who had taken her. They were the same ones who had accosted Darius and me on our way to the tomb two days before.

The man with a pockmarked face sat against the far wall, cradling his right arm. It had been wrapped in a bolt of dirty linen. The others stood over Tijah. One had her scimitar stuck in his belt.

"Stupid bitch," muttered the one with a lazy eye.

"They ought to give us extra bounty," Pockmark muttered angrily. "We still have a long way to go with her. Maybe we'd best break her legs. Keep her from running."

"Oh, she won't run. Not after I have a little fun first. Least we deserve for our troubles," said the last, who was stocky and spoke in a nasally whine. "Her father won't be expecting a virgin, not after five years." He kicked Tijah in the curve of her back. She didn't cry out, although it had to hurt. "For what you done to poor Maaz over there." He produced a knife and bent down to slit her tunic up the front.

Darius and I stepped into the torchlight. The man looked over at us. His first expression was surprise, followed quickly by a sort of relaxed contempt. They were still three against two, and I'm sure I didn't seem very threatening. A short boy barely old enough to shave.

His eyes flicked down at my pinned sleeve. He smiled. A boy with only one hand, to boot.

Then Darius slammed the mercenary into the back wall with air. The knife clattered to the floor. Before he could recover, I darted over and picked it up. The beast inside me howled as I slid it between his ribs at the precise angle to pierce his heart. The next thing I did was I cut Tijah's bonds. She was on her feet in an instant, and the other two died not long after that.

"Myrri," she whispered. "How?"

"Fire. It was an accident."

A sound broke from her, raw and animal. "An accident? What the hell does that mean? *How?*" Her face was so battered and swollen, the words came out like she was speaking through a mouthful of mush.

So I told her exactly what had happened in the tunnels. Tijah was silent for a long minute. Then she went to one of the bodies and started kicking it. Darius and I exchanged a look but neither of us had the heart to stop her.

"The Prophet?" she asked, when a semblance of calm returned.

"Taken. By a necromancer named Balthazar. One of those we met on the plain."

"*What?* We have to catch them." Tijah retrieved her scimitar and sheathed it savagely. "Why didn't you tell me this right away? She can't die for nothing."

"They're gone," Darius said wearily. "It's over."

She stared at each of us in turn. "You didn't follow?"

"It was you or them," I said. "And we chose you."

A tear slid down her cheek. She brushed it away, wincing at the bruises. "I should have been there. Fuckshit! The gods must hate us all. What of Saman? Did he betray us too?"

"Saman is dead," I said. "If he did, it was under torture and I do not blame him."

"What do we do now?"

Darius just shook his head. I had never seen him so downcast. I knew he didn't regret choosing Tijah, not after what would have happened to her. But with Victor gone, all his hopes of saving his mother were bound up with delivering Zarathustra to Persepolae before Alexander razed the city. We had failed. At every turn, Neblis had outwitted us.

"We could follow them to Bactria," I said.

"And do what when we get there?" he asked. Not angrily. It was a real question.

I didn't respond. I had no idea. "We'll decide once we're out of the city," I said at last. "It should be easy to pass through the gates. The whole population is fleeing the fire. We'll be three in thousands."

Tijah spared a moment to spit on the bodies of the mercenaries. Tears flowed freely down her cheeks now, but I don't think she even noticed. We found the horses and began making our way toward the wall, which lay perhaps a quarter of a league distant. The flow of people grew thicker as we approached. It loomed like a black cliff in the night, blotting out the moon and casting the nearby streets into deep shadow. Then we turned a corner and Darius reined up. I saw him stiffen, felt his sudden wariness. For just ahead, a rag-tag group was hurrying for the gate. I counted seventeen children and four amahs, their arms covered from wrist to elbow with gold cuffs.

My first thought was relief that the daēva barracks had been safely evacuated before the flames consumed it. Those innocent children had never left my mind. But one of them must have run a bit too far ahead. I heard a sharp cry and the child fell to the ground, twisting as though tormented by invisible lashes. The others watched with resigned expressions.

"Leave off, Mina," one of the amahs said crossly. "Punish him later. We haven't the time now."

"I told the brat to stay close," the one named Mina replied in a petulant tone. "He is willful and disobedient." She turned on the child, who hunched down, arms crossed over his thin chest. He wore a faded blue tunic two sizes too big. A shock of dark hair flopped over shadowed eyes that reminded me of Darius when we first met. "I should have left you for the flames," she said coldly. "You're far more trouble than you're worth. Get back in line. If you lose your place again, I will flay you alive."

The boy scurried to the back of the group. The others seemed afraid to even look at him. No one passing by paid the least bit of attention.

Over the low rooftops, I could see the upper arch of the nearest city gate. As I'd hoped, it was thrown wide open to permit the panicked populace to flee. Five minutes and we would be through. We might even manage to catch Balthazar on the road. As revolting as this scene was, it was none of my business, I reminded myself. We *had* to get the Prophet back. That was all that mattered now.

Yet I somehow knew we wouldn't. The necromancer was long gone, and so was our last chance to avert a slaughter. Queen Neblis had won yet again. Persepolae would burn as surely as Karnopolis. Victor was dead. Nothing we had done made any difference in the end.

But I could still make a small difference myself. Right now.

Mina had a long, thick braid that she kept tucked over one shoulder. Without thinking very hard about it, I reached for air, my own breath quickening with the effort. An instant later, Mina's head jerked back as an unseen hand gave her braid a savage yank. She spun around, cheeks reddening.

"Who did that?" she demanded. The other amahs turned back, looking at her strangely.

"Someone pulled my hair," Mina insisted. "With the power."

"You're imagining things."

"Don't you dare, Jamileh. I know what just happened. One of these little beasts attacked me!"

The power churned in my chest. Each time I used it now, it came more willingly, like a feral cat I had courted with scraps. But it also came hand-in-hand with a wanton destructiveness I couldn't control. Didn't particularly *want* to control. I'd always had a temper, always been reckless, but this was different. Something in me was awakening. Something that had hibernated deep inside for the last nineteen years.

Once, I had killed for my sister. But I didn't even need that excuse anymore.

Looking at Mina and the other amahs, I could feel the negatory power building in me, the way the air thickens before a thunderstorm. Heavy and charged. They had not yet seen us beneath the awning of a shuttered knife-sharpener's shop, although we were less than twenty paces away.

"What are you doing, Nazafareen?" Darius growled softly. "I despise these women more than anyone, but it's madness to provoke them now."

I didn't reply. He shook his head, sensing my mood. His hand dropped to his sword hilt.

"Did *she* do that?" Tijah asked, jerking a thumb at me.

"Yes," I said.

"Oh, nomad girl." She sounded almost like the old Tijah. "You're even crazier than I am."

Mina's eye fell on a girl of eleven or twelve. "Anuhita!" she snapped.

"I'm holding *mine*," one of the other amahs, a short, buxom woman, drawled in a broad western accent. "It wasn't Anu." She turned to the other nursemaids. "Did either of you let your leashes slip?"

They huffed in outrage at the suggestion. "This is all ridiculous," one muttered.

"Is it?" Mina's black eyes scoured the children. "One of you knows what happened. Out with it!"

Before she could mete out any more undeserved punishments, I pressed my knees to the horse's flanks and urged it forward until I was ten paces away. "Leave them be," I said.

Mina glanced at me in surprise, her thin, arched brows lifted. I doubt whether anyone but a magus had ever dared to address her so on the street. "Mind your business, boy," she said. "You have no idea what you're playing at."

One of the amahs coughed as the wind gusted black smoke down the street. "Enough of this," she said to Mina. "We must go!"

Mina nodded, already dismissing me. "They'll get a proper beating once we reach the temple at Chigaru. Every last one of them. I swear on the Holy Father, this group is the worst I've ever fostered."

I felt lightheaded. *Wrathful.* Mina hadn't a clue, but the daēva children were starting to catch on. They'd been staring at the ground, but now heads turned, eyes widened. They sensed the flood of power lapping at our feet.

"You're unfit to wear the cuffs," I said to the amahs. "Take them off."

Darius emitted a gentle sigh behind me. He would not have chosen this fight, but he wouldn't turn away from it. I still wasn't entirely sure why I'd stopped. Darius was right. It was madness to provoke them. The City Watch couldn't be far off, and each one of these women was bonded to four or five daēvas. Children, yes, but still more than capable of tearing us apart.

And yet part of me whispered that we were meant to cross paths. That if I did nothing, I would forever regret it.

Mina's eyes bulged. I'd finally gotten her attention. She addressed one of the older children, a thin girl with a twisted spine. Her voice was too low to make out, but the paving stones began to jitter with a grinding sound that seemed torn from deep in the earth. A passing family, arms loaded with their meager belongings, screamed and made a run for the gate. The horses whinnied in fear. Tijah's mount reared up on its hind legs, nearly throwing her from the saddle.

"More!" Mina commanded. "Teach them a lesson." The ground shook harder. A jagged crack snaked down the middle of the street. Bone snapped as the sympathetic magic extracted its price from the girl's own body. She cried out in pain, and still the crack widened. Mina's mouth curved in a tight smile. Not only didn't she care that the child was killing herself, she seemed to actually enjoy it.

I clung desperately to my horse's back, trying to bring her under control, as Darius leapt his own mount across the crevice dividing us from the daēvas and their keepers. Mina saw how gracefully he moved, the glint of gold at his wrist. Sudden understanding struck her and she seized one of the littlest children, holding him against her breast not to protect him, but to use him as a shield.

The short amah wisely picked up her skirts and ran. Two

others stood their ground, a raw-boned pair that could have been sisters. One shoved a younger child forward. "Kill them!"

My heart stuttered in my chest. Oh, how it hurt! Like a small fist was in there, squeezing. Blood poured from the child's nose in a scarlet torrent. She had long, tangled black hair. I knew her. We'd seen her at the tomb, Darius and I, watching the starlings. The fury in me built to a white-hot pitch. I didn't want to fight these children. I only wanted their amahs. But the women were clever. All three hid behind their charges, using the cuffs to force the children to attack us. Some had balked. They were now screaming in pain.

Darius dismounted, eyes fixed on Mina, and was thrown back with air. I wasn't even sure which kid had done it. Tijah kept glancing over her shoulder, pain and confusion etched across her face. She was looking for Myrri, I realized. It was the first time in her life she had ever fought alone.

The girl with black hair stared at me, lips pinched in concentration. I held enough of the power that I could clearly see the vein at her temple throbbing as she tried to manipulate the blood pumping through my heart, just as I had done to the Immortal soldier in the village of Karon Komai. My heart strained to keep its rhythm, became sluggish and heavy as the drums of a funeral procession. If she had not been so young, I would have been dead already.

This girl had never practiced on a human before and she fumbled a bit at first. But she was strong and determined and I could feel a terrible pressure building in my chest.

I couldn't use my sword on her. Not on a child. So I focused my attention on her forearm instead. Let the destructive red magic in me come forth.

I knew there was a place in the cuff that held a piece of the daēva and also a piece of the human. Not a physical piece, but spirit. This was the place where the bond lived. And suddenly I could sense it—an infinitesimally small cage constructed from all three workable elements—earth, air and water. But something else bound them together, and that thing was fire.

The cuff was a talisman, I saw that now. And I thought I might be able to break it. But only if I used fire myself.

The smoke billowing into the street grew thicker, stinging my eyes. Darius looked up at me from where he lay pinned in the dirt. Fear flooded our own bond. He somehow understood what I was about to do, and he knew that I wouldn't do it without his permission. If I was wrong, we would both die.

Flashes from my dreams came to me, his body blackened and my own screams as I saw what I had done. Were they a foretelling of this moment, or just my refusal to accept what I truly was?

I looked into his eyes and saw he was afraid of *me* and it broke my heart a bit. But then Darius nodded once, decisively. The Prophet's words came back to me, and I shivered as the negatory magic inside me reached for the flames consuming the city.

Fire begets fire, in mind and deed. The Alchemist must be wary of the price, lest it lead him to evil.

Before I could change my mind, before the fury could sweep me away in a blood-dimmed tide, I let it go, an arrow aimed straight at the cuff. There was intense heat but no pain, like the split second after you know you've burned yourself badly but before you feel the damage. Darius screamed.

Earth.

Air.

Water.

Fire.

Bonded, burned and broken.

Broken.

The girl with black hair still stood there, with the amahs and other children behind her. But she had the oddest expression on her face. Like she was puzzling over a complicated problem. One of the nursemaids moaned. The girl held her wrist up and examined it, then looked down between her bare feet. Metal glinted in the dirt. It was the cuff, and it was shattered into three pieces.

The street fell silent. A wave of dizziness swept over me. For a moment, I stood on the deck of a ship as it tossed in a storm. Darius laid a steadying arm on my arm. The terrible heat was gone. It had dissipated the moment the magic left my body. For I had not used fire alone. To borrow a fancy phrase from the Prophet, I had wielded it *in conjunction* with the other three elements. And that had saved us.

Seconds later the black-haired girl was running away, thin legs pinioning up and down. Her back was straight and whole. She did not look back, not once.

"You must do the rest," Darius said quietly.

I'm not sure if the amahs heard him, or if what had just happened finally penetrated their cruel little minds, but the pair who looked like sisters ran too. They had ten daēva children between them. Mina tried to follow, but Tijah darted forward and grabbed her arm, twisting it behind her back. The woman was white with shock and did not try to resist.

"What have you done?" she mumbled. "*What have you done?*"

I felt I should stop the ones who fled, but they had already turned the corner and vanished from sight. A terrible weakness descended on me. Perhaps it was the price of the magic, or simple exhaustion, but I don't think I could have defended myself against any of the remaining six children if Mina ordered them to attack.

"You're not dead," I whispered to Darius.

"Nor are you," he replied with a grin.

I needed to be angry again, but I couldn't manage it looking at his handsome face, so I turned to Mina instead. She was already recovering from having the black-haired girl severed from her grasp. She was wary of me, yes, and also of Darius. But that would not last long. I thought that within a few moments, she would strike at us using the children again, and this time, they would kill us.

So I pictured Balthazar as he tried to take my daēva from me, and the mercenaries from Al Miraj beating Tijah, and it did the trick. The anger leapt forth, and with it the power of breaking. It was easier this time. Six sets of cuffs fell to the dirt, shattered and empty of their prisoners. The children didn't run, but huddled together, looking to the last of their number, a much older boy only a few years shy of my own age.

He was remarkably calm, considering that impossible things had just occurred. A shock of brown hair fell across his eyes and he pushed it back. I could see from the way he stood that he favored one leg just as Tommas had. It made my heart ache strangely.

"Don't kill her, if you please," he said, meaning Mina. "I've known her since I was two."

"Be quiet, Achaemenes," Mina hissed. "Don't say another word."

The boy turned to her. "You don't tell me what to do anymore." He drew a deep breath. Mina squeaked as her heels lifted off the ground, hair whipping around her face in a whirl-wind. "You don't tell any of us what to do."

"Please," she sobbed. "Please, Achaemenes..."

He stared at her, pity and contempt writ across his face. "You are not a good woman," he said at last. Abruptly, the wind ceased. Mina landed on the ground in a crouch. Her braid had come undone and she had the look of a cornered animal.

"Druj!" she snarled. "All of you. The Holy Father will flay your souls for all eternity." Her laughter was a crazed, brittle thing. "The time of last things is at hand!"

Before any of us could respond, Mina picked up her skirts and ran even faster than the others had. Tijah took a step as though she might go after her, but then her shoulders sagged and she muttered something under her breath. Her fingers flexed, forming signs. I could see she didn't even know she'd done this.

"The fire is coming," one of the children sobbed. "Please, Achaemenes. Can't you feel it? I'm frightened."

Achaemenes nodded gravely and swept the girl into his arms. "I won't let it get you, Anu, I promise." He turned to us with a level gaze. "I don't know who you are, but I would appreciate your help in getting these children through the gate."

Darius hurried forward and lifted the smallest boy onto his shoulders. Tijah ran to the horses, which had wandered only a short distance away, and within a minute the remaining four children had been helped into the saddles. Their ages ranged from six to twelve or thirteen, with Achaemenes nearly of an age to be sent to the Immortals.

Speaking of whom...

"I see the scarlet and blue," warned Darius, whose eyesight had always been better than mine. "Only a few streets away. Come!" He seized the bridle of his own mount and began jogging for the city wall. Tijah and I did the same, while Achaemenes kept pace, his limp hardly slowing him down at all.

We saw no sign of the amahs as we joined the throngs of people hurrying to the gates. They were unguarded and flung wide open. I heard crying and shouting and the frantic howling of dogs. People had dropped all sorts of things in their headlong dash through the wall, clothing and household goods mostly, but I also saw a few strange items, like a wooden foot with perfectly carved toes.

We didn't have the Prophet, but we had saved six children from slavery. And we were still alive.

I had worked fire, and *we were still alive*.

Dawn lightened the sky to the east as we made our way to the Royal Road, just another group of exhausted refugees trudging towards Persepolae.

❧ 24 ❧

BALTHAZAR

althazar stopped only once on his way to the lifeless pond in the woods—the place that was not really a pond but a gate. He stopped because he wanted to savor the vision of the mighty city of Karnopolis burning to its foundations. A thousand rumors were flying about how the inferno had started. Some said Alexander's soldiers had attacked the palace. Others that the magi had loosed holy fire on the Numerators in revenge for their persecution and the blaze had gotten out of control, racing through the temple district and then the surrounding slums like a plague sent by the Holy Father himself. That He had been angered in some way was the one thing everyone agreed on.

Balthazar smiled to himself. No one would ever guess the truth. Personally, he was not sorry to see his birthplace reduced to ashes. It was corrupt and debauched and as worthy of divine retribution as any place he could think of. But as he watched the columns of smoke rise above the city, turning the sun to a dull orange ball in the sky, he found himself recalling the boy from the brothel and hoping he'd managed to escape with the gold Balthazar had given him.

"When you're done admiring the view, you can take this off. I promise not to cause any trouble."

Balthazar turned to the Prophet, who sat before him in the saddle. The old man's long, dirty hair lifted in the breeze. He looked like one of those crazy sages who went naked and ate only on the second Tuesday of each month. One hand rested lightly on the iron collar around his neck. Balthazar had never seen someone accept their slavery with such calm.

"I would like it if you removed this talismanic device from my person," Zarathustra repeated, when the necromancer failed to respond. "I already wear one of my own. I assure you it is not necessary. And it is giving me indigestion."

"We'll see." Balthazar surveyed him warily. It was the first time the Prophet had spoken since they'd galloped through the gate. He seemed little more than skin and bones and Balthazar thought the horse would easily manage to carry them both to Bactria if he could cajole it to enter the gate. It was a shame he'd been forced to leave his own mount, but there had been no time to retrieve it from the stables.

"Are you looking for pursuers?"

"Be quiet, old man," Balthazar said, steering the horse off the verge and into the woods.

Yes, he had expected the Water Dogs to come after him. They could not follow him into the Dominion, so he wasn't especially worried, but he could see no sign of them on the road behind, and the horse stood on a rise that commanded a view of several leagues in every direction. He thought perhaps they had sustained more severe injuries than he'd imagined.

It did not even occur to Balthazar that they had gone after the mercenaries instead. He understood love, and passion, but kindness was beyond him.

Still, he found the female Water Dog deeply unsettling. She'd wielded a type of power Balthazar had never encountered before. Although he could not sense elemental magic, he knew its effects, knew what it could do. When she had thrown his own necro-mancy back in his face, it was beyond shocking. She had simply erased his spell like a wave washing across sand. The pain of the backlash was nothing he cared to experience again.

How close he had been to taking the cuff! He should have just killed the girl quickly with a knife. Instead, he had chosen to show off, and look what it had gotten him. He did not relish informing Neblis that he had failed to bring the son as well as the father, but he thought she would be interested to know about the girl.

And Zarathustra...he was turning out to be a surprise as well. Despite his frail appearance, the old man was recovering quickly. His eyes were no longer watery and vague, although he had aged from the draining. Balthazar knew he was part daēva from Araxa. It amused him to no end that the empire's most potent religious symbol was himself Druj.

They entered the woods and made their way to the clearing. As soon as the water appeared through the trees, all birdsong ceased. It was black, that water, and glassy as obsidian. In the pocket of his robes, Balthazar's fist closed around the shell, its sharp edges digging into his palm.

"What is this place?" Zarathustra asked.

"A border," Balthazar replied shortly.

"To where?"

"I don't suppose there's any harm in telling you, since you'll find out soon enough. This, old man, is a gate." He deliberately refused to use his name or title, but the Prophet didn't seem to take offense. "A gate to the Dominion."

Zarathustra nodded thoughtfully. "The in-between place."

"You know it?" Balthazar's brows lifted.

"I have heard of it, yes."

"And what have you heard?"

"That it is a dangerous place. That the dead walk there."

Balthazar laughed. "The dead walk here too, old man, if you

hadn't noticed. Yes, it is dangerous. But only for those who travel without protection." He produced the oddly twisted shell Neblis had given him. "This will assure us safe passage through the shadowlands."

"To where?"

"Bactria."

The Prophet sucked his mossy teeth. "So your mistress dwells there still? I was born in Bactria, you know. My family was forced to flee when Neblis's Druj hordes descended. We were among the fortunate few to escape with our lives. It was winter, and many died in the crossing of the Char Khala, although at least they died cleanly, sheltered in the hand of the Father. The fate of those left behind was far worse."

"A pity. But war is never a pleasant thing, is it?" Balthazar had not been aware of that, although it scarcely mattered. The first he'd seen of Bactria after escaping his prison cell, it had already been an empty ruin. "Well, I can assure you *Queen* Neblis eagerly awaits your arrival. You would do well to remember the honorific when you see her. She doesn't take well to discourtesy, and in fact has been known to tear out the tongues of supplicants who use them unwisely."

Balthazar expected a surge of fear through the chains at this comment, but the Prophet's mind remained as serene and unruffled as the surface of the pond. He must be mad after all. Few went to Queen Neblis willingly. Even fewer managed not to gibber the entire way.

Balthazar spoke some words in a guttural language. The talisman warmed in his palm. Was that a glimpse of pale flesh rising from the depths? Did he feel eyes upon him, ancient and avid? Balthazar could not be sure, and frankly, did not wish to know. He dug his knees into the horse's flanks, but it refused to enter. In the end, he was forced to dismount and drag it in by the bridle. The Prophet clung to the stallion's mane as the dark water inched up his bony legs. The old man's back was straight, his heart steady and strong. Balthazar felt a touch of admiration. He was certainly no coward.

The necromancer took a last look at the dappled sunlight streaming through stands of ash and beech. He'd lied. The talisman did not guarantee them safe passage. It allowed them *passage*, that's all. He was known as Neblis's envoy to most of the creatures that dwelt in the gloaming, and they generally left him alone, but others would kill him in a heartbeat if they found him. He did not tell the Prophet this because frightening the old man would just make him difficult, and Balthazar had enough to worry about already.

He shivered as the substance that was not water closed over his head. That first moment of crossing the veil in the flesh always chilled him to the marrow. The world dimmed to shades of green and grey. The horse's eyes rolled wildly in its head as it took a quivering step forward. Balthazar spoke quietly to the beast, urging it down the slope to the plateau beyond. He felt a sense of aching loss, but pushed it away and took his bearings. It was easy to lose one's way here. Landmarks vanished, or simply drifted off to other places. Balthazar had spent years plotting maps and carefully recording his own observations, but there were still vast unexplored territories that remained a blank to him. He knew that at the center of the Dominion lay an inner sea, where the dead were summoned for passage to the next plane. All rivers flowed to the shores of the sea eventually, for it was the lowest point in the shadowlands.

"The chain is no longer yoking us together," the Prophet observed as they reached the bottom of the slope and struck out across the plain. "Nor is this damping my power." He held up his own gold cuff. "Yet I cannot sense the nexus."

"Talismans do not work in the Dominion," Balthazar replied. "Nor does elemental magic."

"But you used one to enter the gate."

"Yes, they will open and close the doors, but that is all."

"What manner of creatures live here?"

Balthazar gave Zarathustra a sharp look. "Besides the dead, you mean? Nothing you want to meet, old man." He barked a humorless laugh. "I avoid the natives as much as possible. The Moon Lands, of course, have been sealed for hundreds of years now, save for the one gate where the dead pass through."

"The Moon Lands?"

"Where the daēvas come from. But I suppose you would not know of it." He silently cursed himself for talking too much. "Hold your tongue until we reach the House-Behind-the-Veil. Queen Neblis will decide which questions she wishes to answer."

They rode in silence for a while. Balthazar's impression of being in an underwater realm began to fade, the murk overhead giving way to a grey-streaked sky. The Dominion was different near to gates. Distorted, like a hybrid of the two worlds it joined. Within a few leagues, he could make out the icy spires of mountains in the distance, their granite slopes luminous in the twilight. As always, the light source was indeterminate. No stars or moon shone overhead to light his way, and yet he could see well enough. This was why some called it the gloaming.

Balthazar made for the edge of the vast forest that stretched between them and his Queen's keep. Their path grew much darker among the trees. Evergreen boughs wove a canopy that blocked out the sky, so dense nothing grew beneath. It was an easy ride, cushioned by a carpet of dry needles, but Balthazar kept his wits sharp. Complacency in the Dominion could kill you faster than a striking adder. The quiet stretched out, and he gave a start when the Prophet spoke.

"Where are we going?" Zarathustra demanded. "If this is truly the land of the dead, I suppose I will face the judgment of the Holy Father." He looked around. "It is not as I imagined it would be."

"You are still alive, old man," Balthazar replied impatiently. "I already told you, we are going to see my mistress."

"Does she have any ink?"

The necromancer's white teeth flashed in the gloom. "I do not think so."

"That's a shame." The Prophet looked up, confusion in his eyes. "I'm sorry, have I asked you these things before?"

"Some of them."

"My memory is not what it used to be." His expression crumpled a bit. "I committed a great wrong, and the Holy Father punished me for it." A shaking hand touched the chains. "I think he punishes me still."

"Well, Queen Neblis offers an opportunity to redeem yourself," Balthazar said smoothly. "We have the holy fire. If you would tell my mistress how to use it, I am sure she can find you some ink."

The Prophet blinked. "The holy fire? Do you mean the fourth element?"

"Whatever you call it, it is the magic used to forge the daēva cuffs."

"Xeros took it from me," Zarathustra said bitterly. "He had no right."

"You were a fool to let him know you had it in the first place," Balthazar said, his tone mild. "Those who lack power will always seek to take it from others."

"Spoken by a man who knows this first-hand."

Balthazar grinned and guided the horse to a small stream. "As a matter of fact, yes," he said, dismounting and offering the Prophet his hand. Zarathustra slid awkwardly from the saddle, tangling his legs in the chain binding them together so that Balthazar had to lift him like a child and set him on his feet. Ignoring them both, the horse gave the water a dubious sniff, then began to drink.

"We must rest for a few minutes. I have a bit of bread and wine." Balthazar began rooting through the saddlebags as the Prophet sat down on a nearby boulder. "Oh dear," he muttered, pulling out a figurine of a squat woman with large breasts and six arms. "A pagan goddess. The Water Dog from Al Miraj had no love for the Holy Father, it seems."

"She is free to be a heretic if she chooses."

"How magnanimous of you." Balthazar drew deeply on a wineskin. "Religion is essentially the same as magic. It only works if you believe in it." He had said it to bait the old man, but Zarathustra merely rested his chin on his hand and looked at him with interest.

"And what do *you* believe?"

"Oh, many things. I believe Queen Neblis will win this war. I believe that if she does, the Dominion will fall eventually, and the Moon Lands too." Balthazar tweaked his white tunic in disgust. "I believe I have come to despise these robes, and cannot wait to change back into my normal attire. Playing at being a magus was less fun than I expected it to be."

"But you were one once, were you not?"

The necromancer's eyes narrowed. "How do you know? Do you remember me?"

Zarathustra smiled. "A lucky guess."

"I was eighteen when they toppled you, still a novice. They claimed you were dead." He raised the wineskin in a toast. "To old times!" Balthazar drank. A cheap vintage, but it warmed his belly. He had not intended to speak so much. Something about the old man drew him out. "Would you like to hear a story? It's not a long one, but you might find it informative, as the one who invented the means of exploiting the daēvas."

"Certainly," Zarathustra said, and the necromancer did not need the chains to read the guilt in his eyes.

"Ah, yes. I know you have great regret for what you did all those years ago." Balthazar offered him the wineskin. When the Prophet declined, he shrugged and took another drink. "But without your intervention, Queen Neblis would have met with little resistance. She has you to thank for that defeat. I do not say it to frighten you, since you will be shortly in her hands, but merely to point out that you too meddled with things better left alone. No matter how holy you pretend to be, old man, at heart you are just like me. Did I mention I have the spark? Well, of course, one must to use a talisman. But I digress." Balthazar crossed his arms and leaned back against the trunk of a spruce. Zarathustra was forced to shift forward or be dragged, but he said nothing, only waited with an expectant air.

"One day when I was quite young, I had gone down to the river to bathe with my sister. There was a young man there, in a travel-stained tunic and no shoes. His hair was a bird's nest, but his face was friendly and I was not afraid of him. We got to talking, and he asked if I wanted to see a trick."

"A wild daēva," Zarathustra said.

"Apparently so. We didn't often see them in the cities. I don't know what this one was doing in Karnopolis. I think perhaps he was just curious about us. Anyway, being a small boy, I naturally said yes. And then he did the most extraordinary thing." Balthazar offered the horse a handful of oats he found in one of the saddlebags. The animal nuzzled his hand gratefully. "He made it snow, just over the river, and he made the snowflakes spin in a great wheel. I'd never seen snow before. It seemed a miracle. I asked him if he could teach me to do it, and he laughed and said he had special powers that humans would never have, so I might as well just put it out of my mind. I hated him for that. Apple?"

The Prophet shook his head, and Balthazar took a hearty bite, crunching the fruit between pointy white teeth. "I resolved to prove him wrong, and I have done so," he said. "Magic is merely the impossible made possible." He lifted the wrist binding them together. "I use these chains not because I like them, but because that is the magic available to me. I would wield elemental if I could, but I settle for necromancy." He studied Zarathustra's wasted face. "Magic does not come to you. You must go out and find it. There is magic in everything, old man. *Everything*. The trick is making it do what you want it to do."

"Perhaps. It does find some people, but very few," the Prophet said quietly. He touched the iron collar. "Will you not reconsider removing—"

"No."

"But—"

A howl rent the air. It came from a good distance away, but Balthazar leapt to his feet, dragging the Prophet with him. Moments later, a second howl came, and then a third. The Shepherds hunted in packs, and they must have caught the scent of the horse. The shadows beneath the trees seemed to thicken at the terrible sound.

"What was that?" Zarathustra squinted into the trees. "Are there...animals here?"

"There are sentient creatures," Balthazar corrected, quickly rebuckling the saddlebags. "Some are quite vicious and they hate the living." He let his voice grow harsh. "Without my protection, you would have not a beggar's chance of seeing the sun again. So do as I say, and try not to panic. They are drawn to fear like flies to offal."

"The Holy Father will protect me," Zarathustra said, although his hands trembled as he traced the sign of the flame.

"I certainly hope He does, but I have never seen Him around these parts," Balthazar replied, hoisting Zarathustra onto the saddle and mounting himself. They galloped into the gloom. The howling rose in intensity, then stopped abruptly. The silence that followed was worse since Balthazar could not judge how close the creatures were. He had stumbled across the remains of another Antimagi once, after the Shepherds had caught up with him. Balthazar thought he would rather slit his own throat than suffer the same fate.

The horse needed no urging to run as fast as it could. It seemed to sense what closed in on them. Balthazar silently cursed himself for stopping. He had grown overconfident, knowing the talisman protected him from the things that lingered near the gates. But they were not the real danger in the Dominion.

The minutes passed with no change in the quality of the light. He found it easy to lose track of time since there was no sun to rise or set, nor moon and stars to crawl across the heavens. The glimpses of sky they caught through the trees showed a blank grey slate. The horse was nearly blown, sides heaving and foam streaking its muzzle, when Balthazar chanced to look over his shoulder.

Five dark shapes sped through the woods, red tongues lolling. Their flanks shone a glossy black that merged with the deep shadows beneath the trees. Powerful hindquarters bunched and lengthened, closing the distance with appalling speed. They did not make a sound. Balthazar's spit dried in his mouth.

He dug his heels into the horse's ribs and leaned forward to stroke its neck. Its head drooped. "Run," he whispered. "*Run.*"

They reached an uphill slope and the horse struggled through dense underbrush. Balthazar could hear the Shepherds' panting now, rhythmic and rushing like a great bellows. Behind him, Zarathustra prayed to his Holy Father for deliverance. Balthazar reached for his knife. He would kill them both, if it came to it. That was all the mercy the old fool could hope for.

They crested the hill and Balthazar saw the valley and the lake that sheltered the House-Behind-the Veil. As a gate, it existed in both worlds at the same time, although in the Dominion, its color was slate grey rather than blue, and instead of the rugged Char Khala mountains, a dense forest marched to the horizon. The horse lunged down the slope and splashed into the shallows just as the lead hound sprung for the kill. A tingling wave washed through Balthazar's body. They had passed the first set of wards. The Shepherds did howl then, in enraged unison, an earsplitting rumble that echoed across the valley. He wheeled the stumbling horse around and faced them where they crouched in a line along the shore. Five sets of yellow eyes met his.

"Go on, pups," he said with a shaky laugh. "Go dig up a bone. You won't have fresh meat today."

The largest hound lifted its muzzle and howled at the sky. Then they turned as one and vanished into the trees.

"We are here," he said to the Prophet, steering the horse toward the center of the lake. "Keep your head, old man. Be respectful and answer all questions truthfully. It will go hard on you if you do not. But if you make yourself useful, you may yet find a place at Queen Neblis's feet."

"Do you think she has any ink?" Zarathustra asked, and Balthazar gave him a sharp look. The Prophet's eyes were again watery and unfocused, his mouth slack. Was it all an act? If so, Neblis would see through it, and his defiance would be punished. But that was not Balthazar's problem anymore.

The water had reached his waist when two Antimagi emerged from the lake to greet him. They had felt his arrival when the ward triggered.

"Balthazar!" cried the first, a tall, cadaverously thin man with a shock of yellow hair and permanent frown. "It is good to see you returned to us. Much has happened in your absence."

"Molon." Balthazar inclined his head in greeting as the second antimagus reined up. "Demetrios."

"Is that him?" Demetrios asked, unable to conceal his curiosity.

"The so-called Prophet? Yes, that is him, although his mind is shattered by two centuries of solitude." Balthazar spurred his horse deeper into the lake. "I can find my own way. Where is she?"

"In council with Farrumohr," Molon said. "She summoned him not an hour ago."

Neblis treated Farrumohr as a servant, although sometimes Balthazar wondered if the opposite was not true. She seemed to spend more and more time with the demon of late. Balthazar feared his influence over her was growing.

"Balthazar!" Molon called from behind him. "You should know—"

The necromancer waved a hand, unable to wait another moment to see his Queen, and the rest of Molon's words were lost as the cold not-water closed over his head. As they passed through the second set of wards and the talismanic magic of the chains awoke again, the old man's emotions poured into Balthazar's mind. Mainly fear, intense and animal. It mirrored his own.

NAZAFAREEN

"This is where the necromancer left the road." We all reined up as Darius pointed to a faint track in the grass that led off in an easterly direction toward a dense stand of woods.

"How far are they now?" I asked. "Can we catch them if we push hard?"

Behind me, Tijah waited with Achaemenes and the children. She held the littlest boy, six-year-old Abid, on her hip. Although he was too old to be carted around like that, Abid did not complain, and Tijah rested her cheek against his dark curls. I think the kids were the only thing keeping her together. Yes, she still had me and Darius, but it wasn't the same as the friend she had known nearly from birth, who had shared every fleeting emotion and fought steadfastly at her side. She looked smaller without Myrri, diminished in some fundamental way, and I had no idea how to make her whole again.

"They're gone," Darius said, shading his eyes with his good hand as though it would help him see past the trees. He grunted in frustration and let the hand fall by his side.

"Cloaked from your sight?"

"No, I mean *gone*. Vanished utterly, as if they never existed. We could follow that trail into the woods, and it would lead us on for another few leagues, and then it would simply...end. Do you want to go anyway? Have a look?"

I bit my lip, feeling uncharacteristically hesitant. "What do you think?"

"I think it's a waste of time. The necromancer has some other way to travel. You saw what he did to us back there. We don't know a fraction of what he's capable of." He paused, tired blue eyes boring into me, and I knew what he was about to say. "Besides which, although I would do anything to save the Prophet from her clutches, we don't need him anymore. You can break the cuffs yourself, Nazafareen."

I nodded, feeling a little ill. "So we ride for Persepolae?"

"I don't see any other choice."

"What if we don't make it in time?"

His face hardened. "We have to try."

Of course, Darius was right. I knew I could break the cuffs now. *Why* I seemed to have this ability was another matter. Maybe my bad temper had twisted the magic of the nexus, made it dark and destructive. In the end, maybe the power you wielded was simply a reflection of who you were as a person, and I was savage and violent.

What would the daēvas do when I unchained them? Five thousand, all at once? Would I be averting bloodshed, or unleashing it?

"It has to be done," Darius said, sensing my thoughts.

"I know. I guess I just wish it could be someone else who does it."

I touched the cuff that used to hold Victor. It was just a piece of jewelry now, although I couldn't bring myself to take it off, just as Tijah still wore Myrri's cuff. Could Victor be alive somewhere? And what of Lysandros? I wished they would appear with the holy fire and save me from making a decision, but that seemed unlikely.

It had been days since I'd thought of my own family, but at that moment, I wondered if I would ever see them again. My brother Kian, who would be married with children by now. My mother, whose sharp tongue I'd inherited, along with her fondness for figs and healthy sense of outrage. One of her favorite sayings was, *Men who use their power for evil have too much of it in the first place.* There was a second part that is too rude to repeat, but suffice to say the women who heard it would laugh uproariously while the men suddenly found urgent business elsewhere.

I missed her very much then. And my father too, who didn't speak much but did love all of us in his own stoic way. The lands of the Four-Legs Clan were close to the Char Khala mountains marking the border with Bactria, and I feared that even if they escaped the wrath of the Numerators, an even worse foe awaited them in the north.

Would the free daēvas help us fight Neblis? Put an end to her once and for all? Or would they run as far and fast as they could, like the girl I'd saved from that horrid woman, Mina? Without their help, we would be children throwing pebbles at Bobak.

And of course, there was a third possibility: that the daēva Immortals would kill us all.

Well, as Darius said, it had to be done, and there was no one to do it but me. So I swallowed my fears and we pushed on through the rest of that day, sleeping on the side of the road and parceling out the little food we had among nine people. All the daēva children except Achaemenes flinched every time they looked at me. I tried not to feel hurt, but if I imagined they would view me as a savior, I was sorely mistaken. Instead, they seemed to think I was some kind of freak.

"They're just confused," Achaemenes told me as he used a whetstone to sharpen one of Tijah's many daggers. Darius had forced her to give it up so Achaemenes would have a weapon.

She'd complied without a word, but the way she tossed it down in the dirt made her opinion on the matter crystal clear. She didn't like him, although I had no idea why.

I heard her voice in the darkness, singing softly to the smaller children who huddled together in blankets under the trees where we'd set up a makeshift camp. The tune sounded vaguely familiar, low and haunting. I thought it might be one of the songs Tommas used to sing to Myrri, but I couldn't be sure. It's terrible how quickly we forget the things that really matter.

"They were born to the cuff," Achaemenes went on. "It's a shock to have it taken away like that. They'll need time to adjust. To accept the truth."

"And you?" I asked.

He rubbed his leg, an unconscious gesture. "I'm very grateful."

"That's not what I meant. The Way of the Flame. The Druj curse. It's all a load of horseshit. I hope you know that."

Achaemenes's lips quirked in a faint smile. "Yes, I know."

"Well, that's good. You must tell the others. Make sure they know too."

He gazed at me calmly. "You and Darius are going to leave us tomorrow, aren't you?"

I looked away. "What makes you say that?"

"I heard you talking." He smiled. "Daēvas don't miss much. I know you want to reach Persepolae before Alexander and we're slowing you down."

"All right. I won't lie to you. Yes, Darius and I must go on ahead. We only just decided, Achaemenes. I would have told you."

"And what of the children?" He sheathed the knife. "I've known each of them since they were babes. They are brothers and sisters to me, and I cannot desert them. But if we encounter trouble on the road..."

"I'll ask Tijah to stay with you." I said. "She's suffered a terrible loss. I only ask you to understand if she seems...volatile. But I can promise she will defend them with her life." I looked at him defiantly. "Tijah has more honor than any human I've ever known, man or woman."

Achaemenes only nodded. "We will follow you to Persepolae. Will Alexander help us?"

I nodded. "He believes the daēvas should be freed."

"And yet he would burn the city if you fail to release the daēva Immortals."

I couldn't deny it. "Yes. He will do what he must to overthrow Artaxeros II."

Achemenes regarded me silently for a moment. I had a sense of being judged, although for what I couldn't say.

"And what of your own cuff?" he asked finally. "You haven't broken it."

"That's different," I said, feeling almost guilty. Darius had not asked me to, and I hadn't brought it up either. "We choose the bond."

Achaemenes nodded and I wasn't sure if he believed that, but he let the subject drop. I wanted to say *I'm not like Mina*, but I didn't know him well enough.

"Let's go talk to Tijah," I said.

SHE DIDN'T OBJECT TO STAYING BEHIND—IN FACT, SHE'D clearly expected it—and we said our goodbyes the next morning just as the sky began to lighten in the east. The daēva children were sleeping all tangled together as Darius and I repacked the saddlebags. We left Tijah most of the food and Myrri's horse, which still carried her belongings.

Tijah wept a little as she went through them and I was glad to see it, because she'd been dry-eyed and silent for the last day. I knew all too well that it did no good to bolt the door against one's grief. It would simply lurk on the threshold and if you didn't come out, it would kick the door down and things would go much harder for you.

"Would it be alright?" I said, clearing my throat. "If there's something you don't care too much about..."

"Take this." Tijah handed me a comb with turquoise and pearl inlays. "If your cat fur ever grows out again, you can use it."

"It's much too nice," I protested. "You should keep it."

Tijah shrugged. "The most important things she left me are in here." She patted her heart. "The rest doesn't matter."

"Then thank you. It's beautiful." I carefully stowed it in my bag, lowering my face so she wouldn't see the mist in my eyes.

"If you ride hard, you can be in Persepolae tomorrow," she said as Achaemenes prowled out of the trees. Like a cat's paws, his footfalls didn't make a sound, despite the drifts of dead autumn leaves blanketing the grass. I noticed that while he limped, it was different from Tommas's rolling gait. More a kind of painful stiffness in one knee.

"I don't mean to offend you," I said carefully. "But didn't your infirmity heal when I broke the cuff?"

Achaemenes grimaced. "Yes, it did. My leg is whole. I just...It feels so strange. I suppose I will walk differently in time, but my mind has not yet accepted the change, if that makes any sense."

"Perfect sense," I told him with a smile, knowing we had reached that bittersweet moment when it was time to say goodbye and anything else would simply be awkward.

The night was still around us. Even the insects dozed, and the first birds had not yet begun to greet the dawn.

"We'll see you in a few days," Darius said, sweeping Tijah into a one-armed hug. Then it was my turn, and we clung to each other a little longer than we meant to, but I suppose we both needed it.

"Fare well," Achaemenes said, raising a hand as we mounted our horses.

"And you," Darius said.

We wheeled onto the Royal Road, which led almost due north through low foothills. The number of travelers was sparse at this hour. I suspected most of the residents fleeing Karnopolis had found refuge with friends and family in the nearby farms and villages. With any luck, the fire had been contained by the canals that criss-crossed the city. I thought of Bobak and Ester and Dav and the other boys at Marduk's Spear and hoped with all my heart that they had been spared. Arshad Nabu-zar-adan...not so much. Follower of the Prophet or not, he was still a sleazy flesh trader and deserved whatever fate befell him.

A low mist lay on the road, making it seem as though we raced through a cloudbank. I let my mind drift, idly tracing the complex pattern of air and water that made up the mist. Within an hour or so, it had burned off completely, and the day grew warm. We passed fields of barley, green and gold in the sun, and mudbrick homesteads with thatched roofs. Once, we saw a courier in the livery of the King. He passed us at a dead gallop, heading in the direction of Karnopolis.

"What do you think his message is?" Darius said with a worried expression.

We had stopped to let our own horses rest for a bit. Unlike the couriers, we didn't have remounts waiting along the road, and it would do no one any good to kill the poor animals before we reached Persepolae—a sentiment I'm sure the horses agreed with.

"I don't know. Do you think Alexander's reached the city already?"

Darius muttered an oath that would have made Bobak's hair curl, if he'd had any. "Damn him for moving early! We had a bargain and he broke it. If there was a way to free the Immortals without helping his cause, I'd take it this instant."

"Agreed. But there isn't, so we can't."

His mouth quirked. "No need to gild the truth, Nazafareen. You can speak plainly."

"If it's any consolation, there's a decent chance the Immortals might turn on him too. I say we break the cuffs and run away as fast as we can. Let them sort it out among themselves."

"A sound plan. After we find my mother, of course."

We'd been bantering a bit, but the smile left my face at this. "We *will* find her, Darius, I promise you."

He brushed my cheek with his fingertips. "Thank you, my love," he said quietly, and I flushed to the roots of my cat fur.

The courier's message became clear later that afternoon. We began seeing refugees, but not from Karnopolis. These came from the east. They looked tired and frightened.

"What's happened?" Darius called to the bearded father of a family of six as they passed.

The man spit in the dust. "Druj. They came in the night, burning and killing. Those who weren't put to the torch were taken by the necromancers."

My stomach tightened. "What of the Water Dogs? Weren't they sent to help?"

The man laughed bitterly. "All dead. If we hadn't lived on a farm outside the village, we would be too. But we saw the smoke and ran." He jerked his head toward the Great Salt Plain. "It's the same in every village we passed. The demon queen is no longer quiet." He made the sign of the flame. "Persepolae is the only safe place now."

I shared a look with Darius. The older children held the hands of the younger ones, while the mother clutched a quiet bundle wrapped in rags that might have been an infant. They all had hollow eyes and pinched faces. Neither of us had the heart to tell their father that Persepolae was no longer safe either. Where else could they go? The hope of protection was the only thing they had.

I dismounted and handed the man the rest of our food. He thanked me profusely and I turned away, embarrassed and wishing I could do more.

"You have great kindness in you, Nazafareen," Darius said softly as I stepped into the stirrup. "As well as the other."

We both knew what the *other* was.

"Thank you," I said, oddly touched. "It's only food. Anyone would do the same."

"No," he said. "Not anyone."

My horse gave me a complaining look as I urged her forward, but she was young and strong and I think she secretly didn't mind a bit of wind in her mane. She snorted, hooves kicking up a cloud of dust. With heavy hearts, we closed the distance towards the field of battle.

❧ 26 ❧

BALTHAZAR

He found his Queen in the gardens, by the well. She was leaning over the rim, whispering into its inky depths, and his heart tripped over itself at the sight of her.

Gone was the silver hair and narrow, sharp-edged face she had worn in the gloaming. This Neblis looked older, riper, with full hips and soft, round arms. An ornate gold crown sat atop fiery red curls that made a strange contrast to her black eyes. She knew how to alter her appearance and even Balthazar was no longer sure what she really looked like, although he always knew it was her inside. Something in the way she held herself with fluid, feline grace. Neblis smiled when she saw him and beckoned him closer.

"My prince regent has arrived," she said to the thing in the well. "And he brings me a treat." Her eye fell on the Prophet, glittering coldly. "Your timing is exquisite, Balthazar. I have sorely lacked for your counsel."

The necromancer fell to one knee, dragging the Prophet with him. Despite her flattering words, he wondered if she listened to anyone besides Farrumohr anymore.

"My Queen," he said, bowing his head. "I am afraid I do not have Victor's son."

"It is of no importance," Neblis said, and Balthazar looked up in surprise. "If he is half his father, it would take more than a single Antimagus to bring him to heel. It was foolish of me to ask you."

Balthazar ignored the slight, although she seemed sincere. Why did she not care anymore?

"I had the cuff in my hands, but his bonded used some kind of fey magic against me," Balthazar said. "I have never felt its like, my Queen."

Balthazar sensed the thing in the well stir. Heard a sound like teeth breaking on stone. Neblis turned and peered down. "On your feet," she said absently. Balthazar complied, but the Prophet remained kneeling, seemingly staring at nothing. "Farrumohr would like to hear more about this girl. Pray continue, Balthazar."

He cleared his throat. Standing, he could see partway into the well. Darker than any night, the black had a fathomless density to it. He thought he saw a single red eye.

"I had turned the power of the chains against her, as you commanded. She was dying. There could be no doubt of it. And suddenly it was as though I met a wall." He struggled to explain the intensely discomfiting sensation that had been inflicted on him. "My power simply...well, it vanished, my lady."

Neblis frowned, her smooth forehead creasing in three lines. "Vanished?"

"There is no other word for it. I took Zarathustra and ran before they recovered and tried to stop me."

"Negatory magic," Neblis said, and it was the Prophet she looked at. For an instant, her mask slipped and Balthazar saw another face beneath it. Ancient and cruel and inhuman. Before he could blink, the image faded. "Am I right, old fool?"

Zarathustra finally seemed to notice her. He climbed painfully to his feet. "Who are you?"

Neblis laughed and closed the distance to him in three strides. He reared back as she bent down, but she only patted his head, like a dog. "You and I shall get to know one another. I cannot tell you how odd it is to be here with you. Truly, I imagined you had made the passage to the inner sea and moved to the next plane. How wicked they were to treat you so." She studied his face. "Perhaps you know something of negatory magic too?"

"Never heard of it," the Prophet replied calmly. "I am a simple man. And it is never too late to choose the correct path. Good thoughts, good—"

Neblis delivered a ringing slap across his cheek. "Do not utter those words in my presence. You used my own kind against me, and for that you shall pay dearly."

The Prophet coughed. "I forgive you your ignorance, daughter."

"I don't want your forgiveness," Neblis snapped. "I want your screams. And when my brother comes, I will finish what I started. *All* your lands will belong to the dead."

Balthazar's hackles rose as he detected that half-heard sound from the well again, overlapping voices whispering just out of earshot.

"Farrumohr says the girl is a Breaker," Neblis declared. "I have heard of them, but never found one before. It is a good thing you did not follow my instructions, Balthazar, for this one may be worth more alive than dead."

"What are Breakers?"

Neblis grinned. "Why, just what it sounds like. They break things, magical things." She slipped her arm into his. "Come! I have not shown you our new guests. They only just arrived yesterday." She stroked his wrist, wrinkling her nose at the thick cuff and chain. "Do take that thing off now. Molon will see to him."

Balthazar shed the cuff and led the Prophet through the gardens to the House-Behind-The-Veil. Viewed from the corner of the eye, it appeared to be a grand manor in the Doric style, constructed of white marble with a procession of square columns and a tile roof. But the towers that thrust up at random intervals corkscrewed like the horns of some strange beast, and the lines of the structure tended to trick the eyes if you stared at it too long. Sometimes it seemed to be receding into the distance. Other times, the stairways appeared to ascend in impossible directions, or no direction at all. Altogether the house made Balthazar feel like an ant contemplating a mountain, barely able to comprehend a small part, let alone the whole.

So he kept his attention on Neblis as they passed into the spacious yet austere entrance chamber and Molon appeared to take possession of the Prophet.

"Make him pliable," Neblis ordered. "He is far too forward. Clearly, his former jailers spoiled him. He needs a reminder that he is no longer the pet of the magi in Karnopolis."

Molon smiled. Unlike Balthazar, he was a man who derived twisted pleasure from inflicting pain on the helpless. Balthazar thought of how light the Prophet had been in his arms, like a child.

"He's just skin and bones," Balthazar found himself saying. "We don't want to kill him before we learn his secrets. A dark cell is punishment enough."

He thought Neblis would rebuke him, but she just nodded thoughtfully. "Balthazar is right. We wouldn't want an unfortunate *accident*. Lock him up for now." She turned to Balthazar. "You will see to him later. I want you to take charge of his questioning."

The old man looked at Balthazar beseechingly as he was led away. Balthazar buried his face in a flagon of wine that a mute servant pressed into his hand.

"They had him down in the labyrinth," he said. "We barely made it out alive."

Neblis raised an eyebrow.

"The Numerators set the tunnels on fire," he explained. "They wanted the old man dead, and I thought it would be a useful method of forcing his rescuers straight into my hands. It worked well enough, but the blaze spread much faster than I had anticipated."

"How fortuitous you were there," Neblis said, taking a dainty sip from her own cup. "Of course, I used to wish him dead myself, so I *can* sympathize. What happened to the Water Dogs?"

"One—a daēva—succumbed to the flames. Hired mercenaries from Al Miraj took care of another. I left Darius on the river-bank, along with his bonded." He hesitated. "The Breaker. They did not try to follow."

Balthazar handed off his wine to another scantily-clad servant —Or was it the same one? They all looked alike to him—in exchange for a hot cloth that he used to wipe his neck and jaw, now rough with two days of dark stubble. Passing through the lake always left him with the faint sensation that he had a residue of something foul on his skin, although he could neither see nor smell it.

"Darius's mother is in Persepolae," Neblis said thoughtfully. "Alexander's forces will be there within a day or two."

"Let him raze it to the ground, if he can," Balthazar said as they went deeper into the House, passing rich tapestries and ornaments of gold and silver, haphazardly strewn around other-wise empty rooms. Neblis was a magpie in her fondness for shiny objects. She did not wear jewelry herself, other than the crown, but whatever she conquered, she looted, down to the smallest brass button. Her treasury was a dragon's lair. "Both sides will be weakened, no matter the outcome," Balthazar continued. "Let our enemies destroy each other, my Queen, and we will crush what-ever is left."

"Perhaps. I have sent most of the other Antimagi across the mountains to lead the scouring of the east. They are not strong enough to hold it for long, but that is not their purpose."

"You wish to draw the victor into a trap?" Balthazar guessed.

"Alexander will win at Persepolae," Neblis said serenely. "That is what Farrumohr says, and he has never been wrong. The boy will have no choice but to deal with the Druj ravaging his new empire. So the Macydonians will cross the Char Khala, and when they do, they will get a surprise."

"Culach?"

Neblis seemed not to hear him. Her black eyes glittered like shards of obsidian. "I must have the Breaker. I must! Did you see Zarathustra's face when I mentioned negatory magic? He knows something. And it will be your task to discover what that is."

Balthazar felt pleased. In a strange way, he and the old man were kindred spirits. Seekers of knowledge. What secrets did Zarathustra hold? He looked forward to having someone intelligent to talk to. Molon was a thug and the rest were no better. He resolved not to become too attached though. Once the Prophet's usefulness was gone, he would die. That was certain. The thought pricked at what remained of Balthazar's conscience, but it left his head a moment later when they turned a corner and Neblis stopped dead. The necromancer was not often caught by surprise, but this he had not expected.

Victor was chained to a pillar in the middle of an airy chamber with high, vaulted ceilings. Blood darkened his tunic, but whatever injuries he had sustained seemed to have already healed—a daēva trick Balthazar envied. He was a bull of a man, taller even than Balthazar, and every muscle strained against his bonds, but it was not the manacles themselves that accounted for the desperate look in his black eyes. A brazier burned not four feet away, and sweat slicked Victor's brow as he tried not to look at the hissing flames.

"Look what I found in the lake!" Neblis crowed.

"So this is the guest you mentioned," Balthazar said, moving forward to examine the daēva more closely. He had seen him on the Great Salt Plain, just before the unnatural sandstorm hit. Unleashed, Victor had been rather terrifying. Balthazar had let the other Antimagi deal with him while he sought the holy fire, which had been carried by one of the Purified. When Balthazar had spurred his mount for Bactria, Victor had been striding across the battlefield like some sort of avenging demon, dead and dying Druj in his wake.

"He still wears the cuff of the Immortals," Balthazar observed.

"Yes. I didn't wish to risk his life by trying to use the fire to break it without the Prophet's guidance."

"How long has he been like this?"

"I don't know. Several hours, I suppose."

"Will he not die?"

"Not if he controls himself," Neblis said, a mother admonishing her unruly child. "Victor is old, as I am. With time, we become more practiced at avoiding the temptation to work fire." Her gaze swept across the brazier, but did not linger there. Even Neblis found the flames to be a bane. "He can stand it, as long as he does not try to reach for the power. Would you not agree that is prudent of me?"

Balthazar had a brief recollection of Victor tearing the ground asunder and hurling one of the Antimagi *and* his mount into the gaping hole, then sealing it shut against their screams. "Very prudent, my Queen."

"I think I will try to bond him myself once we learn the secret of forging," she said. "All that power at my disposal. Not that I lack my own, but I am curious about the bonding process. This emotional connection the humans speak of. I wonder if it would work between two daēvas?"

She stared hungrily at Victor and Balthazar felt a stab of jealousy. She never spoke of what had passed between them, but Balthazar suspected that Victor had spurned her somehow. Not that he would dare suggest such a thing.

"Who is he bonded to?" Balthazar asked.

"Nazafareen."

"The *Breaker*?"

"Apparently so."

"Now that I think on it, she did wear two cuffs," Balthazar said. "Will she not track him here?"

"I do not think so. He is behind the veil now." She idly patted Balthazar's cheek. "But I see you do not yet understand, my pet. Oh, come! Do not bristle at me. My *prince consort*, is that better?"

He knew this flattery was an act, and yet it still had an effect. What a hopeless fool he was. "Victor is not our only visitor. Come see." She took the necromancer by the hand and pulled him down a covered portico to an interior courtyard. A second daēva sat, head in hands, on the edge of a dry fountain. He had short black hair and wore the uniform of the Macydonian cavalry, an armored breastplate with a leather skirt over bare legs. Surrounding him were nine abbadax with scales and great leathery wings. They were even uglier than the Shepherds, but unlike the hounds, these served Neblis. And elemental magic had no effect on creatures of the Dominion.

"Lysandros," Neblis said. "One of the only old ones never to be leashed. He fights for Alexander now. He had some misguided idea he'd help Victor take the fire back."

The daēva glared at Neblis with purple eyes. "I have no love for Victor either," he said. "You know that. I come for our people. Their slavery has gone on long enough. Help me end it. You can have Bactria—"

"How generous of you to let me keep what is already mine," Neblis interrupted. "And they are not my people, Avas Danai. They are *yours*. You were bewitched to forget, but we are blood enemies."

Lysandros shook his head. Balthazar could not tell if his confusion was feigned or genuine. "Avas...Danai? Why do you call me that?"

"It is what you are, all of you," Neblis snarled.

"Whatever you think, I understand your feelings about Victor. When he wanted something, he never cared who he hurt to get it. The way he treated—"

Neblis's skin had gone white as snow, save for two spots of color high on her cheeks. "Enough!" she snapped. "I am not here to discuss Victor. I have a task for you. You will bring me the girl. The Breaker. And if you don't...well, I'll move the fire a bit nearer to Victor each day until she arrives. How long do you think he'll have?"

Lysandros shrugged. "And why would I care either way?"

"Because I know you. You wouldn't be here if your precious honor wasn't at stake."

Lysandros scowled at them. "Even with a swift horse, it will take weeks to return to Persepolae, and the same to return."

Neblis grinned. "Not the way you'll be traveling, little fish," she said.

❧ 27 ❧

NAZAFAREEN

The closer we came to Persepolae, the more refugees
flooded the Royal Road. Those willing to speak told
stories of necromancers and revenants descending on
their villages with only the frantic barking of the dogs for warning, of the men being separated from the women and children.
How the strongest were chosen for the chains and the rest were
slaughtered. The raids seemed to stretch from the Khusk Range
all the way to the southern edge of the Great Salt Plain. Tel
Khalujah had barred its gates, but they did not stop the liches.
The city was a graveyard.

My clan would hole up in the mountains, but they couldn't
survive there beyond the summer. I thought of my sister Ashraf,
her face hidden in her hood, long hair streaming in the wind as
the snow fell around us. *Druj*, my uncle had hissed...

I rubbed my eyes. They felt full of grit. Neither of us had slept
more than an hour and my legs ached from too long in the saddle.
Then we topped a rise and I saw the walls of Persepolae some
leagues distant. Darius muttered something too low to catch, but
the sentiment was easy to read.

There had to be twenty thousand men assembled on the open

plain below us. Besides Alexander's own Macydonians with their twenty-foot pikes bristling like the quills of a giant porcupine, I saw Greek infantry and other soldiers of fortune. Siege engines several stories high stood ready to be wheeled up to the walls, their metal sheathing gleaming in the sun.

Behind them were the dreaded catapults. At least a thousand mounted archers waited in orderly lines behind their spoon-like arms, awaiting Alexander's command. The soldiers who manned the catapults had torches ready to light the incendiary substance he planned to throw over the walls.

"Look." Darius pointed as the gates to the city slowly opened and a man rode out.

"Who is it?" I asked, squinting at the tiny figure.

"The soldier who brought you to my cell," Darius replied. "He was also one of the Immortals at Kayan's manor house. The second in command after Ilyas."

"Lieutenant Kamdin?"

"That's the one. Perhaps he will plead for mercy."

One of the Macedonians rode out to meet him. He wore the traditional uniform of breastplate, skirt and helmet with a stiff crest of horsehair. They conferred for a minute or two, and then Kamdin turned and galloped back into the city.

There was an oppressive weight to the air, as if all the world held its breath. I could see the Immortals on the walls in their scaled armor of red and blue. The Persian army inside was nothing to sneeze at. Besides large contingents of infantry and cavalry, King Artaxeros II had scythed chariots and war elephants. Most of all, he had the Immortals. I doubted he was entertaining notions of surrender.

"We must find Alexander," I said.

Darius nodded and we picked our way down the hillside. When a sentry challenged us, I showed him the cuffs and tried to explain who we were, but he spoke in one of the unintelligible barbarian tongues. By the time an officer was summoned, I had grown extremely antsy.

Although I'd never been in any sort of large battle before, I could hardly mistake the signs. This was not a camp, as we had found Alexander before on the shores of the Hellespont. This was a siege.

"You come from Karnopolis?" the officer asked in broken Avestan.

"Yes. Your king sent us there, on a matter of the utmost urgency. I must see him at once."

"Daēva?" He pointed at Darius.

"Yes," I said, trying hard to be patient. "We are expected."

Another runner was summoned and he must have found someone to verify our claims, for after many excruciating minutes, the officer gave us a hard look and waved us on without taking our swords.

I had no trouble spotting the young king's tent. It was the largest pavilion on the plain, although I wouldn't call it fancy. He planned his campaigns in the main part, while his personal apartment and armory took up the rest. Darius and I rode up to the suspicious glares of the special detachment of hypaspists who guarded Alexander's tent. They were his elite shield-carriers, and seemed to take their duties seriously for they instantly moved to block the entrance with dory spears.

"Is he inside?" I demanded, craning my neck to peer around their broad shoulders.

The hypaspists looked down at me with the flat disinterest of wolves regarding a yappy dog, and I had just opened my mouth to say something foolish when one of Alexander's small daēva contingent happened to pass by and recognized us.

"The King is with the Companions," she shouted. "Over on the right. You cannot miss them." At that moment we heard a great roar coming from the direction she indicated. "He is rousing them with a speech," said the daēva with a feral grin. She was free and so had no infirmity, moving with a feline grace that suited her wild hair and fierce eyes.

Somewhere in the distance, drums began to beat, an ominous sound like thunder ahead of a storm.

We waved our thanks and made for the outer edge of the army. The Companion Cavalry was divided into eight squadrons and each man carried a nine-foot lance but wore little armor. Alexander stood up in his stirrups, exhorting them to courage and immortal glory, et cetera, et cetera. I had heard he liked to make speeches before riding into battle, and this one seemed to have been going on for a long time.

"...remember, brothers, that already danger has often threatened you and you have looked it triumphantly in the face! The gods themselves, by arranging it so Artaxeros leaves the open ground and hides behind the walls of Persepolae, have taken up our cause." He swept an arm across the plain. Alexander had not yet donned his helmet, and red-gold hair curled around his pale face.

"We ourselves shall have room enough to deploy our infantry, while they, no match for us either in bodily strength or resolution, will find their superiority in numbers of no avail. Our enemies are Medes and Persians, men who for centuries have lived soft and luxurious lives! We of Macydon for generations past have been trained in the hard school of danger and war. Above all, we are free men, and they are slaves." His mismatched eyes—one brown, one blue—paused on each of his Companions as he rode down the line. "The famous Immortals must be forced to fight with the cuffs, and they are vulnerable to fire. It is their weakness as surely as my illustrious ancestor Achilles was laid low by an arrow to his heel! You are the liberators of the world. They are the oppressors." He squared his shoulders and looked quite pleased with himself.

"And what, finally, of the two men in supreme command? You have Alexander—they, Artaxeros!"

The greatest roar of all greeted these words, and I realized

KAT ROSS

Alexander's men fought not just for gold or glory, but because they really did love him.

"King of Kings!" I cried, falling to my face on the ground.

Alexander looked over and scowled in annoyance. I recalled that he did not demand the full prostration, but old habits die hard.

"Nazafareen!" He rode over as his second-in-command, General Hephaestion, ordered the Companions to form up. "Darius too, I see. You have returned, although I've had no word from Victor or Lysandros. What news of the Prophet? Is it true the city burns?"

"True," I agreed. "We did find the Prophet, although we've lost him again." I didn't mention it was the same necromancer who had bested us before. The truth was too embarrassing. "But I wish permission to address the Immortals."

Alexander's mouth tightened a fraction. "Why?"

"Don't you want to avert a bloodbath, if you can?" I snapped more harshly than I'd intended, adding: "O, King of Kings!"

Alexander was not much taller than me, but he suddenly seemed to loom. "I fail to see the point." He glanced at the gates, which had been shut tight again. "We just had a message from Artaxeros II. He has vowed to destroy my army to the last man. There can be no leniency now."

"If I may?" Darius said, shooting me a quelling look. "She might be able to persuade them. And if she cannot..." He leaned in and lowered his voice. "She can break the cuffs herself."

"Indeed?" Alexander looked suitably startled at this. "But how?"

"I don't know," Darius said. "But she is able to work with fire. The Prophet's writings mention this. I saw her break the cuffs of daēvas in Karnopolis."

The young king, who was now twenty-two years old, studied me for a moment. "How many did you free?" he asked.

"Six."

"*Six.*"

"But I'm sure I can free more. It's just a matter of amplifying the magic." I tried to sound confident, although I wasn't sure what I was planning would work.

"What do you intend to say?" Alexander demanded.

"I will try to convince them to lay down their swords in the name of the Prophet Zarathustra," I replied.

Alexander tilted his head. Then he laughed. *Laughed!* "Go ahead," he said. "Personally, I do not think they will listen to reason. And if you do free them and they decide to vent their rage on the city, I will not stop them. It may be the only way to avert larger destruction."

I took a deep breath, blew it out my nose. "Thank you," I said, palms erupting in sudden sweat. I made a nervous flapping gesture with my left hand. "Well...I suppose I'll go do that now."

Alexander signaled to Hephaestion that he should escort us to the front. Of course, the tall, youthful general was well known to all the Macydonian troops and they watched us go by with curious stares. Darius rode beside me, past the last line of infantry to the open plain. Alexander's phalanxes were practically indestructible, with five rows of spears jutting out from the front ranks. They were the anvil on which the hammer of the cavalry would smash the enemy.

It was dead quiet on the walls. The Immortals watched us come with stony faces.

I had spent the journey from Karnopolis running through this moment in my mind. The Immortals were all raised as slaves, indoctrinated as Darius had been. Their training began quite young, and they were supposed to be fanatically devoted to the King. In discipline and valor, they were unsurpassed. Would they turn so easily, even if I broke their bonds?

I reined up about thirty paces from the gate, thousands of eyes boring into me from every direction. Suddenly, this seemed like an incredibly stupid idea.

I cleared my throat. Darius gave me an encouraging smile. "My name is Nazafareen," I called out. "I was a Water Dog. I am here to tell you that I have just come from Karnopolis." This next part was tricky. They had no reason to believe a word I said, something I probably should have thought of before I came out here. "You have all heard of the Followers of the Prophet. The King and magi say they are heretics. But it is the magi who have lied to you! The Prophet Zarathustra lives and has been held prisoner at the Great Temple for the last two hundred years."

Most of the Immortals failed to greet this revelation with more than stony stares, although a few couldn't contain themselves. Like Alexander, they laughed.

"I have seen his prison cell with my own eyes. It is deep in the tunnels beneath the city." I paused here and decided it might be better to skip the part about the goats. "The Prophet was to be given to the Numerators." I looked around. "And where are they now? How odd, I don't see a single one. They must be cowering in the treasury, waiting for you to shed your blood so they can walk away unscathed."

"Go back to the barbarians!" someone shouted.

"Can you not see that you are brothers?" I yelled back. "Neblis is the true enemy, and after you are done killing each other, there will be none left to fight her. The daēvas are not Druj, surely that is evident! The Prophet was imprisoned because he opposed their slavery in the service of the empire." I glared at them, bubbles of anger rising in my chest. "When I joined the Water Dogs, I had never been outside the lands of my clan in the Khusk Range. I could not read or do sums over twenty. I knew *nothing*. And yet even I could see my daēva was no Druj, once we came to know each other. In your hearts, you know it too. The Prophet knew it. He was good friends with my own daēva's father, Victor. The daēvas never fought for Neblis! They despise her, and she them.

"I beg you: lay down your swords, brothers. King Alexander has pledged to spare all within its walls, and to save Persepolae from certain destruction. This is the dawn of a new day. Let us not greet it with a feast for the vultures."

All was quiet for an endless minute. Then I heard the twang of a bowstring and an arrow came arcing through the air. I watched, transfixed, as it buried itself in the dirt at my feet.

Shouts with the ring of command from Alexander's lines. Ten thousand spears clanking in unison. I couldn't understand what they were saying, but it wasn't hard to guess. *Idiots, all of them.*

"They're releasing the catapults," Darius said quietly. "Nice try though."

Flame streaked the sky as I raised my hands and the beast within opened one yellow eye.

❧ 28 ❧

NAZAFAREEN

Fiery debris from the catapults cleared the walls, provoking a great outcry within. But before the second assault could be released, the Immortals retaliated, causing the earth to roll in a wave toward Alexander's army. Impressively, the infantry in the van stood their ground. They were battle-hardened men who had fought daēvas before. Yet their courage did little good when that tremor struck, and it was terrible to hear the cries as the front lines were swallowed up by a wall of dirt and rocks.

Meanwhile, the gates to the city swung open, and Artaxeros's main force came riding out, flanked by the scythed chariots. From the looks of things, they outnumbered Alexander's army about two to one. Unlike the Macydonian king, who rode at the head of his Companions, Artaxeros himself was nowhere to be seen. The Immortals carried his banner, the roaring griffin in a circle. They looked fierce in their ranks of alternating scarlet and blue, and it was easy to see why they had been the most dreaded fighting force in the world before Alexander came along.

We stood between the two armies as they came together. On every side was fire and smoke and the screams of horses and wailing of trumpets. At the last moment, Darius threw up a shield of air. The wave of dirt and rocks rolled harmlessly by and although the wind whistled and moaned just inches away, it did not touch us.

My little speech—what a pointless exercise *that* had been!—had omitted the fact that I planned to break the cuffs because I feared for the daēvas if their masters had known the truth. Instead, I decided to simply surprise them.

The sheer stupidity and waste of it all made my blood boil, which is just what the magic wanted. This time I didn't try to tamp it down. In fact, I fanned the flames with thoughts of Mina and the magi and the way the Immortals had been raised, to hate themselves. And then I thought about Darius's amah, Taravat, and what she had done to him all those years ago, when he was a little boy.

The line of Immortals was nearly upon us when Darius seized my tunic in his fist.

"Now, Nazafareen! Free them!"

The anger in me coalesced, gained form and substance. A pinch of dust, a breath of air, a stream of moisture from the clouds above. Fire, from the torches that lit the catapults. All four elements, working in tandem, as they were meant to. The whole surpassing the parts and becoming something else.

But this time, I added something new—a hunting instinct that would cause it to seek out the next talisman, and the next, and the next, like wildfire racing through dry pines.

I chose an Immortal wearing the blue. How young he looked, only a year or two older than Achaemenes. Large and muscled, like all of them, with a blade of a nose and shoulder-length black hair. He shouted something and pointed to the catapults with his sword. I knew he meant to destroy them, and that he would die trying.

Before he noticed me, I loosed the magic at that tiny cage where the bond lived, as I had done with the children. The daēva was near enough that I could see his face quite clearly as the cuff snapped in half and fell to the ground. Shock, followed by perfect confusion. His bonded, a burly fellow with a long moustache, could not have looked more astonished if the Prophet himself had walked up and kissed him soundly on the lips.

Ripples ran through the ranks of the Immortals as the magic raced along, faster than thought, shattering their bonds. Twisted backs straightened, once-blind eyes blinked against the light. Many of the Immortals in red—the humans—instinctively stepped back from their daēvas. Not all did. And then it was done. Perhaps half a minute had passed, no longer.

Only one cuff remained. The one circling my own wrist.

I looked down, the lust of Breaking still hot in my veins, and how badly I wanted to shatter it! The magic hated talismans, all of them. *Unnatural constructs of the power.* I drew a shaking breath and then Darius's hand was on my arm, gently pulling me around to face him.

"No," he said.

A single word, spoken softly, but it pulled me back from the brink.

The chariots flanking the Immortals wheeled around in disarray. They didn't seem to grasp what was happening, only that the ranks were falling apart. At least Alexander was holding his catapults to see what came next.

Well, what came next was chaos. Brother against brother, daēva against daēva. Some of them, like the pair of Immortals who had helped us escape from the dungeons, seized their newfound freedom without hesitation. They banded together and turned their wrath against the gates, tearing them off and hurling them onto the plain. Others simply fled the battlefield, wanting no part of what was to come. And yet others remained loyal despite all the wrongs that had been done to them.

But to know who was fighting on what side? From where I sat on my horse, it looked a melee of epic proportions. Blue and red swirling together, swords clashing, and every now and then an eruption of dirt and yell of pain as someone used too much of the power. Seeing an advantage, Alexander's own troops surged forth. I caught a flash of his copper hair on the right, yelling and gesturing. I didn't know if he was rallying them to fight or urging restraint. Some of the daēva Immortals were effectively fighting for *him* now, as he had hoped, but it was far from all of them, and telling the difference was like understanding the workings of a kicked anthill.

"The palace," Darius cried. "We must find my mother before it's too late."

I nodded and we galloped for the gates. I saw some awful things on the way, which made me even angrier. A great deal of dust had been kicked up in the excitement and the surrounding battle flashed in and out like scenes from a nightmare. A poor horse, savagely gutted by one of the scythed chariots. Two Immortals fighting hand to hand, both wearing the red. One in the blue, lying on his back with no mark on his body but blood running freely from his nose.

Then we were through the gates and things quieted down some. Just past the barracks, I spotted the line of a dozen war elephants, abandoned by their keepers. Each wore thin plate armor and carried a large wooden *howdah* on its back to carry armed riders. Their intelligent eyes met mine, and I was very glad they had not been deployed on the plain.

"Hurry," Darius urged. "Once the King realizes the extent of his defeat...Well, just hurry, Nazafareen!"

He was too superstitious to say it, but I knew. Artaxeros II would rather kill Darius's mother than see her taken from him.

The fight was quickly spreading inside the city. Fires burned where Alexander's catapults had struck, but none had hit the palace itself. It stood as I remembered it, a monument to the wealth and power of the King's line. We rode past the huge statue of the Prophet, a daēva kneeling at his side. The first and last time I saw it, Numerators had watched us from the steps, with their red-hemmed robes and arrogant stares. Minutes later, Ilyas denounced Darius as a traitor. I thought of the dungeons beneath our feet and fought back a shudder.

As we approached the long set of stairs leading to the elevated platform of the palace complex, two soldiers came running at us, long lances in their hands. Darius took a huge breath and expelled it in a sharp burst. My own lungs seized up for a moment as though I had been punched in the chest. And then the men flew backwards like dolls, striking the base of the Prophet's statue and lying limp.

The horses' hooves rang out as we ascended the stairs and burst into the Hall of a Hundred Columns. The great room stretched into dimness. My memories of this place were not happy ones. They had held Darius's trial here, when he was sentenced to burn. Although the throne sat empty now, I could see the King there, his hooded eyes and jeweled crown, Delilah crouched at his feet.

"Where are his chambers?" I asked.

"Not a clue," Darius said.

We looked at each other.

"This is bad, Nazafareen."

"I know."

The mutiny of at least half the Immortals had thrown the entire royal household into disarray. Servants, soldiers, concubines, courtiers and cooks all ran to and fro, jostling each other in their eagerness to flee the city. I saw a few ashen-faced Numerators abandon dignity and hike their robes up, the better to sprint down the palace steps.

Darius leaned down from the saddle and grabbed the arm of a court physician wearing the silver raven of his profession. "The King! Have you seen him?"

The man shook his head, tearing himself free. "You shouldn't stay here. They'll kill us all," he mumbled, staggering away. From the sounds outside, the battle had engulfed the barracks and was nearing the palace.

If they decide to vent their rage on the city, I will not stop them.

And he wouldn't. Alexander was nothing if not a shrewd leader. He understood that if the daēvas were cheated of their revenge, they might turn it on *him*. And perhaps it was necessary. But it left us very little time to do what we had come here to do.

"Where are the King's apartments?" I shouted at an aproned woman whose hands were covered in flour. She stared at me like I'd spoken a foreign tongue, perhaps because I was filthy and riding a horse through Artaxeros II's marble audience chamber. "Where, curse you?"

She gestured vaguely at one of the exits. The scale of everything in the Hall of a Hundred Columns seemed made for a race of giants, with doorways more than twice the height of a tall man. This was convenient since we had no intention of dismounting, but it also saddened me to think of it being reduced to rubble. Nearly every inch bore exquisite bas-relief carvings of men and animals, most of them bringing gifts to the King. Inscriptions covered the walls in the flowing script I found so intriguing, even though I could not read it. There was an undeniable aura of power and awe in this room. I supposed that was the intention of its architects—to build something equal to the might of the empire.

Which, in the end, turned out to be more brittle than anyone suspected.

Darius dug his knees in and we galloped past the startled cook, into a corridor lined with gleaming lapis lazuli doorknobs. And so began a long search, through chambers small and large, spare and richly furnished. The sheer quantity of royal possessions was staggering. All the while, it grew quieter inside the palace, and louder outside.

"Maybe we'd better have a look at what's happening," I said as we trotted through the kitchens, their great ovens cold and empty.

Darrius nodded wearily. "What if they're gone?"

"The King wouldn't leave before he knew the outcome of the battle. He's far too proud. But I suppose he could be elsewhere in the city. Let's go see how things stand."

The kitchens were in an el-shaped wing at the rear of the palace, near the stables and gardens. We exited into a courtyard with a terraced wall that gave a view of the gates and main approach to the Hall of a Hundred Columns—the same we had ridden up.

Flames shot from the roof of the famous library, and the Hall of the Numerators. The treasury had been spared, but only for the purpose of being thoroughly looted. Men still fought in knots of red and blue, but I could see the defenders were few now. If the Immortals had not been divided, the Persian side might have withstood Alexander's assault. As it was, they hadn't a chance. The free daēvas were methodically destroying every structure they encountered, no matter the cost to themselves. My worst fears had been realized, and yet I had a hard time blaming them. I just hoped they spared the poor elephants.

"Nazafareen?"

His voice had a funny edge. I turned my head just as the statue of the Prophet began to crack. It was so tall—somewhere north of a hundred feet—that its headlong descent seemed to come in slow motion. Darius slapped my horse on the rump and it scrambled forward. Time stretched out the way it does when you take a running leap into deep water. A shadow fell across the courtyard as dust and shards of stone rained down on our heads. I threw myself from the saddle. My horse screamed. There was a terrible crash that made the entire platform tremble. I curled into a tight ball, knowing I was about to die, as a table-sized chunk of marble hurtled down from the sky.

My ears rang. I huddled in the dirt, pinned but miraculously not injured. Moments later, I saw Darius's feet and the stone on top of me was tossed aside as though it weighed nothing at all.

"Are you all right?" He looked frantic as he pulled me to my feet. Then Darius laughed. "Do you believe in the Holy Father now?"

"What?"

I looked at the thing he pointed at. The concave shelter that had saved my life. It was the Prophet's cupped palm.

"No," I said, although it *was* a bit eerie. "Still a heretic."

His head spun toward a section of the rubble near the kitchens. Without a word, Darius began to run. I looked around for the horses and saw they had managed to escape and were now galloping away from the fighting.

"Wait!" I cried.

He tore through the rubble and then I saw them, forty paces away. The King held Delilah's hand. His hair was white with plaster and blood stained his robes. He looked dazed, but his eyes cleared when he saw Darius.

"Don't come any closer," he shouted.

Just as Darius had a withered arm and Myrri lacked a tongue, Delilah had a milky eye that made her look like a witch, although it wasn't as scary as the black almond eyes of the wights. That dead eye fixed on us now. She wore the sheer gown of the harem and it looked utterly wrong on her, like putting Darius in a Numerator's robes. I couldn't tell what she was thinking as she regarded us. Her face was a perfect blank.

"You're the son," the King said to Darius.

"And you're a coward," Darius replied.

Artaxeros II, divine head of the largest empire the world had ever seen, dropped Delilah's hand and drew his sword. He had only been King for the last ten years, but he'd taken the throne in his prime and the bond had kept him that way. Thick hair and a short beard. Heavy shoulders. A handsome man, I suppose, although I found him repulsive. "I care enough for your mother that I would not make her kill you," he said. "So I will do it myself."

Darius narrowed his eyes. The King couldn't possibly be that stupid, could he? He didn't stand a chance against a daēva—one he didn't control with the bond—and he had to realize it, no matter how self-important and deluded he might be.

Artaxeros turned to Delilah, one hand raised as though to caress her cheek. She looked back at him and behind that mask of indifference lay a boundless contempt that she barely bothered to conceal anymore. Yes, the King loved her, I could see that. But it was a greedy, sick, desperate kind of love. The more he adored her, the more she detested him, and they both knew it.

That sword...it wasn't meant for Darius after all.

"I'm sorry, my darling," the King whispered. He seemed to age ten years, jowls sagging, as he drew the blade back. Darius lunged toward them, knowing he was too far away to stop it. I caught Delilah's eye, the good one. She raised her arm, the flimsy gown falling back to reveal the gold cuff around her wrist. Just the sight of it was enough to make the negatory magic shake itself awake. With a flick of my finger, I snapped the bond. An instant later, Delilah tore the sword from Artaxeros's hand and ran him through with it.

"Where is Victor?" she demanded, as the King lay dying. She did not even spare him a glance as she ran over to us. Blood bubbled on his lips. He sighed, eyes half-closed as if he were falling asleep.

"Gone to Bactria," Darius said carefully. "He hoped to free you with the fire."

Delilah's predatory gaze swung to me. The witchy caul was gone. "*What* are you?"

"My name is Nazafareen," I said, unsure quite how to answer.

The sounds of another sort of destruction—stone shattering, walls toppling, cries of glee—filtered through the rubble. The daēvas had only just begun. I wondered when they would throw the rest of the palace down on our heads. Delilah stood there, waiting for an answer. She looked even thinner than the last time I'd seen her. Arshad said she'd been flogged, although the wounds seemed to have healed.

"You might recall, I am Darius's bonded," I offered.

Her hand snatched at my tunic, lifting the sleeve. "You wear two cuffs."

"Yes, uh..." I glanced at Darius. "The other belongs to..."

"Victor," he finished.

Her mouth tightened. "I see. And how did that come to pass?"

So Darius gave her a very quick version of what had happened since she helped us to escape the dungeons. Delilah listened without expression. When Darius got to the part about my power, she cut him off.

"Why is he still enslaved?" Delilah said to me. "Break it, as you broke mine. My son is not your lapdog!"

"I—"

"That is not what I wish," Darius said quietly.

"Not what you *wish*?"

"No." I could feel his own anger simmering, although he managed to keep it inside. "We love each other and wish to stay bonded."

My heart lurched at the matter-of-fact way he spoke the words.

We love each other.

And we wish to stay bonded.

I couldn't imagine living if he had said otherwise. I badly wanted to kiss him, but thought his mother might use the sword on *me* if I did.

Behind us, the King emitted a death rattle. Delilah did look at him then. She surveyed his blood-soaked robes and fixed, staring eyes. Then she smiled. When she turned back to me, her face blazed with a kind of righteous scorn.

"If you truly loved Darius, you would release him from his infirmity," Delilah snapped. "Do you? Love my son?"

Holy Father, could we get any more awkward? My cheeks flamed as I turned to Darius. "Yes," I said simply. "Just say the words and I'll free you. When I asked you before and you refused...well, it wasn't within my power to grant. It is now." I tried not to fidget under his level gaze, and Delilah's icy glare. "It's fine either way. Really. I understand if you don't..."

He wove our hands together, his right, my left. "The arm isn't so bad, if you don't mind it," he said with a smile.

"I don't." I held up my stump and barked a laugh. "I mean, seriously."

His mother skewered me with a last venomous look. She was actually scarier now that both her eyes functioned normally. "And what of Victor's cuff? Don't try to tell me that he also chooses to be enslaved to a human."

"No," I said. "But our bond is broken. The cuff is...empty."

"What do you mean? Where is he?" She rounded on Darius. "You said he was in Bactria. Tell me the truth!"

"We don't know what happened. It was only two days ago. Nazafareen says the bond suddenly snapped." He reached for his mother, to comfort her, but she stepped back. "I'm sorry. He may still live. A necromancer we followed disappeared in the same way. I won't give up hope until I see his body with my own eyes."

"The fates could not be so cruel," she muttered. "To lose him now..." Distant screams made us all turn. Delilah's mouth firmed in a grim line. "We'll discuss this later. I will find Victor, and I will bring him home. Now I must show the others Artaxeros is dead." Delilah grabbed the King's ankle and dragged him toward the shattered platform. "Maybe it will make them stop."

"Good idea," I said, sliding Victor's cuff off and slipping it into my pocket.

Nothing.

"Your mother hates me," I said as soon as she was out of earshot.

Darius made a soothing noise. "Give her time."

"At least Victor likes me," I said, trying not to sulk. I *had* freed the woman. And did I get a word of thanks?

"I like you," Darius murmured, pulling me close. "Very much." He nuzzled my neck and I stifled a laugh.

"What if your mother comes back?"

"I don't care if she does."

"Are you sure you love a heretic?" I whispered.

He grinned. "Oh, I'll bet I can make you a believer again." His lips brushed my forehead. "Good thoughts." I tasted the salt of his mouth as he pressed it against mine. "Good words." And then Darius lifted me off my feet, and I felt the warmth of his breath against my heart. A kiss at the swell of my breast. A promise. "Good deeds..."

✣ 29 ✣

NAZAFAREEN

Alexander made camp on the plain that night, feasting his victory and making sacrifices to a variety of barbarian gods, but especially his beloved Zeus. The Macydonians had sustained few casualties. Of the Immortals, about a third remained with Alexander's army. Another third had fled, and the rest were dead. Alexander ordered them to be buried in the earth, which I thought disgusting, but I think he meant well.

When the fires beyond the wall had burned themselves out, Darius and I went to see the ruins of Persepolae. The display of Artaxeros II's body had done little to cool the passions of the mob. After they were done tossing bits and pieces of the Prophet's statue around, the daēvas had singled the palace out for special treatment and the only things left standing were a few dozen pillars. We walked among them and it was like a petrified forest, surreal and disquieting. Sand blew in little eddies across the stones. I wondered how long it would take before the desert swallowed it whole and no one remembered there had ever been a city here at all.

"They shouldn't have burned the library," Darius said with a scowl. "I don't care if they looted the Treasury, and I'm glad they pulled down the palace. But the scrolls were priceless. A stupid waste."

"War is a stupid waste," I said. "But we seem to like it enough to do it again and again." I wrinkled my nose. "You can still smell it. The same as the day Tommas died." I could see in his eyes he knew exactly what I meant. The slaughterhouse and ashes smell that lingers over every battlefield. "Oh well. I suppose it could have been worse. At least some of them stayed."

Darius was quiet for a moment. "Will Neblis kill the Prophet, do you think?"

Her name sent a strange chill through me. The daēva who knew how to raise the dead and make them fight for her. She had been a faceless enemy for most of my life and I wondered what she looked like. Why she had so much hate in her heart. It was not the slavery of the daēvas; that had happened in direct response to her invasion. They had been free before. Something else drove her.

"I don't know. She must have some use for him if she sent her necromancer to Karnopolis."

"That's what worries me." He bent down and fingered a bit of charred tapestry, then tossed it aside. "You fought him off, didn't you?"

I nodded. "I'm sorry I lied to you. It...unsettled me. Whatever this power is, it's a strange beast. It feeds on the darkest corners of the heart." I thought of how close I had come to breaking our own bond. "This is no gentle surrender, Darius. It's like something alive, with a will of its own."

We reached the head of the Prophet's statue. It had rolled to the side and lay balanced on one ear, staring blindly into the distance. The nose was gone and fine cracks webbed the mouth and cheeks, as though the daēvas had tried to shatter it and failed.

"I never imagined such a thing was possible," Darius said wonderingly. "It goes against all we know about elemental magic. If I'm not calm, I can't touch the power. That's just how the

Nexus works. To seize it in anger would be like trying to grasp a handful of mist. But adding fire to the mix clearly changes things, just as the Prophet hinted at."

We both regarded the head for a long moment, as though it might open its mouth and start talking.

"What do you think it means?" I asked. "Is it an evil thing, like necromancy?"

"That depends what you use it for."

The bodies might have been cleared away, but I could still feel the specter of death hovering over Persepolae. "I know I did the right thing in breaking the cuffs..."

"But you still feel guilty," Darius said. "None of this is your fault, Nazafareen. The die was cast two centuries ago, by Xeros the First."

"But why, Darius? Why do I have this thing inside me?"

He was quiet. Then he said, "I wonder if you were born with it, or if it chose you because...you have a suitable temperament?"

I tilted my head. "Now *that's* an interesting question. I—"

We both turned as a man galloped through the gate and made straight for us. It was Hephaestion, and his face looked grim.

"What is it?" Darius asked as he reined up.

"Lysandros. He's back."

We looked at each other. Sudden hope bloomed inside me. I touched the cuff in my pocket, but it remained cold and empty.

"What about Victor?" Darius said.

"You'd better hear it from Lysandros himself."

THIS TIME, THE GUARDS HELD THE FLAP OPEN FOR US AS WE entered Alexander's tent. He sat at a table in the rear, talking quietly with Lysandros. They made a striking pair, with Alexander's copper curls and Lysandros's dusky skin and violet eyes. Alexander briefly consulted with Hephaestion on some practical matters involving the vast amount of plunder he'd taken from the city, and payment of salaries to his soldiers. Then he dismissed everyone except for Lysandros, Darius and myself.

Lines of weariness creased the daēva's face. He studied Darius without expression for a moment, and I had the crazy thought that he had only offered to go to Bactria so he could be alone with Victor, whom he blamed for helping Xeros cuff the other daēvas. Victor had had no choice, but Lysandros still held a grudge, and perhaps he had every right to.

"Your father lives," he said.

Darius's shoulders relaxed a little. "I am glad to hear it. The bond was broken. We didn't know...So where is he?"

"Bactria. Neblis has sent me with a message."

"Sent you? Did you not escape?"

Lysandros shook his head, a trace of bitterness in his voice. "I wish I could claim I had. No, I am merely an errand boy, sent to deliver certain demands. If they are not met, Victor will die."

"I will go to Neblis," Darius said without hesitation.

Lysandros gave that sardonic half smile I remembered from the last time we met. "She doesn't want you. She wants *you*." And he pointed at me.

I was just opening my mouth to say he must be mistaken, even though I knew he could hardly mistake such a thing, when we heard raised voices outside the tent flap. It was Delilah, demanding to be let inside. Alexander waved her through.

"I heard you returned," she said curtly to Lysandros. "Where is my husband?"

Lysandros folded his arms. He seemed to look anywhere but at Delilah.

"Tell me!"

The daēva sighed. "Neblis is...keeping him subdued."

"A hostage?"

"Something like that."

"What does she want?"

"Ultimately? I'm not sure. But she suddenly developed a strong interest in that one." He jerked his head at me. "She says if the girl does not come to Bactria, Victor...well, you can imagine."

Delilah looked at me like I was somehow personally responsible for all of it.

"This is madness," she said. "What could Neblis possibly want with her?"

I didn't particularly like the way she said *her*, as if I was the most useless, insignificant thing one could imagine, but I bit my tongue. Delilah had had a hard time of it, and some of that was our fault.

"It is Nazafareen's choice," Alexander said. He had been quietly watching the exchange, but now he stood and pressed his palms on the table. "I will march as soon as the army has rested. Another day. We can be at the Char Khala in less than two weeks." He unrolled a map and weighted it down, pointing to the four neighboring satrapies of Tel Khalujah, Samashna, Tel Rasul and Tel Iskatra. "The east has already fallen. Artaxeros held the Immortals in the capital while Druj ravaged the countryside. The few Water Dogs deployed were apparently no match for them. We've received reports that large numbers of Druj continue to cross the mountains, revenants mostly, but also wights and liches. Those satrapies still standing *must* declare loyalty to me now, but it will be worth nothing if they are overrun."

Lysandros studied the map, then stabbed a finger down on a spot north of the Char Khala, where a river fed into a valley. "That is her stronghold. There is a lake. Her palace lies beneath the surface."

"We will bring the fight to Neblis then," Alexander said with an eager grin. He seemed much older than his years most of the time, but he loved battle the way a child loves sweets.

"At least you have a good number of daēva Immortals," Lysandros said. "They will help you liberate the east."

Alexander nodded, but then a cloud passed over his face. "She already has the fire, and now the Prophet himself." He turned to me. "She must think to use your power in some way. We shouldn't give her what she wants."

"What are you saying?" Delilah demanded.

"That as much as it grieves me, it is perhaps not a wise bargain to trade Victor for the lives of millions," Alexander replied.

"As much as it *grieves* you—" Delilah spat. She'd grown rail-thin in the dungeons, but there was nothing frail about her.

"Do you think I care so little for him?" Alexander interrupted. "Victor is a hero, and now a martyr. If we could ask him, what do you think he would say?"

"I don't want a martyr, I want my husband," Delilah said in a low voice, and I felt power gathering in her, the first time I had sensed such a thing in a daēva I wasn't bonded with. Lysandros knew it too and he looked at Delilah as if she'd gone mad.

"Don't," he growled, filling with the power himself.

"The very reason Neblis wants me will be her undoing," I said hastily, before they started dueling in Alexander's tent. "Whatever her intentions, her elemental magic won't work against me. We'll be fine." In my head, I heard Tijah's mirthless laugh. I had probably just brought ruination down on all of us.

Delilah didn't release the power, but she didn't use it either. Instead, she gave me a grudging nod.

"I have no fear of Neblis," she said contemptuously. "She has made a bad mistake in abusing Victor. Let us cut the head from this snake and be done with it."

Lysandros stared at her but said nothing. Out of all of us, he alone had any inkling of what waited for us in Bactria. From the look in his eyes, it was worse than she thought.

I almost changed my mind then—not that I hadn't fantasized for years about killing the demon queen. Those daydreams usually involved a big battle, in which chance would bring us together. She would throw her head back and cackle insanely. I would be wounded in a dozen places already, but would heroically raise my sword. Darius would spot us but be too far off to help. Neblis would use the power on me and—this next bit was fuzzy—somehow I would turn the tables and thrust my sword into her heart just as my daēva arrived to bear witness. When Neblis died, all the Druj would die too, and Darius would carry me off in his arms to some remote shepherd's hut where he would nurse me back to health.

Unfortunately, I had a feeling it wasn't going to be like that.

"She must know of your ability, although I can't see how," Alexander said to me. "You only freed the Immortals yesterday, and Lysandros left Bactria three days ago."

"I used it against the necromancer," I admitted. "He must have told her."

"I don't care how she knows," Delilah interrupted. "We must leave immediately."

Lysandros and Alexander exchanged a glance. "With all due respect, Neblis did not ask for you," Lysandros said. "Perhaps it is better if—"

"I have not laid eyes on Victor for ten years. Before that, we were held in separate wings at Gorgon-e Gaz. I saw him only when they wished us to breed." Her voice was perfectly emotionless. "You will not keep him from me now."

Lysandros gave a single resigned nod. No one said anything for a long moment.

"How many days to Bactria?" I asked. "If we bring remounts—"

"That won't be necessary," Lysandros said. "We'll be traveling another way."

I frowned. "By sea then?"

"Not by sea either."

Alexander did not look surprised. Clearly, they had been discussing this very thing when we had arrived.

"We will return the way I came," Lysandros said. "Through the shadowlands. Neblis calls it the Dominion."

I had never heard of such a place. "Where is this route?"

Lysandros had an object in his hand. He let his fingers fall open in a dusty shaft of sunlight streaming through one of the rectangular windows cut into the sides of the tent. My first impression was of a seashell, similar to the ones Tommas used to carve. But this was not made of wood. It glowed a subtle pink in the center, tapering to bone white at the edges.

"This is a talisman for Traveling," he said.

I leaned forward a bit. We all did. The magic in me twitched its tail and sniffed the air. It sensed something—something it wished to destroy. I took a breath and shoved it back down, locking it in a box the way I used to do with Darius. I was glad I had acquired the habit. Otherwise, our passage to Bactria would have been lying in pieces on the ground.

The talisman curled in on itself like a snail. I tried to follow its whirling lines to the center but my eye kept sliding away in the strangest fashion. From the blinks and frowns on my companions' faces, the same was happening to them. Then Lysandros abruptly closed his fingers and tucked it away again.

"It will give you a headache if you stare too long," he said.

"How is it used?" Delilah asked.

"I'll show you," Lysandros replied. "But be warned. Elemental magic does not work in the place we must pass through."

"How is that possible?" Darius asked.

"Because you cannot reach the Nexus. It's hidden." He paused. "I believe it is the land of the dead."

"Behind the veil," I whispered.

"Yes. And there are other things there. So arm yourselves with iron."

"Other things?" Darius asked.

"I didn't see them directly, but I sensed them. Watching me." He grinned, but it didn't touch his eyes. "Alexander had suggested he march his army through and surprise her, but I convinced him it might not be such a good idea. One traveler, or even four, might be tolerated. But many more...Well, we could end up like Jamadin."

I knew the story. Every child did. The ancient king who had led his army into the Great Salt Plain and simply vanished. He had been pursuing tribesmen from the south, cattle raiders. This was long before the empire had been stitched together by Xeros, in the distant era of independent city-states (which later became satrapies). Jamadin had six thousand soldiers. Not one was ever seen again, not even their bones.

Many years passed. And then a merchant caravan stumbled on something odd while camping for the night at one of the oases in the no man's land between the plain and the Sayhad Desert. At the edge of a small spring, a single spear jutted out of the sand. Its shaft was inscribed with the words:

And so the light banishes the darkness

The spear had a bronze butt stamped with Jamadin's sunburst.

✣ 30 ✣

NAZAFAREEN

I found Lysandros lying on a hillside overlooking Alexander's camp. The young King was doing his best to help the endless flood of refugees, and a second makeshift camp had sprung up near the river. Soldiers handed out soup and bread, along with blankets and whatever else the army could spare, which was not very much. Hundreds milled around there already, with more arriving every hour, all carrying tales of horror. They seemed too tired to walk any further. I imagine they expected to find safe haven behind the walls of Persepolae, and the shock of discovering that the summer capital had been sacked, their King dead at the hands of his own daēva and the barbarians in charge, was too much. I had seen people sit down in the dirt and simply refuse to get up.

It was clear to all of us that the war was not over. It had only just begun.

"The King is looking for you," I said. "It's almost time to leave."

Lysandros sprawled on a boulder, chin resting in his hand. His cap of short hair gleamed blue-black in the sunlight as he idly toyed with the shell talisman. I'd be lying if I said Lysandros didn't intimidate me. He was very old, even if he didn't look it, and therefore very strong in the power. I had no idea what he thought of me—a former Water Dog and the bonded of Victor and Darius. The only person he seemed to care for was Alexander. I still didn't understand why Lysandros had chosen to fight with him, but they'd obviously grown close.

He turned at my approach, studying me with those purple eyes. "Before I went to Macydon, I spent fifty years in Qin with Duke Xian and later his son, Duke Xiao," Lysandros said. "They were fascinated by my kind, and by magic in general. Duke Xiao had made a study of it and told me some interesting things. Only one in a thousand humans has the ability to wear the cuffs, and one in a thousand of those can do what you do. In Qin they call it *huŏ mofa*. Fire magic."

A tremor of excitement—and relief—ran through me. So I wasn't the only person in the world with this ability. "What else do they say about it?"

Lysandros shrugged. "Very little. It is so rare, you see." He plucked a wildflower and spun it between his fingers. "Wood and metal are held to be separate, so the scholars of Qin count five elements rather than four. But they agree that the price of huŏ mofa is paid not by the body, as it is with elemental magic, but by the mind." He tapped his forehead. "Rage, destructiveness, hatred."

I said nothing. I knew all this already. "Did Duke Xiao tell you why certain people have it? Where it comes from?"

Lysandros shook his head. "He knew only one practitioner of huŏ mofa and the man died young in a duel before his talent could be fully developed. But what you did yesterday..." Lysandros gave me a wolfish grin. "I wish you had been born two hundred years ago when my people were being enslaved, but I suppose late is better than never." His gaze fell upon the shell and the smile faded. "I say all this to warn you that it's quite likely your power will disappear once we enter the Dominion. I can vouch that elementary magic does not work there. That means your bond with Darius will break."

"Forever?" I asked in alarm.

"No. Just while you are in the Dominion. But there are more things than the dead in that place. I was lucky to get out."

"Did you actually see...the dead?" I immediately thought of my sister. I hoped she had found peace in the afterlife, even if I no longer knew what I believed that to be. The Way of the Flame said souls were weighed on Chinvat Bridge. Those found lacking tumbled into the abyss, while those who were pure of heart passed safely over the bridge to paradise. I was supposed to be a heretic now, but I found my dread of Judgment Day was perfectly intact. "Is it like Hell? Heaven?"

"Neither. More like what your priests call *hamistagan*. A place where souls wait to travel onward. And no, I did not see the dead. But I saw other things, or thought I did." Lysandros looked away. "I want you to understand what you're walking into. For *Victor*." He spoke the name like a curse.

"What other things?" I asked, more than a little uneasy.

"I'm not sure." He balled his fists in frustration, the first time I'd ever seen Lysandros lose his composure. "They never showed themselves. But I had the distinct sensation of being watched. And not in a friendly way."

"What does it look like there?"

"Much like this world, but without sun or moon."

I took a seat next to him and watched Alexander's soldiers breaking down their camp. They moved with a purpose and efficiency born of long years campaigning in the field. Tomorrow, the King would march on Bactria. Here and there, I saw the red and blue of the Immortals who had chosen to stay, but their numbers weren't as many as I'd hoped for. Many had simply fled, and who could blame them?

"When you were with Neblis..." I began, clearing my throat. "Do you know what she wants? How she plans to use me?"

He looked at me and I saw pity in his eyes. "I don't, Nazafareen. I would tell you if I did."

"I don't know anything about Neblis really," I confessed. "Except what the magi say. Is it true she's a daēva?"

"Yes. One of the eldest."

"How old is that?"

Lysandros thought for a moment and rubbed his forehead. "I...I don't know. I can't remember. Hundreds of years, I suppose. Perhaps more." He paused. "She called me something else. Avas Danai. I don't know what it means."

A wind swept across the plain, lifting his dark hair and making the dust swirl below us. I heard the distant shouts of men.

"Did you see the Prophet there? Or a necromancer named Balthazar?"

"I saw a necromancer, but she never spoke his name."

"Tall, with a crooked nose?"

"That's the one."

My bones ached as I remembered what he did to me. "Victor said she has powers the other daēvas don't. But where do they come from? How does she make the dead serve her? We've both seen the necromancers. They are human, and their only power derives from the chains. But who made the chains?"

"All very good questions, and ones I don't know the answers to."

"Why does she hate humans so much?"

He shrugged carelessly. "Our races have never been friends, Nazafareen."

"All right." I smiled. He was probably waiting for me to lose my temper and prove him right. "Can you at least tell me how she caught you?"

Lysandros snorted. "I stupidly trusted that Victor knew what he was doing. He'd been there once, shortly after Neblis first took Bactria. This was before the war, but tensions between your kind and mine were already simmering. Neblis offered the lands north of the mountains as a safe haven to all the daēvas. Victor refused. He did not approve of the manner in which she'd cleared the humans out. She took him prisoner."

"So were they...did she love him then?" I asked.

"She'd always loved him," Lysandros said, stretching lazily. "And she claimed he loved her back. Until Delilah came along. From the moment he laid eyes on Darius's mother, no other woman existed for him."

"She must have been upset about that. Neblis, I mean."

"You have no idea," Lysandros said wryly. "She refused to allow him to leave Bactria, but he tricked her and got away. She never forgave him that." Lysandros sat up so suddenly I nearly leapt out of my skin. "I'm sorry," he said with a laugh. It had a distinctly mocking quality. "I forget sometimes how slow humans are. I didn't mean to startle you."

"It's all right," I said, though my heart was still fluttering against my ribs like a caged bird. Lysandros was not as...tame as I was used to. "You were telling me what happened to you in Bactria."

His expression hardened. "When we arrived, we found a few revenants camped on the shore of Neblis's lake, but we managed to slip through their lines under cover of darkness. We intended to watch the house and wait for a chance to search for the fire." Lysandros stared down at the lines of people and soldiers milling about below, but his eyes were unfocused, as though he saw something else. "We entered the lake. I knew immediately that it was no ordinary water."

"Does she live on an island?" I asked.

"No, worse than that. She lives at the bottom, in the dark and murk."

I swallowed. "Go on."

"We did not make it very far before the creatures of the lake found us. And we discovered to our chagrin that they are impervious to the power. Perhaps because they are natives of the

Dominion, I'm not sure. Their bodies are solid enough, but nothing we tried had any effect. It was like sparring with shadows." He paused. "When Neblis saw it was Victor...the way she looked at him." Lysandros shook his head. "I wouldn't be in Victor's boots right now for anything. I think she loves and hates him at the same time, and hates herself for being so torn."

I realized I was gripping Victor's cuff and forced my fingers to relax. "What did she do with him?"

"Chained him near to fire. As long as he must fight the urge to use it, he cannot touch the power."

Holy Father. "Can he hold on?"

"For a while, yes." Lysandros stared at me intently. "Are you sure you want to do this? It is quite likely you will never return."

"Then why are *you* going back?" I retorted. "You don't even like Victor."

"I have no choice," Lysandros said stonily. "You're right. I don't like him. Victor is arrogant and selfish. He traded the freedom of the daēvas for Delilah, and once they were all caught, Xeros still refused to let her go." He gave a bitter smile. "So she ended up in Gorgon-e Gaz like the rest of them."

"But not you," I said.

"No, not me." Lysandros crushed the flower in his fist and tossed it aside. "You would never find your way through the Dominion if I didn't guide you. And I made a promise. It was a long time ago, but now I must honor it."

"What promise?"

Lysandros didn't respond. He looked sorry he'd even mentioned it. For the first time, I wondered if he felt guilty about being the only one to get away.

"Well, I'm glad you're helping us," I said awkwardly. "But I still don't understand Neblis, and I wish I did. None of it makes sense. It's all well and fine that Victor spurned her, but that doesn't explain everything she's done, the thousands of people she's butchered."

Lysandros barked a laugh. "You want an explanation? Go ahead and ask her yourself when we get to Bactria."

I glowered at him. "Maybe I'll do that," I said, although the thought of asking Neblis anything made me feel ill.

To my surprise, Lysandros offered me his hand, pulling me to my feet. "I won't lie," he said. "I've never liked humans very much. But if you can use your fire magic to stop her...Well, maybe I'll take you to Qin one day." He winked, his violet eyes glittering with amusement. "The bird's nest soup is quite extraordinary."

⚬⚬⚬

AN HOUR LATER, WE SAT ON OUR HORSES ABOUT FOUR LEAGUES from Alexander's camp. A river ran through a series of hills rippling with gold-tasseled foxtail grass. It was wide but shallow, and made a cheerful rushing sound that did nothing to lift my bleak mood. The place where Lysandros had stopped was a quiet pool at the bend that only looked to be a few inches deep.

"I am not going into that," I said flatly.

"It's not what you think," Lysandros said, casting me an impatient look. "I already explained it."

"Oh, really?" I dismounted and hunted around until I found a stone the size of my palm. I tossed it at the murky water. It rested for a moment on the surface, then gently sank into the mire. "Tell me that's not quicksand. Go ahead."

"It's not quicksand."

I watched the deceptively solid-looking surface reform. Underneath would be layers of water and loose sand that would trap anything stupid enough to flounder into it as surely as a tar pit. I had seen such places before, at the edges of the Great Salt Plain.

"You go first then," I said. "How would you like your belongings disposed of?"

Lysandros didn't bother replying, just spurred his horse toward the soggy rim of the inlet.

"At least Tijah will know how we died," Darius observed.

We had left a message for her with Hephaestion. She might be angry we had left her behind, but we couldn't wait. It could be two or three more days before she and Achaemenes arrived with the children. And to be honest, I didn't think she could handle another dangerous journey at the moment. Her grief was still too raw.

"If you are afraid, I will go ahead," Delilah said, shouldering her mount up between us. "Lysandros says he emerged from this place. It stands to reason that it is not what it appears." Her horse took several tentative steps forward and made an unhappy sound as it sank to its forelegs. "The talisman will protect us. You heard him. It will make a gate to these shadowlands." She lifted her chin. "If it brought me to Victor more swiftly, I would ride through Hell itself."

"And who's to say you won't be?" I muttered.

Delilah ignored me. She was having enough trouble getting her horse to go any further. Up ahead, Lysandros murmured something too low to hear, the talisman clutched tightly in his fist.

"This is how the necromancer traveled," Darius said. "I'd bet my life on it. Do you remember the way the trail ended so abruptly?"

I stared at the quicksand, my breath growing shallow. Darius knew I was afraid, but he didn't make it worse by pointing out the obvious. He never did. It was one of the things I liked about him.

"Do you think it will be like that the whole way?" I asked. "Like riding through disgusting porridge?"

"Lysandros said it wasn't. Once you pass through the gate, it gets better."

I nodded, more firmly than I felt. "All right. I'll go next."

I took a last look around. At the mountains, a blue smudge in the distance, and the nearer slopes of pine and juniper marking the foothills. The sun rode low in the sky, casting long shadows across the river. It ran in a southerly direction, but the pool was smooth as a mirror. As I dug my knees into the horse's flanks, a kingfisher sped past overhead, its long beak pointed into the wind. I could have sworn it was not reflected in the water beneath.

The cuff around my wrist seemed to tingle as I eyed the mire. The *gate*. Delilah's horse was halfway into it now and thrashing wildly, which only made it sink faster. Lysandros had vanished completely. The current didn't touch the pool, although it swept past just a few feet away.

What had I said to Darius on the ship as we landed in Karnopolis? Oh, yes. That we were skipping into quicksand.

As the horse took a trembling step forward and the water rose to the tops of my boots, I resolved to hold my tongue from then on. Maybe Tijah's gods were listening after all.

EPILOGUE

TIJAH

"You should eat something."

Achaemenes held out a hunk of bread. How could his hands be so damn clean? Tijah glanced at her own fingers, laced tight in her lap. Dirt crusted the nails in black half-moons. His blue tunic looked clean too. She had a dim memory of Achaemenes stripping it off and washing it in a stream the day before, but time seemed without meaning since Myrri's death. All she knew was before and after. Whole and broken.

Tijah turned her face away. "I'm not hungry."

It was past sunset but not yet full dark, and they had stopped in a clearing far enough from the road that the children's loud voices would not attract unwanted attention. She was so tired. She just wanted to sleep and sleep and never wake up.

"You've had nothing at all today," Achaemenes persisted calmly, tucking a fall of brown hair behind his ear. He was always calm. It was starting to get on her nerves.

Myrri had been the same way. Tijah had always taken her serenity for granted, coming to rely on it as though it were her own. As though Myrri's qualities belonged to Tijah. Now she was discovering that they didn't. They were gone, like borrowed clothes torn from her back. When she closed her eyes, she saw Myrri's fingers talking at her. Telling her not to worry so much, that everything would be okay.

But everything was not okay.

Take the kids. Tijah had never especially liked kids, but Myrri did. So Tijah was trying, for Myrri's sake. But it was hard, harder than she thought it would be. She was no mother, not even a big sister. She didn't have the patience for it. All she'd ever wanted was to be the hunter instead of the hunted. To have some say over what happened to her.

What a vain hope that turned out to be.

"If you don't get that bread out of my face, I'll find another place to put it," Tijah muttered.

"All right." Achaemenes popped it in his own mouth. When he finished chewing, he studied her for a minute. "I'm very sorry for what happened to your daēva. You met my own bonded so you know we weren't close, but I'm old enough to understand how it can be."

"I don't want to talk about it."

Achaemenes shrugged. "Suit yourself."

Tijah watched the children eat in silence. If not for Achaemenes, she doubted she could have controlled them. They were both euphoric at being able to touch the power whenever they wanted, and traumatized by years of violent discipline. The littler ones were easier because they mostly left it alone. They were so used to being cuffed that they forgot they weren't anymore.

The older ones didn't forget. And they were even more damaged.

Anuhita, who was nine and kept playing around with air even though Achaemenes kept telling her she would get them all in trouble if they ran into any Numerators or soldiers on the road.

Bijan, seven, and Parvane, twelve, who were brother and sister and stuck to each other like burrs.

Little Abid, the baby of the bunch who was small even for a six-year-old, although Achaemenes said he was very strong in earth.

And lastly, Pegah, whose name meant early morning light. She was thirteen, tall and gangly, with guarded eyes. Like all of them.

"Stop it, Parvane," Achaemenes said. "Just eat your supper."

Parvane snatched the bread out of the air. They'd been batting it around without using their hands.

"I'm thirsty," Abid announced.

Tijah passed him her water skin. He took a drink and snuggled into her side. The warmth of his small body was comforting. She liked little Abid the best. He was sweet and simple and seemed to like her back, unlike the others, who trusted only Achaemenes. Sometimes she felt Abid was the only thing tethering her to reality.

Who am I now? Alone? Tijah wondered. And: *Gods, why do I dislike Achaemenes so much? Is it because he tries to smooth my rough edges just like she did? Oh, Myrri. Tell me what to do.*

"Do you know how much farther it is to Persepolae?" Achaemenes asked.

Tijah shook her head. She didn't care. It was all she could do to get through the next minute, the next hour. She realized—with very little surprise—that she wouldn't mind dying.

"There's someone watching us," Achaemenes observed. "From the woods."

That roused her a bit. "Only one?"

"Seems to be. It's a daēva."

"What do you make of that?" Tijah had left her scimitar next to her bedroll on the other side of the clearing. She could see the scabbard and reckoned she could reach it in about six seconds. Not that she stood any real chance against a daēva. If she attacked, maybe it would kill her quickly.

"Come share our food," Achaemenes called.

Tijah scowled. "What are you—" She fell silent as a man

stepped out of the trees. He wore the blue uniform of an Immortal. The scaled armor was covered in dried reddish brown streaks.

"These children are free," he said, pointing to the wide-eyed group. The kids fell silent and still under his scrutiny, like rabbits huddled beneath the passing shadow of a hawk. Anu jutted her chin defiantly and Tijah thought she would say something, but the girl seemed to think better of it and kept her mouth shut. The Immortal still had his sword. One hand rested lightly on the pommel.

"Yes," Achaemenes agreed. "We are slaves no more. Like you."

And that's when Tijah noticed that both the Immortal's wrists were bare. His arms were tanned acorn brown, but one showed a lighter strip of skin where the cuff had been.

The daēva stopped about thirty paces away. He didn't come any closer, nor did he make any move to leave.

"Do you come from Persepolae?" Tijah asked. "What's happened?"

His voice drifted across the twilit field. "The King is dead."

"Which King?" Achaemenes asked dryly.

"Our King. Artaxeros the Second."

"And the Immortals?"

The daēva shifted. "Divided. Something broke the cuffs. Some magic of the barbarians. Those who remained loyal are also dead."

So Nazafareen had done it. Tijah knew she should be glad, but she felt nothing. Just a dusty, lonely emptiness, like an abandoned house. "And the others?"

"Some stayed with Alexander."

"But not you?" Achaemenes asked.

"I will never again fight for men," the daēva said flatly.

"Where are you going?"

"I don't know. As far away as I can get."

"And the Macydonians? What will they do now?" Tijah asked.

"I believe Alexander marches on Bactria."

"*Bactria?*" Achaemenes echoed. "But what of the other captive daēvas? When word of Persepolae reaches the satrapies, they will be slaughtered!"

"Probably. But there is nothing you or I can do about that."

Tijah thought of the prison Victor had escaped from, of the one hundred and seven daēvas who still languished within its walls. If Myrri were alive, she would not have turned away from them. For the moment the guards knew there was a chance they could be freed...well, they would not wait for Alexander to arrive. They would burn the place.

Achaemenes caught her eye and she knew he was thinking the same thing.

"I cannot continue on to Persepolae," he said quietly. "I cannot."

"Where would you go?" she asked, already knowing the answer.

"Gorgon-e Gaz."

"To free the old ones?"

Achaemenes nodded.

"I've seen it," Tijah said. "It is no place for children."

He bristled at this. "I'm not a child."

You're certainly not a man, Tijah thought, although she didn't say it aloud. Something in his face told her it would be a serious mistake. "Perhaps. But they are." She looked at the rest of their ragged, dirty-faced group, who watched the exchange intently. It was unthinkable that Achaemenes would contemplate leaving her in charge of these little hooligans. "You can't just abandon them. They won't listen to me."

As if to prove her point, Abid exclaimed, "I want to go with Achaemenes. You can't make me stay!"

The others joined in, yelling over each other like drunken monkeys, until Achaemenes hollered at them to shut up.

"Do you even know what Gorgon-e Gaz is?" Tijah demanded of the children.

"I do," Pegah said. "It's a jail. My mother is there."

"And ours," Parvane added. "Our father too, I think."

"I never met my parents," Abid said. "But I'm sure they must be too."

Anu just sniffed and flopped onto her back. "Everyone comes from there, stupid," she muttered.

"If you don't let us, we'll just follow you," Pegah said. She had light brown eyes that reminded Tijah of Nazafareen, except even colder. "We have no place in Alexander's camp. They are barbarians, not civilized men. I want to see my parents."

"You can't do it alone," Parvane said to Achaemenes, ignoring Tijah. "You need us. We know how to fight."

Achaemenes slid an arm around the girl's shoulders. She looked up at him with adoration.

"Do you think they'll remember us?" Bijan asked uncertainly. "I don't even know what my mother and father look like. How will they know who we are?"

"Don't worry, they will," Achaemenes said, ruffling the boy's short black hair. "Parents just know."

Bijan nodded, satisfied with this worthless reply. Then the others erupted in questions and excited chatter about their grand new adventure. It was no use refusing them now, Tijah could see that. Pegah and Anu—especially Anu—were more than capable of lashing out with the power if they felt threatened. But the journey north would take at least a week and it was madness to bring them all the way to Gorgon-e Gaz. Assuming the prison hadn't been torched yet, the guards would still have full control of the daēvas inside. With the cuffs, they could be forced to do almost anything. And if they refused, they would be tortured. Tijah didn't want the children seeing that. It was the sort of thing they would never forget.

No, she would find some safe place for them on the way—if there *were* any safe places left. For the last day, they had seen the survivors coming from the east, heard their stories. They would have to pass through the lands overrun by Druj to get to the prison. First the Great Salt Plain, then over the mountains to the Salenian Sea. She had almost frozen to death the last time.

"All right," she said. "We all go to Gorgon-e Gaz. I'll try to buy some more horses, if anyone in the villages is selling, which I doubt. But I won't have you drawing attention to yourselves with childish pranks, understood?"

They all nodded, although Anu did so with obvious hostility.

"Thank you," Achaemenes said. "For not leaving us. I expected you would want to find your friends in Persepolae."

Tijah gave him a brusque nod. In truth, she welcomed the prospect of a fight. For the first time since Myrri's death, she had a purpose. A reason to go on living, and one she was sure Myrri would approve of. How they would free the daēvas in Gorgon-e Gaz, she had no idea. Perhaps if the Immortal would come too… Gods, the Immortal! How could she have forgotten him?

She scanned the open field. Fireflies flickered on and off in the grass. Beyond, the woods lay dark and impenetrable. It was nearly night, but the moon had risen and she could still see well enough. There was no one there.

The daēva had gone.

Read on for the first chapter of Queen of Chaos, Book #3 in the Fourth Element Trilogy. And if you have a moment to leave a review, they're a huge boost for authors and help us to keep writing books at affordable prices!

CHAPTER ONE
TIJAH

She stretched out flat on her belly in a fold of earth, the late afternoon sun beating down on her bare neck. Goddess, she missed having long hair. Myrri used to braid it each night before bed. Her gentle smoothing and tugging always made Tijah sleepy.

The memory would have brought angry tears to her eyes if she had any left to shed. But after the things she'd seen, and the nights weeping silently so she wouldn't wake the children, Tijah's heart was cold and heavy as a stone.

Oh, sister. I'd give anything to have you at my side again.
Anything at all.

Myrri didn't answer, but that was because she'd never spoken a single word aloud in her life. Also because she was dead.

The silence managed to be more accusing than any imagined response. If Tijah had gone down into those tunnels with her, Myrri would still be alive. She could have saved her with the bond, the way Nazafareen had saved Darius. Or they could have died together, as they were always meant to. She'd never for a moment considered that she might be left behind. Alone and consumed with regret. It was the cruelest fate imaginable.

Tijah squinted through the waves of heat rising from the white, cracked earth. Beads of sweat carved a slow path down the side of her nose. She hadn't moved a muscle in an hour. Hardly so much as blinked. She was watching the village below for any signs of life. There were none.

It looked like the other villages they'd passed in the last four days crossing the Great Salt Plain—a dusty collection of mudbrick houses with rounded roofs and narrow slits for windows to keep out the desert heat. Except this one wasn't a charred slaughterhouse.

Why?

Tijah knew what the necromancers and their Druj did when they swept through a village. She had seen the aftermath a dozen times so far. The first one she'd known was coming because they could all smell it from leagues away. When little Abid saw what had been done to the sheep in their pens, he'd gotten sick to his stomach, vomiting right on Parvane's bare feet. At that point Tijah had ordered Achaemenes to take the five children and give the village a wide berth, cursing herself for not doing it earlier. She was the only one to enter. She'd hoped to find survivors.

There were none.

Tijah heard the buzzing of flies in her dreams now, on those same nights when she woke with a scream trapped in her throat and the image of faceless men standing over her with knives. So many horrors, all congealing together. So many bad men in the world.

She'd made herself count the dead at each village. At first to honor them, to remember the lost. But that's how she came to suspect the Druj weren't killing them all. Oh, there was no lack of burned and tortured corpses. But Tijah could see it wasn't enough. That meant the necromancers were taking fresh slaves at each stop. Maybe the wights too.

Afterwards, when the culling was finished, they would put the place to the torch and carve up every last living creature that remained. From what she could tell, the Undead didn't eat the animals. They killed for the pleasure of it.

But either this particular village had been spared—highly unlikely—or overlooked. Well, it was a stroke of much-needed luck. They'd run out of food and water a day ago. Since the succession of ghost towns, Tijah's priorities had radically shifted. She no longer expected to buy horses or provisions. Her only goal at this point was keeping everyone alive.

She'd thought about turning back. Not herself, but

Achaemenes and the kids. She should have tried harder, the moment they came to that first village.

"Do you care so little for them?" Tijah had demanded. "This plain is a battlefield. Not even that! A charnel house."

"We can handle a few Druj," Achaemenes replied.

"Can you?" She stared at him until he looked away. "Did you know the necromancers use fire? They're not stupid. They know how to deal with daēvas. And they're hard to kill, much harder than the Undead."

She could see from his face that in fact, he had not known about the fire. Very few did. Tijah only knew because she'd fought them once before, but the so-called Antimagi had not crossed the mountains in generations. Until now.

Still Achaemenes dug his heels in. "We're going to Gorgon-e Gaz," he said, iron in his voice. "And we're going to find our parents and let them out." He glanced at the children, sitting blank-eyed in the dirt, waiting to be told what to do. "They need to know who they are. They need to know they're not Druj. You've no idea of the things that have been done to them. The lies they've been told."

Tijah had nothing to say. If Myrri were here, she'd agree. So on they went.

And Tijah found herself warming to the stark, forbidding landscape. The perfect emptiness of it, the silence. She didn't think she could have stood being in a city, with its teeming multitudes and staring faces. That made her remember Karnopolis and what had happened there. But the Great Salt Plain had an austere beauty Myrri would have appreciated. Scorching during the day and cold at night, but oh, the stars! More than she had seen since leaving the golden, shifting dunes of Al Miraj all those years ago.

They had walked and walked, and seen many strange and wondrous things that eased the other horrors: spires of pure white crystals thrusting up from the earth like half-buried palaces, and rivers of salt driven by the wind to look like hair, and a dry lake pitted by some ancient hailstorm that turned out to a morass of sticky mud. They had almost gotten stuck in that one. Afterwards, Tijah was careful to avoid anyplace that didn't have a thick crust of salt.

Most of the villages had an oasis nearby, so Tijah managed to refill their water skins until the last one, where she'd found corpses stuffed into the well. That was yesterday.

Now it was far too late to turn around. And Tijah wanted to go to Gorgon-e Gaz too. Needed to go. It was the only way she could think of to avenge Myrri's death and if it cost Tijah her own, she could accept that.

In fact, she was counting on it.

But the kids.... She still planned to leave them somewhere safe. Tel Khalujah, maybe. There were Water Dogs there and a high wall. Garrisons of soldiers.

So why haven't they been sent here? Why haven't you seen a single red or blue tunic among the dead?

Tijah shifted the tiniest bit to avoid a pebble digging into her right hip. This wasn't the first time that little voice had asked unanswerable questions. The people of the Dasht-e Kavir were helpless as goats staked out for a pack of hyenas, abandoned by both their old King and new. And if none of the eastern satrapies had sent aid either, when news had surely reached them of the massacres by now, that meant....

Tijah didn't want to think about what that meant.

She watched the village until the sun hovered just above the peaks of distant mountains. The one good thing about the Great Salt Plain was that no one could sneak up on you. It stretched flat and featureless in all directions, with nowhere for an army to hide itself. Wherever the Druj had gone, she felt reasonably certain it wasn't here. Besides the lack of bodies and flies and stench, the ground around the village wasn't churned up the way the others had been. The necromancers and their minions were foul, unearthly things, but they left hoof- and footprints just like men did.

Tijah crawled back to the clump of scraggly brown bushes where Achaemenes waited with the children. Like a crucible, the desert had both reduced and hardened him, boiling away any spare flesh along with the last shreds of innocence. His eyes were haunted, but then so were her own.

"Nothing moving down there," she said.

"Someone must have warned them," Achaemenes said, the kids clustered tight around him like ducklings. "They got lucky and ran."

"Probably. Or they're hunkered down. Hiding."

Tijah did not mention Ash Shiyda, the village she'd been called out to with the Water Dogs several years before. A merchant caravan had reported possible trouble in the area. When her company arrived, Ash Shiyda appeared to be deserted. In fact, the Druj had been waiting for them, holed up in the empty houses. That's when she'd killed her first revenant. She remembered the eyes like mirrors, the terrible wounds on its body, squirming with maggots. It held its longsword with cracked, raw hands. The weapon had been nearly as tall as she was. If Myrri hadn't distracted it while Tijah snuck around behind....

"Listen up." Tijah braced her hands on her hips and gave the kids a hard stare. "What do you know about the Undead? About Druj?"

They shuffled their feet. Pegah glanced at Achaemenes for his consent to answer and Tijah wanted to shake her until her perfect white teeth rattled.

"Come on," Achaemenes said, scrubbing a hand across his jaw. His beard was coming in and he had an unconscious habit of stroking the wispy hair when his authority was invoked. "Remember your lessons with the magus. Let's start with liches."

"Like shadows," Parvane said promptly. "If they touch you,

you're dead." She poked Abid, who giggled, stuck his tongue out and pretended to sag to the ground.

"And how do you stop them?"

Most of the kids chimed in with the answer, all except Anu, who, when she wasn't bickering with the others, usually refused to speak at all. "With air!"

"What about wights?" Achaemenes asked.

"Cut their heads off!" Pegah said, eyes shining. She was only four years younger than Achaemenes and worshipped the ground he walked on.

"And revenants?" Tijah said.

"Undead soldiers, returned from the grave," Parvane chanted. Words she'd memorized by rote. "You have to behead those too. When they're born, they come out of the ground."

"Stinky old Druj!" Abid jeered, collapsing in laughter. It had been two days since he saw the eviscerated sheep in their pen, entrails draped across torn bodies, eyes staring glassily into the sun. Only two days. But with the resilience of children, he'd managed to erase the scene from his mind.

Ordinarily, Tijah would envy him for it. Sometimes she wished she had the same amnesia. But not today. Not when all their lives depended on staying alert and *afraid*.

"You think it's funny because you've never seen one," Tijah said quietly, but with a touch of menace. "Never felt the air whistle past your face as you try to keep them from chopping you to pieces with their iron swords."

Abid's grin slid away. Small and scrawny for his age to begin with, he suddenly looked a lot younger than six. Tijah felt a little bad for scaring him but it had to be done. The Druj were no fairy-tale ogres. Maybe it had been a mistake to keep the children away from the villages. Maybe they needed to see.

"You listen to me," Tijah said. "If we come across any liches, feel free to unknit them with air. That's what daēvas do best. Did the magi teach you how?"

The older kids nodded firmly, the two younger ones a bit more uncertainly. Achaemenes just watched, his face unreadable.

"Now wights are fast, really fast," Tijah continued. "A good friend of mine lost her sister to a wight. I've seen them. They look like a person, except for the eyes, which are all black." Tijah touched the corner of her eyelid. "Once they take you, it's over. There's no coming back. So if you see something like that, don't hesitate for a second. It's not a human, not a daēva, and it will kill you in a heartbeat. You run, understand? Same for revenants. They're even worse. We see any of those, you let me take care of them."

The kids stared at Tijah, at the hilt of the curved sword she wore across her back. Pegah looked on the verge of rolling her eyes, but Tijah's expression made her sigh and brush an invisible mote of dust from her tunic instead.

"Abid can make a crack in the earth," Bijan whispered. He was almost as quiet as Anu, and always had a worried crease across his forehead. At seven, he was the closest in age to Abid, and the boys were friends.

"Want me to show you?" Abid asked, bouncing on his toes.

"Not right now," Achaemenes said firmly. "And not without permission. You all know earth can break bones. It's easy to draw too much."

"We don't need anyone's *permission* to use the power," Anu muttered under her breath.

Achaemenes ignored her. Nothing seemed to ruffle his calm. Tijah almost snapped back at her—it wouldn't do to have a mutiny on their hands—but thought better of it. She'd talk to the girl later. They only had a few hours of daylight left, and she wanted to get in and out of the village quickly. They'd yet to see any actual Druj, only the aftermath of their passage across the plain, but she knew they were out there. A whole army of them.

Tijah climbed to the top of the low rise where they had stopped to rest. A series of arid foothills hemmed the village from the west. Otherwise, the Great Salt Plain stretched in an uninterrupted sheet of parched earth as far as the eye could see. Tijah figured they were two or three days from the Khusk Range. Gorgon-e Gaz lay on the other side.

She shaded her eyes with one hand, sweeping her gaze along the flat line of the horizon, where the sky grew soft and fuzzy, as though someone had smudged their thumb along it. It was a trick of the heat, she knew. Just like the shimmering quicksilver pools that looked like water. In the Sayhad, travelers died chasing those pools, which always floated just out of reach.

"So the village is safe?" Achaemenes asked.

"I didn't say that. I said it *looks* safe. See the difference?"

"I only meant—"

"I know what you meant. Too bad daēvas can't sense Druj. That would make it simple. But we have no choice. I doubt there's another water source for fifty leagues. So in we go."

The sun touched the tops of the hills, painting them reddish gold. A flock of birds winged past in ragged formation overhead. They must be migrating. No place was worth stopping at for long in this wasteland. Tijah imagined them going somewhere green and wild, an island in the middle of the ocean surrounded by wave-beaten cliffs echoing with the roar of the sea. The thought made her wistful. How pleasant to be able to simply fly away....

"Everyone stay close," she said, taking the bridle of their mare. The animal barely responded to her touch. Its head drooped, dark eyes fixed on the dirt. The horse had been intended for Myrri. Tijah stroked its muzzle. "There's water down there, old girl," she murmured. "Half a league more. If I can do it, you can do it."

They all needed fresh water, desperately. Tijah herself came from the Sayhad and had a high tolerance for dry heat—more than for cold, that was certain—but even she couldn't go forever on a gulp of piss-warm water.

They picked their way down the hillside, Tijah in front with the horse and Achaemenes and the kids trailing behind, to the rutted road leading to the village. Parvane held her brother Bijan's hand. She was tall for an eleven-year-old, almost as tall as Tijah, who could look most men in the eye. Pegah had taken charge of Abid. As usual, Anu held herself apart from the others, although Tijah noticed she didn't stray far from Achaemenes.

As they neared the village, she saw the tops of walled gardens inside. The people who lived there would have to be self-sufficient to survive out here. They would have wells, and some kind of irrigation system. Tijah scanned a stone pen with a crude thatched shelter that offered protection from the elements. It smelled faintly of manure but the animals were also gone, which Tijah took as a good sign. No bloated bodies rotting in the sun.

The wind whistled across the plain, whipping a fine grit into her eyes. Tijah wished she still had her Water Dog *qarha*, which was easily the most useful item of clothing she'd ever owned. A long scarf that wrapped around the head, it served in rain and snow, dust and wind. But she'd left her old life behind. Now Tijah wore a plain tunic and trousers, once white but scoured to a dingy grey from their journey across the plain. The children still wore the blue of daēva slaves. That color alone would mark them out, if there were anyone within five hundred leagues to see it.

Tijah felt Achaemenes' eyes on her but kept her own straight ahead. He'd finally lost the limp in his right leg, she noticed. His infirmity had vanished the moment Nazafareen freed him from the bond but his mind hadn't accepted it for days.

How we cling to our old ways even when they no longer serve us.

When they reached the opening in the low wall where the road passed into the village, Tijah turned and gave the kids a stern look. Most of them hadn't a clue. They knew, but they didn't really believe. They wouldn't, until they faced their first Undead. But she wouldn't tolerate foolishness.

"Food and water," she said. "Don't touch anything else."

Tijah went into the first house alone while the others waited in the street. The bottom level had served as a stable, with bales of hay stacked against the walls and extra tack. Good news for the horse. She unsheathed her scimitar and slowly scanned the shadows until she felt certain the room was empty. A dark, steep flight of stairs led to the second floor, the stone worn smooth from the long passage of feet. Tijah peered up it, then began to climb, pausing on each step to listen for any sign of movement.

The gods only knew how long this village had been here. A thousand years, maybe. The people of the Dasht-e Kavir were descendants of the pastoralists who had once roamed free with their flocks. She remembered the magus at Tel Khalujah explaining about it in their history lessons while she listened with half an ear, daydreaming about one of the handsome young soldiers in the satrap's personal guard. What had his name been? Farhad? Or was it Farbod?

When Tijah reached the top of the stairs, she waited for a full minute. Just the wind, and the faint voices of the kids outside.

She reached over her shoulder and unsheathed her scimitar. Then she cautiously began to explore the second floor. As soon as she saw the bedroom, her shoulders relaxed. She rolled her neck and was rewarded with a satisfying crunch. It was not like Ash Shiyda, everything perfectly intact except for the people. No, this had been a planned exodus. Clothing spilled from cedar chests as though a few favorite items had been hastily grabbed. She could see the dust-free spots on dressers and tables where sentimental keepsakes had been taken. Likewise, only the smallest, cheapest rugs remained. Most of the food was gone too, although she found half a loaf of hard bread and some shriveled onions.

Tijah gathered up the food and returned to the street.

"I think it's okay," she said. "Let's check the other houses."

"I'm thirsty," Abid whined, pushing the offered bread away.

"There's an aquifer beneath the hill," Achaemenes said. "They use it for irrigation." He tilted his head back and closed his eyes. Finding the nexus. Letting it guide him to water. "The well is in the middle of town."

Tijah hesitated. Goddess, she was thirsty. "All right. Lead the way."

They followed Achaemenes through the cramped, dusty streets. Some of the houses had been carved straight out of the slabs of sandstone that erupted from the plain. They looked like giant termite mounds, with irregular windows and pointy roofs.

The sun sank behind the hills. Deep shadows cloaked the alleys between the buildings. The dark, cave-like doorways and perfect absence of sound, except for their own footfalls in the dust, had a subduing effect on the children. No one spoke until they reached a central courtyard. Sure enough, it had a deep stone well, with a bucket on a rope.

The water was good and cold. Most of all, it was wet. When they'd all drunk their fills and Tijah had tended to the horse, she explored the houses fronting the courtyard. Most of the food was gone, but she had better luck in the rear gardens. A small orchard yielded a walnut tree and a few hard green pears. Tijah squatted in the shade and ate one. It tasted bitter and chalky. She'd probably have a stomachache later, but she was too hungry to care.

"You never told me what happened to your face," Achaemenes said, dropping down beside her.

Tijah looked up at him. The pain was better than it had been a few days ago, although her jaw still ached where one of the Al Miraji mercenaries had punched her. She wiggled a tooth with her tongue. It felt loose.

"Someone asked me too many questions," she said, chucking the core over a stone wall. "You should see *him*."

Achaemenes raised an eyebrow but let it go. "I'm going to look around," he said.

"Make yourself useful then. We'll need provisions. Warm clothing, blankets. This might be the last village standing before the Khusk mountains." She glanced at Abid, scuffing around in the dirt with his big toe. "They need shoes."

Achaemenes nodded.

"Don't go far."

"I won't."

After the kids devoured some scraps of dried meat and part of an old wheel of cheese Tijah had discovered in a cupboard, their spirits picked up. Parvane pretended to be a lich and chased Abid and Bijan around. Anyone who got touched was declared to be out of the game. They moved so fast Tijah could barely follow. Pegah, who was thirteen, obviously considered herself too old for such silliness, so she sat against the well and watched the others with an indulgent air.

Tijah almost put a stop to it, but it was the first fun the children had had in days and it seemed clear the village was long deserted. So she left them with Parvane and went inside one of the houses looking for anything useful. A few minutes later, Tijah heard raised voices outside. Not in alarm, but in anger. When she reached the courtyard, she found Anu and Parvane going at it. Anu gave Parvane a hard shove, knocking her on her bottom. After a moment of shocked silence, Parvane leaped to her feet. She was lunging at Anu when Tijah stepped between them.

"Knock it off," she said.

Anu spit in the dirt at Tijah's feet. Unlike Parvane, who kept her hair neatly combed, Anu's was wild and knotted. She had the Bactrian look, with pale skin peeling from the sun and light green eyes that now settled on Tijah with open defiance.

"I warned her not to touch me," Anu growled. "I warned her."

Tijah turned to the other girl, who crossed her arms defensively. "Why, Parvane? You know how she is."

"It was an accident!" Parvane protested. "Bijan pushed me. I didn't bump her hard!"

"What's going on?" Achaemenes emerged from the mouth of a dark alley. He carried a cracked water jug in one hand and a stack of blankets in the other.

Parvane cast him an appealing look. "Anu's like a wild animal, she always has been, you know that," she said, all batting eyelashes and reasonable tone. "There's something wrong with her. She *likes* to fight. No one can talk to her without getting their head snapped off. She never wants to play. She just sits there with that mean look on her face." And then Parvane did an uncannily accurate imitation of Anu, clutching herself and rocking back and forth with a sour, blank-eyed stare.

"That's enough," Achaemenes said wearily. "I don't care who started it. You're the older one, and this isn't the place for childish squabbles."

Anu kept her eyes on the ground, refusing to defend herself. Tijah had seen it before. The kid just shut down.

"But—"

"I said, enough." He turned to Anu. "You okay?"

No response. Achaemenes sighed, addressing Bijan and Abid, who had stopped playing to watch the outcome of the fight. "Tijah says the mountains we have to cross are very cold. Pegah, take your brother and check out the houses on the left side. Look for food and clothing mainly, but also weapons, needles and thread, anything useful. Parvane and Bijan, you're with me." Achaemenes stepped up to Anu, careful not to get too close. "Why don't you go with Tijah?" he said gently.

Tijah suppressed a scowl but held her tongue. She could see the wisdom of keeping Anu and Parvane apart for now, but she didn't relish the strange daēva girl's company. She didn't relish any of their company.

When the two of them were alone, she looked Anu up and down. The girl was still staring at her own feet like they contained the secret of life. "Don't want to talk, huh? Well, you're in luck because neither do I." Tijah turned her back and started toward a crooked house at the end of the square. A moment later, she heard the whisper of bare feet behind her.

The place was little more than a mud-brick hovel, with a narrow doorway leading to three rooms on the ground floor. The owners had packed in a hurry, leaving little behind. A crude wooden doll with no arms. A comb with half the teeth missing.

"You want this?" Tijah held it up. "Your hair looks pretty ratty. You might want to give it a comb sometime. No?" She tossed it aside, glancing at Anu out of the corner of her eye. "I could teach you some hand signs. That way we can communicate without talking." Tijah hooked her middle and ring fingers together, palms up. "That means go fuck a herd of camels. You can use it on Parvane anytime you want. I don't care."

Anu's lips bunched together as she tried not to smile. It made the girl look more like an actual person.

"I don't know about you," Tijah announced, "but I feel weird and kind of sad invading people's privacy like this, even if they're never coming back, so let's just get it over with, shall we?"

Anu didn't reply but she snapped out of her trance, helping Tijah search the place and piling whatever seemed worthwhile on the living room rug. Along the way, Tijah taught her a few of the more useful signs she and Myrri had devised when they were kids together.

"This one means stop talking so loud, I'm just mute, not fucking deaf," Tijah said, rapidly touching mouth and ear with a gleeful flourish. "This is yes"—a closed fist—"and no"—first two fingers of right hand tapping left palm.

Anu tried the last two out, her face intensely focused.

"Very good." Tijah grinned. "And this one means you're going bald from ringworm, you flaming son of a pimp."

An hour or so later, they all reunited in the square and made a pile of everything they'd found. Some of it was desperately needed —woolen jackets, a few pairs of sturdy leather boots, pickled vegetables in clay jars and salted mutton—while other items had simply caught the younger children's eyes. A toy chariot complete with horses that you could pull behind you on a string. A carved wooden cat.

Pegah took charge of sorting through it all, directing the

younger children to pack the most practical items in a little cart they could hitch to the horse. She and Parvane chattered away, admiring this or that treasure, as Bijan and Abid dutifully followed instructions. The only one who did nothing was Anu. She'd gone off in her own world again, sitting in the dirt near the well and picking at her bare feet.

Tijah took Achaemenes aside, pitching her voice so low she doubted even a daēva could hear it.

"What's the story?" she whispered, flicking her eyes at Anu. "Was her amah a monster?"

Achaemenes shrugged. "No worse than the others. She's always been like this. Different. Awkward with children and adults both."

"Is she slow?" Tijah asked, doubting it. The kid had clever eyes when she bothered to look at you, and she'd picked up the hand signs quick enough.

"The opposite. Anu has a brilliant mind when she wants to use it. She was top of the class in lessons."

"Did the other kids resent her for that?"

Achaemenes shrugged. "Some did."

"So she got it on both sides then. That can't have been easy."

Achaemenes gave her an appraising look. "She could use a friend. I don't know if Anu has ever had one."

Tijah didn't like the way he looked at her, with pity in his eyes. Like he could see inside her. Like he thought maybe Tijah was the one who needed a friend. It made her angry. He couldn't possibly know what she felt.

"Well, she can look elsewhere," Tijah said, and her voice had a nastier edge than she'd intended. "That's not what I signed up for."

Achaemenes's mouth thinned. Tijah felt a surge of petty triumph that she'd finally gotten to him when a prickling sensation made her look across the square, through the thickening shadows, to where Anu crouched by the well. The girl was staring at them. She'd probably heard that last bit since in her irritation, Tijah had forgotten to lower her voice. Goddess-cursed daēvas.

"Shit," Tijah muttered.

"Do we stay here for the night?" Achaemenes asked. She could tell he was disappointed in her.

"Might as well. We'll move on at first light."

He grinned. "You mean I actually get to sleep in a bed?"

"I didn't say that." She pointed down the street. "There's a building over there that should do nicely."

It was the tallest in the village, four stories and solid stone mortared with lime. Tijah had seen it while she was searching a cluster of nearby houses, and had immediately marked it out as an excellent vantage point. The circular style was different from the other buildings, and the stones were much more pitted and weathered, as though the structure predated the village itself. Who had built it was a mystery, but Tijah guessed the settlement had eventually grown up around it. She thought perhaps the tower had been a lookout, dating back to the days when raiders from the hill tribes of Bactria would harry the herders of the Salt Plain.

Whatever it had once been, the villagers now used the tower to store grain. A ladder led to a windowless loft with bales of hay, and then a timbered roof that commanded a clear view in all directions. Tijah tied the horse to a post and gave her a handful of feed. The last faint glow of daylight was fading at the rim of the western horizon as Tijah and Achaemenes reached the top of the rickety ladder. Tijah sat on the edge of the roof and let her feet dangle down. She had never been afraid of heights, although Myrri hated them.

She pushed her sleeve up and touched the gold cuff that still circled her right wrist. If only Myrri had been afraid of enclosed places too. Then she might have stayed with Tijah and the horses by the bridge. The mercenaries wouldn't have snuck up on her and Myrri wouldn't be a greasy scorch mark in the tunnels under Karnopolis.

The soft voices of the children drifted up from the loft below. To Tijah's eyes, it was pitch black inside, but daēvas could see like cats in the darkness and the kids had no trouble scrambling up the ladder and making themselves little nests in the hay.

"How much farther to Gorgon-e Gaz?" Achaemenes asked, settling in beside her.

Tijah let her sleeve fall back down, concealing the cuff. "Two more days to the mountains, another two to cross."

"Do you think we'll make it?"

Tijah looked at him. "We'll make it."

He nodded, but not like he believed her. Just because it was the polite thing to do. "Why don't you get some rest? I'll wake you in a few hours," he said.

Tijah slipped down the ladder and curled up in the straw. The kids were already asleep. She listened to their soft breathing for a few minutes. All her icons—Mami Natu, the fertility goddess with her pendulous breasts; Innunu, Tijah's fierce patron, half woman, half falcon; and Kavi, the nine-headed, nine-armed deliverer of justice—had been lost in Karnopolis. But they lived in her heart.

Bring us safely across the Plain, she prayed. That's all I ask. What happens on the other side is for you to decide.

She felt as though she'd just closed her eyes when Achaemenes was saying her name in the darkness, softly so as not to wake the others. He didn't touch her, which she appreciated.

"You sure you're up for this?" he asked, as she blinked owlishly and let out a jaw-cracking yawn. A pale trickle of moonlight from above let her make out the sleeping mounds of the children. "I can take the next watch too, easy. I'm not tired."

"It's my turn," Tijah replied, stumbling for the ladder.

She sat with her chin on her knees, eyes fixed stubbornly on the eastern horizon. Not even a hint of sunrise yet. She probably had a couple of hours to go at least. That was okay. She could handle it. She'd gone without sleep plenty of times.

The plain stretched ahead of her like a black ocean.

We'll make it. Achaemenes doesn't believe it, but we will.

She sat for a while, then paced the perimeter of the tower. Sixteen steps. It grew cold, the moon set, and she sat back down to huddle for warmth. Whenever her chin would nod toward her chest, she'd pinch herself and get up. Pace some more. In the hour just before dawn, a vision stole over her, clear as if she were seeing it.

Myrri. In the stern of a small boat on that black ocean. Beckoning. Too far off to see her face, but Tijah would bet she's wearing that wry smile, the one that only came out when they were alone together. Tijah is standing on the shore and she understands, even without signs, what Myrri wants.

I'm coming, sister. One way or another, I'm coming....

🌺

Tijah woke to the first lukewarm rays of dawn hitting her face. She stirred, realized what had happened, and cursed fluently and with great feeling. It was the first time she'd ever fallen asleep on watch.

She jumped to her feet, shading one hand against the low angle of the sun. A moment of blindness as she squinted past the village to the desolate plateau beyond and Tijah came fully awake, heart pounding like she'd just run a footrace through the Sayhad at noon.

"Achaemenes!" she yelled, trying to keep the panic from her voice. "Get up here. Now!"

Moments later, a tousled head of brown hair popped out of the hatch. Achaemenes pulled himself up and then he was at her side.

"Holy Father," he breathed.

A huge cloud of dust obscured the plain not a league from the village, and it was moving fast, from west to east. The same way they were headed.

Along the road that passed right through the village.

"That's not a sandstorm," Tijah said, feeling sick and scared and guilty all at the same time. "There's no wind."

"That's an army," Achaemenes finished.

They looked at each other. Then they were running to the ladder. He said nothing about her falling asleep, neglecting her duty, and she didn't either.

Tijah dropped the last few feet from the ladder to the loft, Achaemenes behind her.

"Wake up," she barked.

Sleepy faces, blinking eyes. Pegah shot her an accusing look, like she was being a bitch just for fun.

"There's Druj coming," Tijah snapped. "A lot of them."

That got everyone moving. Bijan let out a whimper, clinging to Pegah's leg. Achaemenes snatched up their blankets and wadded them into a ball that he tossed through the hole in the floor.

"I'll get the wagon hitched," he said.

"We still have time to get out, but just barely," Tijah said, herding them toward the ladder as she did a quick head count: Anu, Parvane, Bijan, Pegah...

"Where's Abid?" Tijah demanded. "Where the *hell* is Abid?"

QUEEN OF CHAOS - SUMMARY

FOURTH ELEMENT BOOK #3

Persepolae has fallen.
Karnopolis has burned.

As the dark forces of the Undead sweep across what remains of the empire, Nazafareen must obey the summons of a demon queen to save Darius's father, Victor. Burdened with a power she doesn't understand and can barely control, Nazafareen embarks on a perilous journey through the shadowlands to the House-Behind-the-Veil. But what awaits her there is worse than she ever imagined...

A thousand leagues away, Tijah leads a group of children on a desperate mission to rescue the prisoners at Gorgon-e Gaz, the stronghold where the oldest daevas are kept. To get there, they must cross the Great Salt Plain, a parched ruin occupied by the armies of the night. A chance encounter adds a ghost from the past to their number. But will they arrive in time to avert a massacre?

And in the House-Behind-the-Veil, Balthazar and the Prophet Zarathustra discover that they have more in common than meets the eye. But is it enough to salvage the necromancer's blood-stained soul and thwart his mistress's plans?

As a final showdown looms between Alexander the Great and Queen Neblis, the truth of the daevas' origins is revealed and three worlds collide in this thrilling conclusion to the Fourth Element series.

Now available for purchase on Amazon!

ABOUT THE AUTHOR

Kat Ross worked as a journalist at the United Nations for ten years before happily falling back into what she likes best: making stuff up. She's the author of the dystopian thriller Some Fine Day, the Fourth Element Trilogy, the Dominion Mysteries, and the new Fourth Talisman Series. She loves myths, monsters and doomsday scenarios.

www.katrossbooks.com
kat@katrossbooks.com

ALSO BY KAT ROSS

ACKNOWLEDGMENTS

Special thanks to Christa Yelich-Koth, Jessica Therrien, Deirdre Stapp, Kat Howard, the design team at Damonza and all the wonderful folks at Acorn Publishing.

GLOSSARY

Al Miraj. The southernmost satrapy of the empire, it is surrounded by the Sayyhad desert. Daēvas are called *djinn* there. Al Mirajis worship their own gods and very few follow the Way of the Flame.

Amah. The nursemaids assigned by the magi to bond daēvas until they are old enough to be sent to the Immortals or the Water Dogs.

Avas Danai. The daēva clan of Victor and Lysandros.

Avas Valkirin. The daēva clan of Neblis and her brother, Culach.

Bactria. The land to the north of the Char Khala range. Once a satrapy of the empire, now the realm of Queen Neblis. It is a wilderness, with all the people who once lived there having fled or been enslaved.

Barbican. The stronghold in the middle of the Great Salt Plain where the daēva cuffs are forged.

Breaker. See *negatory magic*.

Cuffs. Gold bracelets that create a magical bond between a human and a daēva that allows the former to control the daēva's power. In some cases, the wearers will also experience each other's emotions. The cuffs are generally worn for life.

Daēva. Creatures considered *Druj*, or impure, by the magi. Their origins remain a mystery, but they have the ability to work elemental magic. Most daēvas have a particular affinity for earth, air or water and are strongest in one element. However, they cannot work fire, and will die merely from coming into close proximity with an open flame. Daēvas live for thousands of years and heal from wounds that would kill or cripple a human.

Dominion, also called the gloaming, shadowlands or veil. The land of the dead. Can be traversed using a talisman to open gates, but is a dangerous place for the living.

Druj. Literally means *impure souls*. Includes Revenants, wights, liches and other Undead. Daēvas are also considered Druj by the magi.

Elemental magic. The direct manipulation of earth, air or water. Fire is the fourth element, but has unstable properties that cannot be worked by daēvas.

Faravahar. The symbol of the Prophet. Its form is an eagle with outstretched wings.

Gate. A passage into the Dominion.

Gorgon-e Gaz. The prison on the shore of the Salenian Sea where the oldest daēvas are held. It is also where daēvas are bred. The bloodlines of all daēvas in the empire can be traced back to Gorgon-e Gaz.

Hands of the Father. The order of the Numerators that hunts daēvas. Their sigil is an eye with a flame.

Holy Fire. Said to be a gift to the Prophet from the Holy Father. Holy Fire can both forge and break daēva cuffs.

Immortals. The elite division of the King's army. There are always precisely 10,000 Immortals, half of them human and half daēva. They fight in bonded pairs. If an Immortal dies in battle, the cuff is designed to be torn off so the fallen soldier can be bonded by another.

Infirmity. Also called the *Druj Curse*, it is the physical disability caused to daēvas by the bonding process.

Karnopolis. The winter capital of the empire, seat of the magi.

Lich. A thing of shadow whose touch brings death, it can only be unknit using the power.

Macydon. The kingdom across the Middle Sea that invades the empire.

Magi. The priests who follow the Way of the Flame. In the old days, some of them bonded daēvas to help fight the Druj, but this tradition has waned over time.

Moon Lands. The daēva world, reached by gates in the Dominion.

Necromancers. Also called Antimagi. They are the lieutenants of Queen Neblis. Necromancers draw their power from talismanic chains attached to human slaves, and which are imbued with the power of the Dominion. When a slave is killed, five Druj Undead are born. Many necromancers are former magi who now serve Queen Neblis.

Negatory magic. A rare talent that involves the working of all four elements. Those who can wield it are known as Alchemists or Breakers. Negatory magic trumps both elemental and talismanic magic. The price of negatory magic is rage and emotional turmoil. It derives from the Breaker's own temperament and is separate from the Nexus, which is the source of all elemental magic.

Numerators. A powerful order in the bureaucracy of the empire, they collect taxes and hunt down illegal daēvas.

Persepolae. The summer capital of the empire.

Purified. The order of magi that guards the holy fire at the Barbican.

Qarha. A protective face scarf worn by Water Dogs.

Revenant. Said to be the corpses of an ancient warrior race come back to life, they stand close to eight feet tall and fight with iron swords. Must be beheaded.

Satrap. A provincial governor of the empire. Satraps are permitted a small number of daēvas to keep the peace.

Shepherds. Hounds of the Dominion, they herd the dead to their final destination at the inner sea of the shadowlands.

Extremely hostile to anything living, and to necromancers in particular.

Sun Lands. The human world.

Talismanic magic. The use of elemental magic to imbue power in a material object, word or phrase. Generally, the object will perform a single function, i.e. the shells that open gates in the Dominion, the daēva cuffs and the necromancer chains.

Tel Khalujah. The satrapy where Nazafareen served as a Water Dog.

Water Dogs. The force that keeps order in the more distant satrapies and hunts down Undead along the borders. Human Water Dogs wear scarlet tunics, while their daēva bonded wear blue.

Way of the Flame. The official religion of the empire. Preaches *good thoughts, good words and good deeds*. Embodied by the magi, who view the world as locked in an eternal struggle between good and evil. Fire is considered the holiest element, followed by water.

Wight. A Druj Undead with the ability to take over a human body and mimic the host to a certain degree. Must be beheaded.

Zarathustra. Also called the Prophet. The founder of the Way of the Flame and creator of the first daēva cuffs. Considered a saint.

97440728R00204

Made in the USA
Lexington, KY
29 August 2018